USA TODAY bestselling author **Heidi Rice** lives in London, England. She is married with two teenage sons—which gives her rather too much of an insight into the male psyche—and also works as a film journalist. She adores her job, which involves getting swept up in a world of high emotion, sensual excitement, funny and feisty women, sexy and tortured men and glamorous locations where laundry doesn't exist. Once she turns off her computer she often does chores—usually involving laundry!

When **Emmy Grayson** came across her mother's copy of *A Rose in Winter* by Kathleen E. Woodiwiss, she sneaked it into her room and promptly fell in love with romance. Over twenty years later, Mills & Boon Modern made her dream come true by offering her a contract for her first book. When she isn't writing, she's chasing her kids, attempting to garden, or carving out a little time on her front porch with her own romance hero.

ONE NIGHT, NINE MONTHS

HEIDI RICE

EMMY GRAYSON

MILLS & BOON

First published in Great Britain 2025
by Mills & Boon, an imprint of HarperCollins*Publishers* Ltd,
1 London Bridge Street, London, SE1 9GF

www.harpercollins.co.uk

HarperCollins*Publishers*, Macken House, 39/40 Mayor Street Upper,
Dublin 1, D01 C9W8, Ireland

One Night, Nine Months © 2025 Harlequin Enterprises ULC

The Heir Affair © 2025 Heidi Rice

Pregnant Behind the Veil © 2025 Emmy Grayson

ISBN: 978-0-263-34474-5

08/25

THE HEIR AFFAIR

HEIDI RICE

MILLS & BOON

To Abby Green and Amanda Cinelli,
my fellow writing witches, and Theo James!

Who all encouraged me to write my first Greek hero
(in rather different ways LOL).

CHAPTER ONE

'I CAN'T BELIEVE you haven't slept with the Princess yet, Xander. What are you waiting for?'

Alexander Caras held onto his temper at his brother Theo's provocative comment while their limousine edged through the night-time traffic in Port Gabriel, the coastal resort hub of the small but exclusive European principality of Galicos.

'We haven't even announced the engagement yet,' he murmured. It was supposed to be happening at an event the following week. 'And I have no intention of sleeping with her until our wedding night.' After over a year of intensive negotiation with Princess Freya's father, Prince Andreas, Xander should have been overjoyed that the deal to finally secure a merger between Galicos' multibillion-dollar port facilities on the Rivera and Caras Shipping would be finalised with the engagement.

The Prince had insisted Xander marry his wayward oldest child and only daughter as part of the deal before he could buy the land. Xander had been surprised. The concept of an arranged marriage seemed nothing short of medieval. But when he'd been offered Princess Freya's hand as part of the negotiations six months ago, he'd still jumped at the chance. When was a former Athens street rat going to get another opportunity to marry into royalty? The fact there had been not one single spark between them on the two occasions he'd met her hadn't bothered Xander then… But it bothered him now.

Because of the woman he had met five months ago. The woman he could not forget. The woman who had captivated him and excited him and still seemed to have some damn hold over him he could not break.

Poppy. The girl whose surname he didn't even know. He'd met her precisely once, on a hot spring day on the beach in Rhodes. The girl who had insisted on hitching a ride on his jet ski to the island he'd bought off the coast—while having no idea he was the billionaire who now owned the place she'd once visited with her mother while on vacation. The girl whose bright, sunny, sweet smile he could still see, whose sobs of surrender he could still hear echoing in his ears, whose tight flesh he could still feel massaging him to a brutal climax, and whose intoxicating scent—sea and suncream and sultry female sweat—still invaded his senses, every time he had to take himself in hand late at night, trying to forget her.

What the hell had she done to him? Because he didn't like that their one day together was still intruding on his consciousness—and making him regret the engagement that was going to take Caras Shipping to the next level.

It was just sex. Epic sex, to be sure. But once you're officially engaged you'll forget her. You have to.

'Surely banging your fiancée, though, would seal the deal even tighter with her father,' Theo goaded. 'I've heard she's pretty enough. I still don't get why you're being so honourable. It's not like anyone expects guys like us to wait for the wedding night.'

As the glitter of casino lights and the superyachts anchored in the dock flickered in the darkness, Xander tensed, and frowned at his reflection in the limo's treated glass.

'Princess Freya is a virgin, Theo. Or at least her father seems to think so. Showing my future bride some respect and not jumping her the first chance I get is the classier move. Remember that is what we're trying to achieve with this whole damn deal. Class.' He bit out the words, infuriated by his brother's low chuckle.

'Yeah, right, like anyone is going to think either of us have class, no matter how many princesses we hook up with.'

Xander clenched his teeth even harder, frustration and fury grinding in his gut.

His younger brother was a playboy who treated sex like a recreational sport. Which had been great for the Caras brothers' brand up to now—because Theo exuded the sort of hot, edgy charisma that social media and the celebrity press ate up. It had helped put them on the map, given them connections to the circles of the rich and famous, before the business had taken off. But now they'd arrived, their worldwide logistics brand clearing well over two billion euros in profit a year, Theo still refused to take any damn thing seriously— Xander's marriage plans most of all.

Caras Shipping was moving into luxury cruises. Xander wanted to diversify, because they'd reached as high as they could in the container market, even if that would remain the bread and butter of their operation. But to launch the cruise business, he wanted to acquire luxury anchorage on the Mediterranean, to house the fleet of boutique liners they were currently kitting out for the inaugural cruise at the end of next year, which was already fully booked. And Galicos was perfect. There was nowhere more exclusive because no other company had secured a deal there. Plus, Prince Andreas needed the investment, because his high-end lifestyle cost a bomb, and he was rich in property, and legacy, not so much in cold, hard cash.

Xander was the one having to marry the Princess to secure their company's future. A woman he barely knew and didn't even particularly want to bed. Freya was young, but probably more than a little spoilt and entitled, not to mention mercenary. Because who agreed to let their father marry them off to a Greek shipping billionaire if they didn't have their eye on the main prize?

But he didn't begrudge the girl that. He was more ruthless than anyone, because he'd had to be as a kid, to keep him and his brother fed and out of the hands of the authorities. Sentiment meant nothing to a man like him. Because he hadn't been able to afford it as a child, and now all it was likely to do was stand in his way.

The only problem was Poppy, whose luscious lips and full breasts and captivating laugh had crept into his dreams and refused to leave. To the point where he couldn't forget how much he still wanted her, which was a lot more than he was ever likely to want the woman he was supposed to be making his wife.

'The difference is, I don't just want to screw the Princess, Theo,' he lied, because the truth was he didn't even want to do that. Because he could still see Poppy's open, heart-shaped face, the sheen of excitement in her brown eyes when she'd thought they were sneaking into a billionaire's house—without knowing the billionaire was him, and the guy she was with wasn't some random beach bum she'd met three hours ago. 'I'm going to *marry* Princess Freya.'

Perhaps if he said it often enough, he'd start to believe it. And stop questioning the decision he had been so certain of before that chance encounter in Rhodes.

'Seems risky though. How do you know you'll want to marry her if you haven't found out first what she's like in bed?' Theo murmured, not impressed with Xander's restraint. 'What if you find out on your wedding night that she's frigid? I mean, how come she's still a virgin at twenty?'

Maybe because she's not a man-whore like you?

Xander clenched his teeth to stop the knee-jerk response from coming out of his mouth. He'd said all he intended to say on the subject of his arranged marriage, because even thinking about it made him think more about the woman who had got away. The woman he still wanted but knew he couldn't have. The woman whose memory turned him on much more than the woman he had agreed to make his wife.

He stared through the dark glass at the high-end restaurants lining the wharf, which served *cordon bleu* food and vintage champagne to anyone who wished to take a break from the casinos or give the chef on their superyacht a night off.

The car slowed in the evening traffic and he caught sight of a waitress, with her back to him, busy scribbling an order. He blinked and lurched forward, his gaze suddenly riveted to the girl.

What the hell? Could it be her...?

A prickling sensation rippled across his nape as he took in the graceful line of the girl's neck, caressed by honey-brown curls that had escaped her updo. The way she held herself reminded him of that captivating girl and the carefree day out of time he'd spent with her. Was he dreaming, hallucinating, going totally and utterly mad?

He needed to see her face.

Turn, dammit.

Her head moved, and he devoured the sight of her face in profile. The prickling sensation became sharp jagged thorns, ripping through his consciousness, and then turning into red-hot pokers to sink into his groin.

Her smile, those high cheekbones, the dimple playing peek-a-boo with an errant curl, which she swiped away to finish jotting the order down on her pad. The way her teeth chewed on her bottom lip. The same lush lips he had devoured himself.

The rush of sensation throbbed and pulsed.

'Poppy?' he whispered. *It is her.*

'What did you say?'

His brother's voice barely registered. The car began to inch forward. He smacked his hand against the glass partition. Their driver, Dimitrios, slid open the panel.

'Stop the car,' Xander shouted, his breathing laboured, his mind dazed. 'I'm getting out here.'

Maybe he *was* going mad. Perhaps he had conjured her up after too many nights spent alone, frantically trying to masturbate away his memories of that one day like a teenager mooning over a centrefold. But he had to be sure.

The car had barely braked before he flung open the door and leapt out.

'Xander, where the hell are you going?' his brother shouted from inside the car.

'I'll see you at the yacht,' he shot over his shoulder, slamming the door. He headed back along the wharf towards the restaurant.

The waitress had finished taking her order and was making her way inside.

Her walk? That was Poppy's walk, too. Fluid and sensual and so unconsciously seductive it made the heat swell in his groin. The visceral reaction swept through him, turning the nagging arousal at the memory of her in his arms, which had been dogging him for months, into a tidal wave of need.

He strode through the crowds as she disappeared into the restaurant, then jogged past the maître d' standing by a lectern. The man shouted in French, asking if he wanted a table. He waved him off, breaking into a run.

Once inside, he spotted the girl standing at the far end of the bar, her back to him as she collected drinks on a tray.

'Poppy,' he shouted.

The girl's head whipped round, responding to her name. Joy exploded in his chest as the need shocked him. Those eyes, that face. It *was* her. He wasn't going mad. But as he got closer, a brutal blush suffused her whole face, highlighting the freckles across her nose, which he knew she also had across her breasts, because he had massaged suncream into her pale cleavage that day. But as she turned towards him, depositing the tray back on the bar with a clash of glasses, his greedy gaze swept down her figure.

His steps faltered. And he blinked, exhilaration turning to shock, then confusion, then another blast of hunger.

A compact bulge distended her apron where he had once been able to span her flat, narrow waist with a single hand.

He reached her at last, but it felt as if he were walking through waist-high water now, his movements jerky and sluggish as he tried to make sense of all the warring reactions going off inside his head.

'Alex…' she murmured, using the name he had given her that day. The name only she had ever used. 'Hello,' she murmured. But she didn't look surprised to see him any more.

Just shocked he had found her here.

He grasped her upper arm, unable to stop himself from touching her again—still not entirely convinced she was real. She trembled, her instinctive response echoing in his groin, but then she tried to tug her arm loose.

'We can't speak now, Mr Caras,' she said, her voice carefully devoid of emotion. Her gaze flat and direct. 'I'm on shift.'

Mr Caras?

So, she knew who he was. Had she always known? The cynicism that had deserted him for months—every time he thought of that sultry spring day and her—twisted the joy at seeing her again into something bitter and jarring.

That would be the cynicism—the survival instinct he had relied on for years, ever since he was a street kid scavenging for scraps in Athens to feed himself and his brother—that she had suspended that day, with her artless response to his kisses, his touch, his caresses and the confidences they'd shared. Then the heartfelt words she had whispered after they'd made love—which had made him question everything in his life before her—slammed into him, again.

'*You know what, Alex. I've never hated anyone. But I wish I could meet the man who used his wealth and privilege to turn Parádeisos' unspoilt natural beauty into his private pleasure dome. I'd love to be able to tell him what a selfish bastard I think he is. Wouldn't you?*'

He'd laughed with her then, but his laugh had been forced and hollow, because he'd been wincing inside, knowing what had started as a small lie to see where their day—and their extraordinary chemistry—might lead had suddenly become an enormous, insurmountable one. The sweat had still been drying on his skin from their lovemaking, after spending four hours together so full of surprises he was sure he'd discovered genuine joy for the first time in his life. But as he'd lain on his own bed—which she'd thought belonged to someone else—still steeped in afterglow, her words, edged with sadness and derision, had echoed in the soft sea breeze, damning him. And he'd found himself questioning the ruthless ambition that had stopped him from seeing the island she loved as anything more than a good investment opportunity—a place to build a luxury pleasure dome. But worse had been the realisation he could never tell her he was the man who owned the house she thought they had sneaked into, or she would hate him, too.

But as his real name echoed on her lips now, he suddenly understood that might have been an illusion. That while he'd struggled for months to suppress the yearning to find her and call off his planned engagement, she had never been who she had pretended to be either.

Had she played him? Had he been a sap to believe she was really that artless, captivating, rebellious free spirit? The bright, sweet girl who considered love to be more valuable than money. And true beauty to be something you couldn't buy…?

His temper surged, becoming a mix of fury and suspicion and anger at the shame she'd caused him, in that moment. But right alongside it was the possessive urge to stake his claim on her again—here, now, for ever—even though she might have lied to him all those months ago.

But then his gaze snagged on her belly again—and the only question that mattered broke from his dry lips.

'Is it mine?' he demanded.

Flags of colour slashed across her cheeks, but all he heard in her tone was the sting of regret—not the satisfaction he had expected—when she whispered, 'Yes.'

CHAPTER TWO

'WE'RE LEAVING.'

Poppy stared at the man she had believed she was falling in love with. The man she had begged to give her a lift on his jet ski to the no longer deserted island where she had once spent her last truly happy day with her mother. The man who had fathered the baby growing inside her on the beautiful spring day that had unfolded. The day she had remembered so blissfully—until she'd discovered the truth about him. The day that had once had so many wonderful memories, encompassing everything love should be—fun, exciting, tender, passionate, adventurous.

When she'd run down to the beach in Rhodes the next morning, hoping to see him again, instead she'd found no sign of him or his jet ski anywhere. She'd spent the rest of her week-long vacation asking at all the beach bars, trying to find him—or at least something more about him than his first name. Desperate to contact him, even if she couldn't see him again. Desperate to let him know how much their day had meant to her. And to find out his surname.

But no one had heard of a guy named Alex. No one had even noticed the guy with the jet ski, except her.

Why hadn't she insisted on getting his number? Or at least his last name? It had seemed so romantic at the time to keep their identities anonymous—after all, they were both trespassing on a billionaire's private island. She was the one who had suggested they make a pact—just in case either one of them got caught and questioned—not to reveal their surnames to each other, so they couldn't be interrogated into giving each other up.

Their pact had seemed impossibly romantic at the time. Especially as that wonderful day had become a blissful bubble of hope and possibilities and searing passion.

He'd made everything so perfect, even suggested they sneak into the new house the billionaire had built. She'd loved swimming in the guy's pool, with Alex. They'd been two crazy kids, claiming the island back, one last time, from the rich bastard who was going to make it out of bounds for ever as soon as he took ownership in a few weeks' time.

And the sex… She'd come on to him, unable to resist the chance to sweep her hand down his tanned belly as they'd lain side by side on the pool deck. Feeling the bunch of his hard abs, circling the small scars and crude tattoos that had fascinated her, tracing the happy trail of hair to his belly button. Heady excitement had eddied through her body at the sound of his sharp groan when she'd cupped the thick erection in his trunks and stroked the evidence that he'd wanted her as much as she'd wanted him.

He'd insisted on taking her inside, finding one of the deluxe bedrooms, making her feel like a queen—revered and wanted—as they'd stripped off their wet costumes and made love. The shattering pleasure had validated all the emotions he'd stirred in her—his brooding watchfulness giving way to reckless amusement and then dark passion as they'd shared the day together—creating emotions so intoxicating they'd hurt.

She'd known something wasn't quite right afterwards, when they'd ridden the waves back to the jetty where they'd met what had felt like a lifetime ago but had been only four hours. She'd refused to let in her doubts, though, that niggle of panic and regret that she'd said something to offend him without intending to.

When they'd kissed goodbye on the dock as the sun had set, and he'd cradled her cheek, with such tenderness, the passion still making them both ache, she'd tried to tell him her name. But she could still remember his finger pressing against her lips to silence her.

'Don't tell me,' he'd murmured. 'We don't want to spoil our perfect day. And we still might get arrested.'

She'd laughed at his silly joke and felt wild and free. But then she'd assumed, hadn't she, that he'd be there the next day? She'd been so excited that night, unable to sleep, sure that this had to be the start of so much more than a casual holiday fling. So sure he must have felt it too. How could he not when he'd looked at her with such intensity, such brooding passion?

Discovering six weeks later that she was expecting Alex's baby had been devastating and beautiful all at once. She'd redoubled her efforts to find him. Finally returning to Rhodes again, a month ago now, once she'd saved enough money to make the trip...

Only to discover everything she thought they'd shared had been a cruel hoax. When she'd seen a picture in a local magazine—of the billionaire who had bought the island they'd 'trespassed' on together.

Not Alex. But Xander Caras. The Greek shipping magnate who was about to marry a princess.

Not the man she had been falling in love with, then. But a total fraud.

He grasped her upper arm now, and she trembled. Sensation sprinted down her spine—at the feel of his calluses on her skin again. It was the first time he'd touched her since he'd pressed his fingertips to her lips to silence her on the sunset dock in Rhodes. And left her standing there with her heart so full of dreams.

Dreams that had finally been shattered for good a month ago.

Her temper flared, right alongside her shock, the visceral reaction to his touch disturbing her now almost as much as how easily she'd fallen for his lies on that sunny day five months ago.

She yanked her arm loose. 'Let go of me. I told you. I can't go anywhere with you now. I'm on shift.'

It wasn't a lie. She needed to keep this job, not just to earn her passage back to the UK, but also to build up some more savings for when the baby arrived. She'd had to use the last of them to get to Galicos—once she'd discovered from social media he was due to be here to announce his engagement to the Galician princess—so she could have some chance of informing him he was going to become a father.

If she'd been able to contact him in any other way—discreetly, at a distance—she would have. But after the devastation caused by discovering his true identity, it hadn't taken her long to realise billionaires were impossible to contact, because no one would let a complete nobody past the firewall of executive assistants and security personnel who shielded them from the real world.

It was bad enough she'd had to come all the way here, in the hope of maybe discovering where he was staying, just to do the decent thing. She was already at an enormous disadvantage. And she'd spent all her mental and physical energy so far on getting here and surviving until she could figure out a way to deliver her message.

She'd wanted to have this conversation face to face, but had never expected it to actually happen, fairly sure after the lies he'd told her already he'd have no interest in the news he had fathered a child. No doubt he'd done this before to other women—after all, he'd been so good at it. Inhabiting the persona of a gruff, moody beach bum, cleverly using her own innocence and positivity against her when she'd insisted they remain anonymous to make their adventure more romantic.

One thing was for sure, she certainly wasn't ready to have this conversation tonight. And she'd be damned—after the emotional wringer he'd put her through in the past five months—if she'd have it at his convenience and on his terms, instead of her own. She'd been on her feet since noon. She was worn out and seeing him again—having him touch her again—was more than enough to contend with for one night.

Never for a moment would she have expected him to spot her, or to confront her. From the suspicion shadowing his eyes, though—reminding her of the moody, watchful guy she'd first met that day—she suspected his decision to confront her had more to do with him wanting to get her out of Galicos on the eve of his high-profile engagement party and nothing whatsoever to do with the discovery he was going to be a dad. So why shouldn't she let him stew, for tonight at least, while she got some sleep and prepared for tomorrow's confrontation?

'Are you insane?' he snarled, as if he were the injured party. His burning gaze seared across her midriff again. 'You are carrying my child. I will not wait to have this conversation a moment longer.'

The anger in his tone only ignited her own.

How dared he behave as if this were her fault? She wasn't the one who had pretended to be someone she wasn't. Nor was she the one who had made herself impossible to contact for a month.

'Well, tough, because I don't care what you want,' she fired back. 'We'll have this conversation when I'm good and ready and not a moment before.'

His dark brows shot up his forehead—as if no one had ever

said no to him before… They probably hadn't, she thought, resentfully. She prided herself on being the first. It helped to strengthen the tremor in her knees that had started the minute she'd turned to see him standing there by the bar. So tall, so indomitable. His face familiar… But nothing else.

In the expertly tailored designer suit, which hugged his muscular physique like a second skin, he couldn't have looked more different from the man she'd clung to at the back of that jet ski, in old swimming trunks and a soaked cotton shirt, or the man who had gradually come out of his shell that day as they'd roamed the island and he'd listened to her endless chatter without saying much. His watchful presence had made adrenaline surge every time she'd caught him staring at her with that sheen of confused fascination in his eyes—as if he hadn't understood her, but he'd wanted to.

The clean-shaven dashing man who smelled of expensive sandalwood cologne before her now could not have been more foreign to her, or more different from the beachcomber with a day-old beard, and sun-drenched skin, the delicious scent of salt and sweat clinging to him.

But then his brows lowered ominously again over those pure blue eyes that had once captivated her. Not brooding now but burning with fury—all of it directed at her.

'You will come with me, or I will *make* you come with me… It is your choice,' he said, his voice so low she doubted anyone else could hear it.

'Go ahead, then, make a scene.' She forced the bitterness to the fore to cover the hurt.

This wasn't Alex. The rough, edgy, mostly silent beachcomber had never existed. This man was just an arrogant billionaire playboy who thought everyone had to bend to his will. No way would she let his arsy behaviour upset her.

'I'm not sure your royal girlfriend will appreciate you getting caught on camera dragging a pregnant lady out of a waterfront bar in her principality right before you announce your engagement.'

Something flickered in his eyes that looked almost like admiration—and not at all like panic—when her manager and the bar's owner, Serge, interrupted their stand-off.

'Excuse me, sir. Is everything okay?' her boss asked, slanting Poppy a look that said, loud and clear, *Don't worry. I'll handle this bozo for you.*

Serge was a terrific boss who lived by the adage 'the customer doesn't always know best, we just let him think he does'. He'd hired her two weeks ago when no one else had wanted to employ an obviously pregnant woman and been impossibly sweet and accommodating when she'd struggled to get through her first couple of shifts, still exhausted from her travels and her heartache, and the demands of her pregnancy.

Serge was one of the good guys, unlike the man standing in front of her, generating a tidal wave of controlled irritation. But just as Poppy's spine began to dissolve with relief, Caras reached into his jacket and pulled out his wallet.

'I need you to give your waitress the rest of the night off,' he demanded as he tugged out a gold credit card.

Poppy blinked, struck dumb by his arrogance. And her own stupidity.

Seeing him now—the aura of dominance and command emanating off him like a forcefield—how on earth had she ever persuaded herself this guy was a freewheeling beach bum living by his wits in Rhodes who owned nothing more than a much-loved jet ski?

'I'm sorry, sir,' Serge replied patiently. 'We're rammed tonight and short of staff so—'

'I will pay one hundred thousand euros...' Caras interrupted as he slapped the gold card onto the bar. 'To compensate you for the inconvenience.'

Serge's face flushed. But Poppy wanted to hug him when he directed his gaze to her, then back to Caras.

'As it is Poppy's time you seek, Mr Caras,' he said, making it clear he had recognised their irate customer, 'it must be her choice to leave with you.'

Serge's bravery and integrity helped to restore Poppy's faith in humanity... Or rather the humanity of the non-super-rich. Because offering to protect her against a man who was destined to become Galicos royalty was not an easy choice.

'And she should be compensated too,' her boss added.

She stiffened. 'That's okay, Serge.'

The last thing she wanted was any of Xander Caras' billions. That wasn't why she was here. Whatever suspicions Caras might have, she had come to Galicos only to let him know about the pregnancy, and then she planned to leave— as soon as she'd earned enough to give her some financial headroom when she returned to the UK.

How typical, though, of a rich manipulative bastard like Caras to think he could buy her and Serge's cooperation.

She'd opened her mouth to tell him where he could stick his gold credit card, when she spotted Serge's hopeful expression.

She closed her mouth, forced to confront the ugly truth about this situation.

While her boss was determined to do the right thing, whatever it cost him, money was always tight for an operation like his. Even though he catered to a luxury clientele, when you factored in the cost of staff and supplies, not to mention the huge rates the principality charged for a prime location like this one, he'd be lucky to clear more than ten thousand euros in profit a week. One hundred thousand euros would be a major boon to his business.

'I'll... I'll go with him, Serge. If you're sure you can spare me,' she said, untying her apron and dropping it on the bar with trembling fingers, while trying not to reveal to her boss how anxious and frustrated she was with this outcome.

But the truth was, she didn't have a choice. Caras hadn't given her a choice. The rat. She didn't want Serge to lose the money. Nor did she want Serge to risk losing his business—because who knew what a man with Caras' connections might do if she defied him again?

Caras inserted his card into the reader rushed over by one of the bar staff. He barely blinked as he completed the transaction.

Poppy bit down on her frustration—and the surge of disgust. One hundred grand, just to get his own way.

Men like him would never understand the true value of money, because they had no idea what that amount of money meant to people who had to work for a living in menial jobs. Money to them represented power over the little people like her. It sickened her he'd been able to buy her time so easily. But as he tucked his credit card back into his wallet, she consoled herself with the knowledge they would have had to have this conversation eventually. So why not have it tonight, when Serge would be able to profit from it? And while Caras might have been able to buy her time tonight, he would never be able to buy her, because she wasn't for sale.

She stepped away from him, intending to collect her stuff from the staff room.

But he grasped her upper arm. 'Where are you going?'

'I need to get my bag and coat…' she said through gritted teeth, infuriated not just by his domineering behaviour but also by the unwanted reaction to his touch sprinting up her spine again, and making her breasts feel even more sensitive than usual.

'Tell someone else to fetch them,' he said, or rather demanded.

'Let go of my arm and I'll consider it.' She ground out the

words, her jaw locked tight. Determined not to let him win this round, too.

He glared at her, his eyes narrowing, the suspicion in them so galling it was a mammoth effort to keep her cool. But she managed it because, unlike him, she didn't wish to drag any more of her colleagues into this mess.

He released her arm, reluctantly, but the warning in his voice was unmistakeable when he leant down and murmured, 'If you try to run off, I'll come after you.'

She stiffened, the feel of that gruff, accented voice so close to her ear bringing back more memories she didn't need.

'Why would I run off?' she snapped back. 'I've spent weeks getting here just to find you again.'

She pressed a hand to her belly, hating how vulnerable that sounded. And how vulnerable she felt with him so close to her. He had to be at least six feet three. She'd noticed his height before when she'd been clinging to him on the jet ski, those broad shoulders cutting out the sun, and protecting her from the waves… And at the island's hidden cove, when they'd played a game of swim tag and he'd beaten her so easily… And then later… Much later, when he'd boosted her into his arms and carried her to the villa's bedroom… When he'd held her hips and plunged deep…

She shivered, locking the unfortunate memory back where it belonged—in the box marked *You were seduced by a player.*

Her workmate Isa arrived with her things from the backroom—her starry-eyed gaze landing on Caras. 'Hi, Mr Caras,' she said, clearly mesmerised.

'Hello,' Caras replied, but as Isa went to pass the coat and bag to Poppy, the infuriating man lifted both items out of her colleague's grasp and tucked them under his arm. 'Thank you. Let's go, Poppy.'

Before Poppy had a chance to protest, he'd placed a controlling hand on her waist and marched her out of the bar, through the restaurant's terrace tables and onto the cobblestone street by the wharf.

'Will you stop it?' she whispered, finally managing to shrug off his hold.

'Stop what?' he asked absently as he snapped his fingers at a passing taxi.

'You know perfectly well what,' she shot back, flustered now, as well as infuriated, which was somehow worse.

The cab screeched to a halt at the kerb.

He placed the proprietorial hand on the small of her back as he opened the passenger door. 'Get in the car,' he demanded, as if they weren't already having an argument about his high-handed behaviour.

'I'm sorry, who exactly made you the boss of me?' she replied, determined to make a stand now. No matter what. He might be getting his way as regarded the timing of this conversation, but she was not his personal possession. And the sooner he figured that out, the better.

His gaze dropped to her waistline. When it met hers again, the furious light in his eyes made the prickle of sensation she couldn't control become an inferno.

Not good.

'I've just paid a hundred grand for the privilege of your company,' he said, his voice so low she could barely hear it above the sound of the tourists milling around them enjoying the nightlife, unlike her. But she could hear the outrage just fine. Apparently, he hadn't been completely unmoved by the cost of that transaction after all.

Definitely good.

'You need to get into this cab before I lose what's left of my temper,' he finished.

She wasn't scared of him. Or his threats. Nor did she feel remotely guilty he'd been forced to pay such an exorbitant amount to get his way. But as the feral heat seemed to crackle between them in the warm evening air, the need to defuse the situation occurred to her.

The conversation they needed to have would require maturity. And common sense. And having a massive pissing contest in public would not make it any easier. Especially as she could already see some of the tourists nearby had noticed them together and recognised who he was, from the way they were staring so avidly.

As much as she despised this man, she genuinely hadn't come here to upset his plans or his life any more than was necessary. She'd simply come here to do the right thing for her child. Because every child deserved to have their father know they existed.

Of course, when she'd decided she had to tell him, she'd assumed he wouldn't want to know, or would accuse her of lying that he was the father. She had not anticipated his furious reaction, so this situation was already more complicated than she had expected. But she didn't plan to complicate it further. Nor did she plan to give him any ammunition for the suspicions she could already see swirling in those furious blue eyes by drawing more attention to their meeting than was necessary.

'Fine, I'll get in the cab,' she said, shrugging off that controlling hand *again*. 'But FYI, you're not the boss of me, no matter how much you had to pay Serge. Understand?'

His jaw tensed, but he gave a curt nod. 'Noted.'

She got into the car, then scooted across the leather seat so fast she almost got whiplash, while Caras reeled off directions to the driver.

But as he folded his tall frame in next to her, and buckled himself in, she realised two unfortunate facts.

Firstly, his presence was so dominating, no matter how far she scooted he still seemed to take up all the available oxygen in the car. And secondly, she had been so busy scooting, she hadn't paid attention to the directions he'd given the driver. So, when the car sped off into the night, she had absolutely no clue whatsoever where he was taking her.

Definitely not good.

CHAPTER THREE

WHEN THEY ARRIVED at their destination, Xander handed several bills to the driver, his jaw now clenched so tight his teeth ached.

The woman beside him had not said a word during the short drive along the wharf to the marina, but he could feel her animosity.

What exactly did she have to be so angry about? She was not the one who had been unaware she was going to become a parent for five solid months.

He climbed out of the car and headed around the back to open her door.

She peered out, but remained seated. 'Where are we?'

'My yacht is moored in the bay,' he said tightly, annoyed he was having to explain himself. 'We require privacy for this conversation, so that is where we are headed.'

Her gaze met his. 'You don't have somewhere we can go on land?'

'No, I do not,' he replied, which wasn't precisely true. Caras Shipping had hired the penthouse floor and the roof garden at the principality's main casino hotel. It would be the venue for the event early next week celebrating the announcement of his engagement to Freya and the port deal that would base Caras Cruises in Galicos.

But he had not bought property in Galicos yet, preferring to live on the yacht when he was visiting the principality for business purposes. He steeled himself against examining why that was, because he had a bad feeling his decision not to buy a home here yet—despite his planned marriage—had a lot to do with the obsession he had been unable to shake with the woman refusing to leave the cab.

His gaze strayed again to the evidence of her pregnancy. And the knots in his gut tightened. He had no idea how he felt about the prospect of fatherhood. He had never really considered becoming a parent. The truth was, when she had confirmed what he had already suspected—that the baby was his—his first reaction had been shock followed by panic. Because all he had been able to think about in those first moments of dawning awareness were those nights in Athens, with his brother's fragile body curled beside him. Those dark hours before dawn, when he had woken, sweating, or shivering, his belly empty, his heart racing, and the terror had consumed him that he would not be able to keep them both safe and together for another day.

But the fierce protectiveness now towards the life growing inside her was hard to ignore. And went some way to curbing the old fears.

'Get out of the car, Poppy,' he managed, trying not to shout—while she had been belligerent at the restaurant, she seemed more wary now.

She glanced up at him, her expression as tense as he felt, but he could see the flicker of panic she was trying to hide. 'We could go to my hostel?' she offered. 'Pretty much everyone there works nights, so it'll be virtually empty.'

He bit into his tongue, to stop himself from informing her exactly what he thought of that asinine suggestion.

'We will not be alone on the yacht, if that is your concern,' he managed, barely containing his temper now. Did she think he was going to hurt her? What kind of a monster did she think he was? 'I have staff, and my brother, Theo, will also be there.'

The thought of Theo's response though, when he saw Poppy and put two and two together, was hardly reassuring. No doubt his brother would find it hilarious that Xander had just discovered he had got a woman pregnant on the eve of his engagement announcement.

Although Xander couldn't muster much concern for the possible demise of an arranged marriage he had been less than enthusiastic about. The minute he had seen Poppy again, the moment he had realised she was pregnant, and the child was his, he had also acknowledged his arrangement with Prince Andreas might have to be renegotiated. Because his primary concern now had to be this child.

Whatever its mother's motives, the child was innocent in all this and would deserve his protection. He would never shirk that responsibility, because he knew what it felt like to be unprotected and unwanted.

Poppy had captivated him once with her free spirit, her optimism, her reckless pursuit of pleasure and her wild enthusiasm for life. Her irresponsibility, her impulsiveness, her artlessness that day had been like a drug to a man who had spent his life in the single-minded pursuit of his goals.

No doubt that had been an act to trap him into this commitment. But even if that girl had been real, what had once captivated him only concerned him now. How could that girl, who had been so eager and unworldly, so keen to lavish her affection on a man she didn't know, and had thought nothing of trusting so implicitly without even knowing his name, be able to give a child the safety and security it needed to thrive?

And that was assuming she could even nurture it long enough to give birth to it. The concern tightened like a vice around his ribs. He knew nothing about pregnancy, but she had been on her feet working long hours. Was that even safe, for her or the baby?

'I'm not sure that's as reassuring as you think it is...' Poppy murmured, still rooted to the cab seat. 'Let's not forget, you already lied to me once.'

The anger surged. 'I did not lie. We both agreed not to reveal our surnames to each other.' The anger twisted at the realisation that her impulsive suggestion—which he had thought so charming at the time—had come back to bite him on the butt. The suspicion she had known all along who he was that day only made him feel like more of a fool. Why on earth had all his common sense deserted him? The minute she had bounced up to him on the beach and offered to pay him twenty euros to take her to his own private island, with some ludicrous story about wanting to revisit the place where she had spent the best day of her life as a teenager?

Why had he been so eager to buy into her lies? The sob story about her mother? So keen to believe she didn't know who he was, that her motivations were so pure and sweet and genuine, when he had always known that no one did anything without an agenda.

Her eyes flashed with hurt. 'I thought we were trespassing on that island *together*. If you had told me you were the man who owned it, I would never have gone with you, and you know it.'

Really? Did she think he was an idiot?

His teeth clenched as he held onto the retort. He would not engage again with her nonsense. His gullibility that day, the way she had managed to play him, was immaterial now.

'The only thing that matters about what happened that day now are the consequences,' he said, his gaze flicking to the evidence of her pregnancy, pointedly. 'If your intention is to make your condition public, then by all means let us discuss it on the wharf, or in your hostel,' he bit out, deciding to call her bluff.

No doubt that had been her intention all along, to humiliate him, possibly even to extort money out of him—why else would she have chosen to be in Galicos less than a week before his engagement was announced?

'But first you will have to get out of the car.'

Poppy wanted to scream. How had he outmanoeuvred her again?

The cynical glitter in his eyes told its own story though. He thought she had come to Galicos to ruin his wedding plans, when nothing could be further from the truth.

Of course, she had been heartbroken when she had discovered he was as good as engaged. But seeing him now, knowing what he thought of her, was helping to heal her heart the rest of the way. This was not the man she had been falling for. She needed to cling to that salient fact now like a life raft.

Letting her heart rule her head had been her superpower as a kid, her optimism the protection her mum had given her against the harsh realities life could throw at you.

As her mum had often said—when she'd had to work an extra job to pay the rent, or been struggling through another round of chemo—the only way to find the joy in life was to find a positive out of every challenge, every setback, every hard or cruel event.

And the positive now was the baby Caras had given her, however unintentionally.

Dealing with her baby's father was the forfeit she would have to pay for the life inside her—which she had loved as soon as the plus sign had appeared on the pee stick.

She grabbed her coat and bag from the seat and stepped out of the taxi.

Damn him.

After handing the driver another note, Caras closed the passenger door. As the cab sped off into the darkness, she shivered even though the night was warm.

She did not want to go to his yacht, because she had no doubt at all having his wealth thrown in her face would be more than a little intimidating, and she was already intimidated enough. But she guessed that was the only way to have this conversation without the press getting wind of the details. She'd never had to deal with press scrutiny herself, being a complete nobody, but she supposed if you were about to marry a princess, it could be an issue. And the last thing she wanted was for her baby to be exposed to any kind of media spotlight. At least they were on the same page about that.

Without another word, he scooped the coat and bag out of her hands.

'My launch is this way,' he said, his tone surprisingly neutral.

She tried not to react when he placed his hand on the base of her spine, *again*, to lead her towards a speedboat at the end of the dock. But she couldn't seem to control the instinctive shudder.

Double damn him.

But as they reached the boat, his hand dropped away.

Had he felt it, too? Heat burst in her cheeks—and pulsed disconcertingly between her thighs. What exactly *was* that about?

She thanked God for the darkness.

He stepped into the speedboat, steadying himself with ease when the boat rocked, then turned to offer her his hand. The flash of memory, when he'd offered her his hand once before, to help her onto his jet ski—and later at his pool on the island, when he'd pulled her up off the lounger—made the pulsing between her thighs increase. She squeezed her thigh muscles to try and control it... It didn't help.

What was wrong with her? Was this some kind of weird biological reaction to her baby's father? Because she wasn't still attracted to him. How could she be? Now she knew all the lies he'd told to lure her into a false sense of intimacy that day.

Unfortunately, though, there was no way she was going to be able to climb aboard the boat without taking his hand, because she wasn't exactly an accomplished sailor. And she was wearing a pencil skirt.

'It is a little late to be afraid of my touch, Poppy,' he said, his gruff voice snapping her out of her frantic thoughts.

That he had noticed her hesitation made the heat in her cheeks surge. 'I—I'm not,' she replied. From the sceptical arch of his eyebrow, he knew she was lying.

She grasped his hand, bracing against the telltale shiver when his long strong fingers folded over her palm.

But as she stepped from the safety of the dock, the boat swayed alarmingly. She gasped, as his hands dropped to hold her waist and lift her the rest of the way. Suddenly, she was flush against him, her rounded stomach touching him, her lungs filling with the intoxicating scent she remembered, soap and man, detectable now under the expensive notes of his sandalwood cologne and the fresh salty air.

She tried to step back, aware of the heat rising up her neck and sinking deep into her abdomen, but his hold on her waist remained firm.

'Stand still until the boat stops rocking, or we will both end up in the water,' he demanded.

She glanced up—way, way up—to find him gauging her reaction. But instead of the cynicism and disdain she had expected, she saw the flicker of amusement. And the dark awareness she remembered from that day.

'It's not funny,' she managed, her throat as raw as the rest of her, unsettled by the reminder of the brooding beach bum, and the watchfulness that had once aroused her.

'You think not?' he asked, clearly amused now, and at her expense.

The boat finally stopped swaying and he slid his hands from her waist, but not before she got another lungful of his addictive scent.

She scrambled into the passenger seat, so aware of him she was shaking. He seemed unmoved by the brief contact though, as he climbed into the driving seat.

She had to grab the handrail as the boat purred to life, then lifted out of the water.

They sped across the bay, bouncing over the slow tug of the tide, towards an enormous boat—its four storeys lit up like a Christmas tree. Her heartbeat accelerated.

That's a yacht?

From where Poppy was sitting—as the launch circled the enormous hull and Caras cut the speedboat's engine to drift up to the lowered platform at the back—it looked more like a mini ocean liner.

A man appeared wearing a uniform of black shorts and a white short-sleeved shirt with epaulets that had the Caras Shipping logo embroidered on the breast pocket. Caras threw him a line and the crew member tied it off.

'Welcome aboard, Mr Caras,' he said. 'Miss,' he added, giving her a nod of greeting.

'Hi, Jack. This is Poppy,' he said, surprising her. She hadn't expected him to introduce her to his crew, especially as she was obviously pregnant. Wouldn't they ask questions? 'Tell Meghan to prepare the Sunrise Suite for my guest.'

Sorry? What now?

'Is Theo aboard?' he added, while Poppy was still trying to control her shock. Why would she need a suite? She wasn't going to stay.

The crew member shook his head. 'Your brother has not

yet returned. I'll send the launch back for him and let Meghan know right away, sir. Do you and your guest require dinner?'

Stepping off the launch, Caras turned to offer her his hand again. She didn't have much choice but to take it, even though all her alarm bells were going off when he tugged her onto the deck then placed a controlling arm around her waist.

'Are you hungry?' His gaze shifted to her belly. 'Is there anything you would like?' he asked, as if she really were a guest instead of being here under duress.

She shook her head, not able to speak round the ball of outrage forming in her throat.

He turned to his crew member. 'Tell Angelo we're good for tonight. We'll be on the starboard terrace. Make sure no one disturbs us.'

'Of course, sir,' the man said, then bowed and disappeared back into the bows of the ship.

As soon as he was gone, Poppy shifted away from that controlling hand.

'Why does Meghan need to prepare a suite for me?' she hissed. 'As soon as this conversation is over, I'm going back to my hostel.'

He frowned. As if he were surprised by the news. She pushed her frustration with him to the fore, to cover the spurt of panic, and the unsettled feeling in her gut.

She already felt overwhelmed, not just by his enormous yacht, but also by the arrogant way he had of simply taking charge, with no apparent consideration of her wishes or feelings.

'Do you seriously believe we are going to be able to get anything settled tonight?' he demanded. The arrogance from the restaurant was back full force. Why was she not surprised?

'What exactly is there to settle?' she countered, far too aware of the cynical glitter in his eyes. Ever since she'd told him the baby was his, he'd looked at her as if she were a problem that needed to be solved and to his satisfaction. It hurt to realise he had never been the man she'd thought he was, but it hurt more somehow to realise he thought she was as manipulative and mercenary as he was.

'You know very well what there is to settle. If this is my child, I intend to be involved.'

If...

She supposed she should have expected that. But still she found herself flinching inside at how little he truly thought of her. But she was still cauterising that wound when he continued.

'I need to inform my legal team and arrange a DNA test once the child is born. But I do not intend to shirk my financial responsibilities,' he declared. 'So, at the very least, we will need to negotiate a suitable amount, which I am sure you are well aware of or you would not have turned up here on the eve of my engagement announcement.'

The hurt and humiliation curdled in her stomach.

Lord spare her from rich men—was every single thing about money to them?

'Well, that's where you're wrong,' she shot back. 'The only reason I came to Galicos now was because I knew you would be here. The plan was to get a message to you, so you would know you were going to become a father. I thought I owed you that much.'

The naiveté of that mission struck her now. What had made her believe for a single second a man like him wouldn't see her appearance here as some kind of shake-down? It hurt to realise she had been so wrong about him. It hurt even more to realise his cruel assumptions had fundamentally shaken her long-held confidence in the essential goodness of people, even billionaires like him. But she did not intend to make that mistake again.

'I don't want or expect anything else from you. I never did. And that includes your vast hoards of filthy lucre. Nor do I intend to derail your engagement to Princess Freya.' She pressed a hand to her bump. *Her* bump. Not his. And dismissed the hurt that he had fallen in love with someone else so soon after meeting her, because according to the gossip columns his engagement to the Princess had been muted for months. In fact, he might well have already been dating his princess when they had made love in his villa. But that thought just made her feel grubby as well as used, so she tried not to think about it.

'I chose to have this baby, and I intend to raise it, on my own, without any help from you. If you really want to be a part of its life, I will agree to a DNA test after it's born to confirm you're the father. But if you don't want to be involved, there's really no need for one. Because I have absolutely nothing I need to prove to you. And nor does my child.'

She huffed out a breath, glad to have got all that off her chest.

'So now we've got that settled, you can take me back to the marina.'

His frown became catastrophic, but she put that down to the arrogance that made him believe any woman who he slept with had to be after his money.

'Your vast hoard of filthy lucre...' What the...?

Xander was pretty sure he could hear the ticking time bomb of his temper about to explode.

'The hell I will...' he growled, the effort not to yell at the woman in front of him so great he felt as if he were chewing on a rock.

He never lost his temper. Not with anyone. Not even his brother, Theo, who had made it his life's mission to push Xander's buttons. Because he had learned as a boy that when people knew they could hurt you, or provoke you, it only gave them power, while you lost your own.

That this slip of a woman had managed to do what even Theo had only achieved occasionally, and only because his brother was the one person he truly cared about, was even more infuriating. Why did it matter what she thought of him, or his money? It didn't. Nor should it bother him that he might have underestimated her. And her motives.

If she was *not* here to destroy his marriage plans, or blackmail him, he should be rejoicing. Why should he feel insulted that she had decided she didn't need his money, that somehow his wealth was tainted?

But the truth was, he did feel insulted.

His company, and his career, his success in business was the thing he was most proud of in his life... That through hard work, single-mindedness and taking sometimes insane risks he had lifted himself out of the poverty and the insecurity that had marred so much of his childhood. Being driven and determined, with his eyes always squarely on the prize of financial security, was how he had finally buried that unwanted, neglected, brutalised boy who had woken up one morning to find his father gone, and his brother crying with fear and hunger. And he would be damned if this girl would make him feel ashamed of what he had done to protect them both again. Nor would he let her stop him from protecting his own child.

'Are you refusing to take me back to the wharf?' she asked, her voice determined.

But then he noticed the tremor in her body as she wrapped her arms around her waist. And knew she was not as calm and collected as she was pretending to be.

Well, good, because he was no longer calm or collected either. And it was all her fault. She had provoked him, deliberately, and insulted him. But if she thought he was going to let her make him lose his cool, she was very much mistaken.

'You're not going anywhere until we get one thing straight,' he edged out the words, still not yelling, even though he was shouting inside his head. 'Either you do as I tell you, or I will sue for custody once the child is born.'

She stiffened, as if he'd slapped her. 'But you can't do that. I'm its mother.'

'Watch me.' His gaze coasted down her figure again, aware of how much thinner she looked now than she had in April, despite the bump. How long had she been working in that bar? What had the pregnancy been like? He swallowed down the spurt of panic. She should have come to him sooner. While he might be hard to contact, he was not impossible to contact and if any of his assistants had mentioned a communication from a woman called Poppy he would have immediately replied. 'No judge will look favourably on a mother who deliberately rejects the support she needs out of some misplaced sense of superiority and self-righteousness. My money is as good as any man's and it is clear you need my financial support, or you would not be working all night in a bar and living in a hostel.'

Poppy stared, so shocked by his outburst, she didn't know what to say. But right behind it was the niggle of guilt. And the prickle of fear.

'My money is as good as any man's.'

She hadn't meant to insult him. Not about his wealth anyway. Or not specifically. But from the brittle light in his eyes, and the flags of colour on his skin it was clear she had hit a nerve she hadn't been aiming for.

The truth was, his determination to support his child, though, surprised her. And maybe it shouldn't have. But what concerned her more was the realisation he might be able to take her baby away from her. The thought terrified her. Had she been naïve, contacting him at all? She'd believed it was the right thing to do, but now she wasn't so sure. He had wealth and power, why hadn't she even considered that he might use it against her? Perhaps because her own father had been so uninterested in her as a child, she had foolishly assumed Xander Caras would be the same.

A gust of sea air blew through the thin cotton of her work blouse and made her shiver.

He draped her coat across her shoulders, his gaze still locked on hers. She clung to the coat, suddenly feeling desperately vulnerable. And hating it. Because that feeling dragged her back to the days after her mother's death. She'd been powerless then too, when her father had appeared at the hospital to collect her, called by social services. A man she hadn't seen in years.

'Come,' Caras murmured. 'We will discuss this inside where it is warmer.'

Perhaps she should have resisted, shrugged off that controlling arm yet again, but as he led her into the yacht, she felt too listless and confused—and frankly panicked—to object.

They entered a lavishly furnished lounge area, but instead of stopping he directed her to the end of the space and pressed a button. A metal door swished open revealing a mirrored elevator.

'You've got a lift on a boat?' she murmured, dumbstruck again, as she stepped inside with him.

He glanced at her, the quirk of amusement on his lips strangely incongruous. Nothing about this situation was funny. But the light in those brooding blue eyes made the nerves in her stomach relax, a fraction. 'There are four storeys on the yacht and the starboard terrace is on the top.' His gaze darkened, gliding down to her stomach. 'I did not want to over-tax you in your condition.'

The doors closed, confining them in the narrow space, and making her far too aware once again of his size.

'I can walk up a few flights of stairs,' she muttered, determined to believe it even though her knees were rapidly turning to jelly.

Unfortunately, the fragile feeling wasn't just because of his nearness, and the threats he'd made, but also because those few words had struck something inside her, however unintentionally. It was a long time since anyone had cared about her welfare, except herself.

She locked her knees and clutched the coat tighter, refusing to allow the sentimental thought to soften her attitude towards him.

Xander Caras didn't care about her. He'd proved that five months ago by withholding his identity on a technicality. And disappearing the next day. They hadn't made a connection. She'd simply been an easy conquest.

How he must have been laughing at her when she'd told him all about her mum, and sounded off about the man who had bought their special island, not realising she'd just made love to him.

Resentment surged.

Maybe Caras cared about the baby. But even that seemed doubtful, when he'd threatened to take it away from its mother, as if it was a possession he wanted to own, rather than a person who deserved to be nurtured by the woman who had chosen to give it life. She cradled her belly beneath the coat as the elevator's doors opened silently to reveal another lounge area. This one, though, wasn't as open to the elements. Glass walls looked across the bay towards the lights of Port Gabriel on the headland. A six-person hot tub stood on the outside deck surrounded by luxury leather seating, steam rising from it in the night air.

'Shouldn't that be covered?' she asked, without thinking. 'It'll cost you a fortune open to the elements like that.'

She realised how ridiculous that sounded when he chuckled.

'Fortunes are relative,' he said. 'And I prefer it left available for use until I retire for the night. It is one of the ways I use to relax most evenings.'

'Oh,' she said, aware of the new wave of heat hitting her cheeks at the thought of him lounging in the tub, all those muscles and sinews sheened with steam and sweat.

One of the ways?

She blinked and turned, to find him watching her. Arousal swelled and pulsed in her abdomen on cue.

Why did the throwaway comment feel so intimate? And that dark look in his eyes, which she remembered far too well from their day together. She'd misunderstood it then. He hadn't been looking at her with admiration or fascination or even any real interest in her as a person. All he'd really been thinking about was how to seduce her, so he could relax himself with some extra-curricular sex—which she'd been far too willing to provide, after a day spent under that torrid gaze.

'Sit,' he murmured, indicating the leather couches that lined the space, the command tempered by the fact the muscle in his jaw had stopped clenching. It felt like a concession of sorts. 'Would you like anything to drink?'

The offer seemed oddly polite, given their argument, but also strangely conciliatory. Their conversation had got out of control on the lower deck. Keeping things civil made sense, however hard it was for her. He was right about one thing, whatever had occurred five months ago was in the past, and she needed to get over that sense of betrayal—and loss—so she could deal with what happened next.

She'd totally underestimated how complicated this situation was going to be. But adding all those foolish emotions to the mix—which had been based on dreams that had never been real—was just going to make dealing with this man, and her current reality, that much tougher.

She cleared her throat, which was so dry it could give the Sahara Desert a run for its money, and nodded. 'Umm, yes, thanks, a glass of water would be great.'

He nodded. Producing a pricey bottle of mineral water from the fridge behind the bar, he filled two crystal tumblers and added ice and a slice of lemon to each. He brought both glasses over to where she had perched herself on the butter-soft leather.

She shrugged off the coat and took one. Their fingers brushed. The jolt of reaction rippled through her. She took a big gulp of the icy water, in the hope it might cure her dry throat and cool the now radioactive blush.

He relaxed into the seat next to her, crossing one ankle over his knee, and making the fabric of his trousers stretch over his thigh muscle.

She jerked her gaze to his face, stupidly aware again of how easily his presence could make her think of that day. Those hours they had spent together.

She took another long swallow of her water. Was he waiting for her to say something? Or just trying to unnerve her? Because it was totally working.

As she tried to formulate something coherent to say that wouldn't make the whole situation worse, he cleared his throat.

'Have you suffered from any sickness?' he asked. 'You have lost weight, despite the pregnancy.'

The probing question, and the astute observation, surprised her. But not as much as the horrifying surge of arousal when he continued.

'Except your breasts,' he added, his voice husky as his

gaze roamed over her figure with a sense of entitlement that disturbed her almost as much as the way her nipples tightened against her bra under his observation. 'They are even more generous than I remember.'

'Th-that's normal…' she stammered, wishing she hadn't taken off the coat now. 'It's the hormones.'

He nodded. 'And the weight loss, is this normal too?'

'I—I haven't lost weight,' she said, then realised how defensive that sounded, especially as strictly speaking it wasn't entirely true. After her last scan a month ago, the doctor had told her she needed to keep an eye on her nutrition, because the baby was big for dates—not surprising given the size of its father, she realised now—but she was underweight in comparison.

He frowned and then his eyes narrowed, the sceptical expression making her feel even more defensive.

'Who is handling your maternity care in Galicos?' he asked.

No one. The answer sprang into her head, but she managed to prevent it from popping out of her mouth, because she could suddenly imagine how irresponsible that might sound. But, really, she was perfectly healthy. A little tired perhaps— because she'd been working nights. And she'd struggled to gain weight initially, because the morning sickness *had* been brutal for a few weeks before and after her last antenatal appointment. But she was over that now.

'I'm perfectly healthy, Alex,' she countered. The minute she'd used the name he'd given her that day, she wished she could take it back. 'I—I mean, Mr Caras.'

One dark eyebrow arched, and he leaned back in his seat. He took a long draught of water as he watched her over the rim of the glass. He put it down on the table in front of him. How could he look so relaxed, she wondered, when she felt as if her insides were tied in large greasy knots?

'You are having my child, Poppy. I think you can call me Alex,' he said, the husky tone matched by the wry amusement in his eyes.

'Except that's not your name,' she snapped back, reminded all over again of how she'd fallen so easily for his lies that day. 'The article I read in the business press referred to you as Xander Caras.'

She'd only managed to find one article on him, an interview in an investment magazine, when she'd looked for more information about him after seeing the celebrity piece about his rumoured engagement to Galicos royalty, and more recently the social media thread about his engagement announcement and party. She wished now she'd looked a lot harder, because she felt unarmed. She hadn't, for example, really understood how wealthy he was until she'd seen his yacht.

'My given name is Alexander,' he said, hitching one shoulder in a nonchalant shrug. 'Most people call me Xander, it is true, but you are welcome to call me Alex…' His gaze drifted to her waist. 'After all, you are the only woman who has ever been pregnant with my child, so you are not *most* people.'

She let out a breath, trying desperately to relax and not react to the patient tone. It was pointless having an argument about what she was going to call him. And equally pointless to give in to that foolish flush of pleasure that he considered her special in some way. Of course she was special to him now. But only because she was having his child.

'You don't have any other children?' she asked, because she was suddenly curious.

He shook his head. 'You are also the only woman I have ever chosen to make love to without using a condom.'

Her cheeks heated again. They'd used withdrawal that day, because they'd both been desperate to feel him inside her. And neither of them had had any other form of protection with them. It had been a stupid risk. She knew that now. But she couldn't regret it.

'I should apologise,' he added, the flags of colour on his cheeks returning. 'For not pulling out fast enough.'

'That's okay,' she replied, strangely touched he would think an apology was necessary when they'd both made the choice to go ahead. 'When I found out I was pregnant, I wasn't upset. I wanted to have the baby.'

She knew now, of course, the burst of euphoria she'd felt in that moment had had a lot to do with her feelings for him, or rather her feelings for the man she had thought she'd met on the beach that day. But once she'd found out who he really was, she'd already heard the baby's heartbeat and seen it on the ultrasound monitor. However hard it had been to face the fact that what had happened that day was a lie, her excitement about becoming a mother would always be real.

She shrugged. 'And anyway, we both made the choice to take that risk. So, we're both responsible for the consequences.'

Unhooking his ankle, he leant forward and brushed his thumb down her face. She shuddered, the slight contact nothing short of electric. But somehow she couldn't seem to pull away from his touch as he traced his finger across her cheek and hooked a curl of hair behind her ear.

She dropped her chin, disturbed by the fierce light in his eyes, which made her remember the way he had looked at her that day, as if she mattered. As if he cared.

She gulped down the ball of need.

He captured her chin between his thumb and forefinger and lifted her face back to his.

'You must let me support you, and our child, Poppy,' he said, the passion and purpose in his eyes unmistakeable. 'I do not want you working in this condition.'

The words reverberated in her heart, as well as her head,

but then he cradled her cheek and tugged her towards him, adding, 'And I have never stopped wanting you.'

Her lips trembled, the yearning coming from nowhere, when he lowered his head to hers and captured her mouth in a searing kiss.

She sucked in a breath, knowing it was wrong, knowing she shouldn't give in to the passion that made her heart race and pound between her thighs the second his mouth conquered hers. But then his tongue swept across her lips, demanding entry, and her mouth opened to let him in.

His tongue delved deep, exploring the recesses of her mouth, and she probed back, her tongue tangling with his, demanding, desperate to have more. His fingers thrust into her hair as he angled her head to take the kiss deeper. She clung to his shirt front, propelled back to that bright sunny day, when everything had been so wonderful, so exhilarating, so full of promise and possibilities. He'd been so strong, so perfect, so unknowable and yet so exciting—a man who saw her and wanted her.

He broke the kiss first, their ragged breaths a brutal reminder of that day five months before when they'd made their baby. He rested his forehead on hers, the delirious feeling of connection so intense she felt branded, as his thumb stroked her neck.

'I could not forget you,' he murmured against her lips.

The words brushed across her heart, but then the truth struck her. The way it had a month ago when she'd read about his upcoming engagement. And she reared back, dragging herself away from that possessive touch.

She leapt up from the seat and stood trembling, still far too aware of the throbbing sensation where his lips had devoured hers. And her instant, unstoppable reaction to that drugging kiss that had made her forget again who he really was.

'Don't say that, when you know it's not true,' she managed, brutally aware now of how easily she had succumbed again. All he'd had to do was say he wanted her, and she'd been putty in his hands. Even though everything about this situation was wrong.

He unfolded himself from the seat and walked towards her, his face flushed, the piercing blue gaze intense. 'Of course it is true. We have such chemistry. Or you would not have kissed me as you just did,' he replied, so close now she could feel the heat of his body. 'And you would not now be pregnant with my child.'

She took another step back, and wrapped her arms around her waist where their baby grew. 'But you love someone else,' she said, her voice breaking on the words.

His frown deepened, but it was the blank confusion in his expression that shocked her more. As if he had no idea what she was talking about.

'Princess Freya,' she prompted. 'The woman everyone says you're planning to marry.'

The confusion cleared, and she almost felt sorry for the Princess. How could he have forgotten his soon-to-be fiancée so easily?

But then he swore and muttered something in Greek, before stalking across the lounge. He stood with his back to her, every muscle in his spine rigid, as he stared out into the night.

She lifted her coat from her seat. 'I want to return to Galicos now,' she said, hating the tremor in her voice. And the guilt and shame rising up her torso.

She had never intended to get pregnant by another woman's boyfriend. And perhaps he hadn't been dating the Princess when they'd met. But the fact he could kiss her with such fervour even now, when he was about to pledge himself to someone else, said a lot about him. Worse, though, was what that said about her.

He wasn't wrong about the chemistry they shared. Unfortunately, it was as vivid and combustible as it had ever been. But that was all it was, a physical attraction, a biological need. An animal instinct that they needed to control instead of encouraging.

'She means nothing to me,' he said, stopping her in her tracks as she made her way to the lift.

She had to force herself to clamp down on the awful rush of hope at his words, which were swiftly followed by another wave of shame. But before she could think of anything to say about his brutal revelation, he crossed the lounge towards her.

'How…? How can she mean nothing if you are going to marry her?' she forced herself to ask.

He shrugged as if the details were of no interest to him.

'The marriage is part of an arrangement I made with her father, Prince Andreas, to purchase anchorage in Galicos for Caras Shipping's new cruise liners.' The muscle in his jaw began twitching again, his frustration at being forced to explain himself clear. 'It was a requirement of the Prince, because he did not wish to sell land in the principality to anyone outside the royal family. He suggested that a marriage between us would make him more comfortable about selling me the land.'

She sucked in a breath, the pragmatic answer, and the cold tone, somehow worse than the thought he had cheated on the woman he loved. 'You're dating the Princess to secure a land deal?'

The thought sickened her. Who *was* this guy? Really? Of course, she understood people didn't always marry for love, she wasn't *that* naïve. But she was still stunned that anyone could be so ruthless.

His gaze sharpened. 'I am not in a relationship with Princess Freya. I have met her precisely twice. And I have never slept with her.' His eyes darkened. 'In fact, I have not slept with anyone since that day. Because you have a hold on me which I cannot break.'

She stiffened, shocked by the revelation. But even more shocked by the desire to romanticise it, when the brittle light in his eyes suggested he saw her effect on him as some kind of curse. She knew how he felt now, because the feelings she'd had for him, the feelings she'd believed had developed over that one bright beautiful day, had all been a lie.

'If that's supposed to make me feel better, it doesn't,' she said.

She turned, intending to head down to the lower deck and beg his steward for a lift back to the mainland if she had to. But before she could make her getaway, he caught her wrist and tugged her back around to face him.

'Feelings are not important now. What matters is what is going to happen next. You and this baby are my responsibility, and I will not allow you to—'

'I don't care what you'll allow.' She jerked her wrist free, forcing the anger with his arrogance to the fore to cover the hurt. 'I can look after myself without any help from you.'

'And yet it is clear you cannot...' He grasped her wrist again.

But then they both startled at the sound of someone clearing their throat, loudly.

She swung round to see a man—as tall and muscular as Alex, with the same piercing blue eyes—standing with his hip propped against the bar, his legs crossed at the ankles and his arms folded over his chest. His stance was casual, his demeanour a lot less intense and moody than Alex's, but she already knew this had to be his younger brother... She'd read in that same article that Theodoros Caras co-owned the company, but also that he was a devastatingly handsome and charming playboy. She could see that was objectively true—his chiselled features were more finely drawn than his brother's, but they lacked the brooding intensity that made Alex's face so compelling.

A feral light glittered in the man's eyes and a cynical smile twisted his lips.

'Sorry to interrupt your lovers' quarrel,' he said, his English perfect but his accent a mid-Atlantic mix of American and European, unlike his brother's, which was much more Greek. 'But you need to keep the noise down.'

The man's gaze dropped to her stomach, but then to Poppy's astonishment he laughed.

'So, it's true. The Internet is already buzzing with the news Princess Freya's intended was seen escorting a pregnant waitress off the wharf and taking her to his yacht.'

The chuckle turned wry with amusement as his gaze rose back to Poppy's burning face.

'Good to meet you, miss.' He gave her a mock bow. 'I'm Theo Caras, Xander's bad-boy kid brother.' He dipped his head to indicate her pregnancy, his smile widening as his attention returned to his brother, and those blue eyes became eagle sharp. 'But if that's really my brother's responsibility— as he just broadcast to the crew of this yacht and probably every sharp-eared paparazzi with a telephoto lens gathered on the dock a mile away—it appears I'm not the only bad boy in the family any more.'

CHAPTER FOUR

'I'M SO GLAD you find this situation amusing,' Xander growled, switching into Greek to address his brother so Poppy would not be able to understand their argument. The last thing he needed was for his brother's sarcasm to make this impossible situation even worse.

He had never felt more frustrated or impotent in his life—the fact that he was also now brutally turned on after that ill-advised kiss was not helping him control his temper.

His marriage to Freya could not go ahead. That much was already obvious. Not only had he never had any real desire to take the woman to his bed, but his private life had just become a great deal more complicated. Factoring in an arranged marriage now would only make the situation worse. He had no desire to lose the port deal that had been ten months in the making, but his child would have to take precedence.

'Is the baby yours?' his brother asked, taking the hint and switching into their native tongue as well, while getting straight to the point.

'Yes,' he said, because there was no point in denying it. The realisation a part of him wanted Poppy's baby to be his did not escape him either. A part of him that had a lot to do with the furious wave of desire when he had first seen her rounded belly in the bar, and noticed her full breasts, and wanted to believe he had staked a claim to her in the most elemental way possible.

'Are you sure about that?' Theo asked, even as he maintained the relaxed stance—probably for Poppy's benefit so she would not realise the direction of the conversation.

'She has no reason to lie,' he replied sharply, annoyed his brother would accuse Poppy of such a deception, even though he had believed the same thing himself at first. But he hadn't been able to maintain that delusion for long—her open, honest expression and her refusal to accept his help damning his suspicious nature.

His brother let out a harsh laugh. 'Yeah, right. You're a rich man, Xander.' He spoke in rapid Greek now as his gaze drifted to the woman who was still trying to pull out of Xander's grip. 'And she's a waitress. Plus, you're about to marry into European royalty. You don't think that gives her an incentive to pretend you're the father of her kid? How much has she asked for to keep quiet about your little accident?'

'She has asked for nothing. She does not want my money…' Which was the most infuriating thing of all. Before either of them could say more, though, Poppy had struggled loose.

'Sorry to interrupt,' she announced in English, not sounding sorry at all. 'And it's been nice meeting you, too, Alex's bad-boy kid brother,' she continued in the same indignant tone that suggested she had guessed their switch to Greek had been a deliberate attempt to exclude her. 'But I'm going back to shore now.'

'Who's Alex?' Theo replied.

At the exact same time as Xander said, 'No, you are not.'

He snagged Poppy's arm yet again to prevent her marching off.

'You cannot return to Galicos now,' he continued, struggling to contain his increasingly volatile temper at her belligerent expression. 'Did you not hear what my brother said? There are already reporters on the dock.'

He had always hated the press, and had kept a low profile

in the media—giving only a few interviews over the years exclusively to the business press—for the simple reason he did not want people prying into his past, or judging him and his brother for the things they had once had to do to survive.

He wasn't ashamed of those things. But having that part of his life exposed to media scrutiny would allow others to control the narrative and make assumptions about him that might not be beneficial to the image he wished to promote for Caras Shipping. One of the main reasons he had insisted that the engagement to Princess Freya be announced only a few months before their proposed wedding was to maintain his low profile in the press for as long as possible.

But now, Theo's news that Poppy and he had been spotted leaving the wharf together seemed surprisingly fortuitous, as it gave him an opportunity he intended to exploit. He did not want her leaving the yacht. Not until they had got a few crucial things straight. One of which pertained to the baby. And one of which pertained to the insane chemistry—which had not abated in the least in the past five months if that kiss was anything to go by.

He did not intend to let her out of his sight again. And especially not in her current condition. The idea of her supporting herself on a waitress's salary was ludicrous. He understood she had her pride. But he had learned at a young age there were several things more important… One of which was the security only wealth—and lots of it—could give you.

'So what? I'll just ask whoever takes me back to drop me off away from the main dock,' she said, still struggling against his hold. 'Will you let go of me?'

'No, I will not. You are not leaving this yacht. It isn't safe. For you…or my child.' He ground the words out.

'Why not?' She glared at him, freeing her arm a second time. 'They don't know me from Adam, and I certainly don't intend to broadcast our connection.'

His anger flared. Was she ashamed of him, then? Why? What had he done to be treated with such contempt? Had she not kissed him back with the same hunger he was struggling to control?

Before he could formulate a coherent response though, which did not involve throwing her over his shoulder, carting her down to the Sunrise Suite and locking her in, his brother interrupted them both.

'Chill out, guys. There's no need to yell.'

'I'm afraid there is every need to yell,' Poppy yelled. 'To get your brother to listen to me. He promised he'd take me back when I wished and now he's breaking—'

'Hey, don't shoot the messenger, miss.' Theo lifted his hands in a defensive gesture, but the admiration in his eyes suggested he was enjoying Poppy's refusal to see reason.

It figured!

Xander swore at Theo then added in Greek, 'Do not encourage her foolishness. You're supposed to be on my side.'

'I am on your side, *Alex*,' he teased, also in Greek.

'Stop talking in Greek.' Poppy slapped her hands on her hips, which made her blouse stretch over those full breasts. He blinked, trying to ignore the renewed shot of lust and how much he wanted to capture those tight peaks between his lips. Her breasts had been incredibly sensitive that day— would they be even more so now?

'I know perfectly well you're both talking about me,' she continued, looking almost as frustrated as he felt while he tried to drag his mind away from her breasts and back to the problem at hand. 'And it's incredibly rude to discuss me while I'm standing right here in a language you know I don't understand.'

'To be fair, miss,' Theo began, the mocking smile turning into a grin, 'no one has ever accused either one of us of having good manners.'

Poppy opened her mouth again, looking almost as annoyed with Theo now as she was with him. Which was a minor improvement. But before she could let rip at his brother, Theo stepped closer to her and rested a consoling arm over her shoulders.

'Hey, I'm sorry, okay, miss…' He dropped his voice to a friendly murmur. 'What is your name, by the way? Xander didn't introduce us…'

'Poppy… Poppy Brown,' Poppy replied, looked momentarily nonplussed with Theo's familiarity.

The sudden burst of relief that Xander finally knew Poppy's last name was followed by the bigger surge of jealousy.

If his brother didn't lift his arm from her shoulders in the next ten seconds, he would throw him overboard.

Perhaps sensing Xander's anger with him, Theo removed his arm, but he remained by her side, then shot Xander a conspiratorial look that seemed to be saying, *Don't worry, I've got this*... Before he sent Poppy a far-too-charming smile.

'I'm sorry to say, Poppy, that my brother is not wrong about the situation in Galicos.' Theo tugged his phone from his pocket, clicked on something and handed it to her. 'Nowhere there is going to be safe. You were both photographed leaving the restaurant where you work, and it's already hit the Internet.'

Poppy took the phone to examine the photographs. Then pressed trembling fingers to her mouth.

Xander drew closer, to look over her shoulder at the social media app Theo had opened. And got a lungful of her intoxicating scent for his troubles. He forced himself to detach his gaze from the soft skin of her nape, to examine the photos too.

And immediately understood Poppy's distress.

They looked like a couple in the snatched shots. He had his hand on the small of her back, was clearly shepherding her to the cab, while she seemed small and fragile beside him, her rounded belly hard to miss. Poppy flicked through the article on screen, which was written in French and had named the restaurant. The app had a whole series of photos— had there been a photographer on the wharf? The shots were surely far too professional to have been taken by an amateur. And they clearly hadn't wasted any time selling them to the highest bidder, because they had already appeared on this gossip website, with a series of captions identifying him as the man about to declare his engagement to Princess Freya.

Poppy began to tremble, the belligerence of moments ago gone. 'Do you think they'll be able to find out my name?' she asked, but he could already hear her panic.

Theo retrieved his phone, then said, as he cast Xander a meaningful glance, 'Yeah, I do. They know where you work, Poppy. It's only a matter of time before someone you work with gives up the information.'

'But they're my friends. They wouldn't…'

'Money talks, Poppy,' Theo said. 'And you're about to become a big story. You and Xander and the baby…'

'But I didn't mean for this to happen…' she said, and Xander heard the confusion as well as the innocence in her voice he remembered so well from that afternoon.

Before he could think better of the gesture, he pressed his hand to her shoulder, felt her quiver of distress. And wanted to murder whoever had invaded their privacy. He intended to use the press attention to keep her here, but the visceral anger with that photographer felt justified.

He pulled her around to face him and saw hopelessness in her face now as well as fatigue.

'I need that job,' she murmured, sounding devastated. 'The tips are really good, and I don't have any savings left.'

What foolishness was this now?

He frowned. Surely, she had to know she could not return

to work. The restaurant would be besieged by reporters, and so would she. And he had already told her he intended to support her now.

But when he saw astonishment flash across his brother's face, he clamped down on the angry retort. He had already told Poppy he had no intention of abandoning his responsibilities to her or the baby. But losing his temper—and his hurt at her refusal to accept anything from him—had not helped. Clearly, she was exhausted. And more fragile than she realised. He needed to treat this situation with finesse, no matter what it cost him. Because his first priority at the moment was to impress upon her she could not leave the safety of the yacht.

'Serge is already understaffed,' she continued. 'So I can't just—'

'Poppy, this is not rational,' he cut in to her ramblings, as gently as he could, while tucking a knuckle under her chin and lifting her face to his.

The sheen in her eyes, and the way she chewed her lip, made frustration and something a lot more volatile coil in his gut.

'But I—' she began again.

'Listen to me. You will stay here, tonight.' If he got his way, she would be under his protection now for the foreseeable future. But he would have to deal with the logistics of that after he had spoken in private to Theo, because he had to persuade his brother to return to Galicos and break off the engagement—and renegotiate the deal with Prince Andreas without a marriage, as there was no way he could marry the man's daughter now. Theo's greatest strength was his charm—perhaps he could use it to schmooze the Prince into selling them the land without a marriage?

The cruise line had always been Xander's baby. Theo had been against the idea from the start—seeing no need for them to diversify. But they had sunk enough capital into the venture now that Theo would be incentivised to find a solution. And it would have to be his brother's problem to solve. Because buying the land they needed in the principality was now way down on Xander's list of priorities. By far the most pressing problem was the woman in front of him, looking as if she had just been kicked in the teeth. Keeping her safe from the reporters until he could figure out what the hell he was going to do about her and the hold she still had over him—not to mention his child—was what he must focus on first.

'I don't think that's a good idea...' Poppy began again. But he simply brushed his thumb across her lips to silence her. Her vicious shudder of reaction reverberated in his groin.

'I know you don't wish to stay...' he said, as calmly as he could manage. 'But you must think of the baby. Do not be so naïve as to believe the press will go easy on you because you are pregnant and unable to defend yourself against them. They won't. And Theo is right, wherever you go now, they will find you. Especially if you do not have the resources to protect yourself.'

A tear slipped over her lid. She brushed it away with her fist. A flush of embarrassment lit her cheeks, making it clear she wished he hadn't seen her weakness.

'I shouldn't have come here. I didn't think this through at all.' She sighed, her shoulders drooping in defeat.

He captured her waist and went with the urge to pull her against him. She stood stiffly in his arms, clearly unsure about accepting his support, but also unable to stop trembling.

He stroked her narrow shoulders, aware of the compact bump between them. This was a new experience for him too. He had always been a hard man—had always been determined never to let his guard down. Tenderness was a weakness, one he had succumbed to only once before... And this woman had been responsible for those strange urges then, too.

But when she finally stopped trembling and let out a hefty sigh, all he felt was relief.

He drew back. Her chestnut eyes had lost their anger, so the only thing left was vulnerability. He doubted that would last. Poppy was far too independent, and frankly impulsive and reckless, to let her guard down for long. But tonight, she looked too washed out to fight him any longer. And he was glad of that much at least.

'Meghan has already prepared the Sunrise Suite. Let me take you there. You can sleep and then we will discuss what to do in the morning?' He tried to phrase it as a question, even though he had already made up his mind.

They could not remain in Galicos. Not if they were to have privacy and Poppy was to be protected from the fallout when news of the broken engagement came out.

She let out another sigh. 'Okay, but can you tell me how to get to the suite? I just want to be alone.'

He bristled, not willing to let her out of his sight. But he forced himself not to demand she let him escort her… He would have to learn to only fight the battles that mattered, because demanding her obedience only made her more belligerent. Releasing his hold on her, reluctantly, he pulled his phone out and sent a message to Meghan, the yacht's service manager.

'I have requested that Meghan escort you to your suite,' he told her as he put away his phone. 'If there is anything you require, just ask and she will supply it.'

She nodded. 'Thanks.' She pressed her hand to her stomach as she grabbed her bag and coat from the seat. 'And… I'm sorry. It was never my intention to make this so complicated.'

When Meghan arrived, Poppy thanked Theo too, then left with her. The weary set of her shoulders added incredulity to the surge of possessiveness—and determination.

Had she really believed telling him about the pregnancy

would be simple? That he would have no interest in the child growing inside her? Of course, their situation was complicated. But frankly one thing remained clear. As the mother of his child, she would have to deal with him now. And he had no intention of letting her remain alone. And unprotected.

And that had not one thing to do with media intrusion.

'There is a selection of nightclothes in the armoire, Miss Brown, and complimentary toiletries in the bathroom, but if there's anything specific you need—in the way of clothing or accessories—I can get a crew member to pick them up first thing in the morning.'

Poppy turned from contemplating the lavish suite to find Meghan Henri, who had introduced herself as the yacht's service manager, smiling at her.

'No… That's…' She hesitated. The suite was beautifully furnished and appointed, the large picture window looking out onto the shoreline. She'd never lived anywhere so lavish, but something about this level of luxury felt incredibly intimidating, almost as intimidating as the man who owned it.

'You've been so kind and helpful, Meghan,' she said, desperately trying not to be totally overwhelmed. She'd almost burst into tears when Alex had tugged her into his arms and held her. Stupid really, because he was the cause of most of her panic, and that huge bottomless pit in her stomach, which had become a chasm when she'd seen the photographs on his brother's phone. 'But I'm only going to be here for one night.'

'Of course, miss.' The older woman's expression remained gentle. 'Is there anything else you would like, to eat or drink, before you retire for the night?'

'No, thank you.' Poppy shook her head. The last thing she would be able to do right now was eat anything. Her insides felt as if they had been knotted into a pretzel, while everything that had happened in the last hour was still bombarding her exhausted brain. She needed to sleep. Alex was right about that much. Hopefully everything would seem less overwhelming—and insurmountable—tomorrow.

She'd need to find another job, and she would probably have to get out of Galicos. But surely the press wouldn't be *that* interested in the story. Perhaps she would just have to lie if they did track her down, and say the baby wasn't Alex's. She didn't want anything from him, and surely he would have to see reason about supporting her, because it would mean acknowledging he was having a child with a woman who was not the one he was planning to marry.

Even if he didn't have a romantic attachment to Princess Freya, he was obviously invested in the marriage.

She shivered at the memory of his ruthless explanation for the engagement. What kind of man agreed to marry a woman he barely knew to secure a land deal?

She let her gaze linger on the luxury furnishings, the leather upholstery and the silk quilt on the bed, monogrammed with the Caras Shipping logo, and felt the gentle sway of the water beneath her feet.

The kind of man who had enough money to own a yacht the size of an apartment building.

She took a careful breath. The good news was, while Alex's wealth was intimidating, his business was also extremely important to him, which meant he would soon realise it was in his best interests not to claim the baby as his...

She swallowed. Not Alex, *Xander*.

She *had* to stop thinking of him by that name. He wasn't Alex, he had never been Alex. Not really. That man had been an illusion, whom Xander Caras had created to seduce her and she had become besotted with far too easily. The brooding magnetism, the curt, guarded responses of the man she had met on the beach in Rhodes, had called to someone inside her who had always wanted to be seen by a man like him. A man who had appeared to be so emotionally unattainable even then. And so, as soon as he had finally been persuaded to give her a lift to the island, she had made it her mission to make him smile, to entertain him and not make him regret his decision.

And that day. When he had softened, when he had smiled at her and eventually laughed with her, when he had encouraged her to talk about her mum, she had been utterly captivated, while also feeling empowered, because she'd thought she had achieved something magnificent. That she had made this hard, closed-off man lighten up a little. And then, when they'd made love, and he'd been so intense, so focussed, so determined to give her pleasure, she had been intoxicated. And believed she had given him something equally precious in return, when it had all just been a tactic.

She breathed through the renewed swell of loss. The bitter stab of betrayal.

Get over it, Poppy.

Maybe Xander Caras had played her. But she had been unforgivably foolish and hopelessly naïve, too.

You let yourself get played because you got high on his attention that day. And then his lovemaking.

And that hadn't been all Xander Caras' fault. Why *wouldn't* he take advantage of her when she had been such an eager— and willing—participant? So addicted to their chemistry still, she hadn't even been able to resist him when he'd kissed her again, ten minutes ago.

'I'll leave you for the night, Miss Brown,' Meghan said, yanking Poppy out of the feverish internal monologue. 'But if you think of anything, just press the call button.'

'Thank you,' Poppy said again, but as Meghan opened the door to leave, a question surfaced that had been lying in wait ever since the woman had mentioned the selection of nightwear—and even before that, when Alex, no, *Xander*, had talked about his relaxation regime in the hot tub.

'Wait, Meghan… W-would you mind…? Could I ask you something, in confidence?'

The service manager paused, a curious expression on her face. 'Of course, miss.'

'Has Alex…? I—I mean Xander… Sorry, Mr Caras. The older Mr Caras…' She stuttered to a halt, embarrassment making her cheeks burn.

Good grief, could she actually make this any more awkward?

'You have a question about Mr Xander?' the woman prompted, not looking perturbed by Poppy's rambling non-question. Which made Poppy feel hopelessly foolish again—and tongue-tied.

This woman was employed by Xander Caras, of course she would be loyal to him, which meant she would probably refuse to answer a personal question about him. But who else could she ask?

'Does Mr Caras invite a lot of guests on the yacht?' she blurted out, almost choking on her own embarrassment.

Meghan looked momentarily nonplussed. 'He often conducts business on it, yes.'

'No, I meant… Does he have a lot of female guests, you know, like girlfriends?' She flung a hand out to indicate the armoire. 'You mentioned there was nightwear here. I just… I wondered. If having women stay the night onboard is a regular thing.'

The woman's eyebrows rose as she realised what Poppy was asking her. And Poppy suddenly wished she could just chuck herself overboard…

But then instead of being outraged or, worse, offended, Meghan let out a surprised chuckle.

'Actually, no, he doesn't. Not a lot. Since I've been working for him—which is over a year now—he's only brought a couple of women on board socially, and neither of them stayed the night.' The woman's warm smile took on a mischievous tilt. 'And there's been no one at all in the last six months. Mr Theo, on the other hand, is more…' She cleared her throat, discreetly. 'Shall we say sociable? But I can honestly say, they're always very well behaved with the staff. Surprisingly so for men in their position.'

The easy expression sobered. 'Obviously, I'd prefer if you could keep that information between the two of us. Mr Xander, particularly, is very strict about his private life remaining confidential and I wouldn't want him to think I was gossiping about him or his brother.' Meghan's gaze rested for a moment on Poppy's pregnant belly. The kindness in her eyes made Poppy feel stupidly grateful when she continued. 'Although it's clear Mr Xander now considers you to be part of his private life, so hopefully he won't mind.'

'I… Right…' Poppy managed, tongue-tied again. 'I won't tell him what you said, you have my word.'

Meghan nodded and left.

It wasn't until the door had closed behind her, though, that Poppy realised the identity of her baby's father was now not a secret to anyone on the crew. Apparently, Theo had been right about them broadcasting the information to the whole ship during their argument.

But somehow, as she showered and changed into a brand-new silk negligee she found wrapped in tissue paper in the armoire, her stomach unknotted enough to allow the tiredness back in.

As she drifted into a deep, drugging sleep on the thousand-thread-count sheets, listening to the lap of the waves against the yacht's hull, she decided that Meghan's confidential revelations about Xander Caras' not so prolific love life made her feel a tiny, weeny little bit less overwhelmed.

CHAPTER FIVE

'WHAT DO YOU MEAN, you want me to fix it? *You* fix it. The cruise-ship business was your baby...'

Xander splashed ouzo into two shot glasses and handed his irate brother one. He needed something stronger than water right now. A *lot* stronger.

'And now I have another baby to worry about...' he offered, before downing the traditional liquor in one gulp. The aniseed burned his throat. Normally he would dilute the aperitif with water and ice, but right now he needed it neat. His insides were churning, his emotions in turmoil, ever since he had spotted Poppy from the car.

Tomorrow he would have to figure out how to proceed—how to make the woman who was having his child do as he asked. But tonight, he was forced to confront one essential truth. Something *had* happened on that day in April, in Parádeisos, something more than just that instant physical connection that had made him act out of character right from the moment she had approached him on the beach and begged for a lift to his own island, her brown eyes glowing with purpose and passion.

His brother continued to scowl. 'Why are you so positive the baby is yours? I'd want proof.'

He sighed. His brother was the ultimate cynic, a man who believed in nothing and no one—and was reckless and impulsive and followed his passions without regrets. But then

Theo had never known the stability of family life. And those feral instincts had served them both well on the streets of Athens. Domesticating Theo was an impossibility—which was why Xander had offered himself as Princess Freya's groom. At least, that was what he'd told himself at the time.

But having Poppy in his arms again, her lips softening under his mouth, her tongue tangling with his, had told a different story—of why he might have decided to finally agree to Andreas' suggestion of an arranged marriage, the week after that day on Parádeisos. Something about his reaction to Poppy had unsettled him. Wasn't that why he had prevented her from blurting out her name to him on the dock? Why he'd been so determined to leave that night, and never look back again?

No one had ever made him feel the way she had that day. As if his dreams had always been too small, his ambitions for his life too pragmatic. She'd made him want for fanciful things, hope for a connection that could never be real, not for a man like him.

And now she was back and unsettling him all over again. But this time, they had a connection that he would never be able to break, never be able to walk away from. And that concerned him even more.

How would he ever get over her now? How could he ever get his life back on track? Back into that safe, secure place where he was immune to the opinions and approval of others?

'It will be easier to test the DNA once the child is born. You know that,' Xander murmured, even though he didn't need proof. Poppy hadn't tried to blackmail him, hadn't even asked for money, because that just wasn't who she was— which only made her more disturbing to his peace of mind. And more destructive to the wall he had never let anyone breach—least of all a wide-eyed girl with notions of romance and intimacy.

He poured himself another shot, but his brother grabbed the bottle neck.

'Slow down on the ouzo,' he said. He yanked the bottle out of Xander's hand and slammed it onto the bar. 'You need to tell me what exactly you're expecting me to do to fix the situation with Prince Andreas and his daughter. Because I've never even met them.'

Xander flicked open the buttons of his shirt, because the neckline was starting to strangle him. And tried to get his aching brain to engage. But the truth was, he had no plan— nor did he have the bandwidth at the moment to even care about the problems his broken engagement was going to cause.

He'd seen the appalled look on Poppy's face when he'd described his non-relationship to Princess Freya, the practical reasons for their marriage. And for a moment she had made him feel ashamed. *Damn her.* He was a pragmatic, ambitious businessman, and there was nothing wrong with that. She had no right to judge him, when she knew nothing of the struggles he had had to overcome.

He swallowed, a ball of anger forming in his throat. Why was he defending decisions he had made for the right reasons in his own head? He forced himself to think about the problem of Freya and not think about Poppy's shocked expression.

'Contact the Palace tonight,' he said. He glanced at his watch. And cursed—it was close to midnight. 'You'll have to contact them tomorrow. Tell them the engagement is off. And see if you can find a way to make the deal regardless. Perhaps we could lease the land, instead of purchasing it.'

Theo's frown deepened. 'That's it? That's all you've got? We've sunk close to a quarter of our capital into this venture. The first liner will be finished by the end of next year and now we've got nowhere to harbour the damn thing.' He huffed. 'Perhaps we should just sell the whole operation.'

'No,' Xander snarled back. 'We're not doing that.'

'Why not? What the hell is the big deal with the cruise line anyway?'

He glared at his brother. Angry that he was going to be forced to admit what he'd skated around for over two years, while he'd nurtured this part of the business without his brother's input. Or support.

'We need this to finally escape from our past...' he managed, reaching for the bottle again and topping up his glass without his brother's interference. Because his brother was gaping at him as if he had lost his mind.

'What the hell are you talking about?' Theo said, sounding more confused than angry now.

'I can still smell it sometimes,' Xander murmured. 'Stale urine, rotting garbage, cheap liquor...' He contemplated his glass, the clear ouzo bought from the finest distillery in Greece somehow mocking him. 'Those nights, when we would be sleeping in doorways, hiding... That's what I remember most. The stench. The reek of failure, of despair, of desperation. It has a smell. And I don't want to smell it on myself any more.'

Then maybe he wouldn't still be woken at night by the smell of his own fear. The stale sweat of his nightmares. Those terrifying anxiety dreams, that he wouldn't be strong enough to save his brother, to save himself. To keep them together. To make them a family.

The cruise line had been his way of finally rising above the last echoes of that grasping poverty. The container business had done so much for them both. It was what they had always known from those first days as kids, running errands on the docks. But their ships were still anchored in the areas of ports hidden from view, part of an industrial infrastructure that had no status, no class.

Theo stared at him. But instead of the contempt, maybe

even the cynical mockery he had expected to see when he revealed the true reason he had invested so much in the cruise business, what he saw was shock. And sadness.

His brother released a heavy breath. 'Okay, Xander,' he said, his voice gruff with a depth of emotion he never usually revealed to anyone. 'If that's the way you feel. We'll fix this.'

Theo placed his still full shot glass on the bar. Then clasped Xander's shoulder. '*I'll* fix this. You have my word.' His lips quirked into a rueful smile, breaking the tension. 'But I'm going to handle it my way. And you're not going to interfere. You okay with that?'

Xander didn't like the sound of that. Given Theo's propensity to think outside the box, and his willingness to break the rules if he couldn't bend them, his solution to the problem of how to get a new land deal with Andreas was likely to be drastic and quite possibly unethical. But, oddly, Xander found that he wanted his brother to take the reins now, and not just because he doubted Andreas would be receptive to any overtures from him after he had disrespected his daughter. It was past time Theo took more interest in this side of the business. They couldn't continue to grow as a company restricting themselves to the container business. And Xander's full attention needed to be on handling his volatile reaction to the woman now fast asleep in the Sunrise Suite—and not micromanaging his brother. He had to find a way to compartmentalise his feelings for Poppy, something he hadn't been able to do even before he'd found her again and discovered they now shared a life-long commitment.

'Whatever you need to do, do it. You have my full support,' Xander said, forcing himself to let go of control.

Theo could be wild, but he was also smart and shrewd, and his ruthless survival instinct would mean he would find a solution. Maybe it would not be one Xander would have chosen, but he would have to trust his brother.

'Okay. I'll head back to Galicos tonight and stay at the Grande,' Theo said, mentioning the hotel where they'd hired out the top floor so they had a business base in the principality—and somewhere to host the engagement party that wasn't happening.

Xander winced. 'We should cancel next week's event,' he murmured. 'I'll let Lydia know,' he said, mentioning his assistant in Athens who was handling the arrangements.

'Don't worry about any of that. I said I'll deal with it and I will.' Theo's rueful smile widened. 'You need to concentrate on what you're gonna do about your pregnant mistress.'

'She's not my mistress,' Xander replied. But even as he denied it, the wave of heat swept through him again at the memory of Poppy's astonished gasp before her lips softened beneath his.

'Yeah, right,' Theo said, not looking convinced. 'See you around, *Alex*.' He sent him a jaunty salute before he strolled out of the lounge.

Ten minutes later, Xander heard the launch power up. He watched the boat head away from the yacht with Theo at the helm. As it trailed across the dark water then approached the Port Gabriel marina, a barrage of flashes went off on the dock.

Paparazzi.

He cursed in Greek, then reached behind the bar to grab the onboard phone. Jack, the captain's mate—who was on watch for the night—picked up.

'Mr Caras, what can I do for you?' the young man asked in French.

'I'd like to weigh anchor tonight, and leave Galicos before dawn,' he replied in the same language, one decision made at least.

He did not want to wait until the piranhas hired boats and besieged the yacht for shots of him and Poppy, which they would do by first light. He also had no intention of allowing Poppy to return to shore with those bastards lying in wait.

'Yes, sir. Do you have a destination in mind?' Jack asked.

'Yes, Parádeisos,' he said, naming the island he had built a home on, but hadn't visited since that day in April.

If he had Poppy with him, though, there would be no need to stay away any longer. He let out a bitter laugh, aware of the supreme irony. Funny to think he hadn't even been prepared to admit the real reason he hadn't moved into his villa for five months was because he had been determined to forget her, and sleeping in the bed where they had made love would have made that impossible.

There would be no forgetting her now, though.

He heard shuffling papers. Then Jack came back on. 'I'll wake the captain to plot a route, sir. But that's approximately a three-day journey. Would you like us to factor in some stops en route? Maybe in Italy and Sicily or Malta?'

'Sure,' he replied. He didn't want to give Poppy a chance to walk away from him. But he had no idea what kind of a sailor she was, especially in her condition—and they would need to purchase her a new wardrobe, as she had nothing but her work clothes and a coat and bag with her. 'Just ensure we don't arrive at the first stop until tomorrow afternoon.'

She would be angry when she discovered they had left Galicos. Knowing Poppy, and her impulsiveness, he wouldn't put it past her to jump overboard if they were close enough to shore when she woke up.

'Yes, sir,' Jack replied. 'We'll aim for departure in the next couple of hours.'

'Good,' he murmured.

'Do you want to okay the itinerary before we set off?' he added.

'No,' Xander replied. He didn't care where they stopped.

When Poppy awoke he would have to prevent her from leaving the yacht until he got her assurance she would not run off.

But Theo had given him an idea about how to persuade her.

He had never taken a mistress…never even had a long-term relationship. But his preference for casual dating seemed to have died a death the moment he'd met Poppy Brown on that beach, because he'd had no desire to make love to any other woman since. That wouldn't last, once there chemistry had run its course… But still, perhaps the solution to controlling Poppy's headstrong behaviour was much simpler than it appeared.

He placed the phone back in its cradle. And poured himself another glass of ouzo, adding ice and water this time. As the liquor became cloudy, he settled himself on the bench seat.

He sipped slowly, savouring the sharp, bittersweet taste.

His life—not to mention his latest business venture—was a bombsite. But his emotions finally felt as if they were back under some semblance of control.

A smile formed as he listened to the yacht's engines purring to life in preparation for their departure. A shot of adrenaline worked its way through his system, languid and provocative as he pictured the woman in the cabin beneath him—her belly round with his child, her breasts swollen with the hormonal changes his seed had caused.

Heat pulsed and throbbed insistently in his groin, as it had so often in the last five months—every time he had remembered the bright, beautiful girl who had looked at him with such yearning, such hope, and then come apart in his arms with such artless and unbridled passion on that hot spring day…

But this time, he didn't try to control the surge of desire and possessiveness triggered by those recollections.

Poppy was *his* responsibility now, whether she liked it or not. Because they had made a baby together that day. Why should he not use that physical attraction to his advantage— when it would be in her best interests?

She would not be happy tomorrow morning to find herself trapped aboard his yacht as they cruised down the Italian coastline. But happiness was not as important as safety. It was a bitter truth he had learned as a boy. You did whatever you had to do to survive, and sometimes that meant trampling over other people's feelings.

He would not risk his child, or her, but that did not mean that they could not come to an accord that would suit them both. Once she had seen reason about her situation.

He rubbed his hand over his mouth, then licked his dry lips as her heady sigh, that little sob of surrender, echoed in his groin all over again.

Poppy was going to have to confront some difficult truths tomorrow morning. One of which was that, as the mother of his child, she no longer had the luxury of doing as she pleased. But there was no reason why they couldn't both enjoy the fallout. Eventually.

He knocked back the last of the ouzo.

In fact, he was rather looking forward to tomorrow morning's fireworks. Poppy had already proved to be an enchanting and exciting diversion… But, he'd discovered tonight, she was also a surprisingly formidable opponent.

And when had he ever backed down from a challenge?

CHAPTER SIX

'How DID YOU get all these scars, Alex?'
    'Why do you want to know? It is not important...'
    'It is to me. They look...scary.'
    'I guess they were, at the time...'
Poppy jerked awake, the scent of salt and suncream swirling through her consciousness, the vivid dream rich with memory... Deep blue eyes, guarded and wary, a low voice tight with tension. Her heart thundered in her ears, compassion squeezing her ribs again and making it hard to breathe.

It took her several deep breaths to orientate herself, and recognise where the luxury scent of new leather, the whisper of silk against her sensitive skin, and the heavy weight of loss were coming from.

She rolled over, to stare blankly at the cabin's expensive furnishings as the details from last night flooded back... Alex, so tall and indomitable in the restaurant, the journey across the water, his enormous yacht, the angry words, the confusing emotions knotting in her stomach... The force and fury of his kiss.

She gazed at the ceiling, the expensive polished mahogany, inlaid with lights. And struggled to haul herself the rest of the way out of the arresting dream—not a dream, a memory of the conversation they'd had beside the pool that day, when she'd finally got up the courage to ask him about the many nicks and cuts she'd noticed in the sunlight...

Funny to think that of all the things they'd talked about, she would remember that conversation so vividly. Because for one split second she'd seen the tough exterior he wore like a shield dropping, to reveal the vulnerability beneath.

Except what had that conversation really revealed? He was probably just clumsy which was why he had so many scars. And like everything else about him, she'd tried to romanticise it. Casting Alex as some kind of wounded boy, zealously guarding his secrets, instead of a rich, ruthless man who had lied to her deliberately.

Not Alex. Xander, you ninny.

She slid her hands over her stomach, but then she noticed the familiar need to pee.

She sat up, intending to forget the silly dream, only to notice the rumble of background noise that hadn't been there when she'd fallen asleep.

She climbed off the bed and walked to the cabin's picture window then pressed the button to lift the shutter. She stared at the vast expanse of sea—and the shoreline at least a mile away across the water... The moving shoreline!

'What the hell?' she screamed, so shocked her mind went completely blank.

Why was the yacht moving? In fact, it wasn't just moving, it was powering along at a rate of knots. She was still cursing as she dashed for the toilet, struggling to stay upright when the boat slapped a wave.

Once she'd relieved her full bladder, she washed her hands, then rushed back to the bedroom, to peer out—still struggling to get her mind to engage with what was happening.

Where was Port Gabriel? Where was the bay? The shore was much further away, but from the mountainous topography of the coast rushing past, she knew they weren't in the same location as the night before.

When had they left Galicos? And how far had they travelled? Had Xander Caras kidnapped her during the night?

It took her five full minutes of searching the cabin to discover her pencil skirt and the fitted shirt she wore for work had gone AWOL too.

Her mobile was dead, so she grabbed the onboard phone by her bed, planning to call Meghan and demand to know where the heck the boat was going and what had happened to her clothes.

But before anyone picked up, she slapped the handset down again. Having a go at Meghan was pointless. This wasn't Meghan's fault. She would have been following her boss's orders.

Locating a silk dressing gown in the wardrobe, she slung it over the skimpy negligee she'd slept in. And stormed to the cabin door, stupidly relieved when she discovered it wasn't locked. But after she'd wrenched it open, it occurred to her her kidnapper didn't need to lock her in the cabin when he had her trapped on his yacht, travelling to who knew where?

Fury edged out her panic.

She bumped into one of the crew on the stairs, carrying a tray laden with a silver pot and a delicious-looking breakfast platter.

'Miss Brown, you're awake, I was just coming to serve you breakfast,' the fresh-faced young man said with an eager smile. 'My name is Nicholai. I will be your personal steward for the duration of our journey.'

'That's fabulous, Nicholai.' She tried not to spit the words out—it wasn't poor Nicholai's fault either that his boss was a kidnapper. She grabbed a slice of bacon, suddenly ravenous—as she always was in the mornings now. 'But I need to find Mr Caras.'

And demand he turn his damn boat around and take me back to Galicos.

The high-handed bastard. How dared he take off without consulting her?

'Do you know where I can find him?' she asked as she wolfed down the crispy bacon.

'Absolutely, Miss Brown.' Nicholai's eager smile didn't falter. 'He is in the dining salon on the aft deck. He asked that I escort you to him once you were ready.'

Oh, did he, now? The wave of outrage left her breathless. So that was the deal: he was going to pretend she was a guest on his yacht, when she was a prisoner.

'If you give me a moment,' Nicholai offered, looking for somewhere to place the tray, 'I can assist—'

'It's okay, take the tray to my suite. The food looks delicious, by the way,' she interrupted him. 'If you could just give me directions to the salon, I'll come back and eat the meal in a bit.'

She got lost twice in the vast ship trying to follow Nicholai's directions, which did not help with her mounting temper. But she finally found the yacht's dining area.

Xander sat at the far end, at the head of a long glass table. The view of the coastline they were powering past—without her consent—was displayed through the sun deck behind him. A breeze whipped at his dark hair as he sipped his coffee, his attention buried in a business newspaper, the remnants of his own breakfast laid out before him.

Her fury surged. So kidnapping her hadn't ruined his appetite any!

The bastard.

Even in the casual outfit of sky-blue shirt and loose-fitting linen trousers, his feet bare, the dark stubble on his jaw proof that he was now in holiday mode, he looked like a king. Relaxed and in control of all he surveyed.

She stormed into the space, her bare feet silenced by the

powerful hum of the engines and the wind whipping off the water.

'You arrogant bastard...' she yelled, her outrage all but choking her as his head rose.

Damn, but she is magnificent.

Xander had to purse his lips to stop from smiling at the sight of Poppy striding towards him, her honey-brown hair loose now and flowing over her shoulders, her chestnut eyes bright with indignation. The negligee clung to her subtle curves. The matching robe was undone, giving him an un-encumbered view of generous breasts, pert nipples and the mound of her pregnancy barely covered by blue silk.

When she stopped in front of him, her usually open face was taut with fury. She slapped her hands on the table, making him aware of her unfettered breasts swaying under flowing silk.

'Where the hell are you taking me?' she demanded.

He folded his paper and stood up, regaining the height advantage. Then swallowed, because his mouth had dried to parchment.

'I trust you slept well, Poppy,' he said, his voice husky enough to pull a bobsled as he forced his gaze to her face. From this vantage point he could see far too much of her. And the vivid recollection of exploring the line of freckles across her cleavage with his tongue five long months ago made the heat he was trying to suppress pound in his groin.

'Don't patronise me, Caras,' she snapped back, her face now rigid with anger. 'Where are we? And how long will it take to get me back to Galicos?'

'We are not returning to Galicos.'

Her eyes narrowed to slits as her chin lifted, taking on a stubborn tilt. 'Yes, we are. I have a shift starting at four.'

So, they were back to this nonsense again. His own temper spiked as his patience began to fray.

'No, you do not,' he replied. 'My assistant in Galicos has informed your boss you will not be returning and has found a replacement, whose wages Caras Shipping has agreed to pay for the next month.'

Instead of her being grateful for his intervention though, and his generosity towards her former employer, the flush of outrage on her cheeks spread across her collarbone… Drawing his gaze back to her cleavage, annoyingly.

'H-how…how *dare* you?' she sputtered, her hands balling into fists. 'You had no right to contact Serge. He's *my* boss, not yours. I need that job.'

'You do not *need* that job, or any other,' he replied, no longer prepared to pander to her misplaced pride. 'Do you believe I would allow the mother of my child to work as a waitress and be hounded by the tabloid press?'

'A-allow!' She raised her arms, but he grasped her wrists before her fists could connect with his chest. 'Y-you arrogant son of a bitch.'

He held her off—far too easily—as she struggled against his hold. But he could see the sparkle of angry tears turning her chestnut eyes to gold, and the fierce sense of injustice on her face, and regretted provoking her.

He should not have allowed their argument to get so far out of control. He had worked out a strategy during the past two hours as he had waited for her to wake up. Why had he forgotten it the moment she had strode towards him looking like an avenging Valkyrie?

Perhaps because of the brutal reaction he was struggling to control even now. And because her determination not to accept his protection made him feel helpless—which triggered his greatest fear… A fear he had lived with since childhood, that he would not be strong enough, not be good enough to protect the people who relied on him to keep them safe.

She tired quickly, a single tear seeping over her lid as her breathing became ragged and her struggles ceased.

'Let me go,' she said wearily. 'I—I won't punch you… Even though I want to.'

The last of his temper faded, as the ludicrousness of her promise occurred to him. She didn't even reach his collarbone and was half his weight despite her pregnancy.

'That is a good choice,' he murmured, stroking her wrists with his thumbs before he was forced to do as she asked and release her. 'You would have broken your hand on my jaw.'

She stared up at him through moist lashes and let out an unsteady breath. 'Fair point,' she said, the wary concession almost as disturbing to his equilibrium as the defeated expression.

He had not intended to bully her. Or break her.

He tensed against the brutal—and far too persuasive— urge to run his tongue over the lush bow on her top lip, then delve into her mouth again, capturing the heady sobs that had kept him awake—and aroused—most of the night.

Perhaps his own sleepless night was responsible for his inability to control his temper and manage her angry reaction.

Was he required to apologise now? When he had only been acting in her best interests? And how did he do that, when he had not apologised to anyone since he was a boy?

He was still puzzling over how to proceed when she let out a sob of surprise—or was that distress? And pressed her palms to her rounded belly.

'Poppy?' Panic ripped through him as he took her arm. 'Is something wrong?'

She was trembling, breathing too fast, cradling her belly.

Had they harmed their child? With their pointless argument?

'Is it the baby?' he rasped as guilt clawed at his throat. He couldn't see her face. Why wasn't she saying anything? 'Should I call an air ambulance?'

* * *

Poppy raised her head, finally registering the fear in Xander's voice over the leap of joy inside her—from the distinctive tickle of sensation in her belly.

An air ambulance? What?

Her confusion cleared as she noticed the visible pulse in his neck, and the ashen pallor beneath the tanned skin. But before she could respond she felt the little kick again, deep in her abdomen. And grinned.

'No… It's…' She couldn't seem to formulate the right response or process the conflicting emotions bombarding her.

She'd been so furious with him. His arrogance, his high-handedness, his innate ability to dismiss her feelings and ride roughshod over her choices without a qualm had triggered memories of living in her father and stepmother's home.

She'd always known she was an inconvenience to Daniel Brown, the man who had fathered her but had never had any real interest in her life. Because he'd run off almost as soon as her mum had told him she was pregnant and had a whole other family by the time Poppy had been forced to go and live with him at fourteen—because he was the only relative she had.

She hadn't been able to get out of that expensive house in Islington fast enough—which had never been her home. Not like the ramshackle but cosy cottage in Kent where she and her mum had lived, and which had been boarded up ever since her mum's death, because Poppy didn't want to sell it, but nor did she want to live there again with all the memories.

Her father had never been cruel, never been deliberately unkind, he'd insisted on paying for an expensive private school for her—even after she'd told him she'd be much more at home at the local comprehensive. But his indifference to her, and the inability of him and his new wife, Sarah, to hide the fact their two kids—her half-siblings, Jacob and

Ellie—were their pride and joy, and Poppy an afterthought, had made her feel so alone and insignificant as she'd tried to navigate the horrendous grief.

As soon as Poppy had turned eighteen, she'd secured a place at university, got a bursary and a student loan, and declared herself financially independent by working nights and weekends while doing her degree.

Her father had continued to check up on her occasionally, out of duty. But she'd ignored the messages, and eventually he'd stopped calling. She hadn't seen any of them since.

Maybe she didn't have any blood relatives who she was close to and who cared about her. And thanks to her nomadic existence since college, she hadn't kept in close touch with any of her friends. But the most important thing was she had herself. And now she had this baby.

She was strong, she was smart, and her independence mattered, because her ability to make decisions for herself meant no one got to make her feel less than ever again.

And in one fell swoop, he'd tried to make her feel like a burden again.

Her fury ebbed away though at the stricken look on his face. And the panic in those cool blue eyes.

However arrogant and entitled and autocratic this man was—which was a lot—he was also emotionally invested in this baby's well-being. Or he wouldn't look so terrified.

'It's okay, Alex,' she said, forgetting to use his correct name, but suddenly not caring any more about the deceit, the lies. Maybe they were completely incompatible as individuals. Maybe he wasn't and had never been her 'Alex'. But what they did have now, which they hadn't had then, was a shared purpose—to keep their baby safe. Something she had resisted acknowledging up to now—because she didn't want to risk letting Xander Caras anywhere near her heart again.

Was that the real reason she didn't want to accept his

money? Not because she wanted to maintain her financial independence, but because she was terrified she still had feelings for the man she had met on the beach that day? The man who had intrigued and excited her?

Grow up, Poppy, and face the truth. That man never existed.

'It's okay. I just felt the baby properly kick,' she said.

His brows lowered, but his expression remained tense. 'Is this dangerous?' he asked, concern still shadowing his eyes.

'No. It's all good,' she said, unable to control the quick grin. 'It's exciting.'

She'd felt the flutters and a squirming sensation before, but had never been sure if she'd been imagining them. But these were proper kicks inside her, making the sense of connection so strong.

Going with instinct, because he still looked unsure, she grasped his large hand. 'Here, see if you can feel it too.' She pressed his palm to her tummy bulge. 'I think we must have woken up junior with our shouting.'

His gaze locked on hers, the flicker of emotions—guilt and shock—unguarded. That morning's hazy half-formed dream came back to her. The vivid recollection of when she'd asked him about his scars—and for a moment the feeling of connection had been so vivid. The sense she'd touched a part of him he guarded zealously, but which he had let her see for a moment.

Once again, the wary expression disappeared almost as quickly as it had come, but she knew she hadn't imagined it this time.

He swallowed. 'Does it hurt?'

She shook her head. Strangely thankful when his gaze dropped to her belly, where her hand still held his much larger one.

Her heart jumped into her throat, and seemed to pulse between her thighs, as he rubbed his palm across the silk caressing the spot where their baby grew.

The kicks had stopped. But she couldn't seem to swallow past the huge surge of emotion, and the rush of heat, when his eyes met hers again.

'I cannot feel it,' he said, but despite the shadow of disappointment she could also see the desire, reflected in his eyes. Volatile and intense. The spot between her thighs clenched and ached.

She eased her hand off his, suddenly brutally aware of how naked she was beneath the thin silk—and the warm weight of his palm. Her nipples throbbed in time with the heartbeat between her thighs.

She hadn't even stopped to put panties on before charging out here to confront him.

Did he know her sex ached? Could he smell the slick heat building between her thighs? Could he sense the swollen weight of her breasts, the engorged oversensitive nipples, begging for his touch?

She blinked slowly, the charged atmosphere making her forget everything but how close he was. The tantalising scent of soap and sea clung to him. All she could hear was the rough murmur of his breathing, the ragged sound of her own.

His hand skimmed down. He bunched the silky fabric in his fist and tugged her to him, until her body was moulded against the hard contours of his, making her brutally aware of the thick ridge—so strident, so insistent—rising to press against her bump.

Why couldn't she push him away? Why did her arms feel weighted to her sides, her body languid, her mind dazed, her throat so tight she couldn't speak, couldn't seem to swallow down the raw lump of need?

His hands rose, caressing her sides, cupping her heavy

breasts, his thumbs rolling over her swollen nipples, proprietorial, possessive, but also so sure, so certain.

Her staggered breathing became deafening, her back arching into his touch, as if she were a cat, desperate to be petted.

He cradled her cheeks, and lifted her face to his, trapping her in the heated purpose of his gaze. He lowered his head, the scent of orange juice on his breath—and the sultry perfume of the moisture now damping her thighs—invaded her senses when his words whispered across her lips. 'I am sorry, Poppy, for upsetting you. Upsetting our baby.'

His words sounded rusty, his voice strained, as if he was not used to apologising to anyone... But still she could hear what it was costing him, not to command, but to compromise.

'But I will not risk your safety,' he added. 'You cannot return to Galicos. It is not safe for you or the baby there any more.'

She ought to argue with him. He'd had no right to take her job away from her, and he'd been wrong to sail from Galicos without even telling her, let alone asking her. But she needed to be prepared to compromise too. She had to believe however arrogant and autocratic his actions, his motives were less so. And that the gruff apology meant something.

But before she could find the right words, his hands swept down to cup her bottom and tug her closer still—making her brutally aware of that rigid erection. She writhed against it, the mindless desire to take him again, to feel that thick length stretching her, filling her, so overwhelming it shattered her last coherent thought.

'And I want you with me,' he said. 'So we can feed this incessant hunger which has been driving me mad for months.'

'Yes.' Her reply choked out on a sob of need. She grasped his shirt in fistfuls and dragged him to her. Not caring any more about who was right, or wrong. Only caring about feeding the molten, aching heat at her core too.

Grasping her bottom, he boosted her into his arms and strode across the lounge.

She wrapped her legs around his waist, anchoring herself. He grunted his approval, carting her down the yacht's corridor and through a door into a bedroom suite.

She barely had a chance to register the view of the sea through the glass wall that wrapped around the end of the suite—and the balcony beyond—before he placed her on the king-sized bed.

Then all her attention was riveted on him. And the pulsing ache in her abdomen.

Standing, he grabbed the back of his shirt, and pulled it over his head, then thrust down the loose-fitting trousers. Within seconds he was naked. The erection jutted out, so thick, so hard and even more magnificent than she remembered.

The scorching heat backed up in her throat as he knelt on the bed and stroked her thighs, to bunch the silk and expose her bare sex to his gaze. Moisture flowed between her legs, the sweet spot molten.

His gaze locked on hers. As he stripped the robe away, wrestled the silky negligee off. Until she lay beneath him. She covered her belly and her breasts, suddenly shy about the ways her body had changed under that searing gaze as it glided over her—hot and possessive.

'No,' he rasped, taking her wrists to lift her arms free and expose her fully. 'Your body is so beautiful. Even more beautiful now it is carrying my child.'

Gentle, reverent hands skimmed over her breasts, before stroking her distended belly, where their baby lay peaceful now, even as her skin felt alive, her senses rippling with awareness.

She arched up, and into his touch as he cupped her bottom and lifted her sex to his mouth.

His tongue lapped at the tender bud, and she cried out. Already so close. Too close.

'Shh…' he murmured, even as he began to torment her, licking and circling the aching spot.

She threaded her fingers into his hair, tugging, coaxing, panting, her breathing raw, her lungs tight, her need soaring.

At last, he found the swollen nub again and trapped it between his lips. The tension released in a shuddering rush, pulling her into a maelstrom, making her jerk and buck against his mouth.

She cried out again, the wave receding, then building again, harder, higher.

As she crashed over a second time, she was shuddering, shaking with the intensity of her orgasm.

His big body rose over her. He clasped her hips, but as the thick erection probed at her entrance, she could hear the strain in his voice, the fraying control as he buried his face against her neck and murmured, 'Is it safe?'

She gripped his cheeks, to lift his head. 'Yes, please, I need you. All of you.'

Possessive fury flashed across his features, but he eased in slowly, too slowly, filling her to bursting and beyond.

She panted, sobbed, the stretched feeling as immense and overwhelming as it had been before. But even so, she lifted her knees, angled her hips, needing more of him, needing it all.

At last, he was lodged to the hilt. Their ragged breathing sounded deafening as the sunlight sparkled on his hair. The ocean pounded the hull. And she struggled to adjust to his possession.

'I must move, Poppy.'

She nodded.

He pulled out, then drove back. Harder, heavier. And yet still so painfully slow.

The coil tightened anew, deep inside her sex, as he established an agonising rhythm. Each thick stroke forced her to take more, as his pelvis nudged her over-stimulated clitoris. But she rose, moved with him, meeting his thrusts, to take him deeper still, desperate to reach the point of no return. They moved together, the sensual glide of their bodies sending her senses into a frenzy of need. That thick girth embedded deep, so much and yet not enough.

'Please, more, faster…' she demanded in broken sobs.

He increased his speed, rolled his hips, to stroke a place only he had ever found.

The wave barrelled towards her. She lurched up, the brutal pleasure becoming exquisite pain, her nails digging into his shoulder blades, to cling onto sanity, even as he shouted out his own release and dragged her back into the abyss.

CHAPTER SEVEN

DON'T CRUSH HER. Don't crush the baby.

Xander's delirious senses engaged, long enough to use the last of his strength, to roll onto his side, his arms full of soft, pliant woman.

He noticed the moment she came to her senses, when she tensed and tried to tug free of his embrace. He tightened his arms around her. The still hard erection nestled against her bare bottom, as he stroked her belly.

He hadn't felt the baby move, and in many ways he was glad of that. Because the child had been too real in that moment, too much. But now he couldn't stop touching her.

The endorphin rush had him smiling, even as he struggled to make sense of the rush of possessiveness.

He pressed his face into the soft cloud of curls and inhaled her scent.

'We shouldn't have done that...' she said, blunt as ever. But the strain in her voice—and her body—made him more determined not to let her go.

'Why not?' he asked, keeping his voice even, despite his rising irritation. Why could she not accept she was his responsibility now?

She shifted to glance over her shoulder, her face a picture of consternation and frustration.

'Because we're not... We're not a couple.'

He steeled himself against the stab of impatience at her

obstinacy. How could he want her so much when she was so damn frustrating?

His hand roamed over the compact bulge, cradling their baby.

'Are we not?' he asked, keeping his tone neutral and ignoring the renewed ripple of desire—and irritation.

Why he found her curves even more erotic now he had no idea, but he could make an educated guess. Was this how all men responded to the sight of their child growing? Because he had been nothing short of unhinged when he had stripped off the nightgown to find the changes his baby had wrought. Her enlarged nipples, the swollen breasts, the smooth bulge he couldn't stop caressing even now.

But he had no wish to trigger another pointless argument. That first apology had been excruciating enough.

She huffed. 'You're engaged to someone else, Xander.'

The use of his usual name struck a dull chord inside his chest.

Was that regret, sadness? That she no longer thought of him as the man she had met that day? Why would he want her to call him Alex, when he did not want her to see him as that man? Vulnerable, captivated, exposed?

'I am not yet officially engaged to Princess Freya,' he remarked. 'And anyway, it is of no consequence now...'

A sharp frown marred her brow. 'It is to me. I don't...'

He pressed his thumb to her lips to silence her protest. 'Because Theo will inform her and her father today a marriage between us is no longer possible.'

She looked momentarily nonplussed. But if he had been expecting joy, or even gratitude, at this development—he was soon disappointed.

She struggled out of his arms and scooped the discarded robe off the bed to tug it on—covering all those delectable curves, still flushed with pleasure.

Pity.

She banded her arms around her waist, her gaze dropping to his still semi-erect flesh—which he saw no reason to hide. A blush scorched her cheeks.

She walked across the room to stare out at the sea as the yacht powered towards Sorrento. Her shoulders were rigid with tension. Oddly, he couldn't help smiling at her typically complicated reaction.

Interesting that he still found that contradictory mix of innocence and awareness so intoxicating—and her stubborn refusal to bend to his will captivating, as well as annoying.

He sighed, sitting up to drag on his shorts. He didn't particularly wish to get dressed. If only he could keep her in his bed until they reached Parádeisos, in three or four days' time, it would make this whole situation far easier.

But then, nothing about Poppy Brown had ever been easy.

He followed her across the room. Her shoulders stiffened even more as she heard his approach, but her gaze remained riveted to the view from the yacht's bow. The wake churned as they headed across the Bay of Naples. They would be anchored off Sorrento in an hour at most. And he did not want her to demand he let her go again.

Seducing her had seemed like a good way to ensure her compliance, but as soon as he had touched her, and she had responded, any thoughts of subtlety—of seduction—had been lost in a firestorm of need.

'Why are you not pleased by the news that my marriage to Princess Freya is off?' he asked, still confused by her less than enthusiastic reaction to the sacrifice he had made. He didn't want to lose the land deal—or the months of negotiations it had taken to set it up—but still, he had not hesitated to risk it all by calling off the alliance, to concentrate on his responsibilities towards Poppy and their child. Surely she should be happy about his decision?

She looked over her shoulder. 'I didn't ask you to cancel your engagement, Xander.'

The bite of frustration was swiftly followed by something that felt uncomfortably like hurt.

'Do you think so little of me?' he demanded, using his temper to cover the hurt. 'That I would consider marriage to one woman, while another is pregnant with my child?'

Why did he care that she believed he was not a man of honour, when he did not care what anyone thought of him? And she would certainly not have been the first to believe a street rat like him had no integrity.

She turned to face him, her arms still wrapped around her waist, trembling despite the sun's warmth shining through the glass.

'Honestly, I don't know what to think. How can I, when I don't know you…?'

'How can you say this?' he asked, baffled now. Were they speaking a different language? He had always considered his English fluent, but now he was not so sure. 'When we have made a child together…and not five minutes ago, I was so deep inside you I could feel your heart beating?'

The blush on her cheeks exploded, the mottled colour spreading across her collarbone.

'Th-that's… That's just sex,' she said, but her gaze skipped away from his.

'Just sex!' He swore in Greek, dumbfounded, even as he struggled to control the wave of jealousy. Clasping her chin between his thumb and forefinger, he dragged her gaze back to his. 'Have you responded to other men with such passion, then?'

She tugged her chin from his grasp. But as her brows shot up her forehead, and the flush burned, the twist of jealousy released its death grip. Because he could see the answer written on that expressive face.

No, she had not reacted to other men the way she had always reacted to him.

The sex had been as mind-blowing for her. And as extraordinary. His relief was quickly followed by a new surge of need, the yearning to taste her again, to lick her to orgasm, making his insides twist with something far more exhilarating.

'That's not the point,' she finally managed. But she did not look so sure.

'Then what *is* the point?' he said, trying to be reasonable, while hot blood was coursing back into his boxers, threatening to derail his caution all over again.

Why on earth did you sleep with him again? What is wrong with you?

She looked at Xander's furious scowl, making it clear he had no clue what Poppy was talking about. And he was also not happy with her answer.

Unfortunately, she couldn't really blame him for that incredulous look… Or the temper swirling in his eyes and turning them to a stormy sea-blue. She was sending him so many mixed messages even she felt dizzy. And she wasn't entirely sure either what the point was she was trying to make.

The truth was, when he'd told her his marriage was off, she'd felt the leap of joy in her chest—and immediately hated herself for it.

Because it made her feel like that naïve girl again, who had fallen for him so easily five months ago. The naïve girl who had been so captivated by his attention, so enchanted by his interest in her, so intoxicated by his lovemaking, she'd thrown away all her common sense.

That her body was still far too susceptible to him was bad enough. She really did not want to fall down that rabbit hole again—of believing their chemistry and that livewire attraction, the incendiary way she responded to his no doubt practised moves, meant more than it did.

'The point is…' She huffed, trying to figure out what to say without making herself look even more clueless. 'Just because we have chemistry, it doesn't mean that we're in a relationship.'

His scowl deepened and his jaw tightened. 'You are having my child,' he said, his exasperation edging out his fury. 'Therefore, we are in a relationship.'

'You have to care about someone to be in a relationship with them, Xander,' she countered softly.

He blinked, the dumbfounded expression so telling she felt foolish. The man was a stranger. They'd met precisely once before, spent four hours together full of lies and half-truths, and made a baby. Why would she even expect him to care for her when he hardly knew her, too?

'I should return to my own cabin… My breakfast is getting cold,' she murmured when he stood, apparently lost for words, his brow furrowing.

But as she stepped past him, he snagged her wrist. Sensation sprinted up her arm, but she couldn't find the energy to tug her arm free when her gaze met his. Instead of the indomitable, demanding man she had encountered since he had all but dragged her out of the restaurant in Galicos, he looked confused and, for once, less guarded.

'I want you more than I have ever wanted any woman… And you want me, too.' His voice dropped to a husky murmur that brushed over her skin, even as his thumb caressed the pulse point in her wrist. 'The hunger has not died. And I see no reason not to indulge it.'

She wanted to disagree with him, even though her hormones were doing a happy dance at his blunt offer. But before she could utter a word, he pressed his hand to her mouth, trapping the not entirely truthful denial inside her.

'But this we can discuss another time,' he continued. 'More important to me is that I keep you and our baby safe. Why must you fight me on this?' His tone was strained, but from his expression she could see it was a genuine question.

The fact that he didn't know the answer spoke volumes. But maybe communication was key.

She eased her hand from his grasp, because his touch made it hard for her to think clearly. And she didn't want to mess up the chance to explain *why* she was so averse to having him make decisions for her without her consent.

It was obvious he was a man who didn't usually talk about his emotions and that he was also used to giving orders and having them obeyed even more so. That he might never have had to compromise his needs was another a hurdle to overcome. But perhaps she needed to stop being so defensive, too.

He was a rich, powerful man—and that scared her, because she never wanted to let any man have the power to hurt her or reject her again. But if he was only interested in their physical chemistry, and the baby growing inside her, why should he be a threat? She didn't love this man, she hadn't been falling in love with him that day, she'd been falling for the fictitious Alex.

She folded her arms around her waist, aware of how virtually naked they both were, and the ripples of desire still skittering over her skin.

'Could we have this conversation later? I'm really hungry,' she said, knowing it was a cop-out, but also knowing she had to have her wits about her before she had this conversation with him. 'And I need to shower and get dressed.' She frowned. 'Although I have no idea where my clothes are.'

'I told Meghan to have them cleaned,' he said. 'Until I can buy you a new wardrobe.'

Her temper spiked at his arrogance. 'Xander, I don't want

you to buy me new clothes. I just need my own clothes, which you chose to leave behind in…'

'Please, do not let us argue about this…' He interrupted her, his rueful expression suggesting he knew he had crossed another line he was unaware of. 'Again.'

She sighed. And thrust her hand through her bed hair. Having him buy her clothes—because they'd left Galicos without her belongings on his orders—did not seem all that trivial, but she was feeling too raw to argue the point. And at least he had said please… Perhaps that was progress, of a sort.

'Fine,' she said. 'But I would really appreciate it if you stopped making decisions for me. When you tell me you're just trying to keep me safe, but you don't discuss it with me, it reminds me of when my mum died and I didn't have a say in anything that happened to me,' she continued, suddenly desperate to make him understand how his high-handedness made her feel. Perhaps he didn't like to talk about his feelings, or hers, but she would be damned if she would let him take her choices away from her again. 'Everyone said they were doing what was best for me, and maybe they were, but they never *ever* asked me what I wanted. And that sucked. I refuse to let you make me that powerless again, whether I'm pregnant with your child or not. Okay?'

His eyes darkened, his gaze intensifying even more, and the muscle in his jaw began twitching again.

He didn't like being challenged. At all.

She braced herself for the familiar pushback—which she had endured as a grief-stricken teenager and learned to hate so much—the high-handed assumption he knew better than she did what was good for her.

But then something in his expression shifted. The hard muscle in his jaw softened, and the slabs of muscle on his broad chest lifted, and fell, as his breath guttered out on a long-suffering sigh. And then, to her utter astonishment, he nodded.

'I understand,' he said.

'You do?' she asked, wanting to believe him, but knowing she should not trust him too easily. *'How?'*

Did he really understand how she felt? Or was he simply trying to placate and manipulate her again? To lull her into a false sense of security, so he could get what he wanted… The way he'd done on his private island five months ago.

His gaze became shuttered, and wary. And his cheek tensed again.

Yup, Xander Caras is so not big on 'share and discuss'.

When he finally replied, though, his words were so carefully devoid of emotion, they had the harsh ring of painful truth.

'My mother died too, when I was very young… And then…' He let out a heavy sigh. 'Our *baba*…woke me late one night…'

He paused, his gaze shifting to the horizon, but she suspected he wasn't seeing the cliffs topped with grand hotels, the dots of boats moored in the port, or the mound of Vesuvius, which hovered over the Bay of Naples as the yacht powered closer to Sorrento.

'He told me Theo was my responsibility now.' He released an unsteady breath. 'I thought it was all a dream. A bad dream… But when I woke the next morning, my father was gone and we never saw him again.'

She gasped, shocked by his words and what it revealed. His life had not been as charmed and entitled as she had believed.

'How old were you?' she asked, compassion welling in her chest.

'Eleven, twelve… I do not remember.' He shrugged. But even though his expression remained blank, the cautious shoulder hitch made her heart ache for him. 'My age then is not important, as that morning I became a man,' he finished, and she could see he believed that.

But how could that be true? No twelve-year-old deserved to be saddled with that much responsibility. How had he and his brother survived? Had they escaped the authorities, or been taken into care?

Whatever the outcome, though, what he had revealed explained a lot.

Was this why he was so determined to protect her and the baby? Not because he wanted to take her choices away from her, but because his own father had failed to protect him?

'I'm so sorry that happened to you. It must have been terrifying,' she said.

He frowned and colour slashed across his cheeks. 'I do not require your pity.'

'It's not pity, Xander. It's sadness, that any child should have to go through something like that. And compassion for that little boy who had nobody. I lost my mum when I was fourteen and it made me feel so alone, because up to then it had just been me and her.'

How had he managed to keep himself and his brother safe? And how had they both made such a success of their lives, and their business? Surely that explained, at least in part, the single-mindedness she found so intimidating.

'I did not have nobody,' he said, the annoyance in his voice almost endearing. 'I had myself and I had my brother—who, despite appearances to the contrary last night, is not always a pain in the butt.'

She smiled. It was obvious he regretted being so candid with her, but his reluctance to speak of that time in his life—something that certainly had not been mentioned in any of the articles she'd read about him—only made the confidences he'd shared more precious.

He placed a callused palm on her cheek. The contact made

her shudder, the shiver of reaction streaking down to her bare toes. But, for once, she wasn't embarrassed by her response.

'You look tired,' he murmured, the all-seeing gaze unnerving her again. But then he brushed his thumb under her eye. 'Have your shower and get dressed. Meghan will have left your clothes in your cabin.' He glanced through the glass at the end of the space, towards the Sorrento shoreline, which was fast approaching. 'I will order a new breakfast to be served to you in your room, and then we can go ashore...' His eyes narrowed as he let his hand drop. 'If you will promise not to run away from me.'

That was a pretty big *if,* but somehow the hot glow in his eyes, plus the confidences they'd shared, made her feel less inclined to rebel against the string of orders he'd just issued.

Now she had some idea why he needed to be in control at all times—and why his child's safety was so important to him—she was prepared to give him some slack.

'I'll promise not to run away from you, if you promise not to kidnap me again.'

His eyebrows shot up his forehead, but then he let out a gruff chuckle that had her own lips quirking. She didn't need his validation, or his permission, but the glow of approval in his blue gaze had the ripple of reaction at her core turning into a definite hum.

'You drive a hard bargain,' he said, apparently only half joking.

'Do we have a deal?' she countered. 'Or don't we?'

He swore under his breath, looking more resigned than approving, but then he gave a reluctant nod. 'I guess.'

'Excellent,' she said, pleased, because she was sure she had just got a major concession.

Whether he lived up to his end of the bargain remained to be seen. But the fact they'd both managed to share something personal about their past was important, if they were ever going to rebuild trust.

They were *both* going to be on a steep learning curve—as he figured out how to control his insistence on being the boss of all things, and she figured out how to control her determination never to take orders from anyone ever again.

But perhaps spending time with him—on his very luxurious yacht—and getting to see the Amalfi Coast, without having to worry about how on earth she was going to pay for it, wouldn't be *so* bad.

She would have to find a job sooner rather than later, as her financial independence was important to her. But the baby was the responsibility of *both* of them, and she needed to accept that.

On impulse, she pushed up onto her toes and touched her lips to his, in a fleeting kiss. But when he went to grab her and pull her back into his arms, she danced away.

'Let's go and explore Sorrento.' She threw the words over her shoulder. 'I've never been there before.'

She heard him grumbling in Greek as she laughed and dashed out of the door.

CHAPTER EIGHT

HOW CAN SHE be so enchanting and so infuriating at the same time?

Xander stared at the woman in front of him as she bartered enthusiastically with a stallholder to buy fresh figs in her rudimentary but surprisingly effective Italian. The simple summer dress she had insisted on buying with her own money at a small boutique off the Piazza Tasso flattered her figure, while only just accommodating the pregnancy belly that had begun to fascinate him. A shaft of heat eddied through him, at the memory of her nude body—so lush and delicious—laid out on his bed that morning. Dark engorged nipples, full breasts, the compact bump where his child nestled and her rounded hips—so firm in his hands as he plunged into the tight clasp of her sex.

He shook his head, trying to dispel the erotic visions—which had been tormenting him all day—before he embarrassed himself in the open market square.

But he couldn't shake the surge of lust that accompanied them.

Sex had always been a basic physical urge for him, something he enjoyed and had learned to do well but was easily forgotten once he had climaxed. He prided himself on knowing how to please the women he slept with, because their enjoyment enhanced his own. But the burning hunger he felt for Poppy was very different. Something he now suspected he needed to be more wary of. Because making love to her only made him more addicted to her, and had a devastating effect on his usual caution and self-control.

Why else would he have blurted out information about his childhood to her that he had never confided in anyone, except Theo?

He was not ashamed of his past. His father's abandonment and the desperate years that followed had made him the man he was now—driven, focussed and extremely ruthless when necessary. Nor did he see any reason to dwell on those early hardships, or re-examine the effect they might have had on his psyche. Or to revisit the night when his father had shaken him awake, the smell of stale liquor on his breath, and told him he was now the man of the family.

Until Poppy had stood before him so valiantly and given him an insight into the grief that had blighted her childhood—and made him ashamed of not even considering her feelings when he had chosen to leave Galicos without her consent.

He did not regret that decision. It had been the right one to make at the time. But even so, he had wanted her to know he understood her distress. He didn't believe it would change anything, nor did he really understand the knee-jerk decision to confide in her. And that disturbed him. Because surely letting her see such a weakness would give her ammunition against him?

Weirdly though, instead of exploiting that moment of weakness, Poppy had shown compassion for that boy—even though that boy was long gone.

He did not understand her willingness to forgive his autocratic behaviour either. But he was not about to look that gift horse in the mouth, if it meant they could visit Sorrento without her trying to escape from him.

While he had no illusions she would allow him to make

all the decisions that needed to be made from now on—in a strange way he no longer resented her refusal to obey him as much. While her insistence on buying her own dress had annoyed him, the battle of wills that had followed had been... well, hot.

'Fabulous and only four euros!' She held the newly purchased bag of figs aloft like a prize, her triumphant smile dazzling him... And reminding him of that day in spring when she had looked at him with the same sunny expression brightening her face.

He had missed that smile.

She plucked a fig from her haul and tore one open, peeling away the purple skin to reveal the red seeded flesh beneath. 'They smell so fresh and delicious,' she said. Then she bit into the fruit. 'And they taste even better.'

Not as good as you do.

She grinned, licking the syrup off her lips.

The vicious shot of arousal made him tense.

She held out the half-eaten fruit. 'Have a taste.'

His throat dried at the artless invitation. Did she have any idea how seductive she was? Her lips shiny with juice, her eyes bright with accomplishment and her expression open and uncomplicated again, as it had been the day they'd met.

He captured her wrist to guide her hand to his mouth, then angled the fruit so he could bite into the flesh in the same spot her lips had touched.

Her eyes widened as he swallowed the mouthful then devoured the rest of the sweet, fragrant fig, dragging his teeth across the skin. He plucked the used fruit from her fingers to drop it into a nearby bin, then lifted her wrist, and licked her fingertips clean.

Each slow lave of his tongue made her shudder. He captured her thumb between his lips, and drew it into his mouth, sucking it the way he wanted to suck the bud of her sex until she came. And suddenly he knew, whatever the complications of this relationship, and the many arguments no doubt in their future, he would not be able to let her go—not for a while.

'Delicious,' he murmured, finally releasing her hand.

Her breath guttered out in a sob of surprise. And awareness.

He banded an arm around her hips, unable to resist the invitation in her eyes to drag her closer.

Shocked arousal had dilated her pupils to black. Flush against him, with her protruding belly cradled between them, she had to be able to feel the reaction he could not control.

He leant down to whisper against her ear.

'Let us return to the yacht and finish the figs in my bed,' he said. 'Then we may return to Sorrento later if you wish, before we set sail.'

It wasn't a question.

She bucked against his hold, but he could see the desire she was trying to control when she flattened shaky palms against his chest.

'I—I haven't agreed to sail away with you, Xander,' she said, trying to sound firm, even though her voice was husky with need.

The spike of temper—at her refusal to admit how much she wanted him—threatened his self-control, but he bit down on the urge to argue with her in the busy market square, aware of the tourists and locals milling around them.

Not the time, nor the place, to argue this point.

He released his hold on her hips, annoyed with himself now as well as her. He had planned to be subtle during their outing in Sorrento, had even arranged for his assistant to book them a suite at the Grand Hotel Excelsior Vittoria, which overlooked the bay—so he could persuade her to return to Parádeisos with him over a shared meal. And already he'd blown it.

But as soon as she had sunk her teeth into the fig, all he had been able to think about was the desire to have her again.

What was happening to him? Because she made him behave like that feral boy again, desperate to grab what he wanted and gulp it down before anyone could take it away from him…instead of the sophisticated man he had made himself become. A man who had the world at his fingertips and could indulge himself in his own time and at his own pace.

He forced himself to step back and take a breath, to calm his rampaging heartbeat and the need pounding in his pants.

She looked wary and tense, the bright, playful smile gone, the paper bag of figs clutched in her fist.

He swore softly.

'You haven't even told me where we're supposed to be going, Xander,' she added, the wary tone shaming him for the second time in one day—which had to be a record.

But beneath the wariness he didn't hear the resistance he had heard before. She had asked him to include her in his decision making. And while that was a much bigger ask than she probably realised for a man who had built an empire on never taking no for an answer, perhaps all that was really required here was more finesse.

He nodded. 'We can discuss the details of our journey while we eat,' he offered, tightly. 'Before we return to the yacht.'

As much as he would like to drag her back to his cabin now and ravish her again, he could see it would not get him any closer to his goal. While he could not give her a choice over whether she accompanied him or not—because he had no intention of leaving her in Sorrento—he could at least attempt to solicit her consent first.

He had been in difficult negotiations before—especially in the early days of setting up his business, when he hadn't had the power and financial clout he had now. He knew how to coax and cajole, even if those skills were rusty… All he had to do now was suppress his more basic urges and be patient.

'How about we discuss whether I'm actually going to go on this journey with you, first?' she countered.

Clasping her hand, he brought it to his lips and kissed her knuckles.

She shuddered deliciously, and the kick of irritation at her rebellion faded.

You've got this, Xander, because she wants you too.

'As you wish,' he said, but he couldn't control the smile as he led her through the narrow cobblestoned streets towards their waiting car and felt her shiver.

Suppressing this feral need was going to be a struggle, but then she was fighting the same losing battle. So why not use this incendiary attraction to fight his corner…and show her that a trip to Parádeisos would have some delicious advantages.

Poppy inhaled an uneasy breath as she sat on the private clifftop terrace in the penthouse suite at the Grand Hotel Excelsior Vittoria. The sprawling city of Naples could be seen thirty miles away along the rocky coastline against the hulking shadow of Vesuvius, with the ancient ruins of Pompeii visible inland. Capri and Ischia rose out of the vivid blue waters ahead of them, completing the breathtaking view from this vantage point, gilded by September sunshine.

But the view was not as breathtaking as the man sitting opposite her, his tanned face set in stark lines of determination.

'When you mentioned eating, I thought we'd be having pizza in a local trattoria, not a five-course meal in a private suite in one of the most famous hotels on the Amalfi Coast,' she murmured, trying for amused, rather than overwhelmed.

The hotel itself—its grandiose fin-de-siècle architecture

a throwback to a bygone era of elegance and exclusivity—had been a sight to behold perched on the cliffs overlooking the port as they'd driven through the streets in the chauffeur-driven car that had appeared on the quay that morning when they'd disembarked. Discovering Sorrento, with Xander as her guide, had been exhilarating, the bustling streets and alleyways both picturesque and yet buzzing with life. And with the summer season over, the locals had started to outnumber the tourists.

She'd loved browsing the artisan shops and stalls selling everything from hand-painted ceramics to the finest extra virgin olive oil. And the weather was still warm enough for the stylish summer dress she'd found in a second-hand boutique. Xander had made a face about her paying for the dress herself, of course, and she'd ignored him.

But as their car had arrived at the gates of the opulent hotel and the hotel's manager had rushed out to greet them personally, the panic caused by their almost-kiss in the market had begun to ramp up again. As the older man escorted them through a secret garden of citrus and orange groves, then staterooms decorated with impressionist art and antique furniture and crystal chandeliers, before guiding them up a sweeping staircase to this enormous private suite, Poppy had begun to wonder if she'd been thrown back in time, too.

She knew luxury hotels such as the Excelsior Vittoria existed, but she'd never even worked somewhere this exclusive, so the idea of being a guest made her stomach clench. The view from the suite's wide terrace and the table elegantly set for two only made the experience more overwhelming.

Imposter syndrome, much?

If Xander was trying to intimidate her again he was doing a very good job.

'We needed privacy for our conversation,' he said, with

typical pragmatism. 'But I am sure pizza may be arranged,' he added. 'If that is what you wish to order.'

She smiled at his puzzled expression, and her panic receded, even as the hot blush climbed into her cheeks.

Apparently he was *trying* to be a bit less intimidating.

'If it's not too much trouble, that would be great.' Perhaps putting a slice of pizza on the gold-rimmed plate would make her feel less like a scullery maid playing dress-up... Enough that she might actually be able to swallow some of it.

Xander was extremely wealthy. She needed to deal with her inferiority complex because that wasn't going to change.

And what exactly was so intimidating anyway? Maybe she wasn't rich in money, but she had rebuilt her confidence from the ground up since her mother's death, and there was no need to feel threatened just because he could afford a suite in a place like this. She was his equal, but only if she didn't allow his wealth to intimidate her.

'I've never had real Neapolitan pizza,' she added, filling the silence a little desperately, because the brooding look as he studied her was starting to make her feel like a bug under a microscope. 'I've heard it's amazing.'

Plus pizza was much more her vibe than cordon bleu cuisine.

His frown relaxed and his lips curved. Which unfortunately drew her gaze to his mouth... She shivered involuntarily at the memory of those same lips sucking the fig juice off her fingertips in the market square.

Hmm, perhaps the wary tension in her tummy wasn't just about the exclusivity of their venue, and also about the far too vivid memory of him sucking her fingers earlier—which had almost made her spontaneously combust in front of a few hundred tourists and local market-goers.

'Real Italian pizza is indeed delicious,' he said, his gaze

darkening again as it had during Fig Gate, making her wonder if they were still talking about their menu options.

Apparently, Xander's wealth was *not* the most intimidating thing about him. Not even close.

'Although it is not as delicious as freshly made souvlaki from Nico's in Piraeus,' he finished.

'Piraeus, that's in Athens, right?' she asked, trying to redirect the conversation to something less incendiary... But also intrigued by the affectionate tone.

He didn't strike her as a sentimental man but clearly he had fond memories of the restaurant he'd mentioned.

'Piraeus is the city's port and the largest passenger port in Europe, yes,' he replied. 'It is where Caras Shipping's container business is based.'

'And Nico's is a restaurant there? That you frequent?' she prompted, keen to get him to talk about himself.

Other than the incident he had mentioned with his father, she really knew very little about him. During their day together in April she had done nearly all the talking because he'd encouraged it, apparently fascinated to hear about everything, from her holidays in Greece with her mum, to her taste in music. And while she'd talked incessantly, basking in his attention, Xander, or rather the man she had known as Alex, hadn't really told her anything about himself, except that he was from Athens originally. She had realised how dopey she had been not to get more information out of him that day when she had discovered the pregnancy. When she had found out his true identity, she had convinced herself he had been deliberately evasive. But now, seeing his expression tense at her questions, she wasn't so sure. Perhaps his reticence to talk about himself had a much deeper root than just the desire to keep his identity a secret from that smitten girl.

He stared at her for the longest time, saying nothing, even though her question had been innocuous. She could almost sense him weighing up whether he would be giving away too much information if he answered her. But then he shrugged.

'Nico's wasn't a restaurant, it was a stall, on the docks. Nico sold souvlakis to the dockworkers.' The warm expression softened the harsh planes and angles of his face. 'My brother and I would celebrate with souvlaki whenever we had extra coin to spend—and Nico always gave us extra, probably because we were both so skinny.' He sighed. 'Nico was also one of our first investors—he lent us money to buy our first tugboat. It is a good memory.'

Her stomach muscles clenched at the wistful tone. And the suspicion that most of his childhood memories were not good ones.

'You grew up in Athens?' she prompted, keen to push for more. She wanted to ask about his father, about what had happened to him and his brother after the terrifying night he had described. But she sensed the shutters lowering again. And heard the careful distance in his voice when he replied.

'Yes. I was born there,' he said, stiffly, as if he was bracing himself for more intrusive questions.

'What happened to you and your brother, after your father left?' She made herself ask the question that had been bugging her since that morning, despite the frown reforming on his brow. 'How did you survive? And stay together?'

'Why do you wish to know these things?' he countered, not answering the question. 'When it is ancient history now?'

Ancient? She didn't think so. Not when he was so reluctant to talk about it.

'Don't we need to know more about each other? To build trust,' she replied.

Why beat about the bush? She had given him so much of herself that day on Parádeisos, while he had kept so much of himself hidden, which put her at a huge disadvantage now. 'Isn't that why you wanted to have lunch on neutral territory?'

she added. 'So we could talk in private? About our plans for the future? But how can we plan what happens next when we're virtual strangers?'

He let out a rough chuckle. 'I wanted to return to the yacht and lick fig juice from your breasts. Eating here was my idea of a compromise,' he countered. The brazen statement and the intent in his gaze sent erotic shivers through her body she did not need. The memory of Fig Gate was still far too fresh. The breasts in question then puckered into tight points, almost as if he had his lips on them already.

She crossed her arms over her chest, but when his gaze darkened she had the awful thought he had already seen her reaction.

The blush burned her cleavage, which suddenly felt far too exposed in the light summer dress, and she was reminded all over again how her innocent offer of a bite of her fig had turned into a moment charged with passion.

But then pretty much everything Xander did and said was passionate, and seductive. The man was a walking sex machine.

Reaching across the table, he held one of her wrists and gently unfolded her arms.

'There is no need to hide your reaction, Poppy,' he said, the sensual smile making it clear she had not been wrong about his powers of observation. 'I am already aware of how responsive your nipples are. And how much you enjoy having my mouth on them.'

'Xander!' The blush exploded into her cheeks. 'Would you please stop trying to derail everything with sex?' she added, exasperated now, and far too aware her nipples were pressing against the bodice of her dress like torpedoes ready to launch. What she wouldn't do right now for a padded bra. Or better yet an armour-plated one. 'And don't think I've forgotten that completely inappropriate thumb suck in the piazza,' she continued, then felt annoyed he'd made her sound like a prude. 'Which I did not appreciate at all.'

'Did you not?' he questioned, the sensual smile widening. Still holding her now clenched fist, he drew it towards him, then prised open her fingers—far too easily. 'And there I was thinking that purring sound you made—like a cat begging to be petted—meant you enjoyed my attentions very much.'

He drew his thumb across her palm in lazily circles, his gaze hot on her now burning face.

She ought to tug her hand free, ought to call him a liar. But she was powerless to do anything but stare, and tremble, as he lifted her palm to his mouth. He bit lightly into the flesh under her thumb. Sharp, heady sensation geysered up from her core and the sob of arousal that rumbled out sounded exactly like a purr. *The bastard.*

He laughed—as she snatched her hand back.

She shoved her sizzling fingers into her lap and glared at him, her face now so hot it felt radioactive.

'You're incorrigible,' she declared grumpily, but her admonition didn't carry the weight it should, because they both knew he'd just proved her the liar and not the other way around.

'There is no need to be ashamed, Poppy,' he said, the patronising tone almost as galling as the triumphant twinkle in his eyes. 'We have an exceptional chemistry. Why should we not enjoy it?'

Before she could come up with a suitable comeback to that suggestion, without making even more of a fool of herself, he leant forward, the amusement turning to a heated promise.

'Perhaps sex is the best way to get to know each other, also? If this is what you need? Instead of raking over the sad details of our pasts?' he said, sounding so reasonable—and persuasive—she almost didn't see the great gaping hole in his logic. *Almost.* 'I have no desire to go back there, and, from what you have confided in me about your childhood, neither do you.' He took the other hand she now had resting on the table and lifted it back to lips to kiss her knuckles. 'We have made a child together. This is not something either one of us can change. But if you must learn to trust me, then come back to Parádeisos with me, so we can start over again.'

She shuddered, the tangle of emotions streaking through her at the bold suggestion hard to identify, let alone understand.

'You want to go back to the island?' she asked, stunned. And extremely conflicted, even though she couldn't deny the excited leap in her heart rate.

What was that even about?

But then her head finally caught up with her thundering pulse—and all the pheromones that had gone into freefall again at the determined look on his face.

Was he manipulating her again—not just with the physical desire she couldn't hide but also with her emotions?

He knew, because she'd told him all those months ago, how special Parádeisos was to her. How much being there had meant to her that day, not just because of him and the friendship she'd thought they'd been forming. But also because of her mum and the summer day she'd spent with her there as a teenager… Before the island had been purchased by a billionaire.

Was that why he wanted to go back there—because he knew how raw it made her feel, and how easily she had fallen for him the first time?

'That is where we are headed, yes,' he said. 'And yes, I want to take you there again. You are right when you say we must rebuild trust. I see no better place to do it than there, where we can be safe from any press intrusion. And we'd also have the privacy we need to discuss the practicalities of our shared future.'

Our shared future.

When he said it like that, it struck at the heart of all her insecurities. The desperate yearning to have a home again, to have the kind of love and approval that had disappeared with her mother's death…

She tensed, hating the sudden pulse of longing, and how vulnerable it made her feel. She couldn't afford to turn into that needy teenager again, looking for scraps of affection from someone who had never really cared for her. She'd looked for that from her father, and never found it… Looking for it from a man like Xander would be equally pointless.

She'd dived into a relationship with him once before, when she'd thought he was someone else… Someone who was on her level, not just financially, but also emotionally. However moody he'd been when she'd first met him, she'd thought he'd let his guard down by the time they'd made love that day. But of course he hadn't, because he'd never been who he'd said he was… And this man—this billionaire, who had the world at his fingertips and answered to no one and nothing—was even more closed off and emotionally unavailable.

She was still puzzling how best to respond to his offer though—not that it had really been an offer, more a foregone conclusion—when a waiter appeared on the terrace to take their order.

Xander and he had a short conversation in rapid Italian—making her wonder how many languages he spoke fluently, because she'd already heard him speak in perfect English and French as well as his native Greek.

'Our waiter says the chef is happy to make you a real Neapolitan pizza, with any toppings you wish…' His lips quirked. 'Although he says the chef will not put pineapple on a pizza, even for the King of England.'

She choked out a laugh, suddenly desperate to lighten the mood—because her stomach was already in knots trying to consider all the angles here and she didn't want him to know how much his offer of a return to Parádeisos had unsettled her.

'I'm happy to go with anything he says is good. There's nothing much I won't eat…' she said, then flushed again, when Xander's gaze intensified. 'Except maybe anchovies…' she added hastily, trying to yank the conversation back into the PG zone. *Again.*

For Pete's sake, how did he make her think of sex now with a single look? This was getting ridiculous.

Xander rattled off more orders in Italian to the waiter.

Once they were alone again, though, her reprieve was over. Because that intent, all-seeing gaze settled back on her face.

'So, what is your answer, Poppy? Will you return to Parádeisos with me?'

'For…for how long?' she asked. 'I'm not sure I can afford to—'

'Do not say this again,' he interrupted her, his tone sharpening. 'You cannot work in menial jobs when you carry my child, Poppy. Surely this must be obvious. If you must buy your own clothes, I will allow it.'

Her back stiffened. 'Oh, will you now?' she said, working up her outrage to cover her panic at the way he was taking charge again. She couldn't let herself rely on him, or her independence would be gone—why couldn't he understand that? 'How very accommodating of you.'

'Stop. That is not what I meant, and you know it,' he interrupted her again as frustration swirled, turning the pure blue of his eyes into a stormy grey. 'I don't care about your clothes, but I do care about you. You must not continue to fight me on this. There is no shame in letting me support you,' he added as his gaze dropped to where her pregnancy bump was visible over the tabletop. 'And I could not live with myself if anything happened to you or the child while I have the means to keep you safe.'

She blinked back the swell of tears—and emotion—at his outburst, as one phrase echoed in her head.

I do care about you.

She clutched her hands in her lap and stared down at them—forced to acknowledge what she'd already guessed. That his need to support her—and their baby—wasn't actually about her. It was rooted in that little boy who had been deserted by the man who should have protected him—however much Xander might want to deny it.

'I just, I don't want to lose my independence, that's all,' she said, suddenly feeling small and foolish for finding it so hard to get past that feeling of needing too much from people who would never give it to her…

Her fear wasn't about Xander, it was about her dad, and those years spent living with the family who mattered to him the way she never would. But why did it have to be about Xander too? When she'd already realised the foolish feelings she'd had for him in April had been an illusion?

How insecure was she that she was linking his need to protect his child to all her own insecurities? And how exactly did she think she was going to support herself waitressing when she was having a billionaire's baby? Because she wasn't convinced now her panic had ever been about the money. Had it always been the fear of relying on Xander emotionally, when he had never even offered her that?

She let out a hefty breath and lifted her head. Perhaps she just needed to have more faith in her ability to remain emotionally independent? Surely it wouldn't be that hard, now she knew who he really was?

'But I get where you're coming from too,' she conceded. 'I don't want to put our baby at risk either.' She shrugged.

'Not that I think working as a waitress is dangerous when I'm healthy and strong, and...'

'Poppy...' he admonished.

She trailed off, because he had that indomitable look on his face that told her he wasn't going to budge on this. And in a weird way she found that reassuring.

She just needed to ensure she didn't kid herself again that he cared about *her*, per se. Then it didn't have to be a bad thing that he wanted to support his baby. Right?

'I want to be reasonable, but this...' he said slowly. '*This* I cannot be reasonable about. Not when you are having *my* baby. And what about the child? It will be my heir—this will make it extremely vulnerable. The kidnap threat alone will have to be managed. You must understand that I must protect you too, as its mother, for the child to be safe.'

Kidnap threat?

She balked, shocked into silence by the serious expression on his face.

Had she been impossibly naïve and immature? Not to have even considered the full impact of having a man as wealthy as Xander Caras as the father of her child?

'Okay, I guess... Maybe we do need time and space to talk about how this is going to work,' she said wearily, aware for the first time of how much her life was likely to change. She sighed. 'There's definitely more at stake here than I thought.'

He smiled, but his gaze remained shuttered, his expression strained. Reaching across the table, he scooped an errant tear off her cheek.

'Do not cry, Poppy. It will not be so bad. Believe me, it is much better to be too rich, than too poor. I know.'

'Yes, I suppose so,' she murmured, although she wasn't so sure.

One thing her mum had never had to worry about, when

her father had walked out on her for another woman, was whether her child would be kidnapped.

But even so, she felt ashamed now at her naiveté. And her sense of entitlement.

After all, she'd judged him and his motivations, and made assumptions about his past, to justify her own hurt feelings. Assumptions that she now knew were totally false. She'd held his extreme wealth against him, even despised him for it, believing he was a man who had been born into privilege. But, from the little he'd divulged about his past, she now knew that was not the case.

If he tried to use his money to control her, she could fight him on that. But thinking she could go back to being a free spirit, or a free agent even, wasn't going to fly. Not if she was going to do what was best for her baby.

She let out a shuddering breath.

Their baby.

She pressed unsteady palms to her rounded belly—and rubbed the place where she'd felt the baby move that morning.

It was past time she stopped thinking only of herself. The truth was, however determined she was to maintain her independence, she also hadn't really put a whole lot of thought into the practical considerations of what her life would look like once the baby was born. She'd just assumed she could wing it, as her mum had, and as she had ever since she'd left university and embarked on a nomadic existence of temporary jobs and insecure accommodation. She'd enjoyed not knowing where she was going and what she would be doing next. It had felt like an adventure… Not being beholden to anyone, not being tied down. Perhaps because whenever hard times had hit when she was a kid, her mum had turned it into an adventure.

They'd always been the two musketeers. And when her mum had gone, and she'd been stuck in her dad's home, she'd convinced herself she could still be the one musketeer. Her ability to be upbeat and positive even at the lowest points in her life had been her greatest strength. Even after she'd found herself pregnant and alone, she'd been so excited at the thought of becoming a mum.

But had her greatest strength also been a weakness?

Because always assuming her life would just fall into place, that things would work out okay in the end, if she worked hard and kept her options open and didn't let the doubts get her down, had also left her without a coherent plan now—because how exactly was she supposed to protect herself and her baby from kidnappers? When she didn't even have enough money at the moment to get back to the UK, or fix the roof on her mum's old cottage in Kent where she'd had some vague plan of living?

'You will come back to Parádeisos with me, then?' he asked, although it didn't really sound like a question.

'Yes, okay… Yes.'

'Excellent…' The fierce frown became an even fiercer smile. 'I will have to work occasionally, but the island is beautiful at this time of year, and I have spent no time there. So I will make time to explore it with you.'

Before she had a chance to process his meaning, he skimmed a proprietorial finger down the side of her face. 'And we can also enjoy more of the chemistry that created our baby.'

The familiar jolt of arousal hit all her erogenous zones at once.

'No.' She jerked away from his touch. 'I… I don't think us sleeping together is a good idea. It will just complicate things even more.'

'How does this complicate anything?' One eyebrow rose in a quizzical expression. Maybe she was—because the echo of pleasure from that morning was pulsing in those damn erogenous zones again too. 'Surely this is the only thing which is very simple,' he said. 'We both enjoy making love to each other. And we are good at it.'

Except they wouldn't be making love.

They'd be scratching an itch. Unfortunately, she was a lot less experienced at scratching those itches, and she'd certainly never scratched them with a man who could do it so well.

He wasn't the first man she'd ever slept with, but he was the only one to make her forget everyone but him. She could so easily become addicted to his touch, his taste, the way he made her feel cherished and important while he was bringing her to orgasm with ruthless efficiency. He'd done it that morning, when, for a few precious, terrifying moments, he'd held her. And while she'd been steeped in afterglow, she'd almost fallen back into the trap of believing their spectacular connection meant something more.

She couldn't afford to go there, especially now she was having his child.

After Fig Gate, she knew he could use their chemistry like a weapon against her. And remain aloof. If he ever found out exactly how fast and hard she had fallen for 'Alex', how easily she'd confused their physical intimacy that day for something else, and all the hopes and dreams she'd poured into a relationship that had never existed, she would be even more vulnerable than she was already.

But how to tell him she didn't want to 'enjoy their chemistry' without him realising exactly how vulnerable their physical connection made her feel?

'Honestly, I'm just pretty exhausted,' she finally said, not honestly at all, because she was mostly over the fatigue that had hit during the early weeks of her pregnancy.

'I see.' His brow furrowed, but when twin flags of colour appeared on his cheeks, she knew she'd used the right tactic. Because for the first time since she'd met him, he looked unsure. 'But you are well?' he asked.

'Absolutely. I'm fine.' She dismissed the trickle of guilt that he had been concerned about her health. 'But making a baby is a lot of work. It would be nice to take some downtime, a proper holiday… Just sit around the pool and concentrate on the baby-making when we're not busy discussing stuff. And get lots of early nights.'

In truth, she couldn't think of anything more tedious than sitting around a pool doing nothing—or more boring than going to bed early, because she'd always been a night owl.

But she could explore the island she loved while he was working, and if she recalled correctly—from when they'd crept into the palatial villa he'd built there—he had an impressive entertainment suite and a huge library. She'd just have to hope the games and films and books in there weren't all in Greek. And that hopefully he'd be far too busy growing his already enormous shipping empire to notice she was busy avoiding him.

The crease on his brow became a chasm, and she had the disturbing thought he had already smelled a rat. But then the waiter arrived with a service trolley, laden with a mouth-watering array of local foods and an enormous pizza. The delicious scent of grilled mozzarella and garlic had her empty stomach growling loudly.

He sat back in his chair, still studying her with the intense scrutiny that made her feel totally transparent, while the waiter sliced up the pizza and reeled off the toppings the chef had added.

But once the server had left again, Xander's sensual smile had heat eddying down to her core.

'Eat,' he said, his voice so husky it brushed over her skin like a caress. But as she lifted a slice to her mouth and bit into the heady combination of thin chargrilled bread, sweet

tomatoes and creamy, chewy cheese, it wasn't just the fla-
vours of her first authentic Neapolitan pizza that had her
whole body exploding with sensation. It was the intensity in
his eyes as he watched her eat.

'We must ensure you keep your strength up,' he said as he
helped himself to a slice of the pizza.

But as she watched him fold the slice and devour it with
equal gusto, she had the strange feeling that, instead of keeping herself safe from any misguided emotions where the father of her baby was concerned with her white lie, she'd just
thrown down a gauntlet to a billionaire player who never lost
a challenge he wanted to win.

CHAPTER NINE

Three days later

'I MET YOUR princess last night, Xander. She's a lot more… intriguing than I was anticipating.'

Intriguing? Xander frowned at his brother over the video call. Why did that sound like a euphemism for something else entirely? And why did Theo look a lot less relaxed than usual?

'She's not my princess any more, Theo,' he clarified, deciding not to question his brother further. Theo might be a player, but he was not the type to seduce virgins, especially not regal virgins who came with irate fathers attached.

And Princess Freya was certainly that. Xander had phoned Prince Andreas himself, after he and Poppy had returned to the yacht in Sorrento, to confirm what Theo had already told the man that morning—Xander was pulling out of their marriage bargain.

He thought he'd owed the man and his daughter that courtesy. But the Prince had still been furious. Xander had been unimpressed with the man's surly tone and insinuations, forced to explain in words of one syllable he would not be bullied into an arrangement that no longer worked for him when Andreas had threatened to kill the land deal unless he reconsidered.

If Andreas was stupid enough to destroy a deal that would

bring immense financial benefits to his principality over a point of pride, that was his decision.

Now he thought about it, Xander was relieved not to have to contemplate having the man as a father-in-law. From the accusations the Prince had thrown around, it was clear he had never considered them equals. So to hell with him.

After hanging up on the irate prince, Xander had messaged Theo and told him to find another location for the harbourage they required for the cruise-ship business. It wasn't ideal, because there was nowhere as luxurious and exclusive as Galicos—and the opportunities to buy enough land for the terminal were limited elsewhere in the Mediterranean.

Given they were now looking at other options, though, Xander was surprised to discover Theo was still in the principality, and had not called off last night's engagement party...

'Why the hell did you go ahead with the party?' he asked. 'I thought I told you we weren't pursuing a deal in Galicos now.'

'And I thought you agreed to let me handle this from here?' Theo shot straight back.

Xander noted his brother's belligerent expression. What was *that* about?

He forced himself to control his irritation, though—well aware his impatience had a lot more to do with Poppy, and her virtual refusal to come out of her suite in the last three days, than it did with the demise of the Galicos deal, or his brother's strange behaviour. She'd barely even thanked him when he'd had her belongings collected from the hostel in Port Gabriel and flown to Sicily, so they could be returned to her when they stopped in Syracuse to refuel yesterday.

It was Xander's turn to scowl, annoyed her lack of gratitude was still bothering him so much. It was almost as if he had been trying to win her favour with the gesture, when he hadn't needed anyone's approval since the night his father had abandoned him.

He took a long gulp of his morning coffee and inhaled a lungful of the sea air tinged with the scent of the olive and citrus groves cultivated on Rhodes, and the clean earthy scent of the Aleppo pine forests that grew in abundance on the island.

The impatience and frustration that had been sitting in his stomach like a brick since Sorrento began to throb.

He scanned Rhodes' vibrant interior from the yacht's deck—the verdant green of the forested hills splashed with colour from the oleander and myrtles that grew wild on the island—and the ribbons of pristine beaches.

Greece was home. Wherever he went in the world, however much wealth or influence he acquired, he always came back here. Because he felt the pull of these shores, this culture, even though for much of his early life it had not been kind to him.

He frowned, the sentimental—and self-indulgent—thought even more galling.

He had purchased Parádeisos and built a home on it because this area of his homeland was so much less hectic than Athens. Serene and steeped in history, Rhodes and the surrounding islands were also at their best at this time of year, when the sun was still hot, the water warm, but the tourist season winding down...

So why had he allowed his one day with Poppy to rob him of what he had built here? And why did his insistence on returning here with her not seem like the easy fix it had a few days ago?

He'd assumed she would come to him, that she would be unable to resist their chemistry. But he was the one who had struggled, not her.

'Trust me, Xander,' Theo said, interrupting Xander's thoughts. 'The Prince still wants this deal, and he needs it more than we do if the rumours I've heard are correct. Once he realises he's running out of time, and we're his only option, the arrogant ass will do what I tell him.'

'Should I be concerned about your tactics, Theo?' Xander asked, because Theo's usual devil-may-care charm seemed to be in short supply this morning.

Although making a success of the cruise business mattered to him a lot less at the moment than solving the problem of Poppy Brown, which spoke volumes about how she had managed to distract him from his priorities.

'Don't concern yourself with my tactics. I will only employ the nuclear option if absolutely necessary,' Theo said.

'What's the nuclear option?' Xander asked as he took another sip of his coffee and tried to show an interest in his business.

'I kidnap the virgin princess and marry her myself.'

Xander spat out the coffee but was chuckling as he disconnected his brother's call.

His brother's joke had managed to stop him brooding—but also made him realise something that he should have realised days, maybe even months ago.

He was overthinking the problem of Poppy Brown.

He had become obsessed with her, during the past five months. And had allowed his sexual frustration, over the last few days of their voyage, while she had been hiding in her cabin, to demolish his usual pragmatism.

Hearing how her father had also let her down, over their pizza in Sorrento, had made him feel exposed again, as he had that day on Parádeisos five months before, when for a few fleeting hours he had felt a connection with her that went beyond the physical... A connection that scared him, because it felt out of his control.

But it was obvious to him now he had confused his physical desire for her and her unique ability to frustrate him with something else. The only connection they really shared was the knowledge that it was pointless to rely on anyone's affection and support because it could be withdrawn so easily.

Of course, the existence of the child made him determined to protect her... Because he would never be like his father, a man who abandoned his responsibilities to his own flesh and blood. But he could fulfil his responsibilities to Poppy and his child by giving them a secure home—perhaps even on Parádeisos, which he knew she loved. Showing her what her life could be like, as his mistress as well as the mother of his child, would surely make her better able to accept the loss of her financial independence.

More importantly though, he was through letting her call the shots. His obsession with her was physical—the last three days of mounting torture had confirmed as much—so it was time to be a lot more proactive. They would anchor off the coast this morning—and take the launch to Parádeisos. And then Poppy would no longer be able to hide from him so easily. Or the vicious desire that had woken him up each night, hard and ready for her.

'No wonder this place is called paradise, Pops. Imagine living here?'

Poppy stood on the cabin balcony, her mum's voice echoing through the years, as emotion pummelled her chest at the sight of Parádeisos across the sparkling blue water, its verdant interior and beautiful beaches still untouched, despite the deluxe villa she now knew stood on the opposite side of the island.

She released the breath she felt as though she'd been holding for days now... Ever since she'd agreed to return here, with Xander.

Avoiding him on the yacht had turned out to be easier than she'd expected, simply by eating in her cabin and only venturing out to thank him when her rucksack had been delivered. But when she heard the sharp rap on her cabin door, and her heart jumped into her throat, she wondered if keeping such a low profile had been the right choice. Because now she was even more on edge than she had been in Sorrento.

She trooped to the door and opened it to find Meghan and Nicholai, the young steward who had been serving her meals, outside. But the wave of relief was short-lived.

'Mr Caras has the launch ready to escort you both to the island, Miss Brown. Nicholai will pack your belongings.'

'It's okay, I'm already packed,' she said. It hadn't taken long to stuff her tiny wardrobe of shorts, T-shirts and a few summer dresses into her pack. But when she went to lift the rucksack off the bed, Meghan stepped forward.

'Please, Miss Brown, you must let Nicholai carry your bag,' she said, her smile strained.

Poppy wanted to argue. The pack wasn't heavy, and having it escorted by the uniformed steward only made her more aware of the worn fabric, and the meagre collection of clothes inside it. But she forced herself to drop it back on the bed. Because, she had no doubt at all, Xander would reprimand his staff if she carried her own luggage. And she didn't want anyone getting into trouble simply because being waited on made her feel so uneasy.

'Of course,' she managed. 'And thank you, I really appreciate it.'

When they arrived on the main deck, Xander was chatting with the superyacht's captain.

He immediately broke off the conversation though when Meghan informed him of Poppy's arrival. His gaze raked over her figure with the dark intensity that she had been busy avoiding for three days as he strolled towards her.

He brushed his thumb down her cheek, the gesture both

intimate and proprietorial. Heat flushed through her system on cue.

'You are well rested, I hope?' he said, the husky tone not doing much to disguise the edge of irony. Because they both knew it wasn't fatigue that had kept her hiding out in her cabin since Sorrento.

She nodded. 'Yes, thanks.'

'Good. I thought we could go for a swim and then lunch at Seirína's Cove while our luggage is transported to the villa.'

Seirína's Cove? The place where she had instigated an energetic game of swim tag on that bright, sunny afternoon in April? The place where he'd won easily, and thrown her over his shoulder to cart her out of the cool, crystal-clear water and onto the white sand beach? The place where she'd wriggled out of his arms, only to realise she wasn't the only one who had been impossibly aroused by their water play—make that foreplay. The place where she had been only too eager to agree to his suggestion that they sneak into the billionaire's villa—so she could throw caution to the wind and jump him?

Terrific.

He was doing his mind-reading thing again, the dare in his expression unmistakeable.

If she said no, he'd know what a chicken she was. Not that he didn't already know, given that she'd spent three whole days reading every single book on her e-reader. And if she said yes, she would be walking straight into the lion's den with nothing to protect her but her bikini and the knot of anxiety in her gut—those provocative memories an even more powerful aphrodisiac than the longing that had only intensified since the last time they'd made love…

Time to woman up, Pops.

Stepping away from his callused palm, and the thumb that had slid down to press against the rabbiting pulse in her collarbone, she stuck out her chin and sent him her best *Whatever* smile.

'Sounds delicious, I can't wait,' she murmured.

He chuckled. 'Neither can I.'

It was only as he took her hand to escort her onto the launch that she realised her show of bravado was about as useful as a string bikini, when it came to dealing with Xander Caras' bad intentions.

The water was the same pure and iridescent turquoise she remembered as Xander drove the Jeep they'd climbed into at the dock down the rocky track towards the hidden cove. As he cut the engine, she could hear the murmur of the waves as they lapped gently onto powdery sand, which looked almost pink in the sparkle of noon sunlight. The rocky outcrops that edged the cove only made the beach look more idyllic, while a grove of olive trees created a natural shaded area where a couple of cool boxes had been left on the sand, beside an outdoor sofa and a low table—which must have been brought out here especially for their picnic.

Their very deluxe picnic.

She climbed out of the Jeep and sighed, her heart aching for so many things—all at once.

The last time they'd been here together, she'd told 'Alex' all about her mum and their magical holidays in Greece. Of finding this island on their final summer, and how this had become their 'special place' after they'd borrowed a boat and landed on this deserted beach… How they'd lain on the sand after a picnic lunch—and the plans her mum had constructed, about buying a plot of land on this paradise island and building a cabin to live in. All fanciful nonsense, of course. But it had seemed such a wonderful idea, and somehow so possible to twelve-year-old her—because she'd always believed her mum could do anything. That love would find a way.

By the following summer her mum had been sick. And by the next year, she'd been gone, and it was as if she'd taken all those possibilities and Poppy's belief in the power of love with her. But when Poppy had come back here with 'Alex', those dreams had felt tantalisingly close again.

But the memory of the day she'd spent here with her mum so many years ago was hazy and sentimental, compared with the adrenaline overload when she recalled her time here with Xander this spring.

He'd made her feel special that day. So beautiful and seen. Like a siren, in complete control of her own destiny. During that day, she had been sure again the dreams she'd once spun with her mum didn't have to be out of reach if she just had the courage to take what she wanted and damn the consequences… Which was why she'd reached for him later in the villa, why she'd asked him to kiss her, and demanded he make love to her.

And when she'd fallen asleep later that night, in the small bed and breakfast hotel where she'd been staying on Rhodes, not knowing they'd made a baby together, she had convinced herself she could find a place to belong, with him, even if it couldn't be here.

Had he brought her back to Parádeisos to unsettle her again? Because it was working, the tug of connection as strong as the pulse of awareness.

'Tell me something, Xander,' she asked carefully. 'Were you laughing at me that day? When I told you all the silly plans I'd made on this beach with my mum?'

She had to know, because the thought he'd been secretly amused by the confidences she'd shared with him was what had hurt the most when she'd discovered he was the island's new owner.

His brows lowered. 'No,' he said. 'I was not laughing,

because I did not think those plans silly. I found them enchanting.'

The spurt of relief had the knot of anxiety releasing.

'But also hopelessly naïve…' he added.

'Why naïve?' she asked, her heart pulsing heavily at his hollow tone.

'Because those plans could never be more than pointless dreams when your mother had no way to achieve them. Dreams do not feed you or clothe you. And they cannot keep you safe. For this, you must always face reality.'

Her heart slowed. She could see he meant it, from his harsh expression.

She shivered, despite the warm day.

Of course, on one level, she knew he was right. Her mum hadn't ever really had a coherent plan—they'd coasted from one financial cliff-edge to the next, forced to move around constantly until she'd bought that broken-down cottage in Kent where the roof leaked if it rained too hard, and the walls got damp in the winter. But despite having to wear cast-off clothing, never being able to afford to go on school trips, Poppy had always known her mum loved her unconditionally, and that had made her feel so supported and secure, regardless of their money worries. Kind of like that cheesy but also impossibly sweet Dolly Parton song, which her mum had loved to play at top volume, about a rag coat that Dolly's mom had made her. Poppy had insisted on playing it at her mother's funeral.

Her dad had been rich by comparison, but she'd known the money he spent on her was a replacement for the love he couldn't give her.

Xander's insistence that dreams weren't practical made her feel sad for him. Because without dreams, how *could* there ever be hope? And without hope how could there ever be love?

Xander climbed out of the Jeep and she turned to find him watching her, with that guarded but intense expression on his face, as if she were a puzzle he wanted to solve. Strangely his curiosity made her feel a little less insecure about being here with him again. Perhaps he wasn't a hopeless cause after all? He'd just been forced to give up his dreams too soon, much sooner than her, because of the insecurity of his childhood. Had he ever been allowed to be carefree? Ever felt unconditional love? It seemed doubtful given what he'd told her. How could he understand the power of dreams without that?

'Would your mother not be happy,' he said, 'to see you here again?'

'I guess.' She smiled, because it was a surprisingly sentimental question for such a defiantly unsentimental man. 'Although it wasn't really Parádeisos she wanted for me, so much as the dream of it.'

'I see,' he said, although it was clear he didn't see, from the confused frown on his face. But then he relinquished eye contact, to stare out into the cove, and she wondered if he was uncomfortable at having revealed more than he'd intended.

'We should swim,' he said, suddenly.

She blinked at the abrupt change of tone. But she couldn't help the laugh that popped out. Or her desire to lighten the mood, too.

'I don't have a swimsuit with me,' she said, cursing the stupidity of not thinking to grab her bikini before they got into the Jeep. But then she hadn't been thinking at all when they'd stepped onto the dock—in the grip of the emotions this island always stirred.

'I had Meghan pack swimwear for us both,' he said, reaching into the Jeep's back seat for the beach bag he'd thrown in at the quay. 'But if you want to swim naked, I have no objections,' he added, a provocative smile curling his lips.

She tensed, the fierce rush of longing so intense it hurt.

'You bastard,' she murmured, but she couldn't seem to conjure up the indignation she wanted to feel. 'You knew, didn't you,' she said, 'that there was no way I'd be able to resist you here?' She wanted to be mad at him, but the only person she was really mad at was herself, for making this physical attraction that much more potent by trying to deny it.

A schoolgirl error. And she was a grown woman—who was going to become a mother in a few months' time.

'Yes,' he said, with typical arrogance, but then the awareness in those pure blue eyes flared. 'But I still do not understand why you would want to deny us both this pleasure?'

Because I don't want to fall for you. Not again. Not until I can trust my feelings for you.

But that fear felt somehow juvenile and silly—and cowardly too—in this stunning place. She had chosen to have this man's child. That decision would bind them always, no matter her feelings or his. And being here again made her even more aware of how fleeting life could be, how unreliable and insecure. And she suspected he knew that, too, from the small insights he'd given her into his past.

Xander Caras guarded his secrets jealously, his emotions even more so, probably because he'd once been so vulnerable.

He'd lied about who he was that day, plus he still hadn't really explained why he'd decided not to tell her the truth. She wasn't buying the excuse he'd only been adhering to her wishes that they remain anonymous, given that he must have known there was no chance of them being accused of trespassing. But did his silence that day, the decision not to admit he was the billionaire who had purchased her precious island, mean nothing else they'd shared that day had been real either? Had the intimacy, the connection she'd felt so strongly, when they'd mucked about together and then made love, and he had listened to her dreams, all been a lie too? And how would she ever discover the answer to that crucial question, if she didn't have the courage to see where their time together here might take them?

Didn't she owe it to her baby, *their* baby, to find out if they could have a future together as more than just its parents? And didn't she also owe it to that fanciful pre-teen, who had once lain on this beach with her mum and spun silly dreams that had seemed so close five months ago with the brooding beach bum who had turned out to be a billionaire?

He dumped the bag on the ground, pulled out two scraps of red spandex. And dangled them from his finger, just out of her reach.

'You look hot,' he murmured, the provocative smile making it clear he wasn't just talking about the sweat dampening her neck. 'The water is perfect at this time of year, cool and refreshing but not too cold.' His saturnine features darkened, making need gush between her thighs. 'Say please, and I may let you have the bikini.'

It was another dare, pure and simple. So, why not up the stakes?

She began unbuttoning the front of her dress. She'd already lost this round, but she intended to lose it in style.

Two can play at that game, buster.

His eyebrows rose, the colour slashing across his cheekbones as she tugged the dress over her head then kicked off her sandals. Standing before him in nothing but her bra and panties, she could see she had surprised him—even as desire turned his gaze to a deep cobalt, even more vivid than the sparkling turquoise sea.

'You can keep the bikini,' she announced as she reached behind her back to unsnap her bra, then flung it away. Her tender breasts felt swollen and heavy, the nipples tightening as his gaze—possessive and hungry—raked over them.

He groaned and cursed in Greek as the bikini in his fingers dropped to the sand. But when he reached for her, she darted away, a laugh bubbling out.

Why had she denied herself the chance to make him ache, the way she ached for him?

Another schoolgirl error, Pops! Time to turn up the heat.

Power rushed through her as she sprinted towards the sea, aware of him cursing as he struggled to undress as fast as was humanly possible. She waded into the crisp, clear water, then dived under the surface, letting the coolness revitalise her skin.

When she came up for air, he was striding into the waves, gloriously naked, his expression fierce with determination. His tanned skin gleamed in the sunshine. The sculpted muscles of his pecs were dusted with hair that trailed into a thin line between washboard abs. Lean hips, long legs and broad shoulders completed the picture of a man in his prime.

She took the opportunity to look her fill, while her breathing accelerated and the knot in her throat dropped to pound between her thighs.

He was spectacular, like the mock-ups she'd admired as a girl of the Colossus of Rhodes, the bronze statue that had once stood in the ancient harbour, although... Her gaze edged down his happy trail to his groin, where dark hair bloomed around his impressive cock.

Already semi-erect.

Her breath caught as she studied him.

Who knew? Xander Caras was even more magnificent—and intimidating—than an artist's impression of one of the seven wonders of the ancient world...

She stood her ground, determined not to hide any longer from the hunger that bound them both. She smiled as he stalked towards her, feeling like the sirens the cove was named for, luring him to her, aware of his gaze riveted on the tight nipples already begging for his attention. She just hoped he couldn't tell how shaky her knees were under the water or sense the liquid heat turning her belly into an inferno.

Power rushed through her as he reached her, and grasped her round the waist, to drag her against him.

Her pregnant belly butted against the strident erection, not diminished in the least by the cool water as he lowered his head and with a hungry growl closed his mouth over one aching breast.

She bowed back, thrusting the tip into his mouth. Threading her fingers into his hair, she pulled him closer as the exquisite sensations threatened to send her over too soon. She panted, her hands fisting, the water doing nothing to cool the inferno building inside her as he devoured her breasts—sucking, licking, nipping. Devastating desire arrowed down to her aching core. He lifted his head, tugging his hair from her grip, to stare into her eyes while his hand slid into her panties.

She sobbed, already close to cresting, as he parted the swollen folds, slick with her juices. But instead of caressing the perfect spot, he thrust one finger, then two inside her. Stretching her tender flesh, but not doing the one thing that would take her over.

'Xander, I—I need more,' she moaned, frustrated, impatient, rocking against his hand, clinging to his shoulders, desperate to find the friction she craved, to end the torment.

He laughed, the deep rumble strained but thick with masculine satisfaction—and she realised he was tormenting her on purpose.

'You deny me for three days, and yet you expect instant gratification…' Clasping her head with his other hand, he captured her lips, his tongue tangling with hers in a dance of dominance and submission.

She kissed him back but choked out a sob when he removed his hand from her panties. Before she had the chance to beg, he scooped her into his arms, strode out of the surf, and across the sand until they reached the sofa under the trees.

Placing her on her feet, he kneeled to hook his thumbs in the wet panties. She had to steady herself on his shoulder as he lifted one foot then the other to strip them off. When he stood, towering over her, she could see the ruthless desire in his face, feel it in the rigid erection pressing against her belly. But as she reached to circle his neck, he grasped her wrists and turned her away from him, folding his arms around her, the erection now nestled against her back.

'I want to take you so deep you will feel me everywhere,' he murmured against her neck, his low voice guttural with tension, but also rough with desire. 'But I don't want to hurt the baby.'

'Y-you won't,' she managed as emotion bloomed alongside the visceral heat, the concern in his voice touching something deep inside her.

Memory swirled as she recalled their first time, and the care with which he'd eased inside her, aware of his size.

'Good,' he murmured, but then he bit into her earlobe. Raw sensation pulsed in her sex, focussing her attention back on the pleasure that he had denied her.

Taking her hands, he placed them on the back of the sofa, forcing her to kneel on the seat, the strident erection brushing her bottom.

'Tell me if it is too much,' he groaned.

Awareness shimmered through her as he held her hips, the huge head pressing against her entrance from behind. He slid deep, in unbearable increments, her slick flesh easing his way, until he was seated to the hilt.

She sobbed, her muscles clenching, and releasing, struggling to adjust to the thick intrusion, the stretching feeling overwhelming. But then he cradled the mound of her pregnancy, caressing the tight skin, and whispered into her hair.

'I love what my child has done to you,' he murmured, his voice husky with need. 'You are mine now, always, in the only way that counts,' he finished, the words so low it was as if they had been wrenched from his soul.

The emotion rushed back, pressing against her ribs like a boulder, wrapping around her heart—the connection she had sensed all those months ago like a band now around her chest, restricting her breathing.

He pulled out, then rocked back, again and again—faster, harder—until he had established a firm, unstoppable rhythm. Her fingernails dug into the sofa cushions, her body shaking as the vicious climax barrelled towards her, each thrust so deep it felt as if he could touch her heart.

His grunts matched her moans, the pleasure building, drawing, tightening like a vice, until his hands moved from her belly to caress the perfect spot at last.

The orgasm—hot, basic, delirious—tore through her body. She cried out, the fierce pleasure exploding in unstoppable waves, like the tide slapping against the rocks.

He shouted out his own pleasure behind her, his body covering hers as they plummeted into the beautiful, bright oblivion together.

But as he pulled out of her, her knees buckled. He yanked her back, cradled her against him, turning so she collapsed on top of him on the sofa.

They lay, together, spent, drained, her body shimmering with the vicious afterglow, her skin slick with sweat, her mind drifting.

He shifted, to press a kiss to her cheek, then spread his hands over the place where their baby grew.

'Okay?' he asked softly.

She nodded, unable to speak as the boulder resting on her ribs rose up to choke her.

And the words he'd said in the heat of passion reverberated in her heart.

You are mine now, always, in the only way that counts.

Did he mean that? Did she really matter to him now, the way she hadn't mattered to anyone for so long…?

She tried to contain the desperate surge of hope. But the wave of emotion pressing against her ribs felt too huge, too wonderful to be cautious.

So she basked in it, let it warm her heart, while the sun warmed her skin.

She closed her eyes, and gave herself up to the foggy feeling of blissful exhaustion… While the dreams she had convinced herself she needed to forget flooded back in again, regardless.

CHAPTER TEN

THE REST OF the day passed in a haze of hormones while Poppy attempted to focus on the stupendous sex and not her wayward emotions.

She'd woken on the sofa, to find a cotton towel draped over her naked body to shield her from the sun, and Xander swimming in the cove. She'd located the discarded bikini and put it on to join him—because she didn't want to be too much of a pushover by joining him naked! But when he'd insisted on carrying her back to their sofa to apply suncream to her 'pale English skin', it hadn't taken her long to realise he had a hidden agenda.

Their long, lazy lovemaking though, both before and after their deluxe picnic lunch—during which Xander had insisted on licking pomegranate juice off her breasts, as her 'punishment' for stopping him from licking fig juice off her breasts in Sorrento—had been its own reward. And she had acknowledged that, not only did pregnancy make her super horny, but having great sex with her baby's father, could be a fabulous distraction when it came to dealing with the emotions threatening to bombard her again.

If she could just keep everything in perspective, she could use their stay on Parádeisos to get to know Xander better—and discover if their spectacular chemistry could lead to more—but she didn't want to risk letting the endorphin rush mean too much... Too soon.

She'd had dreams about Xander before, about them becoming a couple, but she was much more wary now. She needed more from him than just the promise of great sex—and the responsibilities of shared parenthood. She wanted to be open and honest with him about her feelings, but she needed him to be more willing to share his own emotions. Today at the cove had been a start though, making her realise that perhaps Xander wasn't immune to love, he was just even more wary of being vulnerable than she was.

After their day of blissful isolation, arriving at his villa, where a full staff had now been installed, made her aware once again how different her life goals were from Xander's. He had acquired so much, so young.

The housekeeper, the personal chef, the gardener and the two maids—none of whom, except the housekeeper, Elena, spoke anything but Greek—had been noticeably discreet, disappearing as soon as Poppy had been introduced to them, and Elena had shown Poppy to a spectacular suite on the first floor.

She was grateful to find herself and Xander alone again, a lavish supper of delicious Greek delicacies laid out for them already, once she had showered and changed and ventured out to join him for the evening on the villa's rooftop dining terrace.

He stood with his back to her, watching the sunset, looking tall and indomitable in a light linen shirt and trousers. From this vantage point the view from the terrace was spectacular. She could see the lights of Rhodes dotting the shoreline across the water, while the sinking sun turned the sea to a fiery orange. It made her recall their farewell kiss on the dock all those months ago, when they'd parted, and she'd been so sure she had met her soul mate. She'd believed then he was a man content to drift through life the way she did, never worrying about where she would end up next, because she wanted to enjoy the ride and keep her heart open to all the possibilities.

She knew now Xander was the opposite of that guy. He wasn't moody and enigmatic and rootless, he was focussed and driven and intense. But she could see now that so much of his drive and ambition was linked to his need for the security that had once been denied him.

She released the breath that had been clogged in her lungs ever since their arrival on the island, really, as she stepped onto the terracotta tiles.

He turned towards her. His hair—damp from his recent shower too—gleamed in the twinkle of fairy lights that had been threaded through the grapevines on the lattice that enclosed the terrace. Hunger for her shone in his eyes.

And in that moment, she knew, she no longer wanted 'Alex', who seemed oddly shallow in comparison to this man.

Her heart bounced into her throat. Uncovering Xander's secrets would be tougher, but more rewarding than uncovering Alex's. Because Xander was more of a mystery, and so much more guarded with his emotions.

'I have asked the staff to give us privacy while we are here,' he said as he approached her. 'I know you do not appreciate their presence.'

She was touched that he'd noticed her discomfort and attempted to alleviate it. But it also disturbed her that he could read her so easily, when she found it so hard to read him.

'It's nothing to do with them personally, I just…' She hesitated. How to explain the situation, without making herself too vulnerable again? 'I guess it makes me super uncomfortable to be waited on by anyone. It feels weird, you know…' She began to babble as he placed his hand on her cheek and stroked the skin lazily with his thumb. The possessive touch made her pulse accelerate. She drew in a sharp breath and soldiered on. 'Like I think I'm better than them. And I don't want to make anyone feel that way.'

His brow creased, as if he was trying to figure her out again, but then he smiled, his expression softening.

'Have I ever told you how delightful you are, Poppy?' he murmured.

She swallowed heavily, trying to force her heart back where it belonged. But then his hand cupped the back of her neck to inch her closer. Until she could feel his breath on her lips.

'I'm not sure you felt like that a week ago,' she countered, determined not to make too much of the glow of appreciation in his eyes. Was that a genuine compliment, or was he simply trying to seduce her again? It was hard to tell, because his thumb was now stroking the thundering pulse in her collarbone, making it impossible for her to concentrate.

He let out a deep sigh and raised his head to meet her gaze.

'I was so frustrated that you would not do as I told you.'

'I noticed,' she replied, but her comment came out on a husky breath, because she was oddly touched by the sincerity in his eyes.

He let out a gruff chuckle, but his gaze remained fixed on hers when he continued.

'I find your free spirit and your determination to see everyone as your equal captivating, too,' he explained, the honest appreciation in his eyes disarming. 'But you must not concern yourself with the well-being of my staff. I pay them exceptionally well—and I pride myself on never making unreasonable demands, because I know what it is like to have no power when others have too much. I have been ruthless to make Caras Shipping a success, and I will never apologise for that, but I would never take advantage of those less powerful or wealthy than myself,' he finished.

'I—I know,' she said, humbled by his impassioned explanation—and aware that he wasn't just talking about his staff now, he was also talking about her.

'Do you?' His smile returned, but with a rueful tilt. 'Does this mean you no longer hate the billionaire who purchased this island...?'

She stiffened, registering the defensiveness behind the deliberately amused expression. 'You remember that?'

Cursing softly, he released her and walked back across the terrace—to stare out at the sunset again. His shoulders were rigid as he thrust his fingers through his hair, raking it into rows. 'Forget I mentioned it,' he murmured.

She followed him across the tiles, her chest hollowed out by the controlled irritation in his stance. He wasn't angry with her for the words she'd said that day, she realised, but with himself for having let them matter to him.

She couldn't remember exactly what she'd said after they'd made love. But what she did remember, all too vividly, was the way the atmosphere between them had changed abruptly as soon as the afterglow had faded. How the playfulness, the openness, the heat and longing—and the intimacy—that had been building all day had suddenly disappeared.

When she had discovered Xander's identity, she had assumed the abrupt change had been because he had been keen to get rid of her once he'd got what he wanted. But now, she realised, it must have been that offhand comment.

'I'm sorry, Xander,' she said, softly. And meant it. She'd hurt him. And she had carried on believing he was a man who couldn't be hurt. But the fact he'd held onto that criticism for so long told a different story.

He swung round, his expression carefully blank. 'You have no reason to be sorry. You did not know the man you spoke of was me.'

'You misunderstand me, Xander.' She touched his forearm, desperate to sooth the tension crackling in the air between them. The muscles hardened but he didn't pull away. 'I'm not sorry for what I said about that billionaire, because you're right, I didn't know him then. But I know more about who he is now and, for that reason, I'm sorry what I said hurt you.'

Xander flinched, shocked not just by the unnecessary apology, but also by the fierce compassion in Poppy's eyes. Why did her compassion, her kindness, feel like a strength, when he had always considered vulnerability of any kind a weakness?

And why did her stalwart belief that he was a good man, despite everything, make him feel like that terrified boy again, who had woken to find himself and his brother alone…? It was almost as if everything he had worked so hard for—the security, the safety, the money—had been for nothing, because he couldn't defend himself from this slender woman—or resist the tenderness in her eyes.

Shame and embarrassment washed over him.

Why had he mentioned her comment? Had he really allowed himself to stew over that remark for months? How pathetic.

He drew his arm away from her fingertips, resisting the powerful urge to drag her into his embrace and kiss her until they were both breathless.

If only he could tear off that dress and make love to her, until she was crying out his name again, massaging him to climax, so he could obliterate this foolish conversation. But somehow the brutal need to have her only made him feel more defenceless. Because his inability to control the constant hunger felt like a problem now, too.

He bunched his hands into fists and shoved them into his pockets, to stop himself from reaching for her. If for no other reason than to prove he could.

'You did not hurt me,' he said, determined to reject her

sympathy, her pity. She couldn't hurt him, not unless he let her. And he could not open himself to that again, however much he might desire her.

'Okay,' she said. But then she blinked and the sheen of moisture in her eyes gleamed in the moonlight, disturbing him even more.

'And I certainly do not require an apology,' he added, annoyed by the defensive tone. 'If anything, I should say sorry to you, for not being honest with you that day, about who I was…' he finished, realising the apology was long overdue.

She nodded, but just when he felt as if he could breathe again she asked: 'Why did you keep your identity a secret that day? Was what happened between us always just about the sex for you?'

Yes. Because I knew you would never sleep with me if you knew I was him.

He opened his mouth to give her the answer he wanted to be true. The answer he'd managed to convince himself *was* true, five months ago, when he'd walked away from her on the dock, determined to forget her. But her sincerity—and that bottomless pit forming in his chest—made it impossible to lie to her or himself any longer.

'It is true I wanted you very much,' he said. 'From the first moment you approached me on the beach. You were so fresh, and guileless and fierce… When you spoke of your mother with such passion, it moved me, and I am not a sentimental man.' He paused to ease the tightness in his chest. 'And as the day progressed, I could see you desired me, too.'

But what had happened that day had always been more than just sexual attraction. Because she still unsettled him, causing emotions he did not recognise, he hadn't expected, and he did not want to acknowledge even now. But maybe if he stopped pretending nothing had happened, he would finally be able to control those unthinkable emotions. She was the mother of his child. She would always be a part of his life now. So it was important he found a way to rationalise and eventually overcome the feelings that continued to disturb him.

But he could not admit any of that to her, or it would expose him even more.

'When you suggested we remain anonymous,' he added, choosing his words with care, 'it seemed the perfect solution for us to take what we both wanted without consequences.'

His gaze drifted to her stomach. He pressed his palm to the bump and let out a wry laugh.

'Ironic, given our circumstances now.'

She covered his hand with both of hers. His heart jumped, making him aware that the pit in his stomach was still there, and still bottomless. What he saw in her eyes—soft and warm and real—terrified him more. But even so, he couldn't look away when she smiled.

'Ironic, yes, but somehow wonderful too,' she whispered. 'Don't you think?'

He wasn't entirely sure what she meant by that, but even so, he nodded, the rush of possessiveness hard to ignore. 'Yes, I am glad you are having my child,' he said, surprised to realise it was true.

He doubted he could love a child, and he knew he could never give it what it would need emotionally. He had been forced to give up all those weaknesses on the streets of Athens as a boy to survive—and he did not regret it. But as its mother, Poppy would be able to give their child that so easily.

His role would be as it had been with his brother. To protect, to shelter, and to give their child financial security.

She beamed at him, tears glistening in her eyes now. It made her even more beautiful, and desirable. He tugged his hands out of his pockets to cradle her face, and brush away the tears with his thumbs, ignoring the weightlessness in his belly.

'Do not cry, Poppy. I will take care of you both,' he said, wanting to reassure her. As well as himself.

She sniffed, then smiled. 'I can only let you do that if you'll let me take care of you, too.'

He frowned, her offer making no sense to him. But then decided he could live with that, if *her* role was to bear his child, to nurture it, and to take away this constant nagging ache that only she had ever filled.

Tugging her towards him, he slanted his lips across hers, devouring her soft sob of surprise and surrender, determined to seal their deal the only way he knew how.

He angled her head to take the kiss deeper and make her aware of the thick ridge forming against her belly. The hunger intensified as she returned his kiss with equal fervour.

Sex was simple, uncomplicated. This was what he wanted from her, and all he would ever need. To feed the hunger, soothe the longing, sate the desperation.

She was his now, but on his terms. And when they were tired of each other, he would ensure she and the baby would always have what they needed.

Lifting her into his arms, he strode across the terrace, towards his suite.

'Xander, our dinner?' she asked, dazed and delightfully flushed.

'It can wait. It is you I am starving for now,' he said, grinding out the words as the ruthless need consumed him.

She didn't object as he carried her to his bed.

Much later—after they had eaten in the moonlight, then made love again—he lay in his bed, staring out of the open terrace doors at the starry sky, the sea breeze cooling his heated skin while he held her warm, exhausted body a little too tightly.

As he caressed her stomach, the fierce hunger returned.

As well as the hollow pain, the old fear, that she might leave him when he needed her still. And suddenly he could think of only one solution.

They must become man and wife.

He would have to handle the proposal with care. She would be resistant, because of that maddening independence that captivated and frustrated him in equal measure.

She was resistant to the life of luxury and leisure he could offer her. But she already understood the 'freedoms' she had once taken for granted came with a cost their child would have to pay. So, surely it would not be impossible to convince her she and the child needed the protection of his name. Once the child was born, she would have to nurture it and that would be a full-time job. But surely, given her compassionate nature and her excitement about the pregnancy, being a mother would give her more satisfaction than the menial work she had done before?

He recalled the sheen of deep emotion in her eyes earlier that evening.

Why shouldn't he use her passionate nature, her sweetness and naiveté and her belief in dreams, to overcome all these other obstacles?

She sighed softly then shifted in his arms, her movements agitated—almost as if she had sensed him making decisions for her again.

He gathered her close, ignoring the prickle of guilt. He pressed his face into her hair, breathing in the scent of her— suncream and summer flowers and female musk—and the familiar heat pounded between his thighs. He could not let her go, he had to make her stay, that much was non-negotiable.

He had already arranged to conduct his business from Parádeisos for the next couple of weeks. Why not use the time to lay the groundwork for a marriage at the end of their stay here? He had always been ruthless in the pursuit of what he wanted, so why should this situation be any different?

He could not stay on Parádeisos indefinitely. But once they were married, she and his child could live here.

And, once she was living in the place her mother had once dreamed of making her home, she would understand her independence was a small price to pay for a future as his wife, and the mother of his heir.

He had learned, even if she had not, that love was a trap. It was fickle and dangerous because it forced you to rely on other people. And he could never offer any woman that.

But a home—a home that no one could take away from her—that was achievable and real, if… He paused, his arms tightening around her until her restless movements stilled and she relaxed back into sleep…

No, *when* he made her his wife.

CHAPTER ELEVEN

Two weeks later

POPPY FLASHED A quick grin into the foggy bathroom mirror at the muffled rap on her bedroom door.

Well, that was new. Xander Caras bothering to knock. Not that he had much cause to knock on her door, as she was usually in his room. Grabbing a towel, she wrapped it around her freshly showered body and rushed through the suite to open the door.

Her smile faltered when she saw the villa's housekeeper standing on the other side with her arms full of shimmering silk.

'Oh, hello, Elena. Hi...' she said, feeling awkward and trying not to show it. Elena and the rest of the staff at the villa had been wonderful in the past fortnight, tending to her and Xander's needs while also giving them the privacy they needed.

And, boy, had they made the most of it.

The last fourteen days had been wonderful in ways she never would have expected. She was getting to know Xander better, even if he didn't want to talk much about his past— she *still* hadn't got any more information out of him about his childhood—but in every other way, their time together on Parádeisos had been a revelation.

The sex, of course, had been epic, and exhausting, in the

most delicious way possible. She'd become totally addicted to him. All he had to do was look at her now, the fierce awareness darkening his gaze, and her body quickened, preparing to take him inside her. But more than that, each time he touched her, each time he brought her to another shattering climax, then held her afterwards, he made her feel precious, and cherished, and seen. What they had together wasn't just sex, she knew that for sure now. They had strengthened the connection that had always been there, even on that day when she'd thought he was someone else.

Xander was a sexual being, and so was she. Their connection had been forged in the fire of their physical attraction—but that didn't make it any less real.

And there was also his enchanting reaction to the pregnancy.

He spoke about the baby often and seemed fascinated by the child growing inside her. To the extent that she suspected he had been disappointed he still hadn't been able to feel it move the way she had. She had been impossibly touched when he'd arranged for them to go to a top obstetrician in Rhodes two days before, to have a check-up and do an ultrasound. As they'd sat in the suite together, and she'd watched his face flush with fierce emotion as the grainy image of their baby had formed on the doctor's screen, it had been a seminal moment for her, too.

Because she had understood he wanted this child as much as she did. She had been so happy, partly because she would never have expected him to be so invested, but mostly because she hadn't realised how much his commitment to coparenting their baby meant to her. She hadn't wanted to rely on his involvement. In fact she had tried to keep her expectations in check. But knowing she didn't have to do that any more was exhilarating.

Maybe Xander didn't talk much about the feelings growing

between them, but she was sure now that would come too, she just had to give him time. She didn't have to fear enjoying this first flush of love any more, because so much of what Xander did now convinced her he was falling for her too.

He locked himself away in his study most mornings, for a couple of hours, to catch up on his emails and all the other important business that running a shipping empire must entail. But he was delegating a lot of work to his brother to spend time with her, which—given he was clearly a workaholic—meant a lot to her.

Each afternoon they devoted themselves to spending quality time together. And while a lot of that quality time involved overdosing on the endorphin rush of good, hard, sweaty sex, whenever and wherever they could, they'd also found time to do other *stuff* too. He'd taken her sailing, because of course he was a brilliant sailor. They'd been snorkelling on the reef near Seirína's Cove and explored the ruins of a fishing village on the far side of the island that had been abandoned centuries ago. They had spent one memorable afternoon with him teaching her how to drive his motor launch, which she'd loved, the rush of speed almost as exhilarating as having his big body cradling hers so he could direct her hands on the wheel and encourage her to go faster than the wind.

Not quite as much fun had been the afternoon he'd had a personal stylist flown in from Paris with a ton of designer wear and insisted on buying her a whole new wardrobe. She'd resisted at first, because expensive haute couture was so not her thing—seriously, who paid thousands of euros for a pair of high-heeled sandals?

But when he had explained she would need the necessary wardrobe to attend the functions and events he got invited to, she'd sucked up the familiar wave of panic and agreed to let him buy her a couple of outfits. When he'd ignored that instruction and insisted on buying out the poor stylist's whole inventory, she'd continued to bite her tongue, because he obviously enjoyed spoiling her so much. If she never got a chance to wear all those clothes—because frankly she really didn't want to spend too much time being seen with him in public when it was so much more fun to spend time with him in private—perhaps she could get him a refund.

Other than the designer-wardrobe-buying spree, the only other issue had been the argument—or rather the non-argument—they'd had when she had mentioned finding a new job before the baby was born. He had refused to talk about it, and when she had tried to press, he'd distracted her with sex.

She'd felt uneasy about her capitulation at the time. But she'd let it slide since, because even thinking about how exactly a life with Xander was going to work felt daunting. And she knew there would be arguments in their future about it.

But they would have to talk about it tonight, because she'd overheard him talking on the phone to his brother this morning and arranging to be in Athens in a couple of days' time. So she knew their time together on Parádeisos was coming to an end.

Why did it have to be an insurmountable problem, though? He wasn't the autocratic man who had sailed off with her nearly three weeks ago without even telling her. Surely, he was avoiding the issue for the same reason she was, because he didn't want to ruin the time they had left here. But she was ready to take the bull by the horns.

She wanted them to be a family and she knew he did too now from his reaction at the ultrasound. And for that to happen, they would both have to make compromises. The good news was, after two weeks of basking in the intimacy and connection they were building together, they were in a much better place to have that conversation than they had been when he'd spotted her at Serge's restaurant in Galicos, with so many secrets and lies between them.

So, she was oddly touched when Elena held the shimmering silver gown in her arms aloft. Poppy recognised the stylish mini dress as one from the vast designer wardrobe Xander had purchased for her and which the stylist had said would take a week to alter to accommodate Poppy's burgeoning figure.

'Mr Caras has asked me to deliver your dress for this evening.' Elena held up a pair of heeled silver sandals. 'And your shoes. He has a special supper prepared for you at Seiriná's Cove.'

Poppy's pulse skipped, the trickle of anxiety at the conversation they needed to have tonight comprehensively drowned out by the thought of wearing the dress for him at their cove. And the surge of anticipation. Perhaps Xander was ready to have that conversation too now? Why else would he have planned a special dinner?

'A special supper?' she asked eagerly. She really didn't need the trappings of romance, but it felt validating to know that tonight meant a lot to him too. It made her more sure that, even though their time on Parádeisos was nearly over, the last two weeks had made a difference—a *big* difference—to what their future could hold.

Maybe she should tell him tonight she was falling in love with him?

Sensation rippled over her skin alongside the whisper of nerves and excitement.

She hadn't said as much yet, but she suspected he already knew. And why was she keeping it a secret? She wasn't scared of her feelings for him now. And while he might not be ready to say the same to her…yet…it would be a good way to introduce a conversation about what happened next. So he would know she was committed to this relationship—when she explained that they would *both* need to make adjustments, to figure out how to make it work. Because while their time here had been precious and wonderful, they couldn't spend the rest of their lives on vacation together.

'Yes, very special, I think.' The housekeeper beamed, entering the room to place the dress on the bed. 'I will ask Amara to assist you. She has experience with hair styling.'

'Oh, thank you.' Poppy pushed at the mass of wet curls dripping onto her shoulders. It was a long time since she'd been able to afford a hairdresser. But it would be fun to get all dolled up. For Xander. 'That would be terrific, if it's not too much trouble.'

Elena nodded. 'I will inform Amara to come to the suite.' The housekeeper smiled as she crossed the room. 'Dimitrios will escort you to the cove when you are ready.'

'Th-that's wonderful,' Poppy murmured, but the housekeeper had already closed the door behind her.

She turned to stare at the dress, her nerves settling, despite the fact the whisper of jewelled silk was insanely revealing—the skinny straps and the panels of material that draped seductively over her breasts making it impossible to wear a bra. Imagining Xander's reaction when he saw her in it, though, made the ripple of sensation become a flood.

She wanted to look and feel amazing when she told him she loved him.

The only problem would be getting the words out before he jumped her.

She grinned. But once they'd taken the edge off, she wasn't nervous any more about the conversation they needed to have afterwards because, frankly, afterglow should never be underestimated as a means of getting a man like Xander to see reason.

The sea breeze caught the hem of the floaty dress as Dimitrios helped Poppy out of the Jeep onto the path leading to the cove.

'Efcharistó,' she said in her rudimentary Greek. The older man smiled and nodded, then climbed into the Jeep and drove back up the track.

As the vehicle disappeared through the trees, she stepped onto a hessian runner that had been placed on top of the sand. Her excitement increased as she headed through the line of olive trees to the cove. Seriously? He'd had a carpet put down to accommodate her heels?

The temperature had been in the high twenties Celsius all day even though it was early October and was still un-seasonably warm as the sun set. Warm enough that she had chosen to leave the villa without a wrap. But now she felt exposed in the beautiful dress, her emotions as naked as her flesh. Perhaps because she'd spent the past hour, as Amara did incredible things with her hair and make-up, going over and over in her head how Xander might react when she told him how she felt about him.

Maybe she shouldn't tell him yet, after all? Because what had felt validating and exciting earlier now felt like a bit too much. Was it still too soon to feel this way? Would he think she was asking for the same commitment from him? She didn't want to put too much pressure on him, and how would her revelation play out in the context of the much more prag-matic conversation they needed to have about where she was going to live and how she was going to support herself? Be-cause while she had to accept his help in some respects—and she'd come to terms with that—she didn't want him trying to take control of her future again. Or treating her indepen-dence like an inconvenience.

Anticipation flooded through her system, though, on a wave of emotion when she stepped past the last olive tree shielding the beach.

Xander stood by a table on a platform, built in the same

location as the sofa where they'd made love so furiously when they'd first arrived two weeks ago.

The lit torches beside the platform illuminated the shadows on his face cast by the setting sun when he swung round, as if he'd sensed her arrival.

He took her breath away. His tailored linen suit clung to the muscular physique she had come to know so well. A light breeze caught his hair, ruffling the dark waves as he strode towards her. The purpose in his stride triggered a wave of need as his gaze swept over her, landing on the mound of her pregnancy.

Her nipples had tightened into painful peaks to stand proud against the sheer fabric by the time he reached her.

The new tangle of nerves unravelled. This was Xander, the man she loved. Of course it wasn't too soon to tell him, how could it be, when she trusted him now?

Instead of dragging her into his arms for the fierce kiss she was anticipating, he cupped her cheek, his touch oddly restrained. She leaned into the caress and forced down her disappointment.

That he was treating her with reverence, with tenderness, was a good thing.

'You are so beautiful, Poppy Brown,' he murmured, before placing a gentle kiss on her forehead, then releasing her. Grasping her trembling fingers in his, he led her back across the sand, towards the table. 'Come, we must eat. We have much to discuss.'

Hope blossomed under her breastbone.

Was he finally ready to discuss their future, too? She had been right to wait. He was being restrained so they could get this done *before* they jumped each other.

It was all good.

As they stepped onto the platform, she noticed the table draped in a white cloth had been laid with fine china, silver cutlery and crystal glasses while all her favourite cold dishes were displayed on gold serving platters, which gleamed orange in the dying light.

His thoughtfulness made her heart swell. He'd made an effort to make their last night here extra special. And that had to mean something too. Didn't it?

Pulling out her chair, Xander waited for her to be seated, before taking the seat opposite her. He lifted a bottle of chilled champagne from the ice bucket by the table and poured some into the crystal flute in front of her before filling his own.

'I know that you are avoiding alcohol because of the baby,' he said as he lifted his glass. 'But a small toast to celebrate will not do any harm.'

'Yes, I'm sure one sip won't be a problem.' She raised her own glass. Hope and anticipation thundered against her ribs as she clinked her flute to his, then took a swallow of the dry, bubbly champagne.

'So what did you want to discuss?' she asked as casually as she could.

His sensual lips stretched into an indulgent smile. 'Us.'

The single word shot through her like gold dust, illuminating all the secret corners of her heart that she had kept in the shadows for so long.

'And our wedding, tomorrow morning,' he added.

The sparkle of desire in his eyes was so intoxicating, the planes and angles of his face bathed in silvery moonlight so breathtakingly hot, and the bubble of hope pressing against her ribs so huge, it took her a moment to register the words.

'Our *wh-what*?' she said as her flute dropped to the table, and the giddy excitement became sharp and discordant.

Had she heard that correctly?

He placed his own flute back on the pristine tablecloth and gave a heavy sigh, before reaching across the table to clasp her trembling fingers and squeeze.

'Do not look so shocked, Poppy. Surely you know this is the only solution for us, for our baby.'

Her whole hand started to tremble, so many conflicting emotions rushing through her—hope, excitement, panic, fear—she wasn't sure how to process any of them.

Of course, she wanted to be with him, so much. She loved him. And she wanted her baby to have a father who was present and involved in its life, the way her father had never been, and never wanted to be. And even in the short space of time they had been together here, she had seen so many facets to this man that she adored. Not just his ability to give her pleasure beyond her wildest dreams, but his playfulness, his purpose, his protectiveness, even that fierce possessiveness whenever he held her late at night, or talked about their baby. The truth was his focussed attention had always been intoxicating and validating.

But marriage? *Tomorrow morning*!

It felt like way too much, way too soon, when he hadn't even been willing to discuss where she would live up to now.

Plus, was it even a proposal? Because he hadn't exactly asked her, he'd told her, making the wedding sound like a fait accompli—the decision already made, without her input— the patient demand reminding her of the day her mother died, when her father had appeared and taken all her choices away from her.

'I didn't know you wanted to marry me,' she said.

Even saying it out loud felt scary. But why did it? He wanted to make a commitment, the ultimate commitment, to her and the baby. Shouldn't that make her feel good? Instead of terrified?

He nodded. 'Well, now you do.' He tugged her hand back, lifted her fingers to his lips, to buzz a kiss across her knuckles. The familiar shiver of sensation reached into her sex, pulsing, persuasive, but the instant, unstoppable arousal felt scary now too. Because it was stopping her from thinking clearly.

She tugged her fingers free and buried her hand in her lap. The warm breeze off the water did nothing to soften the knot of anxiety forming like a fist in her chest.

'But *why* do you want to marry me?' Would he tell her now, the words she needed to hear to make this less terrifying? Perhaps that was the real problem, not that he seemed so certain about marriage, but that it felt as if there were so many more steps they needed to take—together—before they could possibly make such a huge commitment.

He frowned, as if the question made no sense. Then let out a harsh laugh.

'Poppy, you are having my child. And you fascinate and excite me, beyond measure. Is this not enough?' he asked, but his tone was flat and devoid of emotion. As if her objections were a problem that needed to be managed, rather than the conversation about their future that she had been anticipating.

But what about love?

The thought echoed in her head, but she didn't want to sound too needy, because she already felt too exposed, so she settled for something a bit more pragmatic: 'No, that's not enough, not for a marriage,' she managed.

His brows rose, but then a muscle in his cheek tensed, reminding her of the man she had met almost three weeks ago, who had stormed into Serge's restaurant and demanded she leave with him.

'Perhaps the wedding gift I have for you will persuade you…' he said, before reaching into his jacket.

He pulled out an envelope and handed it to her across the table.

She opened the crisp ivory paper, embossed with some kind of official seal. Inside was a stack of legal documents—written in Greek. The final page had her name typed across the top—as Poppy Brown Caras—and his signature scrawled across the bottom. 'What is this?' she asked, feeling clueless now, as well as scared.

'It is a deed of ownership to this island. The land and all the property built on it. Parádeisos will become yours, as soon as we are wed. So, you may live here always, with our child.'

He wanted to give her this island? She dropped the papers on her empty plate, shocked, not just by the gesture, but also by the way it made her feel.

Terrified.

'But that's… It's too much, Xander,' she said, but her voice sounded as if it were coming from a million miles away—hollow and confused and unsure. 'I—I can't possibly accept it.'

The brittle smile became genuine, and all the more disturbing for it, the intensity in his expression making his blue eyes shine like diamonds in the torchlight. 'Yes, you can, Poppy. It would be your due as my wife. And the mother of my heir.'

'But, Xander. You can't just give me an island.'

'Of course I can…' Standing up, he stepped to her and clasped her hand to tug her out of her chair. He banded his arm around her waist, drawing her flush against him, until she could feel his erection, as insistent as the determination in his eyes. 'You need a home, somewhere safe, for you and our child and this was always more your island than mine.'

The fist continued to punch her chest. His gift was so generous, and so over the top, but also somehow so Xander. So why did it feel like a bribe?

She cradled his cheek, trying to soothe the muscle twitching in his cheek. Trying not to freak out, not to overreact, not to let her own insecurities misinterpret what was really going on here.

Maybe this extravagant gift and the marriage proposal were simply the only way he knew how to tell her he loved her.

He turned his face to kiss her palm, nipping into the flesh

under her thumb and making sensation sink into her sex, even as her nipples began to throb painfully.

'Do you remember, you told me once this was the last place you were truly happy as a child...?' he murmured against her hand. 'Let me make you happy again, here. Parádeisos is yours, Poppy. But you must take my name—that is the deal.'

Her heart swelled against her ribs. Even as her panic increased.

It *was* a bribe. A bribe she could never accept, because it would mean they could never be equals. But the fact that he had remembered the dream she'd told him about that day and wanted to give it to her felt significant. And moving.

She tried to concentrate on that, and not the fear.

She threaded her fingers into his hair, to pull him to her. 'I don't need the island, I don't want it, all I want is you, Xander,' she whispered against his lips. 'Make love to me,' she managed, suddenly desperate to show him how she really felt about him, even if she was too scared to say it out loud.

'Yes. Yes.' He growled, then captured her mouth at last in a mind-numbing kiss.

Sweeping everything on the table onto the sand, he grasped her bottom and lifted her until she sat on the edge. She ripped open his shirt, desperate to touch him and validate their lovemaking as he grappled with his flies to release the huge erection. He pressed her to lie back on her elbows, her knees raised. Then hooking her panties to one side, he plunged into the tight sheath, his hand clasping her hip as he thrust deep.

She writhed, impaled, the thick intrusion forcing her to take the full measure of him. The climax rose up like a tsunami, sudden and frantic and shattering, sweeping through her like wildfire, scorching everything in its path—and burning away the doubts, the panic, in the bright, incandescent beauty of their physical bond.

He panted against her neck, the afterglow already like a

drug as he rocked into her one last time and shouted out his own release.

She clung to him, letting him hold her, his breathing as ragged as hers, as their bodies shuddered through the final waves of the titanic climax.

She raked her fingers through his hair, feeling his hot breath on her swollen breasts.

'I love you, Xander. So much,' she said, needing him to know, ashamed of her cowardice.

The words seemed to float on the salty air and the funky smell of sex like a promise, a validation, until he stiffened. He raised his head, the huge erection still firm, still *there* inside her. But his expression looked haunted in the moonlight.

'We will be wed tomorrow, then, Poppy. And the island will be yours.'

The afterglow faded, leaving her feeling shocked and strangely numb.

Hadn't he heard what she'd said? Why did she suddenly feel as if her feelings didn't really matter to him at all? Just her obedience?

She'd told him she loved him and, for a moment, he'd looked stricken.

He pulled out of her, then stepped away from her to rearrange his clothing.

He helped her off the table, held her when she wobbled, her knees becoming shaky as all her old insecurities crawled back.

Why wasn't he looking at her? Why did the wreckage of the table setting—and all the delicious food, which had been swept onto the sand—feel as destructive now as the soreness in her sex, the feel of his seed on her thighs?

'We will have to return to the villa to eat,' he said, his voice gruff.

'Okay,' she said, not hungry at all, because the fist was punching her chest now in double time.

As they returned to the villa in the Jeep he'd taken to the beach he spoke of the arrangements for the wedding tomorrow. She listened in a daze, the damning evidence of how he'd manipulated her echoing in her head with every word.

How long had he been planning this? Why hadn't he included her in any of the arrangements? Was this why he'd avoided talking to her about their future plans—because he'd always intended to ambush her with marriage?

When they arrived at the villa, he helped her out of the Jeep. But when he went to press his lips to hers, she shifted away from his kiss, suddenly brutally aware of how easily she'd let herself be used.

'I will have supper served in our room and we can discuss the wedding,' he offered.

She jolted. The persuasive statement was edged with demand.

'I—I'm not that hungry. And I'm really tired.' That much at least was true because she'd never felt more exhausted and heartsore in her life. She needed time and space to process all these emotions. To make sense of what he'd done, before she told him she couldn't go through with the wedding. 'Would it be okay if I went to bed in my own room?'

He frowned, clearly not happy with the suggestion. But then he cupped her chin and lifted her gaze to his. 'Is everything okay, Poppy?'

Nothing was okay, she realised, but even so the tiny bubble of hope refused to die. Forcing her to ask the question that mattered most of all.

'After our marriage, where would you live, Xander?'

Maybe she'd got it all wrong. Maybe this didn't have to be as bad as she thought. Maybe he wasn't trying to control her, or take her choices away from her. Maybe he just wanted to make a much bigger commitment than she'd anticipated. And she was the one freaking out, because she'd never been able to handle too much change, all at once.

'My business is in Athens, Poppy,' he said, the hint of frustration like a bolt to her heart. 'And I must travel a lot. For this reason, I cannot live with you and the child here. But I would visit often.' He cupped her bottom to drag her against him. 'And when and if our chemistry ever dies, this will always be your home because it will belong to you.'

The hope she'd nurtured for two whole weeks burst like a popped party balloon inside her.

He wasn't giving her Parádeisos because he loved her. He was giving her this island to get her to agree to this marriage, which he was using to control her. And rob her of the autonomy she'd worked so hard to earn.

He kissed her lips, his tongue pressing seductively against hers. She opened her mouth instinctively, unable to resist the desire even now. But when he released her, she rushed to her room.

She showered off the scent of their lovemaking, then packed her rucksack with shaking fingers.

If she'd had the courage, she would have stayed until the morning, she would have told him how she really felt about his proposal and argued the point with him. But she felt too much like that broken child again, who had wanted her father to look at her as something other than a burden... And she couldn't do it.

She'd told Xander she loved him, and he hadn't even responded. The stricken look on his face kept coming back to her as she crept down to the dock in the moonlight.

The boat he'd taught her how to drive stood on the quay. She untied the line, and climbed on board, breathing a panicked sigh of relief when she found the key in the ignition.

She turned to glance up at the room where he slept, her

heart shattering as she stroked the place where their baby was sleeping.

Eventually she would have to contact him, once their child was born.

As she turned the key, punched the ignition, and let the boat drift at half speed out to sea, her heart felt fragile and exhausted.

She loved Xander. She would probably always love him. But she couldn't stay, when she was convinced now he would never love her in return.

CHAPTER TWELVE

Two weeks later

POPPY LISTENED TO the rain pounding on the cottage's slate roof, while dragging a bucket across the kitchen floor—which she'd spent yesterday scrubbing clean—to catch the drips leaking through the ceiling. The miserable weather outside was a perfect accompaniment to her miserable mood. All the panic and doubts she'd pushed to one side—while fleeing Xander and Parádeisos, while travelling back on the never-ending coach journey from hell to the UK, reopening her mum's old cottage, and finding a job at the local supermarket—started to crowd in on her again.

On her first day off a week ago, she'd written him a long letter, to explain everything—why she couldn't marry him, why a relationship between them would never work—and told him she would get in touch again once the baby was born to discuss visitation rights. She had no clue how exactly that was going to work, but she'd just have to cross that bridge when she came to it. Because she was still trying to cross the biggest bridge of all first—how on earth she was going to recover from the devastating loss of what she'd thought they were building together.

She returned to the living room. The old furniture she purchased—worn, mostly second-hand, but comfortable—reminded her of her mum. She pressed a hand to her chest, but knew the ache there was nothing to do with that old grinding grief that she'd spent the last eight years trying to escape. Funny to think she'd been too scared to come back here, to live here again. Only to have that loss feel comfortable now. Because it was nothing compared to the wrenching pain of losing Xander.

She let the sadness seep into her bones as she chucked another log on the open fire, but the leaping flames couldn't warm her chilled skin—the way he had every time he'd put his arms around her.

She swore softly, hating the regret almost as much as the miserable grinding grief.

For goodness' sake, Pops, get over yourself. You didn't lose Xander. You lost the dream of him, of what you could be together, which was always your dream, not his.

She rubbed her pregnant belly, aware of the swooping pressure of the baby's movement.

You've still got your baby. His baby. Who you can lavish with the love he didn't want.

She jumped, the loud banging on the front door cutting through the thundering rainstorm and her maudlin thoughts.

It was close to eight o'clock on a Saturday night. Who on earth could that be?

The cottage was at the end of a cul-de-sac, near the river. Concern cut through her misery. What if it was the local council's officer, come to tell her they were about to be flooded?

She crossed the narrow living room, still holding her belly, and opened the door.

Shock came first, swiftly followed by the devastating wave of love and longing. But before she could process her conflicting, contradictory emotions, the irate man standing on her doorstep, his expensive coat soaked through, his wet face set in grim lines of fury, shoved open the door and marched into her living room.

* * *

'You coward!'

Xander Caras was so incandescent with rage, he could hardly breathe. But what disturbed him more was the realisation that the fury that he had been stoking for two whole weeks—ever since he'd woken up on Parádeisos to find Poppy gone and while he'd searched like a lunatic to find her—began to fragment into something much more devastating as soon as he stalked into the dilapidated cottage.

That she'd rather live here, in some cold, stormy part of England, in a place that was so small and squalid, instead of on Parádeisos felt like the final insult.

This place's proportions reminded him of the cramped, unkempt apartment in Athens where he and Theo had spent some of their childhood. The inclement weather outside was not unlike the first January after his father had left, when they had huddled together at night because they could not afford heating. And under the light perfume of flowers and herbs and charred wood in this room, he could detect the smell of damp earth, which was too close to the stench of rotting garbage, which had permeated that apartment whenever it rained.

He could smell the poverty here that he had worked to escape, and which she had chosen over him.

'Xander, what are you doing here?' she asked, her face flushed, her eyes wide with shock, even as she held her belly over the thick sweater she wore. As if she were protecting their baby, from him!

The rage rose into his throat, thankfully covering the well of hurt. And the desperate longing for her he had *never* been able to control. Not for the five months after he'd lost her the first time... And certainly not now.

How could she have this hold over him? Still? When she had treated him with such contempt? Such callousness?

She hadn't even given him a return address, in that insane letter she'd sent him, full of platitudes and sentimental nonsense. Did she really believe that would excuse her behaviour? Or make her treatment of him, of their baby, any less appalling?

'You had no right to run away from me.' His voice rose to a shout as the emotions he had tried so hard to keep under lock and key exploded in a fury of fear, of loss. 'You had no right to leave me. I wanted you. I needed you…'

His voice broke on the words, the bottomless pit in his stomach twisting into a great gaping chasm of rage and pain. He gripped the back of the sofa, aware that his knees were shaking. The humiliation of that, though, was no worse than the emotional overload of seeing her again. And the battle he was waging to separate the man he was now from the boy he had been then. The boy whose own father hadn't wanted him.

'Xander, sit down, you look tired…' Her words came from far away, through the fog of memory and the scalding pain of all the tears he had never shed for that boy.

But then she placed her hand on his cheek and his head rose to see the regret in her eyes. And the compassion.

Tears ran down her cheeks, and instead of the indifference he had expected, she looked as devastated as he felt.

'I'm sorry. I'm so sorry,' she said, her voice breaking too as she held both his cheeks now, stroking, soothing, her palms shaking. 'I was so scared, and you're right—I was a coward.'

He nodded, his own eyes stinging, as everything inside him gathered and spun. The emotions were so raw, so vibrant. And so painful. But also somehow safer, now he had found her again.

He lifted his hands from the sofa to wrap his arms around her, to hold her.

'Don't ever leave me again. I can't bear it…' he managed.

He sank his face into her hair, to gather her warmth into

his heart, and inhale her intoxicating scent—flowers and sultry musk—to banish the smell of his nightmares.

Gradually as they stood there together, in the cluttered room, his thundering heart began to slow for the first time in two weeks. Until the heat from the fire seeped through his wet coat, and wrapped around his chest, to sink into her heart. And he could drag himself back from the precipice he had been standing on the edge of ever since she'd left him.

He caressed her shoulders, her back, feeling the bumps of her spine, the curve of her bottom. Imagining her under him. Arousal flared, as it always did, but when he groaned, and pulled her closer, she shifted, and flattened her palms against his chest.

'No, Xander,' she said, her voice trembling with emotion, but firm. 'We have to talk first. I can't come back to you, not like this…'

His mind screamed as he jerked back.

'What?' he demanded, the raw fear returning. 'Why not? If I forgive you? We can rearrange the wedding.'

She'd left him, but why did that matter now, when he had found her again, and she'd apologised? She loved him, she'd said so herself. He didn't know why she'd run, but right now he didn't care. All he wanted was to have her back.

'I can't marry you, Xander,' she said, the determination in her eyes only terrifying him more.

Why the hell not?

It was what he wanted to say, but he bit down on the retort.

'Okay. I will not insist on marriage again. Until you're ready,' he forced himself to say. Ready to concede that much, even though having her take his name felt like the only way to give him the peace of mind he sought. But perhaps he shouldn't have pressed for marriage so soon. He realised that, now he could think clearly again. Trying to railroad her into a commitment she wasn't ready for had been a mistake.

He slid his hand under the sweater and the T-shirt beneath, to caress her stomach, addicted to the feel of her skin, his thumb drifting over her protruding belly button.

He felt the delicious shudder that always signalled her arousal, but when he kissed the pulse point in her neck, and grazed his hands around her waist to sink his fingers under her loose sweatpants and cup her bottom, she resisted him again. And pushed him back more firmly this time.

'Stop, Xander. I can't…we can't…' She squirmed and wriggled until she could wrench herself out of his arms.

'Why can't we? When I've missed you so much. And I can smell you've missed me too,' he demanded, the familiar spice of her arousal filling his lungs and making the erection throb in his pants.

But instead of falling into his arms, of begging for release as he'd hoped, so they could take the pain away, together, she took another step back and folded her arms over her chest.

'I shouldn't have run away that night. You're right, it was cowardly and selfish,' she said, her voice shaking. 'And if it's any consolation, I've been miserable since, but I was scared… *You* scared me.'

'*How?*' He blinked, the pain and sadness in her voice like pouring the icy rain outside over his rampant body.

'The marriage proposal? The gift you tried to give me? How long were you planning all of that?' she asked, the accusation in her eyes his undoing. 'While at the same time refusing to talk about what *I* wanted? What *I* needed from our relationship?'

He cursed, in Greek, turning to thrust his hand through his hair and stare into the flames leaping in the fireplace, but which could do nothing to warm his chilled skin.

He didn't want to talk about this. Didn't want her to know how scared he'd been when she'd mentioned returning to England to find a job.

'I told you I loved you, Xander. And you had nothing to say. Even though you wanted to marry me. That doesn't make any sense.' He flinched, hearing the sadness in her voice, the disappointment. But also the strength.

A strength he wasn't sure he'd ever had, despite all the things he'd had to endure to survive.

As much as he wanted to sink inside her and make her come and come and come and come again, until he could persuade himself the last two weeks had never happened, a part of him knew she was right.

Because in his darkest moments over the last two weeks, when he hadn't been sure if he would ever be able to find her—because there were about a thousand Poppy Browns in the UK and she appeared to be the only one under twenty-five without a digital footprint—all he'd felt was despair.

'I need a moment,' he rasped, his throat raw, his fear so huge now he could hardly breathe. Because he knew he had been a coward too. And now he was going to have to find the courage to admit it.

CHAPTER THIRTEEN

Five minutes later

'HERE, I HOPE it's strong enough for you,' Poppy said as she handed Xander the cup of black coffee, and then went to sit on the armchair opposite him.

She folded her legs under her and blew on the mint tea she'd made for herself.

She tried to concentrate on the balloon of hope under her breastbone as she watched Xander take a gulp of the coffee—which had to taste like tar, but that was the way he preferred it. He set the mug on the occasional table by his sofa, his hands shaking.

He'd taken off the drenched coat, the figure-hugging black cashmere polo neck he wore beneath making her brutally aware of his impressive chest.

She'd been impossibly grateful for the chance to dash into the kitchen and make them beverages that she was far too worked up to actually drink. Because she'd needed time to process all the emotions threatening to choke her.

As soon as he'd appeared in her doorway, she'd known she had made a colossal mistake two weeks ago. She shouldn't have run. She should have stood her ground, and demanded answers from him. Because it seemed so obvious to her now that, while she'd been panicking about whether or not he would ever love her, she had somehow missed the obvious: that Xander had massive abandonment issues.

Was that why he'd found it so difficult to tell her how he felt about her? Why he'd demanded marriage, while at the same time wanting to keep her on Parádeisos, and visit her at his convenience? Because he was scared of committing to a real relationship that would leave him vulnerable too? But how could she know or understand his motivations if he wouldn't talk to her?

They'd both been in the wrong. She shouldn't have run, but he shouldn't have shut her out the way he had. And if she let him get away with not talking about it again—they'd be right back where they started.

But as he sat opposite her, she could see the fear he'd struggled so hard to hide, and she knew it was not going to be easy for him.

Then her gaze caught the photo of her and her mum together on Parádeisos that summer, which she'd found in an old shoebox upstairs and placed on the mantel.

And she could hear her mum's voice, still loving, still supportive the last time she'd been fully conscious:

'I hate to leave you, Pops. I wish I didn't have to. But always remember to fight for your dreams.'

She blinked, the tears filling her eyes. She didn't know when it had happened, when loving Xander and having their baby had become her dream. But when his head lifted, and his gaze met hers and she saw the lost look in his eyes, she knew what she had to do now was stop running, and fight for him, too.

'Was it because he left you, Xander? Were you scared I would do it too? That's why you didn't want to give me a choice?'

He looked away, his cheeks heating. But she'd seen the shame on his face, before he could mask it. And her heart broke for him, even as it seemed to swell against her ribs, the bubble of hope expanding to impossible proportions.

She wanted to go to him, wanted to tell him it would all be okay, because she loved him. But she remained rooted to her seat, knowing she had to wait for his answer. Knowing she deserved it.

The fire crackled, the rain beat down, cocooning them in the small cottage. She could hear his harsh breathing, see the tense muscle in his jaw flexing, and sensed the battle he was waging to admit the fear that had haunted him for so long.

But finally, he turned towards her. And gave her a stiff nod. 'How did you know?' he asked.

'Because I know what it's like to be vulnerable, to be alone, Xander. To be terrified that you're somehow unlovable.' Except she'd always had her mum, even after she was gone.

'You cannot love me, Poppy,' he said, staring at the hands he had clasped above his knees.

The weariness in his voice shocked her, almost as much as the ashen colour of his skin in the flickering firelight.

'What? Why?' She leaned forward.

'Because I am not a man anyone could love.'

'Why would you think that?' she asked.

He shrugged, the movement stiff and unyielding—and so defensive her heart hurt.

'We were forced to beg, to steal, to scavenge for scraps, to lie and keep on lying, simply to survive.' He shook his head, staring at his whitening knuckles. 'I made a promise to myself then, I would never be that vulnerable again.' His gaze rose to hers, the bleak acceptance in his eyes devastating. 'That is why I wanted this marriage. To trap you. To keep you. I didn't want to give you a choice, because I was terrified that, eventually, you wouldn't choose me, any more than he did.'

He looked so broken in that moment, she went with instinct and rose from her chair to go to him.

Kneeling on the sofa, on either side of his thighs, she sank into his lap. Resting her round belly against his much flatter one, she cradled his cheeks and pressed her forehead to his. 'I hope you realise,' she whispered against his lips, 'that's complete crap.'

A raw chuckle broke from his throat as he lifted his hands to stroke her spine, then dragged her the rest of the way into his embrace. He held her so tightly, wrapping his arms around her body, his heart beating against hers.

'I don't know if I can ever love you back, Poppy,' he said, the sad acceptance in his voice nothing like the arrogant, demanding man she had come to know. 'Something died inside me when I was a child. I killed it because I had to, and I don't know if I can ever get it back. Even for you.'

Yes, he could. She knew he could. He had been through hell and back to support his brother. He had been invested in this baby, determined to protect it the minute he'd known about its existence. He'd treated her with care, even when they'd been driving each other nuts. And he'd shown her he needed her, that he wanted her, already in so many ways. Not least by trying to give her an island. And if that hadn't convinced her, his desperate search to find her, the agony on his face when he had, were more than enough to persuade her that she mattered to him already. A lot.

But they had time, so much time, to figure all this out. And she didn't want to hurt him any more than she already had, by demanding more than he was ready to give.

'I don't need that, Xander. Not yet.' After all, they were just words. 'I just need you to be honest with me. To tell me how you feel. And to give me choices, so I can have an equal stake in our future.'

'I can do that.' He nodded. 'But you must promise not to run from me again. I couldn't bear it.'

She smiled, the sunlight bursting inside her a direct counterpoint to the cold and damp outside. 'I promise.' She took his hand and pressed his palm to her belly. 'Me and junior both.'

He rubbed the bump, his eyes flaring with an emotion so raw it took her breath away.

His hands rose up her spine to ease her back into his arms and he captured her happy sigh with his lips. The kiss was hard and deep, the way they both liked it, going from thankful to carnal in a heartbeat, but just as he slipped his hands under her sweater to pull her even closer, she felt the flutter of movement. And he stilled.

'What is *that*?' he asked.

'You felt it, too?' She grinned, the joy exploding through her nerve endings alongside the arousal. 'It's your daughter... Or maybe your son, saying hello.'

He laughed, wonder shining in his eyes as he pushed up her sweater and T-shirt to gaze at her bare belly. 'Hello, junior,' he murmured.

Just as she thought her heart would burst, watching him talk to his child for the first time, he kissed her bump, then proceed to drag off her sweater and T-shirt.

'Now go back to sleep,' he said, still caressing her belly, before he unclipped her bra. 'I have important business with your mother,' he added, his face fierce with longing.

And the hunger she loved.

EPILOGUE

A week before Christmas

'YOU HAVE A beautiful baby girl, Mr Caras.' The nurse beamed at Xander as she handed him the precious bundle, the mewling cries coming from it full of indignation.

His arms trembled as he held the tiny, squirming baby. The woman left the room, leaving him alone with his family at last. His daughter's red face screwed up into a ball of anger as she yelled out her frustration at having been thrust into the world a week ahead of schedule. Her dark hair was plastered to her head and her tiny little fingers were clenched into fists so small they were barely the size of his thumb.

He had never seen anything more incredible in his entire life.

Tears stung the backs of his eyes, and the rush of love was so intense it felt as if someone had reached inside his chest and ripped out his heart.

She was his now…just like her mother.

'What do you think, Daddy?'

His head rose, speech deserting him as he gazed at the woman he loved more than life itself. Her sweaty hair clung to her cheeks, her tired eyes were sheened with emotion and exhaustion, the new nightgown the nurse had helped her into drooped where the monitor was still stuck to her chest.

She'd never looked more beautiful to him.

He swallowed past the lump in his throat, trying to find the words to tell her how he felt. They had made a promise to each other in that cold damp cottage in Kent, that they would always try to be honest about their feelings. A promise he had not been sure at the time he would ever be able to keep. But, astonishingly, she had made it easy for him to discuss his emotions over the days and weeks that followed, while they settled into their future together. Because there was no judgment, no demand, only acceptance and love.

They still argued, quite frequently, because neither of them had a lot of experience with the fine art of compromise, but they had managed to make a life for themselves. In Athens and Kent—where he had bought a house close to her mother's cottage—and also here on Parádeisos, where they had settled for the last month to await the baby's birth.

Of course, they still had to fully discuss the issue of Poppy's future employment. But luckily, he'd had a reprieve on that decision after she'd finally agreed to marry him and had been busy dealing with the challenges of preparing for the baby's arrival and hosting their wedding on Parádeisos.

But right now, with his child in his arms for the first time, he was lost for words again.

Poppy had been so brave, so strong, so dogged and determined, while he had been scared to death, watching her labour through eight hours of agony to bring their daughter into the world. It humbled him. He had always considered himself tough. How wrong could he be?

'She is perfect…' he managed at last, his voice as rough as the emotions threatening to overwhelm him.

How did other men stand it? Watching the woman they loved go through such pain?

He stared down at his daughter, who had stopped squirming and crying after having discovered one of her fists and thrusting it into her mouth. 'But so tiny...' he added, the awe choking him again.

'Easy for you to say.' Poppy laughed, the musical sound he adored helping to calm his own rampaging heartbeat. Just a little.

His daughter began to cry again, having dislodged her fist.

Pushing up in the bed, Poppy lifted tired arms. 'Here, I should try to feed her again. The obstetrician said she would be hungry and it'll probably take several attempts.'

He watched as his wife bared her breast, and tamped down on the familiar spike of arousal. It wasn't hard to control it, when he recalled the dark hours before dawn, as he had stroked Poppy's forehead and she had panted through the waves of agony.

He shifted his daughter, holding the baby's head the way the nurse had shown him, then placed her gently in his wife's arms.

Pinching the plump nipple, Poppy pressed it against the baby's open mouth. The mewling cries stopped instantly, as his daughter's head swung round and her lips clamped the rouged flesh.

'Ouch!' Poppy flinched as the baby latched on, sucking ferociously. No wonder—his daughter was tugging on her mother's nipple as if she were starving to death.

'Does it hurt?' he asked, concerned.

She shook her head. 'Not compared to everything else.'

He wasn't particularly reassured by that assessment, but then Poppy's head rose and she smiled at him over the baby.

'Isn't she amazing? I think she's cracked it already,' she said, the pleasure in her voice helping him to relax.

'Of course...' He beamed back at her, the pride in his chest almost as overwhelming as the love. 'She is a Caras.'

Poppy chuckled again, stroking her daughter's cheek. 'She's also a Brown.'

'True,' he said, smiling with her. She never let him get away with anything, but he had learned to love that too. How had he ever survived without her there to make him realise he could not control everything? The good news was, he didn't feel the need to any more.

Leaning forward, he placed a kiss on his daughter's tiny head, breathing in the scent of soap and milk, then transferred his lips to his wife. The kiss was tender and achingly sweet, a celebration of their daughter's birth, but he was forced to wrench his mouth away before the heat in his groin rebelled again.

There would be no reigniting their sex life until Poppy was fully recovered from the birth, and he had recovered from the trauma of watching it… Which would no doubt take several decades.

Poppy smiled, aware of her husband's flushed skin and the flare of passion in his eyes, which was almost as compelling as the deep well of love.

'Do not tempt me, Poppy. It isn't fair,' he said, the quelling tone delighting her even more.

The last thing on her mind right now was sex. She was sore and exhausted, and her nipple hurt where her daughter seemed to be attempting to swallow it whole. But that dark intense expression on his face would always be its own reward.

'Frankly I think you deserve to suffer a little, Caras,' she shot back. 'After what you've just put me through.'

He laughed, as she'd known he would, his gaze warm with approval. 'Touché.'

He settled onto the bed beside her, and placed his arm gently around her shoulder, to draw her and the baby against his side. 'We must decide on her first name now, too,' he said.

'I know.' It was the one thing they hadn't been able to agree on, despite their endless discussions—which some people might refer to as arguments—on the topic.

'I vote for Ariana…' she said. 'Or Penelope.'

He nodded, but then pressed his lips to her hair and murmured, 'What was your mother's name, Poppy?'

She glanced round at him, surprised by the question. The one thing they had agreed on was that their baby's name would be Greek, because Xander seemed much more attached to his heritage than she was.

'Gemma,' she said. 'Why?'

'I like this name very much,' he said.

'Really?' she asked, tears forming in her eyes. It hadn't even occurred to her to give the baby her mum's name, but it suddenly seemed so perfect now he'd suggested it.

'Of course,' he said, gently wiping away the tear on her cheek with his thumb. 'Our daughter should be named after a strong woman, like her mother.'

She nodded. 'I agree,' she said, the happy tears sliding down her cheeks now.

He kissed her again, just as his phone vibrated in his pocket.

'Take it,' she said, sniffing back the emotion in her throat. 'It might be your brother.' And she needed a few minutes to get a grip and stop crying happy tears all over her daughter.

Xander nodded and got off the bed to take the call. He had been trying to contact Theo for half an hour, eager to tell him he had just become an uncle.

But when he stared at the screen, his brow furrowed.

'What is it?' she asked. She knew that frown, it was his confused and concerned look.

'It is a private message from Prince Andreas,' he said, his voice tense.

'The Galician monarch?' she asked, confused too now. 'Why would he be messaging you?'

Theo had taken control of the cruise business, and the negotiations for the land in Galicos, months ago. And she knew Xander hadn't spoken to the Prince since he'd called off his engagement with the man's daughter way back in September.

Xander's gaze rose to hers, his blue eyes blank with shock. 'He seems to believe my brother has just kidnapped his daughter!'

* * * * *

If you couldn't put The Heir Affair *down,*
then be sure to look out for
the second instalment in Heidi's
Claimed by a Greek duo,
coming soon!

And why not try these other stories
by Heidi Rice?

Revenge in Paradise
After-Party Consequences
Queen's Winter Wedding Charade
Princess for the Headlines
Billionaire's Wedlocked Wife

Available now!

PREGNANT BEHIND THE VEIL

EMMY GRAYSON

MILLS & BOON

For Mom and John, always.

For my son and daughter. I love watching you grow.

For my brother and his endless encouragement.

For my dad and his editing skills.

For Dr. Farmer, for teaching me so much.

CHAPTER ONE

Alessandra

MY HAND TIGHTENS over the small swell of my belly as butterflies flutter inside.

Not butterflies. A baby. *My* baby.

I smile as I gently tap my fingers against my skin, wondering if he can feel it yet. I'm nineteen weeks along, although I've only known for two. But in those fourteen days, my entire world has shifted, my focus narrowing to the tiny being growing inside me.

My eyes flicker to the millions of lights sparkling just beyond my window. Like a field of stars against the backdrop of New York City's skyline. The last traces of clouds from an early-evening thunderstorm are drifting away, leaving traces of violet and orange in the night sky.

I've had this view for over a year now, ever since I earned my specialist certification in estate planning. It came with a salary increase, my corner office and even more work. I love it. I love the variety in my work, seeing the impact I have and making a difference with one of the most prestigious estate law firms in the world.

My gaze drifts away from the window, passes over the boxes scattered around my office, the half-empty shelves, the blank spaces on the walls. Fingers reach into my chest, grab my heart and squeeze. In that moment of pain, I feel every second of the last thirteen years: days jam-packed with classes, endless nights of clerking and study-ing, receiving the call that I had gotten my dream job.

All gone because of a foolish one-night stand.

My fingers tighten on my stomach. Before that day in the doctor's office two weeks ago, I would have given everything to go back in time and turn away as Michail walked across the bar. Or, better yet, toss my drink in his face.

But once the doctor spoke the words "You're going to be a mother," the regrets disappeared, replaced by a fierce, inherent love for my unborn son. I'd never ad-mitted to myself how much I wanted to be a mother, not when my longest relationship had barely passed the six-month mark. Nearly two years ago, I realize with some surprise.

So no more regrets. No more wishes for what might have been. Yes, my future includes a career change in-stead of keeping my corner office and becoming a partner at Kingston. But it will be an adventure, one that comes with an incredible gift. Tonight is the last step before I'm finally free to move on to my new life.

Now I just have to tell my one-time lover he'll be a father in before the year's out.

Cold tendrils sneak in and steal the warmth from my chest. My smile evaporates as his name whispers through my mind.

Sullivan.

Except it's not Sullivan. No, it's Michail. Michail Sul-livan. Self-made billionaire, internally renowned home and private security expert and recently discovered ille-gitimate son of the late Lucifer Drakos.

The same Lucifer Drakos who, until his death nearly three months ago, had been my wealthiest and most hated client.

The cold sinks deeper. I stand and rub my hands up and down my arms as I pace from my desk to the window. I didn't know anything about Michail when we locked eyes in a cliffside bar in Greece five months ago. I only saw the rock-hewn jaw, the full lips curved into a half smile, the desire that flickered in his eyes. Even when he told me whatever we shared would begin and end in one night, it hadn't tempered my desire. The illicit nature of a brief affair made me want him even more.

One night. One night of fiery passion, of pleasure unlike anything I'd ever experienced. And, unexpectedly, moments of tenderness, secrets whispered in the dark as the moon colored the room silver. Moments that had opened the door to a different desire when I'd awoken to the morning sun making his tan skin glow. The desire to know this man, to spend more time. To imagine something beyond one night.

I turn away from the window. There had been zero tenderness when he'd walked into my office ten weeks ago. Hope had flared for one bright, beautiful moment when I'd looked up and seen Sullivan staring at me from the doorway. When I thought he'd come for me.

And then reality hadn't just intruded. No, it had kicked the door in, blasting it to smithereens as I saw Sullivan's eyes by the light of day for the first time.

Pale, pale blue. Eyes just like Lucifer's.

I'd slept with a client's son.

Nausea climbs up my throat. I stop and breathe in deeply, then out. I've never once violated the oath I took when I became a lawyer. Violating my ethics in such a spectacular manner, even unknowingly, makes me sick to my stomach.

Michail hadn't bothered to disguise his disgust as he glared at me throughout the will reading. A meeting that had left him and his two half-brothers in shock when I'd revealed that Lucifer had made it a requirement for Michail and his younger brother, Gavriil, to marry within a year and make it to their first anniversary. Michail's older brother, Rafael, was newly married but still had to reach the first-anniversary mark.

I'd counseled Lucifer to take out the clause. Then, for the first time in my career, I'd argued with a client. But still he'd refused, leaving me to deliver his manipulative stipulations.

Gavriil had been mad but determined. Rafe had been his usual reserved self. But Michail...

It had been like watching a volcano about to erupt. His eyes had blazed, furious flames of blue, his hands curled into fists. He'd told us he would join Lucifer in hell before ever marrying or accepting a single dime. He'd stalked to the door, turned and fixed that burning gaze on me.

"And if anyone tries to persuade me otherwise, they won't like the consequences."

Tame compared to the accusations he'd flung at me four weeks later at Gavriil's wedding reception. Wild theories like working with Lucifer to blackmail him into marriage, of seeking Michail out for myself.

Of being just like the other women who had set out to conquer him and his fortune.

I hate that his last allegation stabbed so deep. Not only did he consider our night together to be just like all his other affairs, but he labeled me an opportunist. A gold digger. A liar. How could I have been so damn stupid as to think he saw me, really saw me, in those moments we spent together? All he saw was a willing body and the chance for quick, no-strings-attached sex.

I was the idiot who saw him as someone I could fall for.

The shrill ring of my office phone cuts through my musings. I glance at the screen, recognize the number. Our front desk, manned by our night security guard, Donnie, when everyone else goes home.

I let it ring once, twice. Then I punch the talk button. "Hi, Donnie."

"Evening, Miss Wright. Your visitor is on his way up from the lobby."

A thickness fills my throat. "Thanks."

Donnie clucks his tongue. "I hope you don't work as hard at your next job. You should go out with friends, maybe a date."

"Are you offering, Donnie?"

His booming laughter gives me a much-needed boost.

"If I was thirty years younger and unmarried, Miss Wright, I'd…" His voice fades. I hear him murmur something, then come back on the line. "Your client is here." Another pause, then he drops his voice. "Need me to come sit in your office with you? Man looks like he just chewed rocks."

"He probably did." The knock on my door makes me flinch. "I'm okay, Donnie. I promise."

"I'm checking on you in ten minutes."

"Hopefully he'll be gone in five."

I hang up, smooth my hands over the silky material of my skirt as I suck in a deep breath and walk to the door. Each step echoes in my bones as dread wars with memories of a hard body pressing me into bougainvillea blooms cascading over a stone wall and kissing me like I was his last breath.

God, I need this to be over.

Another knock sounds, sharper and louder, as I reach for the door handle. Irritation gives me something to grab onto other than illicit memories and misplaced hopes.

I straighten my shoulders, lift my chin and open the door.

Too close. He's far too close, his massive frame filling up the doorway as he towers above me. Hands tucked into the pockets of his black pants and a navy dress shirt molded to his chest. Sleeves rolled up to his elbows and the top button undone as if he couldn't be bothered with it. Wealth and power and confidence wrapped into one extremely tall, muscled body. Heat radiates off his skin. A rich yet woodsy scent drifts toward me, teasing me as it tries to pull me back into the past. Not just our night together, but the shock I'd barely managed to conceal when he'd walked into my office over two months ago and I'd realized that Michail Drakos and Sullivan were one and the same.

Reluctantly, I tilt my head back to look up into a glowering, handsome face. His square jaw is visibly tense beneath his dark beard. Full lips that curved into a sexy smirk the first time I saw him are now flat. And his eyes…pale blue, like his father's, his brothers. I didn't make the connection in the dim lighting of the bar, the darkness of Santorini's winding streets, the moonlit villa where I let down my guard to a stranger who, for one night, made me feel like I wasn't alone in this world.

But now, as suspicion and anger glimmer in the depths, I know I'm a fool. For so many things. As soon as he'd walked into my office and I'd seen him next to Rafe and Gavriil, the family resemblance had been obvious.

"I see patience is still not a virtue of yours, Mr. Sullivan."

His eyes narrow. "Thought you might have changed your mind and left. As usual."

My spine stiffens. I don't owe him an explanation for why I left his bed at dawn. Not when he had made it abundantly clear the night before that our affair would go no further than one night. No questions, no commitments, just sex.

And as for the last time we saw each other at his brother Gavriil's wedding, I left because the man had been a coldhearted, vicious bastard. I deserved far better than cruel accusations and ridiculous conspiracies.

I step back and gesture for him to walk in. His gaze darts back and forth, as if he's waiting to see if I came up with a trap in the three minutes since I agreed to let him up to my office.

"I'm not going to murder you."

His glance flicks to me, his eyes hard and suspicious.

"Tempting though it may be," I add with a sweet smile.

His gaze narrows, as if he's trying to figure out if I'm serious or teasing. I'm not quite sure myself. When he finally walks past me, that damn aroma of earth and spice trails behind him. I steel myself as I close the door and move to my desk. He glances at the boxes.

"Moving to a new office?"

"In a manner of speaking." My heart twists in my chest. Leaving feels like yet another failure. But it's the right thing to do. "I've accepted a position with Regent Capital Planning."

One eyebrow raises up, surprised yet judgmental. "Financial advising? You're leaving Kingston?"

I gesture to the chair across from my desk as I sit, but Michail shakes his head. Instead, he stands with legs slightly spread, shoulders tense, his body coiled tight. A predator ready to lunge—a cheery thought as I prepare to throw his world into chaos.

"I was fortunate that the firm allowed me to continue on with your father's estate after I reported our liaison—"

"You what?"

I frown at his sharp tone. "I reported our liaison to the firm's partners and agreed to meet with our internal ethics committee." A meeting that was decidedly uncomfortable for all involved. Nothing like sharing your sex life with your bosses and a committee made up of your coworkers. "Once you'd confirmed via email that you had renounced your share of the inheritance and wanted no further contact with Kingston or me, I was allowed to continue working under the guidance of an oversight committee."

He blinks. "I'm surprised you told them."

I resist the urge to touch my stomach and forcibly lay my hands on the armrests of my chair instead. "It was the right thing to do."

His derisive snort punches through my defenses.

"The right thing," he repeats.

My fingers tighten on the leather of my chair. What had I hoped for? That six weeks apart since our horrid encounter at the wedding might change his mind? Erase the viciousness of his words?

"Contrary to the charges you leveled against me, I prioritize ethics and integrity above all."

"Integrity," he repeats, dragging out the word in a long,

slow drawl. "You and I must have different definitions of the word, Miss Wright."

By some miracle, I force myself not to hurl any of the remaining objects on my desk at his smug face.

"Given the fantasies you spun about our affair in Greece, yes, we probably do."

A thundercloud of anger darkens his face. "Suspicions. Justifiable ones."

"Hmm." I tap one finger against my lips. His eyes follow the gesture, his jaw hardening as his gaze locks onto my mouth. Traitorous heat pools in my belly, thankfully countered by the feminine satisfaction that curls through my veins and gives me a boost of confidence. The man might hate me, but he still thinks about that night, too.

Good. He deserves a little suffering.

"I think my favorite theory was that I followed you to Santorini, strategically placing myself in locations you *might* frequent in the off chance you saw me, approached me and fell madly in lust with me." My smile is sharp enough to cut glass. "Or the one where I was conspiring with your father to seduce you into marriage and bend you to his will."

He doesn't say anything. Just stands and broods and stares. It's too much to hope he realizes how foolish it all sounds.

I shake my head. "Perhaps for your next career you could be a writer. Your active imagination and dramatic bent would serve you well."

"Were you and Lucifer lovers?"

Okay, I might actually throw up.

"I underestimated just how low of an opinion you had of me." I hold up my hand when he starts to speak, to justify his latest idiocy. "Lucifer was well over twice my age, mean as a viper and unfortunately my client. All but one of our meetings were conducted by video conference or phone due to his declining health. The one time I saw him in person was the day after I met you." I stand, fury vibrating through me. "I would never sleep with a client."

"Just their heirs?"

Blood drains from my face. I'd thought I was cold before, but it's nothing compared to the ice coursing through my veins.

Except this is good, I tell myself as I breathe out, steady myself. This is just further confirmation that he isn't, and never will be, the kind of man capable of being a good father.

I raise my chin. Time to end this. Telling him is the right thing. But so is keeping him far away from my baby.

"I asked you to meet me so I could tell you I'm pregnant. You're the only possibility."

The slight widening of his eyes, the flare of his nostrils, is vindicating, a pleasure that goes straight down into my bones.

"I don't really care if you believe me or not." I sit and fold my hands together on top of the desk. "I'm only telling you because it was the *ethical* thing to do. I'm comfortable raising this child alone. I don't want anything further from you." I nod toward the door. "Thank you for coming, Mr. Sullivan. You can see yourself out."

CHAPTER TWO

Michail

THE FAINT SHRIEK of a siren travels up from the streets. Cool air shushes out of the vents. Somewhere a clock is ticking. My heart pounds against my ribs so hard it hurts.

I stare at her. She stares right back: calm, cool, collected. As if she hasn't just dropped a bombshell that changes the entire course of my life.

Alessandra Wright. Stunningly beautiful, almost untouchable with elegant cheekbones and a well-defined jaw that serve as physical manifestations of her confidence, offset by large green eyes and full lips.

The beauty is the same. But the woman I knew as Lexi for one fleeting night let her auburn hair hang loose and wavy. Alessandra has it bound up in a bun at the base of her neck. Lexi smiled the kind of smile that made her eyes sparkle. When Alessandra smiles, it's a cold gesture, as if she's ticking a box rather than expressing true emotion.

I have no idea who this woman is. The woman supposedly carrying my child.

Pieces of the puzzle start to fall into place. Ever since I walked into Alessandra's office and realized the woman

I'd slept with months ago was also Lucifer's estate lawyer, I'd been trying to figure out what her end game was.

Now I know. The day I met her was the same day I met Lucifer Drakos for the first and last time. My birth father. The man who told me how proud he was of my success, as if he'd had any hand in it, before adding that I could be even wealthier by marrying within a year of his passing. The mask of suave, confident billionaire had slipped, revealing a weak cockroach of a man who threw a temper tantrum when I'd told him I'd rather go to hell than do anything he wanted me to.

It had been deeply satisfying to tell him no. But I hadn't anticipated him having a backup plan already waiting.

Alessandra.

My gaze shifts from her face down to her stomach. The desk impedes my view. If she's faking it, her hoax will be short-lived. A couple of calls will ensure she's disbarred before the clock strikes midnight. If it's someone else's child she's trying to pass off as mine to get at my inheritance, I'll sue her for attempted fraud.

Except as I stare at her, searching for any hint of deceit, doubt pierces my resolve. If she's not lying, if Alessandra is truly pregnant with my son or daughter, there's no way in hell I'm going anywhere.

Is she trying to emotionally manipulate me? Dangle the supposed baby just out of reach and rile me up so I'll be more likely to agree to whatever her demands are? Whatever she's doing, I won't sacrifice an innocent child or leave them fatherless to satisfy my own vendetta against my birth father.

"I want a paternity test."

She shrugs. *Shrugs*, as if we're talking about the damn weather. "If you wish. Though it hardly matters."

I swallow my fury before I let it take control of my tongue. "Hardly matters?"

The frigid ice in my tone has made more than one Fortune 500 CEO pale. Miss Alessandra Wright merely cocks an eyebrow.

"I'm not asking for child support." Her eyes rake up and down my body, but not in the hungry way she devoured me with her smoldering emerald gaze before ripping my shirt off in Greece. Now her assessment is clinical, disinterested. "You don't strike me as the fatherly type, so visitation won't be an issue."

None of what she's saying makes sense. My jaw tightens. I don't like not having answers. Not being able to rid myself of the craving I've been carrying for Alessandra since she disappeared from my bed is making me even crankier than usual. Even now, despite the suspicion and anger on the surface, a different heat floods my veins. Full breasts press against her blouse. The curve of her bare neck captures my gaze. I imagine pulling the pins out of her hair and letting that fall of auburn cascade over her shoulders before I fill my hands with it.

Blood rushes to my cock. Desire and anger clash, heat my body to dangerous degrees. I haven't been this close to losing control since our night together.

One breath in. Then a slow, measured release. I wait until my pulse returns to a semblance of normal. I'll have to deal with this pesky attraction. But later. The immediate problem is determining if she's lying. If she's not, I have bigger problems to deal with.

Starting with wrapping my head around becoming a dad. Being a father may not have been a part of my life's plan. But if Alessandra is pregnant, if the baby is mine, I will be there for it the way mine never was.

"*If* you're pregnant, and *if* the child is mine, I'm not going anywhere."

Her eyes widen as she leans forward, the movement sudden and slightly frantic.

"What?"

"If the child is mine, I'm not letting you raise it alone."

The color drains from her face. Fear glints in the depths of her eyes before she shuts it off like she pushed a button.

I mentally curse. I'm good at reading people. A skill I honed as a police officer and fine-tuned as I turned Sullivan Security into an international success. Something's off. Not once during our night together did I get a hint of any sort of manipulation. The setup, too, is odd. She never contacted me, not once, between our night together and when I walked into her office. If getting pregnant had been her goal, or seducing me into marriage, why leave before I even woke up and not reach out again?

I glance toward her office door. When I walked through that door the first time and saw her, the first thing I felt was a bone-deep relief.

There you are.

I've never lost my head over a woman. I enjoy them but keep them at a distance. But when I woke up after my night with Lexi to an empty bed, disappointment had settled in the pit of my stomach, a weight that shouldn't have existed but persisted for weeks every time I thought of her.

A weight that had alleviated for a heartbeat when I'd seen her standing behind that desk, auburn hair tied back into a bun, her tall form clad in a navy suit with a skirt that clung to her hips and followed the lines of her long legs past her knees. A weight that had crashed down even harder once I'd registered the blank expression on her sculpted face, her professional greeting. To make the connection that the woman I'd been lusting after for the past few months was connected to Lucifer.

Funny how quickly lust and desire can turn to disgust, to wrath. I know how easily people can disappoint you. Yet I let my guard down for the first time in decades because I saw a sad, beautiful woman in a bar.

A woman who now looks anything but sad as she glares daggers at me.

"Let me make myself clear, Mr. Sullivan. This is my child." Alessandra's voice lashes out, a whip fashioned of ice. One hand moves to her stomach, an unconscious gesture that speaks volumes. My chest tightens. "Not yours, not ours, *mine*. I don't need you and I certainly don't want you involved."

A knock cuts through the tension. My head snaps to the side. Alessandra turns toward the door. In that moment, I see the small curve pressing against the fabric of her dress.

Possessiveness grips my chest, a vise that tightens with every step she takes toward the door. The same possessiveness that reared its head when I witnessed my half-brother Gavriil flirt with Alessandra during the will reading. Then, I was able to dismiss it, harnessing my shock and fury to push away any of my former feelings.

But now, as my world narrows to her and that tiny swell, I want to go to her, tuck her away somewhere private before demanding answers.

My fingers curl into fists as she opens the door.

"Hi, Donnie."

I blink at the sudden change in her tone. Warm, welcoming. Her voice catapults me back to Santorini when our eyes first met, when she gave me a smile that made me want to possess her as much as it made me want to worship her. When she said "Hi" in that husky voice that slid over me like hot silk, as if she'd been waiting for me all night.

"Just checking on you, Miss Wright."

Donnie's gaze darts to me. I stare back at him. The man had it out for me as soon as I stepped out of the elevator, greeting me with narrowed eyes and a flat voice as he directed me back to Alessandra's office.

"We're okay. Mr. Sullivan and I are just wrapping up. I'll let you know when we leave."

The smile in her voice stirs up a nasty swirl of jealousy. Ridiculous that I'm feeling anything over a minor kindness she's showing a coworker old enough to be her father.

But it's there. It's there and damn it, I have to manage it.

Alessandra closes the door behind him. When she turns back to me, her face is once again set in that cool mask.

"Your coworkers seem to like you."

Her mouth thins as she blinks once, twice. The mask slips just a fraction.

"They're good people."

"Yet you're leaving." I glance at the numerous boxes scattered around her office. "Because of the baby?"

A long moment passes, then she nods once. Unwanted guilt pricks between my shoulder blades.

"Kingston was never my forever plan. I hadn't anticipated leaving so soon." She looks around her office. "But I'll handle it."

"And you want nothing from me?"

The investigation I ordered on her the minute I walked out of her office three months ago revealed no unusual financial history, no outstanding debts. In fact, Alessandra lived leanly given the salary she earned. A one-bedroom apartment in Queens's Astoria neighborhood. A frequent traveler on New York's subways. She can afford to support this child on her own.

But I've met several women who could pay their own bills and still chose to come after my money. I don't know what Lucifer promised Alessandra in exchange for trapping me: money, a better position, something else she desired.

She blinks. Her full lips part. I shove away the brief flash of disappointment and steel myself for her demands.

"I don't want you around my child. I don't want to ever see you again."

I stare at her, waiting for the punchline. But it doesn't come. No, instead her words stab into me. The conviction in her voice, the certainty that she would be perfectly content to banish me from her life and our child's, is a hit I never saw coming.

"Our last two encounters haven't been cordial," I finally say, "but for good reason."

A harsh laugh escapes her lips. The brittleness of it crawls over my skin.

"Cordial? No, cruel. Petty. Hurtful."

She spits the words out like machine gun fire.

"I had a right—"

"To be suspicious. To ask questions. To request a meeting with me, even with my bosses. Not to accuse me of being a conniving seductress or your father's lackey."

Her voice darkens on the word *father*. My eyes narrow

as an uncomfortable suspicion forms. One I never suspected because I had been too fixated on my own anger.

"Did he force you into this? Hurt you?"

She blinks, surprised by the change in conversation. "Why would you care?"

I run a frustrated hand through my hair. "I'm not a monster, Alessandra. Yes, I'm angry. But that doesn't mean I want harm to come to you."

Her shoulders slowly drop down. "No," she says softly. "He didn't hurt me. He didn't pressure me. Into *anything*," she adds with such ferocity I almost believe her. "But as a client, he wasn't kind."

Perhaps the nicest way I've heard him described as the bastard he is. The man emotionally and mentally abused my mother for the first ten years of my life. On his death, instead of righting the wrongs he did to her, he tied the one thing he left her in his will to my fulfilling his wish of getting married.

"Why work for him?"

"Because he requested me. It was the biggest account I'd ever been assigned to, and I wasn't going to turn down an opportunity like that. And while he wasn't the kindest of men in the beginning, I didn't get to see his true face until the morning after I met you."

My fingers curl into fists. "What did he do?"

"It doesn't matter."

I stalk forward and plant my hands on her desk. "Tell me, Alessandra."

"Attorney-client privilege," she fires back. "And even if I did tell you, you wouldn't believe me."

"Try me."

She stands slowly, defiance and confidence written in the determined set of her chin and the thin line of her lips.

"I owe you nothing, Mr. Sullivan. Now, I'm tired. It's late."

I want to argue. I want to demand that we stay as late as we need to and sort this mess out. Starting with why she was in Santorini and how she came to be in that cliffside bar.

But my current tactics aren't working. I switch my approach. "How are you getting home?"

"The same way I always do."

I ran plenty of calls in New York's metro system during my first years on patrol as a police officer. There's no way in hell I'm letting the pregnant mother of my child hop a subway train this late at night.

"I'll drive you."

"No. Thank you."

She grabs her purse off the desk then winces slightly, her hand drifting to her temple. Alarmed, I start to circle around to her.

"What's wrong?"

"Nothing." She steps back. "Just tired."

I follow her out of her office and down the hall. The earthy red tones in her dark brown hair catch the light. My eyes drift down to the sway of her hips, the curve of her backside beneath her dress. Blood pumps through my veins as desire stirs.

Five months. Five months of waking up with my body hard and the memory of throaty moans echoing in my ears. Even after learning who Alessandra was and realizing that she had most likely been in Santorini on Lucifer's orders hadn't dimmed my lust.

We walk into the lobby of Kingston Estate Law: white walls, gray wood floors glinting beneath the lights of a domed ceiling. Donnie sits off to the side at a curved desk in front of a bank of monitors. He glares at me before his eyes dart to Alessandra.

"I'm headed out, Donnie."

"Don't know if you saw on the metro app, Miss Wright, but your subway line is down."

Alessandra stops so quickly I nearly run into her.

"What?" Her voice pitches up.

"Mechanical issue."

"I see."

Her tight tone has me biting back a smile.

"I'll splurge on a taxi."

My eyes narrow on her back.

"Good idea," Donnie says with an encouraging nod to her and another scowl in my direction. "You have a good night now."

I follow her into the elevator, ignoring her pointed movement to the farthest side of the car. Donnie's staring daggers at me. I waggle my fingers at him as the doors close.

Alessandra sighs. "You do like to needle people."

"I perfected it in elementary school."

Neither one of us speaks for the next ten floors. It doesn't bother me. During my time in NYPD's Special Crimes Division, I spent countless nights on stakeouts, in interrogations waiting for a criminal to crack under the weight of silence.

What does bother me, however, is her scent. I'd forgotten it. But now, enclosed in this tight space, the faint traces of her perfume are stirring memories I've been trying to suppress and setting my blood on fire. Jasmine, rich and sweet, reminds me of how her fingers tangled in my hair as I slid into her wet heat. Rose, gentle and floral, reminds me of how she woke me with a kiss when the moon was full in the sky before moving down my body and taking me in her mouth. And that faint whisper of amber reminds me of holding her in my arms, tracing my fingers up and down the curve of her back, as we both shared small pieces of the pains that had driven us to Santorini.

Focus. My brain listens to the order, but other parts of my anatomy are slower to respond.

"My car's right outside. We can talk on the way back to your house."

"Pointless since there's nothing to talk about."

I face her, wait until she's looking at me so she can see my determination, feel the weight of my intention.

"That's where you're wrong. I meant what I said before. If it's mine, I will be involved. If you try to keep my child from me, I'll take you to court. I will win."

She holds my gaze even as her pulse pounds at the base of her neck. I don't want her to be afraid. But if that's what it takes to get her to accept that I'm not going anywhere, so be it.

"I won't have my son or daughter growing up thinking their father didn't want them."

She's so still it's as if she's turned to stone. Then, at last, she exhales.

"It's a boy."

Reality shifts, morphs into something more. Something far more important than my existence.

A boy. My son.

Her hand drifts down to her stomach again, pressing her skirt against her body. The possessiveness that reared its head in her office now coils my muscles into tight springs. I tell myself to slow down, to wait for the results of the paternity tests.

"A boy," I echo.

"Yes." The elevator slows. A moment later, the doors slide open. Her other hand curls into a fist at her side as she raises her chin. "And I don't want him to be hurt."

Anger edges out some of the joy and adds heat to my next words. "Why do you automatically assume I'm going to hurt him?"

Pain darkens her eyes. "Because all you've done is hurt me."

Stunned, I stand where I am, rooted to the spot as she walks out of the elevator. Guilt burrows deeper into my skin as I watch her, shoulders thrown back, her movements confident and her pace steady. But I also see other signs: the clenched fist at her side, the rigid set of her shoulders, the slight tilt of her head as if she's resisting the urge to glance back.

I'm not the kind of man to question, to hesitate. But for a second, I wonder if I need to walk away. If Alessandra does relent, am I capable of being the man a child would need me to be? Will I hurt the baby as she claims I've hurt her?

I'm capable of inflicting such pain. I've done it before.

The elevator doors start to close. I slam my arm against the metal to stop their progress and step out. Even if I'm not capable in this moment, I will do anything to become the father a child deserves. My past actions were selfish but, unlike Lucifer's, unintentional. I've spent years locking away my emotions to ensure I never harm anyone again. And if I've hurt Alessandra, I'll make it up to her. Show her I'm the man she and the baby can depend on.

But there are questions that need to be answered first, tangled threads to unweave about the past five months.

There is no way in hell I'm letting Alessandra slip through my fingers until I know the truth about everything, starting with the paternity of the child she's carrying.

CHAPTER THREE

Alessandra

AM I A coward for walking away from Michail and not giving him a chance to reply? Probably. But I'm also five months pregnant by a man who hates me, on the last day at a job I loved but had to give up, and I'm alone.

I'm allowed a few cowardly moments.

My flats slap against the floor and echo in the massive space of the tower lobby. I prefer heels, enjoy the confidence boost that comes with every click on the marble tile. But between my swollen feet and utter exhaustion, I've had to make a change.

So many changes, I think wearily as I near the glass doors leading out onto Broad Street. Discovering Michail wants to be involved in my son's life just might take the prize for most unexpected. I'll have to confront that sooner rather than later. I can't risk going to court. I'm very comfortable financially, but I don't have a bottomless bank account to fund the kind of lawyers I'd need to even come close to competing with Michail.

Disappointment has me slowing just before the door. The rare times I pictured having a child, I imagined doing so with a partner. Maybe not one I was head over heels in love with, but someone I cared about, someone I was happy with. I'd known better than to expect happily-ever-after with Michail. He'd told me flat-out that we'd have one night and one night only. So when the doctor had told me I was pregnant, I'd been content with the alternative of being a single parent, of getting to raise my son the way I saw fit. The thought of having Michail involved, of the arguments and fights we're sure to have while his distrust keeps a wall between us, drags me down until I barely have the strength to push open the door.

But I do. I step out onto the sidewalk. The recent rain left a freshness in the air that eases some of the tension from my muscles. Upbeat jazz plays from a colorfully decorated food truck parked halfway down the block.

I breathe in. A normal New York night. I need to remember little things like this, especially when the world feels like it's spinning too fast.

Except…it is spinning. The music blurs in my head as the ground tilts beneath my feet. I try to blink away the dizziness, but it's too fast; everything's too fast and I'm falling. I wrap my arms around my stomach and turn so that I'll at least land on my side, maybe my back. Keep my son safe.

"Alessandra!"

I hear the voice from far away as the ground rushes up to meet me. I scrunch my eyes shut so I can't see. Brace for the impact.

But instead of landing on hard pavement, strong arms wrap around me, hold me close.

"Hang on. I'm calling an ambulance."

His words rumble through me, pierce the tornado whirling around me. I curl into the heat, the strength, my body turning traitor even as my mind tries to regain control.

My tongue is thick, my mouth dry. I manage to force my lips apart.

"I told you to go away."

And then I slip into the dark. Not completely. I'm still dizzy, nauseous. There's a rapid thumping next to my ear, one that sounds too fast yet offers some comfort. I murmur that I'm too heavy, that he needs to put me down. Maybe he hears; maybe he doesn't. Then a distant hum that sounds like someone's talking, but I'm underwater and can't understand what's being said. The shrill shriek of a siren briefly penetrates. I try to open my eyes, but it's so much easier to just rest.

Jostling. The warmth disappears, replaced by something firm at my back and bindings across my chest and legs. Then voices pierce the darkness. One is brisk, efficient, but unfamiliar. The other…the other moves through me, a heavy blanket that soothes the dizziness still whirling at the edges of my mind.

"…far along is she?"

My eyes shoot open. Bright light temporarily blinds me. I blink as I try to push myself into a sitting position. Straps press against my skin. My heart pitches into my throat.

"Ma'am!"

Firm hands grab my shoulders and ease me back down.

"What…?" I try to turn my head and nearly throw up.

"You fainted, ma'am." The efficient voice is closer. A hazy face appears above me, a man with round spectacles that glint in the light. "You're in the back of an ambulance on the way to the hospital. I'm going to keep the straps on while we're en route, okay? Just a safety precaution."

"Where is—"

"Your fiancé is here, ma'am."

Hysterical laughter bubbles in my throat. Is this a dream? Or am I caught in some alternate reality?

Michail's face swims into view, blurry at the edges but no less handsome. God, why is he still so attractive even when I feel like I just got hit by a truck?

"I'm here, Alessandra."

A strong hand wraps around mine. This time the thickness in my throat isn't hysteria or nausea. No, it's emotion. Temptation to lean into the comfort he's offering.

My mother's voice whispers in my ear.

Don't give a man your heart, Alessandra. All he'll do is break it.

My fingers stiffen in his grasp.

He leans down. His lips brush my cheek in a tender gesture that has me closing my eyes against a hot sting of tears. I hate him for whatever game he's playing. I hate myself even more for wanting the fantasy, especially when I feel so weak.

"I had to let them know you were pregnant." His voice is quiet, but I have no problem hearing him with his mouth right next to my ear. "I told them I was the father and that we're engaged so I could ride with you to the hospital."

I keep my eyes scrunched tight so I don't do something foolish like try to take a swing at him. Not when I can barely look around the moving ambulance without feeling sick. But, I resolve as I slowly open my eyes, I will get him back for this.

Later. He's not the one I care about in this moment. My arms are lead weights at my side.

"My baby," I croak out. "Is he okay?"

A young woman moves into my line of sight. Her kind

smile flashes against her dark brown skin as she pulls gloves on.

"Miss Wright, my name is Jodi and I'm a paramedic. I'd like to check your baby's heartbeat."

"Yes." My attempt at a nod is swiftly met with regret as a stronger headache begins to pound in my forehead.

"Lay still," Michail orders.

I mentally tally all the ways I'm going to exact my revenge as the medic lays a sheet over my lap before discreetly pulling up my skirt. Jodi spreads a small amount of cool gel on my lower stomach. The rest of the sounds fade away: the crackling radio static, the other medic's voice as he converses with Michail, the honking horns and screeching brakes of New York traffic passing by.

Jodi presses the device against my stomach. I hold my breath...

And there he is. That beautiful thumping, like a wild horse galloping across a prairie.

My breath rushes out as I sag in relief. We're not out of the woods yet. But for now, this is enough.

A tight pressure on my hand makes me look to the side. I'd forgotten Michail was holding my hand. His pale eyes are fixated on the doppler. Wide with shock and, I realize with a painful clenching in my chest, wonder. Like he's actually excited to hear the baby's heartbeat.

I know in that moment I have no choice. I'll set boundaries, expectations. He makes one wrong move and I will kick him out of our lives faster than he can draw breath.

But I can't deny Michail the opportunity to know his child.

And if he is a good father, which is the best possible scenario for my son, Michail will be a part of my life whether I want him in it or not.

* * *

Michail

The line on Alessandra's heart monitor moves up and down in a reassuring pattern I've been observing for hours. The line on the screen next to it moves in the same pattern at twice the speed. A pace the nurse assured me was normal for the baby.

My fingers tighten on the paper in my hand. There's no doubt now. Alessandra is carrying my son.

I glance at the clock on the wall. Nearly seven in the morning. It's been eleven hours since we arrived at the hospital. Alessandra didn't mention anything more about my decision to tell the paramedic I was the father, although I could tell she was less than happy about it.

My jaw tightens. Tough. There was no way I was letting her ride to the hospital alone.

My gaze shifts to her asleep in the hospital bed. There's color in her face now. When I caught her just before she hit the sidewalk, her skin was so pale, her breathing too shallow. Every time I've tried to sleep, I barely close my eyes before adrenaline rockets through me as I remember seeing Alessandra fall, over and over again. I was halfway across the lobby when I saw her start to sway. I've never run so fast in my life. I burst through the doors in time to see her twist so that she was falling with her back to the concrete.

That possessiveness that first reared its head in her office at the sight of her slightly rounded belly turns primal, a deep and potent emotion that fills me every time I look at her. She turned her body to protect the baby. Sick and losing control, her last thought before she passed out was to keep our son safe.

I still don't know her. But I know she'll be a good mother.

She stirs in the bed, murmuring softly. One stray tendril of mahogany hair falls from the looser bun she pulled it into just before she fell asleep around midnight. Even in a hospital bed wearing a shapeless gown hooked up to several machines, she's beautiful. Peaceful.

My lips quirk. She wasn't peaceful when she was wheeled into the elevator and realized we weren't being taken to the emergency room but up to the hospital's exclusive eleventh floor. A luxury room complete with a living room, views of Central Park and a dedicated concierge. I have no doubt she would have argued, perhaps even attempted to get off the cot and walk down to the emergency room, if she hadn't still been nauseous.

I don't care if she sees it as overkill or not. The entire unit is locked down, with strict protocols for who comes in and out. Privacy is important to both of us. Until we figure out how we're going to move forward with co-parenting our son and the story we'll tell the public, we need discretion.

My eyes move back to the fetal monitor. Watch the line bounce up, slide down, then up again. A substantial donation to the hospital's foundation at ten o'clock last night fast-tracked all of Alessandra's tests. Everything was normal. Under the doctor's gentle prodding and my sterner follow-up questions, Alessandra had admitted to being nervous about our meeting and having nothing more than a smoothie for breakfast. A fact that had me biting back words that would have only deepened the divide between us.

I don't want there to be something wrong. But what if they missed something? What if this happens again?

I don't like the uncertainty, the possibility of something else lurking in the background. The uncertainty is harder to control.

The paper crinkles as I unfold it and read the results for the dozenth time: "99.99% probability Michail W. Sullivan is the biological father."

When the doctor had rattled off the tests they would be performing, I asked for them to include a paternity test. To his credit, the doctor didn't even bat an eye at my request. I wanted to be able to trust her. But the fact that I wanted to believe her was a problem in itself. Emotions are volatile creatures. The last time I let myself hope, truly hope, was also the day a man I'd never met ripped my seven-year-old heart apart.

The paper in my hand, however, is concrete proof. Whatever happened in Santorini, whatever Alessandra did or didn't do, doesn't change the fact that she's pregnant with my son. I'm not going to let him grow up without me in his life. There will never be a day where he questions where I am, if I care, if he did something to drive me out of his life.

My grip tightens on the paper, creating creases in the print. The man who fathered me taunted me for years with the promise of his presence, only to never show. Learning he had kept my mother on a financial tether during my early childhood, offering meager handouts as long as she sent photos like I was some damn trophy, deepened my hatred for a man who only seemed to be happy when he was hurting others.

I couldn't hate my mother, though. She worked herself to the bone trying to claw us out of poverty. She loved me and let me know it every day, even on the days she struggled to keep herself together.

Even when I broke her.

My throat tightens. I don't like that she accepted Lucifer's handouts. But I can't say I wouldn't have made the same one if I'd been forced to choose between having a roof over my child's head or the streets. And given that I hurt her nearly as badly as he did, I have no room to judge. That she loved me through it all is more than I deserved.

I think back to the will. The one I finally pulled out and reread a month ago, only to discover Lucifer's last attempt to break me: a bequest for my mother. Specifically, paintings. Paintings she had completed that summer when she was an eighteen-year-old art student with stars in her eyes and fell for a much older man who accept her work as he seduced her for his own pleasure. Even after he'd abandoned her, he'd held her works in an iron grip for over thirty years. Taking the art she gifted him and hoarding it simply because he could.

I resist rubbing at my temples as a headache creeps in. My mother will never get them back if I don't get married within a year of Lucifer's passing. She gave up the life she could have had to be my mother. Forewent her parents' promise to welcome her back into the wealthy lifestyle she grew up in if she put me up for adoption and pretended like I never existed.

My mother chose to raise me in a one-room apartment in the Bronx's Hunts Point neighborhood instead.

I don't want to get married. I saw what falling in love did to my mother. Saw plenty of examples in our rundown apartment building of men and women trapped in dead-end relationships by the people they cared about. Even if I wanted to risk it, I'm not capable of opening my heart up to a woman. It took me years to master my emotions, to choose control over anger, sadness, heart-ache. I'm not good husband material.

But how can I not get married? How can I deny my mother the chance to finally have her paintings back? To do something so monumentally important for the woman who never gave up on me even when I'd given up on myself?

A rustling sound makes me look up. Alessandra stirs. Her eyes flutter, her gaze landing on me. Her full lips curve into a soft smile. Blood pulses through my veins as my body tightens. I remember the last time she looked at me like that, except it was moonlight that caressed her face, not the glow of a sunrise.

Then she blinks. Her gaze sharpens as her mouth thins into a straight line. I feel her shut me out like she just slammed a door in my face.

She sits up as her head snaps around toward the monitors.

"He's okay."

My voice rises above the various beeps and ticks of the machines. But her shoulders bunch up until she sees the steady pulse for herself. Slowly, she sinks back into the pillows. Her eyes shift to the window. The room overlooks Central Park, the flourishing greenery a stark contrast to the skyscrapers and buildings that ring the perimeter.

"Any more updates?"

Her voice is huskier than it was last night, her tone firm but with a trace of worry beneath the bravado.

I debate for all of two seconds if I should wait for the doctor. No. Alessandra and I need to be able to have hard conversations, just the two of us. She's not going to like what the doctor has recommended after she's discharged. But to me, it's not a recommendation. It's common sense that will keep her and the baby safe.

"All the tests have come back normal. He wants to keep you for another twenty-four hours for observation."

She's still, almost unnaturally so, as she watches me. Then, at last, she nods. "What are you not telling me?"

Admiration flickers through me. Smart woman. It's easy to picture her as a lawyer, someone who observes and evaluates. I still want answers. And I need to broach the subject of the will and the bequest for my mother. Once she's feeling better, she will be a valuable resource.

"The doctor recommended you have someone stay with you for at least a week."

The obvious solution hangs in the air between us. I know it. Judging by the instant hardening of her face, she knows it, too. She lives alone and, as of three months ago, wasn't dating anyone. Aside from the occasional happy hour with her coworkers at Kingston, she rarely socializes. All details included in the lengthy investigative report one of my employees conducted following Lucifer's will reading three months ago.

"If the doctor recommends it, I'll make it work."

I cock my head to one side. "You're staying with me."

"No."

"Yes."

"I'll stay with someone else."

Jealousy flares in my chest. Did she start to date someone before she found out she was pregnant? I loathe my reaction as much as I do this faceless, nameless person she would prefer to stay with.

"Who did you have in mind?"

She folds her hands primly in her lap. "None of your concern."

I hold up the paternity results. "This paper says otherwise. It's not just about you, Alessandra. It's making sure the baby is healthy, too."

The sudden sadness in her eyes throws me for a loop. She shakes her head.

"So that's it, then. Now that you know I'm not lying, at least about you being the father," she adds with a snarky glance in my direction, "you think you suddenly have a say in my life."

"I want you both to be safe." She blinks as if that surprises her. And, I acknowledge with reluctance, it's understandable given how our interactions have gone the last two months. "My penthouse is secure. I'll be there most of the time, but all rooms are wired with state-of-the-art cameras and alarms that can alert first responders if I'm not and you have an episode like you did last night. You don't have someone that can offer you that kind of reliability and stability as you heal."

She looks down at her hands. Her fingers are threaded together so tightly her knuckles are white.

"No," she finally whispers, her voice hoarse with grief. "I don't have someone like that in my life. Not anymore."

I force myself to stay seated even as my mind goes back to that night. We lay side by side, harsh breaths mingling as we recovered from our second bout of mind-blowing sex. She had been lying on her stomach, her back bare. Need guided my hand to her body, my fingers drifting over her heated skin with a light tenderness I'd never felt for anyone. Every time I touched the rises and falls of her body, the curve of her spine, the swell of her hips, it felt like leaving traces of me embedded in her skin.

I'd looked up at her then, seen the glint of tears in her eyes. I'd moved to her, pulled her close in the dead of night, cradled her as she'd cried. Her tears had flown hot against my neck as she'd leaned into me and taken every bit of comfort I'd offered. Even as she'd grieved, I'd been floored by her acceptance, her trust.

As her tears had dried, she'd told me about her mother. The woman who had raised her alone, fighting against odds to give her a shot at a successful life. For the first time in my life, I had shared, too. Felt seen by someone who had lived an almost identical experience to mine.

We'd gotten out of bed after that, donning robes to sip champagne on the terrace as our conversation shifted to more mundane topics like our favorite places to travel. But those revelations had forged a connection. One I had felt as I'd knelt before her on the balcony, undoing the belt of her robe and spreading her legs before I'd feasted on her in the moonlight. Then, with the taste of her on my tongue and her body warm and pliant in my arms, I'd carried her back into my room and made love to her again.

I remember the sex, yes. But I remember that moment, too, when something more than simple lust bonded us. Remember her grief as I see it etched on her face now, her loss juxtaposed by the steady beep-beep of the heart monitor. New life growing even as she mourns someone who won't be around to see it.

It's hard not to go to her in this moment, to offer comfort as she grieves her mother. My mom is one of the few people I still trust in this world. Alessandra has no one.

"I'll hire someone."

Alessandra's pronouncement wipes away the sentimental bullshit and reminds me that whatever we had that night is gone.

"You would rather waste money on a stranger than let the father of your child help?"

"Look at us, Sullivan," she snaps back. "Three out

of four times we've ever seen each other have been a disaster. How are we going to survive an entire week? And how can you give up—" her voice trails off and she waves one hand in my direction "—whatever it is you do with your security company to just monitor me on the off-chance I keel over?"

"To answer your first question, given that we're going to be connected for a lifetime, we better be able to figure out a week." The color drains from her face. "And as to the second, I own the company. I can delegate any work I need to. This is more important."

Silence stretches between us. The machines continue to beep relentlessly in the background. At last, Alessandra speaks, so softly it takes a moment to register.

"All right."

There's no sense of victory. No rush of success. Just a hollowness as the mother of my child looks as if she's lost something very important.

She eases back down onto the pillows. "I'd like some time to myself."

I want to lay a comforting hand over hers or offer a shoulder for her to lean on, the desire to touch her so strong it's almost a compulsion.

So I step back, skirt around the bed and head for the door. She needs space. So do I. Given how strongly I'm reacting to her, time apart to evaluate everything that's happened is in both our best interests. My reactions to her are understandable given the nature of her revelation and the massive upheaval to my life. But I need to get my guard back up, solidify my walls before she comes to stay with me for a week.

I open the door and walk out without a backward glance.

CHAPTER FOUR

Alessandra

I THOUGHT MY view of New York from my corner office was unparalleled. But as I sit on the terrace of Michail's penthouse ninety-one floors above Fifth Avenue, I'm forced to admit it doesn't hold a candle to this.

The entire city is spread out beneath me. As night rolls across the sky, lanterns flick on in Central Park beneath me, dots of gold glimmering behind leafy trees. The lake is a wandering, dark shape toward the north end of the park, a natural oasis amid steel and stone. Skyscrapers, towers and the thousands of other buildings that make up Manhattan glitter with millions of lights.

It's beautiful. Stunning. The kind of view most people will never see in a lifetime. But instead of relaxing and enjoying myself, I'm tense, waiting for Michail to make an appearance. We've seen each other a few times today. But almost all our interactions have been less than five minutes and consisted of Michail asking if I was okay, if I was eating, and then disappearing upstairs to his office.

Leaving me torn between relief and irritation.

A chilly breeze stirs my hair and makes me shiver. The doctor finally cleared me to leave this morning. A nurse wheeled me out a private entrance where Michail was waiting with his car, a sleek Rolls-Royce with tiny lights embedded in the ceiling and black leather seats that felt like I was sinking into a cloud. He thankfully turned on the radio for our thirty-minute drive to my apartment in Queens. He insisted on walking me up. I countered with ordering him to stay in the hallway. When I go back, I need that space to still be mine. To not carry any memories associated with Michail.

I packed a few essentials, then dosed for the ride back to Manhattan. I woke up when Michail pulled into the private parking garage beneath Central Park Tower. The three-minute ride from beneath New York to one of the tallest floors in the world felt like an eternity. He stayed on the other side of the elevator, his handsome face dark and brooding, his gaze fixed on the control panel. Once we reached his penthouse, he gave me a quick tour of the four-bedroom, five-bathroom space, including my own bedroom with more jaw-dropping views and a marble soaking tub.

It took every ounce of control I had not to let my relief show on my face when he had to go into the office for one last meeting before working from home the rest of the week. It gave me an hour to explore my new surroundings and, yes, snoop. The penthouse is inherently masculine, black-trimmed furniture with hunter green cushions, offset by pale-colored walls and the massive windows that made me feel like I was on the same level as the sun. The rooms practically glowed in the midday light.

But my exploration was jarring, too. Glimpses of the man behind the seductive lover I knew in Santorini and the cold, calculating scion of his own security empire. A spy thriller left on an end table with a bookmark stuck between the pages. A surprising number of watercolors, mostly landscapes, on the walls.

I hadn't gone past the threshold of his room; that would have been creepy. But I did stand in the doorway and glance around, noting the massive bed with a black headboard and a divan in that same shade of dark green arranged in front of another epic window. I could easily imagine lying there on a day when the clouds hung low over the city and feeling like I was living in the sky. And then turning as Michail entered the room, stretching out my hand as I invited him to join me—

I'd slammed the brakes on my runaway imagination and turned to leave when I'd spied the framed photograph on his bedside table. Michail and an older woman with silver hair falling over her shoulder in a long braid. He had one arm wrapped tightly around her shoulders, a huge smile on both their faces.

His mother.

His smile had slammed against the walls I'd constructed around my heart. So too had the protective, loving way he held his mother against him as they stood on a cliff overlooking the ocean.

I'd wanted to learn more about the father of my child. And I did, including that he likes to read and enjoys brandy, judging by the very expensive bottles I spied in his pantry. And chocolate. The man has enough bags of M&Ms in his kitchen pantry to last through an apocalypse.

But the experience was also intimate, little insights into a man I crave and detest in equal measure. I'd gone back downstairs and grabbed a fantasy book off the shelf in his living room before settling into the deep cushions. No more snooping. No more insight into a man who continues to tempt me to break every promise I ever made to my mother to keep myself safe.

To not make the same mistake she did and fall for a handsome face hiding an ugly soul.

I tuck a bookmark between the pages of the novel and close it. I can't remember the last time I read for pleasure. For a few hours, there were no controlling billionaires, fainting episodes or worrying about the future. Just a young woman learning to navigate a world of dragons and treachery.

A quiet whoosh sounds behind me. A door sliding open. The hairs on my arms rise up as my heartbeat quickens.

Another problem I didn't anticipate: my wild hormones making me very, very aware of Michail. Aside from that forty-five-minute break, he's been here the whole day. Us being in separate rooms for almost all of it didn't make a difference to my body. Every time I heard the deep murmur of his voice as he made a phone call or the creak of him going up the stairs to the second floor, my pulse ricocheted as the muscles between my thighs tightened.

"Are you cold?"

I grit my teeth. His husky voice sweeps over me even as the question itself kindles my irritation. Part of the problem is me. I'm used to doing things on my own. The only person who ever took care of me, who I felt like I could trust, was my mom. Having someone who doesn't even like me that much sliding into that role with such confidence is uncomfortable.

Slowly, I make myself relax. It's not a weakness to ask for help. I'd always encouraged my clients to reach out to relatives and loved ones. To be aware of when they need support.

But to be the one to acknowledge that I need help, that I can't handle something on my own, feels like failure.

"It is breezy."

Something warm and soft wraps around me. I stiffen against the melting sensation inside my chest as Michail drapes a blanket over my shoulders. His woodsy scent drifts up from the fleece. I barely resist the urge to bury my face in the cozy fabric and inhale.

"Thank you."

He walks around my chair. My breath catches in my chest. His hair is rumpled, thick locks falling over his forehead as if he's run his fingers through it repeatedly. The top two buttons of his dress shirt are undone. I glimpse tanned skin in the dimming light. His black pants hug his thighs and emphasize his sheer size as he walks across the terrace to a chair right next to the wall. With New York City at his back and the encroaching night, he looks like a dark, mythical god.

I glare down at the book. No more fantasy for me.

"How was your day?"

His tone is conversational, as if we were any other ordinary couple catching up at the end of a long day. The pang of longing is thankfully short-lived. We're not a couple. We never will be. He can't stand me, and despite my physical attraction, I'm not a fan of his, either.

"Fine. Yours?"

"I took another look at Lucifer's will."

Not at all what I was expecting him to say. But a safer topic than the baby or what we'll do after he's born.

"Is anything wrong?"

His lips quirk into a sexy almost smile that makes my heart do a small flip in my chest.

"Aside from his manipulative stipulations, no."

I glance out over Central Park again. Lucifer had first mentioned the marriage clause when I'd visited him in Santorini. The first and thankfully only time I ever met with him in person. Never in my career had I had a client demand something that devious and controlling. His threat to have me fired hadn't fazed me. But his oath to wreck Kingston and ruin the careers of everyone in the firm had.

A shudder passes through me. That was the day I got a glimpse of the devil people had whispered about. The man may have been dying, but his impending demise hadn't dampened his ability to hurl vases against walls or fling cruel insults designed to cut so deeply you couldn't help but wonder if he saw something no one else did.

"I didn't agree with it."

"Yet you wrote it in?"

My back straightens, but unlike the previous times we've argued, there's no malice in his tone, no anger on his handsome face. Just curiosity.

"No. The original will evenly divided his assets between Rafael and Gavriil with no stipulations. He told me he wanted it included, but when I raised doubts, he ordered me out of the house. I was surprised when he didn't reach out, but I thought maybe he saw reason." I sigh. "The updated will included both the marriage clause and you. Although if he had decided to ask me to make the change, I would have been obligated to abide by his wishes."

A fact my boss, Lauri, had reminded me of when I'd traveled back to New York and requested an emergency meeting. But she hadn't taken his threats lightly, either. She'd stopped by my office later that day to tell me she had had a personal phone call with Lucifer and issued her own ultimatums if he ever threatened one of her people again.

A lump forms in my throat. I really enjoyed my job. And I liked working for Lauri and Bethany. Leaving was the right thing to do. But it was also another loss. Another reminder that there is very little in this world I can depend on.

"You didn't know who I was when I walked into that bar."

I shake my head. "No. I didn't know who you were until you walked into my office."

He stares at me. Assessing, evaluating. Then, at last, he nods. My shoulders sag as some of the tension eases between us.

"Ever since I made my first million, I've been the target of more than one woman trying to date me for my money or even trick me into marriage."

I think of the pictures of him from the past few months, always with a beautiful woman on his arm or a bevy of admirers circled around him like a fan club.

"Sucks to be rich."

Michail blinks, then throws his head back and laughs. Truly, deeply laughs. The sound ripples over me, slides into my skin and drifts down to my core. I press my legs together and focus on a point over his shoulder.

"There are downsides I didn't anticipate." He leans forward. "Gavriil mentioned the will you read during our meeting had been delivered by courier that morning. So you hadn't seen the updated version?"

"No. I didn't even know Lucifer had a third son until six hours before you walked in."

"Was the new will completely rewritten?"

Unease creeps over me. "Everything was still my work

except for the marriage clause and the amendment naming you as an heir."

"Who wrote that section?"

"A lawyer from Athens your father had—"

"He was not my father."

The revulsion coating his words sends a shiver down my spine. I don't like my birth father, either. From what little I can remember, and based on the few things my mother said, he was lazy and selfish at best. The two memories I have of him are starkly different. The first is me sitting on his lap the Christmas before he left opening a present. Warm, safe, happy. The second is him and my mother screaming at each other around Easter just a few months later right before he walked out. Scared, sad, hurt.

But I never experienced even a fraction of the bone-deep loathing Michail feels for Lucifer.

"Okay," I say carefully, "Lucifer flew a lawyer in from Athens a few hours before he died. The lawyer drafted the amendment."

"Is it legal?"

My unease flares into alarm. "The will? Of course it's legal."

"No way to break it?"

A dull throb begins to pulse in my temples. "I don't understand. I thought you wanted nothing to do with the inheritance."

"I don't want anything from him." My relief is short-lived as Michail leans forward, determination burning in his eyes. "But I do want something he took from my mother."

The throbbing turns into sharp stabs, like a tiny pickax being dug into my skull. I remember there being something about a bequest for Michail's mother. A collection of paintings. But Lucifer had tied it to the stipulation that Michail marry in order for his mother to receive it.

The man really had been a snake.

"I understand that." I sigh. "I know the lawyer who authored the amendment. He does things by the book. You could try fighting in court. But I wouldn't expect it to be broken."

I brace for an argument, for him to push. But he simply continues to regard me, his face pondering.

"Then I only have one option."

I stare at him. "You mean get married?"

His nod carries the weight of a death knell. It feels like someone plunged their hand into my chest and squeezed my lungs so hard I can barely catch my breath.

It shouldn't matter. I didn't want him to be involved with the baby's life. Why do I care if he gets married?

"What's wrong?"

I feel like a bug under a microscope with how closely he's watching me. I force a small smile that probably looks more like a grimace. "Nothing. Just tired."

"I apologize. I shouldn't have brought this up so soon."

Irritation gives my flagging energy a small boost. "I'm not a porcelain doll, Michail. I can handle reviewing a will and making some inquiries."

He stands. "You need to rest."

"I have been. I barely left my bed in the hospital, and I've been doing nothing but sitting and reading since I got here." I fold my hands together and inhale deeply. "If you're marrying purely for the sake of the will, then it doesn't really matter. But if you're considering proposing to someone who might be involved in your life, then we would need to discuss the potential impact her presence could have on the baby."

The thought of another woman holding my son, of sharing those moments with Michail, creates an ugly swirl of hurt and envy inside me. It's just because of the baby. Nothing to do with Michail.

Yeah, keep telling yourself that.

His deep chuckle interrupts my thoughts. I frown. "What?"

"I'm not marrying someone else, Alessandra."

"Oh." My relief is short-lived when he kneels in front of me. The weight in my chest shifts, gravitates downward toward my stomach. Surely he can't be suggesting that we…

"You and I will get married."

CHAPTER FIVE

Alessandra

SHOCK TETHERS ME to my seat. A million thoughts rush through my head, ranging from heart-wrenching disappointment that my first proposal is more of a business proposition to barely contained fury that Michail would dare to suggest something so preposterous.

"An interesting idea." Slowly, I stand and move over to the balcony. "Not a good one, but interesting."

He arches a brow as he stands, too. "Running away already?"

I bristle. "I don't run away from my problems."

He advances toward me. A predator stalking its prey. I stand my ground even as the urge to flee pulses through me.

"You left my bed in Santorini. You damn near sprinted across the lobby two nights ago to get away from me. And now you're walking away again."

I stare up at him. My mind fumbles for words, trying to find a way to argue the point.

Except he does have a point. I woke up just before sunrise in Greece with Michail's arm wrapped around my waist and his face buried in my hair. The urge to stay there, in his bed, in his arms, had been so fierce it had been frightening. I was certain in that moment that even though we'd only known each other for a few hours, this man had the power to not only bring me to incredible heights, but to crumble my heart into pieces so tiny I'd never be able to piece them back together.

So yes, I'd run. But I'm not the only one. He didn't stick around to talk things out at the will reading.

"I understand you want the paintings for your mother." I grab onto the railing with one hand, the cool metal a balm against my heated skin. "But you need to find someone else."

"I don't want someone else."

Yearning weaves through me for one blissful second before reality crashes in. His words aren't tender or loving. They're calculating. I'm the easiest and most convenient candidate.

"No, you want me because I'm carrying your child and it would be another way to bind me to you."

His jaw hardens. "You need to accept that I'm a part of his life, Alessandra."

My head snaps up. "Don't you dare tell me what I do or do not need to accept." Anger boils over at his nerve. "I've been stuck on an emotional roller coaster for nearly a year, and every time I think I'm about to get off, it just plummets down another hill I didn't see coming. You rejected me not once but twice, and the only reason you're here now is because I'm pregnant. We both know if there wasn't a baby involved, you'd still be in the Hamptons or London or Paris, anywhere but here." I let go of the railing and stab a finger at his chest. "So don't you dare tell me what I need to accept."

Silence falls. The wind stirs my hair, teasing stray strands over my face. The baby moves, a frantic sort of flutter as if he can sense my distress. I pause, suck in a deep breath and slowly move my fingers in a soothing circle over my stomach.

He closes the last bit of distance between us, stopping so near I have to tilt my head back to look up into his face.

"You and I are bound together, Alessandra. There is no escaping that. I won't promise you a lifetime of love and romance. I'm not capable of such things."

I look away. "I know. You told me before."

"But I can offer you and the child almost anything else." His breath is warm on my lips, his mouth inches away from mine. "Name it, Alessandra, and it's yours."

The deep timbre of his voice is a devil's song, his conviction a dark melody that could tempt an angel to sin. The thought of spending a year married to Michail, of bringing my child into a home with a loving father and having that dream of a loving family is all too alluring.

But it would be a transient dream. One with a very firm deadline and no happily-ever-after. The ache I felt as I walked away from his villa in Santorini had hurt enough. I can't begin to imagine the kind of pain I'd feel after living for a year as a family. Michail isn't the kind of man to give his heart away to a woman. And I won't settle for anything less than a man's love.

"Nothing you can provide."

His gaze hardens. "Try me."

"There's nothing, Michail. My answer is no." One corner of my mouth twists into a slight smile. "Ironic, isn't it? You thought for months I was only out for your money, only to learn I want nothing to do with it."

"What about the baby?"

I tense. "I swear to God, Michail, if you threaten me—"

"Don't, Alessandra." The warning in his voice is lethal. "I would never separate you from the baby."

"Then what—"

"You told me the one thing your mother never gave you was a father."

I hate him. In that moment, I hate him and the fact that he remembers what I confided to him in the dark. That he's now wielding my own words as a weapon against me.

"Yes. But she made up for it."

"Did she?" His voice is quiet, yet the certainty in his tone is as strong as steel. "I'm not negating what she did. But you wanted a father."

"We don't always get what we want." I lean in, nearly falter when he doesn't pull back. As if he's testing me to see how close I'll get. "She was twice the parent my father ever was."

"A conviction I'm intimately familiar with." He cocks his head to one side. "My mother is a strong woman. She sacrificed a great deal to give me every chance at success. That didn't stop me from craving a father. Even after I accepted my birth father was a bastard, I imagined life with someone who gave a damn. Someone who wanted to be involved."

I don't want his words to resonate. Don't want to re-member how it felt to sit on my father's lap as he helped me unwrap a doll with a red ribbon in her hair and gather me into a tight hug as he told me I was ten times pret-tier than any toy.

"We both imagined a lot as children." I force the words out, stand my ground. His proposal is the definition of insanity. "I grew up. Fairy tales don't exist."

"Fairy tales, no. But an involved father who can be

responsible and committed to your child? That can be a reality."

A fact I thought I could accept. Except Michail wouldn't just be a dedicated parent; he'd be the one man who would break me the same way my father broke my mother. But unlike her, I have ample warning that any type of relationship with Michail will end.

"I can offer you stability. Support. A guarantee that I will care for our son and give him everything both of us wanted."

"Not love."

He pauses. His eyes drop down to my stomach.

"When I read the paternity results, I knew there wasn't a single thing in this world I wouldn't do to be in his life." He looks back up at me. "I don't have to think about it. I just know."

My eyes grow hot. I know what he means. I felt the same thing in the doctor's office when I first learned I was pregnant. I just never expected Michail of all people to talk about love like this. To feel it unconditionally.

"Children can break your heart, too."

A shadow crosses his face. "I know. And one day that may happen. But I can do everything possible as his father to help him grow into the kind of man who doesn't hurt others."

I fight for control, to keep my eyes trained on his even though I want to lean into him, to just let go for a few moments and revel in the strange intimacy of sharing such an incredible feeling with the father of my child.

Michail's disclosure alters things. If I take myself out of the equation, I know what he's offering is the best thing for our son. But if the thought of one week with Michail was enough to make my chest ache, what will an entire year do? Or more?

No, I can't think like that. My attraction to Michail is something I'll have to deal with. What he's offering is worth far more than a stupid crush rooted in really good—okay, great—sex. Even if it means making a deal with a man who just days ago could barely stand the sight of me.

"How long would we be married?"

Triumph flashes in his eyes. If he wasn't offering me the chance of a lifetime, I'd be tempted to tell him to take his proposal and shove it before walking out of the penthouse.

"The baby's first birthday. Then we can reassess our relationship. You and the baby will live here during that time."

I glance over his shoulder at the penthouse. It's stunning, but it screams wealthy bachelor, not family of three.

"Could we lease a different apartment?"

He frowns. "What's wrong with mine?"

"It's just…it's your space. Not mine."

"We'll make it ours."

Ours. A tempting word that threatens to rekindle my yearning for something more.

I step back and cross my arms over my chest. "I need to think about that."

"Do you want to go back to work after he's born?"

"Eventually."

Another big disappointment of having to switch careers. The leave I built up with Kingston would have allowed me to take six months off. Now, I'll be lucky if I can scrape together three months with Regent before I have the abby.

"But you wanted more time with him?" Michail presses.

"I had hoped for it, yes. But I can't just take a year off from working."

"If you reside here with the baby during our marriage, I'll pay for the rent on your apartment and all of yours and the baby's expenses here, as well as creating an account you may use at your discretion for personal spending."

My mouth drops open. "What?"

"You want time with the baby. I'm offering a way to make that happen."

The bastard should have been a lawyer. "I don't want your charity."

"It's not charity if I'm offering to help make the best scenario possible for both you and the child a reality."

I grit my teeth. "But you'd be giving me an allow-ance—"

"A spending account." His eyes narrow. "You think I don't know how hard a parent's job is? My mother sat with me for hours trying to help me with homework. That was after working two jobs and before she went off to night school. I barely saw her for years, but the times I did, I knew how much she cared about me. I've already seen how much you care for our son. Giving you the op-portunity to have the kind of time she never did, the kind of time your own mother probably didn't have, is a gift for all of us."

I fall silent. Michail inserting himself into yet another part of my life is almost too much. A week ago, I would have told him to go to hell. But the opportunities he's offering are enticing. Yes, he's presenting everything in his controlling, pushy way. Yet his reasons reveal more of the depths I glimpsed in Santorini. A man who rose above abandonment and betrayal to incredible success as still remembers and honors the woman who helped him achieve that.

A man who loves my child.

I run my tongue over my lower lip. "And our living arrangements?"

"You'll have your own room. I won't demand or force anything, Alessandra. Ever," he adds with heavy emphasis. "If we decide to mutually enjoy each other's company, so be it. Otherwise, we'll have our own quarters while maintaining fidelity for the duration of our marriage."

I'm relieved. And I hate myself for that. Why does it matter if Michail does or doesn't sleep with someone else?

I need to take him out of the equation. Focus on the baby. Focus on now and what could be possible for us in the future.

The wind strengthens, whipping up over the balcony and tearing at the leaves of a redbud tree. I'm on the precipice of a second monumental decision in less than a week. One that has the potential to bring me incredible happiness even as it deepens the bond between a man who has the power to break my heart. A decision that makes me feel as though I'm betraying my mother and everything she ever taught me about being independent, resilient.

Yet I know if she would have had the chance to have more time with me, she'd have taken it in a heartbeat.

The wind fades. The leaves overhead still. My lips part.

"Yes."

* * *

Michail

I don't know of a single person in my acquaintance who wouldn't have jumped at the chance to spend a year at home with all of their expenses paid while living in a luxury penthouse.

But as I'm coming to learn, Alessandra isn't most people. Something I took into consideration this morning when I decided to propose if the will couldn't be broken. I know she cares for our son, to the point of putting herself in harm's way to keep him safe. Her continued insistence that she wanted nothing to do with me, coupled with her lack of demands, led me to the conclusion that our time in Santorini had truly been chance.

Leaving me with a solution to my two biggest problems: the will and being a part of my son's life.

Another torrent of wind rushes over the railing, catching her hair and pulling strands of auburn across her face. She frowns and futilely tries to push it back. With her hair wild and loose and that fierce frown on her face, she looks more like the woman who caught my attention in Greece than the cool, calculated professional I'd met at Kingston.

Warning pricks the back of my neck. Living with Alessandra for a year will test me in multiple ways. But the alternative options, either letting my mother's paintings be destroyed or marrying someone else, are not viable. I will not let Lucifer hurt my mother any more than he already has. And the thought of marrying another woman when Alessandra is pregnant with my child disgusts me.

I hold out my hand. She eyes it like it's a snake about to strike.

"Scared?"

My taunt does the trick. She slides her hand into mine. My fingers tighten around hers as I bring her hand to my mouth. Her sharp inhale is primitively satisfying, as is the tensing of her fingers in my grasp.

Just one more touch. One simple touch to satisfy my craving for her. I brush my mouth over her knuckles, watch her eyes widen and her chest rise and fall.

"Deal," I whisper against her skin.

She yanks her hand out of my grasp. A shutter drops down over her eyes as a small shudder passes through her.

"All right." She looks out over the city. "When?"

I stare at her profile. The possibility of indulging in sex during the course of our marriage hadn't been a primary factor when I'd first thought of proposing. But now, after voicing it during our negotiations, it's at the forefront of my mind. Judging by the pitch in her voice and the blush staining her cheeks, she is, too.

The spell woven that night that has kept her in my dreams will break with time; all spells do. That doesn't mean we can't enjoy ourselves until fantasy gives way to reality.

"Next week."

Her head jerks back around. "That soon?"

"If your doctor approves after your next appointment, yes."

I force my focus back onto one of the two main reasons I came up with this idea: the paintings. The will stipulates they can be released to either mine or my mother's possession upon proof of marriage. Until I have them, I won't be able to rest.

I'm also not giving Alessandra any more time than necessary. Time to ruminate, to dwell.

To run.

A dull sensation tugs at my chest. I reached for her when I woke that morning after we'd met. Like I had been waking up next to her for years instead of the first time. I'd pushed aside the shock of encountering empty sheets and immediately yanked my walls into place. Walls that had been tested time and again by the memory of her, of the passion we had shared.

Her hand moves back to her belly, cradling it in a way I've seen her do when she's unsettled or perceives a threat to the baby.

Our baby.

Resolve hardens my heart.

"Do you have any preferences?"

Her lips part and she blinks, like a wild animal caught in the glare of headlights.

"Preferences?"

"Location, flowers, music." When she blinks again, I hold up a hand. "We can discuss details later."

"I assumed we'd have a civil ceremony. Something quick and efficient."

"A small ceremony is fine. But I want my mother in attendance."

"Your mother?" she repeats faintly.

"My mother never thought she would see me get married or have a grandchild."

I can easily imagine her joy as she watches me say my vows, as long as she doesn't know the true reason behind them. It's been years since her breakdown, the one that finally penetrated my wall of anger and helped me get myself under control. But I hear the long-ago echo of her sobs in the principal's office after being called away from work yet again to come get me after a fight. Can still feel the panic when she hadn't been able to stop crying and the principal had called for an ambulance. Can still see her eyes when I visited her in the hospital, her gaze made vacant by medication and exhaustion.

"She doesn't know about the will or the paintings. We're going to keep it that way."

Alessandra arches a brow at the firmness in my tone. But she doesn't push.

"We could get married in private and just tell her after."

My lips quirk. "How is it that you weren't afraid to be lawyer to the devil himself but the thought of saying your vows in front of my mother has you quaking?"

"Because Lucifer was business. Your mother…" She shakes her head. "Tomorrow. We'll figure it out tomorrow."

Part of me wants to reach out to her, to run my fingers over her temples and smooth her tangled hair back from her face. A far more intimate touch than just sex. A line I crossed with her once before. Never again.

"Tomorrow then."

She goes inside, leaving me alone on the terrace as I mentally compile a checklist of things that will need to happen in the next week, from finalizing the details of the ceremony to updating my will and creating a prenup.

I glance over my shoulder. A light comes on in her room. Her shadow appears in the window. My jaw tightens as her shadow moves, pulling her dress up over her head and—

I turn my back on the penthouse and stand on my terrace a quarter mile above the street below, gazing out over a city of eight million people. A sight that normally makes me proud, the skyscrapers and lights and endless stream of traffic a visual reminder of all I've overcome and conquered to get to the top.

But tonight, my thoughts aren't on my accomplishments or future goals. They're focused on the woman who's just agreed to be my wife.

CHAPTER SIX

Alessandra

A BLANKET OF pillowy white covers most of New York City, broken here and there by a tower or skyscraper defiantly pushing through the clouds. With the sea of white below me and the sky above colored the same shade of blue as a robin's egg, the view can only be described as magical.

My tired sigh fills the room. The same can't be said for my wedding. In four hours, I will legally be Mrs. Michail Sullivan, saying false vows in front of Michail's mother and brothers. My former clients.

God, I just want this day to be over.

Michail asked me again yesterday over breakfast if I was sure there wasn't anyone I wanted to invite. My abrupt no shut down any further conversation. I can only imagine the reactions, not to mention judgments, I'd get if I invited anyone from Kingston. My grandmother is still alive, but I haven't spoken to her in twenty-four years. I saw her at Mom's funeral, which surprised me. She didn't talk to me, though, which wasn't a surprise. She'd placed me in the same category as my father before I was even born; someone who had ruined my mother's future.

Michail wouldn't understand. His mother is still an

important part of his life. I was surprised he invited Rafael and Gavriil. Obviously things have changed between those three since I saw them all together at the will reading. Despite Michail's grizzly bear personality, he has people in his life who care about him.

I don't. I've kept people at arm's length for so long, telling myself that time with my mother, the occasional happy hour with coworkers and my career would be enough. That one day I'd get around to dating, to working on those trust issues and open myself up to love, to marriage and a family of my own.

Now it's too late. I'm hitting all the milestones I'd dreamed of as a little girl, dreams I hadn't even realized I still harbored, and I have no one to share it with.

Everyone coming to the wedding knows Michail and I are expecting a child together. But only Rafael and Gavriil and their wives know about the marriage clause. I don't know who I'm more nervous about seeing: my future husband's mother or his half-brothers he just learned about three months ago? I'd only met with Rafe and Gavriil a few times during my tenure with Lucifer, but they'd always treated me with respect, even appreciation for taking on their beast of a father. How will they treat me now after learning that their father's estate lawyer had a one-night stand with their illegitimate half-brother and is now pregnant with their nephew?

I groan. When did my life become a soap opera?

A knock sounds on my door, breaking through my melancholy thoughts.

"Yes?"

"I have something for you."

Michail's voice reverberates through the door. Things

would be so much easier if he had a high-pitched voice or a nasally twang.

I cinch the belt on my robe tighter before I answer the door. It would also help, I think irritably, if the man wasn't so handsome. His black tuxedo is molded to his powerful frame. Yet he wears it with such arrogance, such masculine confidence, it's not hard to picture him ripping it off the first chance he gets.

My eyes travel down to his white shirt and the row of buttons. I can easily picture grabbing the fabric and pulling it apart, scattering buttons as I slide my hands up over his muscular chest—

I cut the thought off before I go too far. Next time I go to my doctor I need to ask her if this is normal, this heightened level of lust and the accompanying vivid imagery.

"Nice suit."

Michail's lips quirk. "Thanks. Nice robe."

"The latest in maternity bridal fashion."

His quiet, husky chuckle flows across my frayed nerves, warm and soothing.

He holds up a small black box. "I have something for you."

I stare at the box as my heart starts to pound. He flips the lid open. I can't help the sharp inhale as I gaze down at one of the most exquisite rings I've ever seen. Delicate threads of silver twist and twine over each other, like branches from some magical forest. Tiny diamonds glimmer in the spaces between. In the middle sits a stunning emerald cut in a circle.

He pulls the ring out and pockets the box before holding out his hand. I swallow hard as I place my left hand in his. Sensation shoots up my arm from where his fingertips rest on my skin. He slides the ring onto my finger.

I blink back against the sudden heaviness behind my eyes. It's nothing more than window dressing, a prop for an elaborate play we're putting on. My mind repeats this over and over again, but my heart doesn't get the memo. I can't help but be touched that he not only thought of something like this, but that he selected something so beautiful and unique.

I hold my hand up. "I've never seen anything like it."

"Anthony told me it was the most expensive piece he had in."

My joy dims. "Anthony?"

"He owns a jewelry store on Madison Avenue. He sent it over this morning."

All traces of happiness evaporate. He didn't pick it out. He just shelled out thousands of dollars, if not more, for the priciest ring in the store.

Don't let it bother you.

"It's beautiful. Thank you." My quick smile probably appears wooden. "I need to finish getting ready."

His eyes narrow, his gaze searching my face. "Everything all right?"

"I'm not going to turn into a runaway bride, if that's what you're worried about."

I meant the words as a joke, but his jaw tightens beneath his freshly trimmed beard. "I know you'll keep your word, Alessandra. I was simply asking if you were all right."

The ring grows heavy on my finger. Our time together in Santorini was natural, effortless. We talked for nearly two hours before he asked me to dance. As soon as I placed my hand in his, I knew where the night would lead. He made me feel beautiful, cherished, intelligent.

Now, we might as well be speaking different languages.

"It was meant as a joke, Michail. I'm fine. Just tired." I don't even bother with a fake smile this time as I start to close the door. "I'll see you on the terrace."

One hand comes up, his palm thumping against the door. Irritation kicks in as I glare up at him.

"Yes?"

Before he can say anything, his phone rings. He pulls it out and glances at the screen. His tension vanishes as his lips curve up into a slight smile and he hits Answer.

"Hello, Mom."

My fingers tighten on the doorknob as he listens for a moment.

"See you soon." He tucks the phone back into his pocket. "My mother's in the elevator. Would you like to meet her now or later?"

I'd like to just close the door and take a nap. A very long nap where I wake up married without having to face my future mother-in-law. But that would be delaying the inevitable. Better to know what I'm facing before the ceremony.

"Now's fine. As long as you don't mind me meeting your mother in my robe."

"She won't care what you're wearing." A hint of his earlier smile reappears. "She just wants to meet you."

I lean against the door as he walks down to the first floor. I know nothing about Sarah Sullivan other than she single-handedly raised Michail. Will she be excited her son is finally tying the knot? Or will she be like my mother and think no one can measure up to her ideals of the perfect woman for her son? That no one is worth the risk of having your heart shattered?

Worst of all, will she be like my grandmother? Reject her grandbaby before it's even born?

A feminine voice travels up the stairs, husky with age and warm with affection, followed by Michail's deep voice. I swallow hard as they come into view. She's only a few years older than my mom was, a beautiful woman with a heart-shaped face framed by blond hair tinged with silver strands. I see Michail in the sharp cheekbones and the full lips as she smiles up at him. He's returning her smile with an endearing grin of his own.

Her head turns in my direction. Uncertainty roots me to the spot until I see the sparkle her eyes as she looks at me.

"Hello." Her hand flies to her chest. "I'm Sarah." Her gaze drops down to my stomach. A lone tear trails down her cheek. "I'm... I'm so happy to meet you. Both of you."

The knots of fear loosen a fraction.

"Hello." I step forward and offer my hand. "Michail's told me a lot about you."

Sarah clasps my hand in both of hers, her gaze darting between my face and my belly. "I'm just..." She blinks rapidly. "I'm sorry. I just never thought I'd ever experience this." She turns back to Michail and grasps his arm even as she keeps one hand wrapped around mine. "Not that I didn't respect your decision. But now that she's here and the baby..." Her head whips back around. "A boy?" I nod. Her smile is bright enough to light up the hallway. "That's wonderful. Do you have names picked out?"

I see Michail's gaze sharpen out of the corner of my eye. I had names picked out. I'd even narrowed it down to two before Michail planted himself in my life. As much as I want to make that choice myself, it wouldn't honor the partnership we've agreed on.

But I'm not ready to have that discussion. Not after I've already given in on so much.

"Not yet. We should have some time on the honeymoon to narrow down a list."

Something in his face shifts, a slight softening about his eyes.

"Of course, of course." Sarah squeezes my hand once more before releasing it. "Just know I'm here for anything you, Michail or the baby need."

The difference between how Michail's mom is reacting to the news of her grandchild compared to how I once heard my own grandmother describe me as my mother's "second-worst mistake" is a blessing I desperately needed today. Even though thinking about my son never knowing my mother is a raw wound I'm not sure will ever completely heal, I'm comforted knowing my baby will have a loving grandparent in its life.

"I really appreciate that." I give her a small smile. "Maybe we can spend more time together when Michail and I get back to the States."

Michail's phone rings again. He mutters under his breath as he answers. "Yes?" His brows draw together in a deep frown. "You're four hours early."

There's a burst of talking from the other end, loud enough that I can hear it. My stomach drops as I recognize the voice.

Gavriil.

"Fine." Michail hangs up and shoves the phone back into his pocket. "Gavriil and Rafe are here with their wives."

Sarah's shoulders climb up a fraction as her smile tightens. I've seen the same reaction before, especially during will readings. Feuding family members who haven't seen each other in years, a man seeing his ex-wife with her new husband for the first time. Sarah has probably never met Gavriil or Rafe, the other children of her ex-lover. I inwardly wince. Rafe is almost an exact replica of his father. I can't imagine what kind of shock that will be for her.

Anger for Sarah, for Gavriil and Rafe's mothers and I'm sure other women who suffered under the weight of Lucifer's selfishness, spurs me to action.

"Why don't you go greet them?" I place a hand on Sarah's shoulder. "I'm having trouble picking between a couple things for the ceremony. Do you mind?"

Michail's frown deepens, but Sarah shoots me a grateful smile.

"That sounds lovely."

I step back to let her in. Michail crosses his arms as he continues to stare. My anger swells. I understand all too well struggling with trust. But I'm putting myself out there, placing an entire year of my life in this man's hands. Forgiving the cruel things he's said over the past six weeks even though his explanation didn't include an apology.

And he can't stomach the thought of me being with his mother for five minutes?

It's only through sheer will that I keep my voice low as I step out into the hall.

"If you can't trust me to be alone with your mother in the amount of time it takes for you to walk down to the elevator and back, we can call this ceremony off right now."

His eyes harden. His lips part, but before he can say anything, I turn and walk back into my room, closing the door with a soft click even as I imagine slamming it with enough force to rattle the paintings off the wall.

Bastard.

I push my anger aside and focus on Sarah. She's standing by the window, arms folded protectively across her chest as she gazes down at the clouds.

"This view is incredible."

I join her at the window. "It is. Your son's been very generous."

With some things, I silently add.

She smiles at me. "He is generous. Sometimes to a fault." She takes a deep, shuddering breath. "Thank you. For noticing."

"You're welcome." I pause, unsure of what to say, not wanting to hurt but also wanting to make her feel more comfortable. "Gavriil and Rafe are good men."

"A miracle given they lived in the same house as Lucifer." She shakes her head. "I'm grateful Michail is getting to know them. I imagine I will, too, if they're comfortable with that."

"Gavriil will be. Rafe is quieter. But from the little time I've spent with them, they both seem kind."

Sarah continues to stare out the window, her gaze distant. She may be looking out over New York City. But I know she's not seeing the clouds and spires. She's seeing the man who nearly ruined her life.

"Rafael looks so much like him." Her words are barely a whisper. "I've only seen pictures. I know he's not Lucifer."

"Knowing and feeling are two different things."

Her smile is deeper, more genuine. "I appreciate the grace. Michail wouldn't have invited him here if he was anything like Lucifer."

I remember the tightly leashed fury in Michael's voice when he had rejected Lucifer as his father. "No."

With a quick shake of her shoulders, she turns from the window. "I'm ready." She reaches out and lays a hand over mine. "Thank you, Alessandra. Unless you actually had something to show me and weren't just creating a pretense for an old woman?"

My eyes dart to the closet. My first inclination is to tell her I'm fine, that I thought she could just use a helping hand. But she's looking at me with trust in her eyes, an affection based on one fleeting encounter and an elaborately concocted lie. Guilt intertwines with a need to involve Sarah, to have her be a part of the wedding in some fashion.

I cross over to the closet. "I could actually use your advice, if you don't mind?"

"No, not at all."

The delight in her voice makes me smile even as my heart clenches. Sarah and my mom could have been very good friends.

My hand stills over the first garment bag. My mom kept herself locked up tight. She was friendly but didn't make friends. She took lovers but didn't allow herself to love. An existence I admired for years. There were no fights, no drama, no broken hearts.

But now, as I glance over my shoulder at Sarah, I realize there would have been no room for the kind of connection I just experienced. If I had met Sarah when my mother was still alive, I would have helped her, but I wouldn't have asked her to stay.

How much have I missed out on living my life inside a bubble?

I swallow past the lump in my throat, pull the two bags down and move over to my massive bed.

"I purchased two dresses." I lay them on top of the silk comforter and unzip the smaller bag. "I bought this first. Tea length, empire waist, cap sleeves."

Elegant. Simple. Practical, almost indistinguishable from my daily work wardrobe aside from the ivory-colored material.

Sarah, I realize, would be a worthy adversary in a poker game. Her face displays zero emotion as I hold the dress up.

"What do *you* think?"

I blink at her unexpected question. "It's lovely."

"Mmm." She nods her head toward the other bag. "And the second?"

I take extra care with removing the other dress from its bag. Filmy sleeves, a bodice crafted of delicate lace and a mermaid skirt of silk. I indulge myself in one fleeting touch of the lace, the soft ridges and swirls, before I hold it up.

Sarah stares at it for a fraction of a second before her eyes dart to mine. "You already know which one."

I pause. "I know which one is the practical choice."

Sarah smiles. "I don't think practicality should take the place of desire on one's wedding day."

"It's just…" Heat creeps into my cheeks. "Michail told you how we met." At Sarah's nod, I rush on. "It feels strange to wear something so sexy and revealing given the circumstances."

"Oh, dear." Sarah grabs my free hand and squeezes it. "How do you feel about the baby?"

Emotion stings my eyes. "I love him."

Unshed tears brighten Sarah's eyes. "And Michail?"

"He surprised me," I answer honestly. "I didn't expect him to want to be a father." The memory of his shocked gaze when he'd heard the baby's heartbeat for the first time is burned into my brain. "But he wants to be involved."

There are many uncertainties when it comes to my relationship with Michail. One of the few things I'm sure of, though, is his commitment to being there for the baby.

Tears slide down Sarah's cheeks as she gives my hand one more squeeze. "Then I would say this is an occasion worth celebrating." She releases my hand and wipes away her tears. "Now I'm going to meet my son's half-brothers and hopefully not cry any more before the ceremony."

"Sarah?" I slowly reach out, grasp her hand and squeeze it as she did mine in the hall. "Thank you."

Her smile is so full of joy it nearly blinds me. "You're welcome."

I wait until the door closes behind her before I sit down with the mermaid gown across my lap. Is it more curse or blessing that I like Michail's mother? I don't doubt her kindness or her enthusiasm for her first grandchild. But will she still offer the same warmth in a year when Michail and I divorce?

A problem for another day. Today I have her support and the presence of at least one person I know will genuinely be happy to watch me walk down the aisle.

My fingers sink into cool folds of silk. I'm almost giddy at the thought of wearing something so beautiful.

What will Michail think of it?

I bat the thought away. It doesn't matter what he thinks. We've agreed to a marriage in name only. Convenience, not passion. Mutual benefits, not love.

Lace whispers over my skin as I slide my arms into

the delicate sleeves. The fabric cradles my stomach and leaves zero doubt about whether I'm pregnant. Yet as I face myself in the mirror, I don't feel embarrassed or apprehensive. I feel…proud. Beautiful, sexy. When I walk down that aisle, I'm going to do so with a confidence I didn't feel an hour ago. I'm going to make the most of this chaos and craft a wonderful life for myself and my son in the process.

Michail's face flashes in my mind, his expression shifting from cold suspicion to fiery intensity. Yes, he tempts me. My body craves him with a need that's almost impossible to ignore.

Almost, I remind myself as I turn away from the mirror. But the desire to protect my own heart overrides simple lust. I'll make the most of today, embrace the positives of having a father in my child's life and keep my desire on a tight leash. I can resist Michail.

For my sake, and my son's, I have to.

CHAPTER SEVEN

Michail

IN LESS THAN ten minutes, I'll be a married man. I never saw myself as a husband. But I never saw myself as a father, either. One role is tied to the other.

I glance at my mother out of the corner of my eye. When Alessandra invited Mom into her room, I was suspicious. It didn't make sense that the woman who had been nervous at the thought of having my mother witness our vows was suddenly inviting her in for a private chat right before the ceremony.

But when my mother had come down the stairs, glowing and happy, I'd been forced to admit I had made an error in judgment. Again.

I pull one of my cuffs down over my wrist with a hard enough yank it's a miracle I don't tear the fabric. I don't want to trust Alessandra. Yet every time I've assumed the worst, she's proved me wrong.

Am I looking for reasons not to trust her? Trying to keep her at arm's length even as I fight to keep her and my son in my life? The thought that I'm not giving her a fair chance, that I'm acting in the manner of the same man who made me feel like dirt as a child, makes my chest tight.

I glance over at Rafe and Gavriil, who are talking with my mother. When Lucifer told me I had two half-brothers, I hated them almost as much as I'd hated him. Reading up on their successes had deepened that hatred until it became a deep wound that constantly tested my control. I'd assumed the worst of them, that their fortunes had been made by Lucifer simply passing the reins.

When Gavriil had invited me to his wedding, I'd thrown the invitation in the trash. An hour later I'd dug it out. Morbid curiosity had sent me to California. The sheer luxury of Gavriil's wedding had confirmed my suspicions.

Until a conversation with Rafe's wife, Tessa, had taken some of the fight out of me. Her vague references to what life had been like for Rafael growing up in Lucifer's household had altered my views. Gavriil's reaching out for help a few weeks later, trusting me to assist him with the company he obviously cared about, had forged a tentative bond between us. A bond deepened a month later when Gavriil roped me into helping Rafe reunite with Tessa. I'd gone, grudgingly and with numerous protests. Deep down, though, helping my brothers had started to fill a void I hadn't even been aware of. One I had thought fulfilled by my relationship with my mother and my work. But being a son of Lucifer is a unique club that, as far we know, only the three of us belong to. We may have known the bastard for varying lengths of time. But he left his mark on all of us.

I hadn't realized how apprehensive I had been at the thought of Mom meeting Rafe and Gavriil. I'd noticed her subtle flinch when she'd met Rafe. But my older brother had put her at ease with a surprisingly warm smile. Gavriil, of course, had swept her into a hug and complimented everything from her dress to her fortitude and raising "a lumberjack." A sentiment that had startled a genuine laugh out of my mother and wiped away any possible tension.

My brothers of course know about the will and its ties to my impending marriage. They also know to keep their mouths shut. As much as I want my mother here, want her to finally have her moment as the mother of the groom, guilt haunts my every interaction with her. If she knew that I was getting married to satisfy a clause of Lucifer's will, one that primarily benefited her, she would demand we stop the whole wedding. Yet the alternative, her earliest life's works destroyed, can't come to pass.

"You look awful gloomy for someone who's about to get married."

I smile as Rafe's wife, Tessa, stops her wheelchair next to me.

"Just thinking." I nod at the terrace. "Everything looks wonderful."

Tessa's smile is infectious as she gazes around at her handiwork. Cane-backed gold chairs with ivory seats are lined up in a row, separated in the middle to create an aisle. The inner seats are marked by low vases overflowing with scarlet flowers. Café lights crisscross above the patio for the small reception we'll host after. A simple arch decorated with white gauze and wrapped with vines of vivid red flowers marks the spot where I'll become a husband.

"Thanks. I didn't really get to plan much of my own wedding, so this was fun."

"I didn't realize that."

Tessa nods. "My mother took care of a lot of it. I wasn't nearly as confident as I am now." She turns her head and

I follow her gaze to Rafe, who's looking at her with such adoration I feel like I'm intruding.

The first time I met my older brother, he reminded me of a block of ice. But now, when his face softens as he gazes at his wife, an uncomfortable sensation flickers through me.

Envy.

I brush it aside. Yes, Rafe and Tessa found happiness, as did Gavriil with his wife, Juliette. It's possible for people to be happy in their relationships. But I know myself, and I know my limits. Not only do I have zero interest in opening my heart up to a woman, but I'm not capable of trusting her enough for us to have a successful relationship.

The last time I trusted someone carved scars into my heart that will never heal. I won't let them. They're a reminder of what happens when you let down your walls. When you allow yourself to hope that maybe you'll finally meet the person you've dreamt of for years, the person you imagined as the hero of your story...until you finally accept he's not only not coming, but he didn't care enough to tell you.

The officiant walks up the aisle, thankfully stopping my trip down the memory lane from hell.

"If everyone could take their places, please."

I stand by the arch draped in gauze and flowers. My mother sits in the front row, beaming proudly as music filters from speakers hidden around the terrace. Gavriil sits in the chair next to her, an empty seat next to him as Juliette lingers in the background with her camera in her hands. I doubt Alessandra will care if we have pictures of the ceremony, but it adds a touch of authenticity to the proceedings. Rafe and Tessa sit on the other side.

"Please rise," the officiant intones.

My brothers and Mom stand. Tessa angles her wheel-chair slightly toward the makeshift aisle. I look up toward the door.

And freeze.

Alessandra stands framed in the doorway, auburn hair flowing over her bare shoulders. The dress clings to every curve, from the long, see-through sleeves to the lace that hugs her pregnant belly before cascading into a waterfall of some silky material that rustles as she walks. The bouquet of red roses in her hands matches the vivid scarlet painted on her lips.

My heart thunders against my ribs. Raw need curls through me, an almost feral desire to go to her, take her hands in mine, dare anyone to take away what's mine. I manage to stand my ground, but barely, as she moves down the aisle with a seductive grace that has alarm bells clanging even as I devour her with my eyes.

Alessandra glances at my mother and gives her a small smile. My mother nods as she presses a handkerchief to her lips, tears glimmering in her eyes. The sight of that moment, that connection, punches through me. When Alessandra looks back at me, I know.

One year is not going to be enough.

No, it's not love. But I like Alessandra, respect her. She agreed to let me be a part of the baby's life because she thought it was the best thing for the baby, even though she wanted nothing to do with me. She will be a great mother to our child.

And I want her so much it's turning into a physical ache that hurts. More than I ever thought I could have with a woman.

The thought of her leaving, of her and the baby living

somewhere else, of another man possibly stepping into my role, has me clenching my fists.

She stops in front of me. Uncertainty passes over her face. I unclench my fingers and reach out. Time slows as she stares down at my hand. My heart thuds once, twice. It's as if everyone on the terrace is holding their breath.

And then she places her hand in mine. My grip firms and I repeat my action from the night I proposed, bringing her fingers up to my lips. But unlike that night, when I merely grazed my lips over her, today I press a firm kiss on her skin.

"You look beautiful."

Her eyes widen a fraction. A blush steals over her cheeks. "Thank you."

The ceremony is quick, our vows simple and straightforward. Yet as I say "I do," I make my own vow. Before our first anniversary, I will convince Alessandra that a divorce is not in our best interests or the interest of our son.

"I now pronounce you man and wife. You may kiss the bride."

I arch a brow at Alessandra in silent challenge. She narrows her eyes even as she tilts her face up. I slide my fingers along her jaw, savor the flare of desire in her eyes and her quick inhale before I lower my head and cover her lips with my own.

Lust takes hold as I savor the taste of her. Her lips part beneath mine. I take the kiss deeper for a single moment, a torturous second, but one I don't regret as she softens against me and leans into my chest.

The press of her stomach jolts through me. I want to touch her, to feel our son growing inside her.

I pull back. Slowly, her eyes open. She stares at me

with a glazed look of desire and something else. A dark, fleeting emotion.

Fear. A feeling I know all too well as those scars on my heart start to pulse with warning. Reminders to enjoy what I have without letting myself go too far.

My hands tighten on her hips before I consciously loosen my grasp.

"Are you all right?" I whisper.

She blinks, then slowly nods. The click of a camera cuts through the moment. We both look over to see Juliette in the middle of the aisle with the camera aimed in our direction.

"It is my honor to introduce Mr. and Mrs. Michail Sullivan." The officiant's voice booms out over the terrace, boisterous and seemingly ignorant of the drama playing out between us. "Congratulations!"

We turn to face the guests. My mother is smiling through her tears. Tessa's watching me, her smile dimmer and tinged with curiosity. Rafe claps, while Gavriil puts his fingers to his mouth and lets out an ear-piercing whistle as Juliette continues to click away.

I twine my fingers through Alessandra's. Satisfaction spears through me as her hand grasps mine. A small step. But a step nonetheless.

My first battle was convincing Alessandra to let me be a part of the baby's life. The second was agreeing to the marriage.

Now, as we face my family—our family—I know those battles were just the beginning in what will be a long and challenging war to convince her to keep my ring on her finger.

A war I will not lose.

CHAPTER EIGHT

Alessandra

MOONLIGHT DANCES ACROSS the waves of the Atlantic several thousand feet below Michail's plane as it climbs into the air. Behind us, New York City glitters like someone dropped thousands of jewels across the night landscape. Ahead of us, the sea blends into the night, a carpet of midnight dotted here and there with the occasional ship glowing on the water.

It's easier to focus on what's outside the plane versus what, or rather who, is inside. Two pilots man the controls of the most luxurious plane I've ever been in. A flight attendant brought me a cup of tea with honey just before takeoff. Now she's working with a chef—an actual Michelin-star-rated chef—to prepare dinner in the front galley, which is the same size as the kitchen I had in my first apartment back in college. Seated toward the front in one of several plush white seats is a nurse practitioner from my doctor's office. And sitting at a desk with his laptop opened in front of him and his phone pressed to his ear is Michail.

My husband.

I breathe in deeply, then slowly release. It's been two days since we said our vows. I spent most of those in my room or on the terrace with my laptop, making plans for the next year. I decided to follow through on my plans of working for Regent Capital Planning through my delivery date. I can't spend the next four months lying around Michail's penthouse. It's just not me. My new boss at Regent was surprisingly understanding when I told him I was now planning on taking a year to stay home with my son, and said we could see how the next few months go, then talk about the future after the baby arrived.

With that stress removed, I was able to finally start focusing on things like a crib and how I wanted to decorate the room next to mine that would become the nursery.

The baby moves, his fluttering stronger. I glance over my shoulder at Michail. He's seated with his back to the pilot's cabin, his thick brows drawn together in a frown as he listens to whoever is on the other end of the line. His dark hair is combed back in thick waves from his forehead. He's wearing a white suit shirt, the sleeves rolled up to his elbows and the top shirt unbuttoned. Usually when I see him first thing in the morning, he has on a suit jacket. But by midday, the jacket is gone and by afternoon, the sleeves come up and the button is undone.

Not that I mind. It gives me an opportunity to fantasize about undoing those buttons and revealing the broad, muscular chest underneath. After that searing kiss he gave me on our wedding day, I need the fantasy. Otherwise I might be tempted to take him up on his offer to enjoy the physical aspects of our union.

My thighs clench. I shift in my seat, trying to relieve the ache that hasn't quit since he kissed my fingers. Michail glances my way. His eyes travel down my body and back up, as if he knows the source of my discomfort.

Judging by the slow curve of his lips, he knows exactly what I'm thinking.

Damn it.

I can't figure the man out. Right before the ceremony, I was ready to call it quits over his suspicious attitude toward me inviting his mother in. When I walked down the aisle, he looked thunderous, fists clenched at his sides and his face tight.

But then he relaxed, kissed my hand in the most sensual way possible in front of the guests. He didn't let go throughout the whole ceremony, gripping my fingers as if he expected me to bolt.

And then that kiss... God, that kiss. It rekindled every moment of our night together: the passion, the desire, those moments of intimacy that added a layer to our lovemaking I'd never experienced before. One that heightened every pleasure, enhanced every peak he brought me to.

I press my legs together as pressure builds. A pressure I have no way of relieving because the only thing that will truly satisfy it is the man I need to stay away from. A task that grows more difficult with each passing day.

I look back out the window. New York City glitters one last time. And then the plane ascends above the clouds.

It's not just my deepening desire that presents a problem. No, it's spending more time with Michail, seeing more and more glimpses of the man I thought he was back in Santorini. The past two mornings I've woken up to breakfast on a small tray next to my bed. He accompanied me to my doctor's appointment yesterday to make sure I was cleared to fly to Greece. He brought me tea on the terrace and, when he saw that I was looking up things for the nursery, asked me questions and even made a couple suggestions.

Yet aside from helping me in and out of taxis, he hasn't touched me. Not once. He's treating me with respect, shooting me the occasional heated or appreciative glance, but otherwise honoring the rules we agreed on.

I don't know what to do about it.

Although, I remind myself, there are still some things he's overbearing on. Like the nurse practitioner. He asked my doctor yesterday about the safety of flying at this stage in my pregnancy and with my recent fainting. She was reassuring, but as soon as she said "There's always some risk associated with travel," he insisted on hiring a nurse to travel on the plane to and from Greece. It didn't matter what argument I came up with; he simply rejected it.

"I'm not risking you or the baby," he'd said.

"Mrs. Sullivan?"

It takes a moment for the name to sink in. I look over my shoulder at the flight attendant.

"Sorry, I'm still not used to my married name."

The flight attendant smiles. "Not a problem, ma'am. We'll be serving dinner in a few minutes."

"Thank you."

I move to the front of the plane and sit down in the seat across from Michail. The more time I spend with him, the more tempted I am to let down my guard. It would be enjoyable while it lasted. But Michail isn't a happily-ever-after kind of man. Yes, he's close to his mother. And he's slowly developing relationships with Gavriil and Rafe.

But I still sense a distance there, a wall he keeps between himself and his half-brothers. Similar to the wall he maintains between us. A wall I recognize because I've lived behind a similar one for most of my life.

Michail hangs up and closes his laptop.

"That was the lawyer in Greece. He has to leave Monday to meet with a client in Japan."

"What about the paintings?"

"Per the will, the lawyer has to meet you and me in person before agreeing to release the paintings to me. He's attending a charity gala tomorrow night and has invited us to join him. Once he meets us, he'll authorize the delivery of the paintings to my home in the Hamptons."

"At least he's getting us in before he leaves." I frown. "Although I'll need to stop by a store or boutique when we land. I didn't bring anything appropriate for what I'm assuming is a black-tie event."

Michail waves his hand in the air. "We'll take care of it."

"I'll take care of it." I hold up a hand when he starts to argue. "Michail, I'm making a lot of concessions. A lot. When I tell you I can shop for my own dress, I mean it. I've been dressing myself for over twenty-five years."

Our conversation is interrupted by the flight attendant setting salads in front of us with plump grapes, walnuts, and feta on top of a bed of arugula. I try to focus on the salad and not my simmering irritation.

As I stab my fork at a grape, my phone buzzes. A text flashes across the screen. I glance at it, then do a double take when I see the message.

"Why is there four million dollars in my checking account?"

He arches an eyebrow. "I told you I wanted to set you up with spending money."

"I could live off the interest generated by four million for the rest of my life. I don't need that much for 'spending money.'"

His brows draw together in a frown as his eyes narrow. "Then don't spend it. Invest it. Keep it as an emergency fund."

"I don't want to, Michail. One percent of that would be more than enough for me to keep myself entertained and buy things for the nursery."

"I already ordered the furniture for the nursery."

My mouth drops open. "You what?"

"Once you showed what you wanted, I placed an order. It should be set up when we arrive."

I can physically feel the last bits of my independence draining away. I lay my fork down and stand.

"Alessandra—"

"Don't." I'm all too aware of the flight attendant and the nurse trying to pretend like they don't see the drama playing out in the cabin. "Just don't."

I stalk down the center of the plane toward the bedroom in the back. I walk in and close the door, lean back against it as I bury my face in my hands. The four million feels like a transaction, a stark reminder that this is a business arrangement, not a real marriage. His buying the nursery furniture without talking to me is another sign that he has no interest in talking to me, really talking to me. He's going to make his decisions without me.

I pull my hands away and look down at my engagement ring and wedding band. Day three and I'm already struggling.

A knock sounds.

"Go away."

"Let me explain." His voice is muffled by the door and the hum of the plane's engines.

I yank open the door. He fills the doorway, his face shadowed.

"Explain what? That you're making decisions without

consulting me? That you're treating me like a child in-stead of a co-parent?"

"Yes."

His simple answer momentarily stuns me into silence.

He glances over his shoulder. "We can either continue this discussion now in private, or we can talk once we land in Greece."

Part of me wants to just shut the door in his face. But I also know once we land in Greece, things will move forward at breakneck speed.

Reluctantly, I stand back and hold the door open, clos-ing it quietly behind him. When Michail gave me a tour of the plane, I thought this bedroom was huge. The same white walls as the main cabin, the space dominated by a king-size bed arranged with a mound of pillows and a dove gray silk comforter. A mini bar sits in one corner and the plane equivalent of a cozy armchair in the other.

But as I turn to face my husband, the room shrinks. His scent curls around me, woodsy and tempting.

"Explain."

"Yes, I ordered the nursery furniture without talking to you."

Disappointment tightens my throat. "Why?"

"Partially because I wanted to surprise you." The ten-dons in his neck tighten. "And because I'm used to mak-ing decisions on my own."

I sigh and run a hand through my hair. "You can't just make decisions for me. If this is going to be a co-parent-ing relationship, a partnership, you have to talk to me. You also have to accept you can't control everything so that it meets what you want. That's what…"

My voice trails off, but it's too late. A shadow drops over his face.

"What were you going to say, Alessandra?" His voice is a low growl.

My stomach rolls. "Nothing."

"No, please. Enlighten me." He crosses his arms over his chest, his muscles straining against his shirtsleeves. "That's what Lucifer used to do?"

There's no getting around this. "Yes, my mind went there. I'm sorry."

"Nice to know what you truly think of me, Mrs. Sullivan."

"Oh, don't you even try to play that card," I snap. "Not after the way you treated me for weeks."

His chin comes up. "I explained that."

"Yeah, explained but didn't apologize! Yet I have gone along with everything you've asked. I've accepted help, even though that's hard for me. You've taken every capitulation, and now you're trying to force even more down my throat without talking to me about it!"

"I'm not forcing anything on you," he ground out. "Donate the money if it bothers you so much. Send the furniture back. I'm not threatening you with it."

How did I think that things had improved the last couple of days? We were just coasting on the residual happiness left over from our wedding ceremony. We are two very different people, and he will never understand me.

"Do you know what happens when you surrender your independence? When you trust someone else? When a man accidentally gets you pregnant and encourages you to drop out of college to raise the baby, but then decides a couple years later he needs time to 'find himself'? Or when your parents suddenly decide that you're not good enough, that nothing you ever do will be good enough, and their handouts come with conditions designed to make you feel as small as possible? I saw my mother suffer that. It wasn't until she took a stand and started relying on herself that she was happy. The people who should have loved her and held her up instead crushed her under the weight of unrealistic expectations."

My voice trembles but I don't back down.

"Two weeks ago, you thought that I was only out for your money. And now, after you've finally accepted you were wrong, all you want to do is push your wealth on me to satisfy your own need to control."

A vein pounds his neck. "You see this as me trying to control you. I don't know what your mother went through. But I can tell you what mine went through. How one of her biggest regrets was missing out on almost all of my early years because she was working two, sometimes three jobs, trying to keep us in a mold-infested apartment on the wrong side of the tracks."

My heart pitches down to somewhere around my knees.

"Michail…"

"And instead of making her life easier, I made it harder because I wanted a dad who kept promising to come visit but never showed. Instead of appreciating the parent I had, I got into fights and stirred up trouble, adding more stress on her shoulders." He pauses, his hands clenching into fists, as if he can hardly bear to think of the past. "Yes, two weeks ago I was wary of your motives. But things have changed. If wanting to provide a better life for the mother of my child so she doesn't have to suffer the same hardships my mother did makes me controlling, so be it."

I start to retort. My eyes drop down to his lips. The angry charge between us shifts, heightens. Electricity crackles across my skin as I remember the way those lips felt on mine, on my neck, my breasts, lower still.

I swallow hard. I don't want to look at his eyes. I don't know what I'm more terrified of: that I won't see the same need, the same desire, or that I will.

His fingers settle on my wrist. Just a graze of his fingertips, but it might as well be a live wire with the effect it has on me. My heart shoots into my throat as my breathing quickens. Slowly, he trails his hand up my arm, leaving behind a burning trail of sensation.

His hand moves to my face, deliberate, slow. Giving me time, I realize with a sudden clench of my heart, to pull away. To stop him. And I should. I really should.

But I don't want to.

He cups my face. Tilts my head up. I lean forward and our lips meet.

Passion explodes. The first touch of his mouth on mine makes me moan. I lock my arms around his neck and press myself against him. Wanton, wild. Everything I'm not, but that he brings out in me.

He groans. The sound fills me with feminine power, as does the hard length pressed against me. Emboldened, I slide one hand up his neck and into his thick hair. His hands clamp down on my hips and pull me tightly against him. He slides a tongue along the seam of my lips. I don't even hesitate opening for him, savoring the intimacy.

One hand slides up, grazes the side of my breast. My hips rock against him as need becomes a physical ache inside me. I want him, I need him, need him to take me inside and strip us both naked as he—

His other hand shifts, grazes the swell of my stomach. He freezes.

Reality crashes in. I let go and step back so quickly it's a miracle I don't trip and fall.

We stand there, breathing ragged, chests rising and falling. The breeze intensifies, cool against my heated skin.

I stare at him. His blue eyes are sharp, his jaw tight. His hands are clenched into fists at his sides.

I want him. I want him so bad it hurts. But I learned the hard way watching my father walk away from my mother after their last fight, hearing her cry at night those first couple of years as she tried to figure out how to pull us out of the poverty he'd left us in, that it's often the people we care for the most who have the power to destroy us.

"I'm not spending that money." I raise my chin. "And no more kissing."

I wait for... I'm not sure what. Anger, persuasion, anything but the steady gaze fixed on my face.

"Is that what you want?"

No. "Yes."

He watches me for another heartbeat. Eyes on mine, searching, penetrating. Then he nods. Walks past me. A moment later I hear the door open, then close again with a soft click.

I suck in a shuddering breath as I sink back down onto the bed. I have nothing to feel guilty about. Nothing. The kiss was amazing. Incredible. Just as potent as the kisses we shared back in Santorini, but with a sensual knowing we didn't have before.

But kissing means nothing without trust.

CHAPTER NINE

Michail

THE PAVESTONES OF VOUKOURESTIOU STREET gleam in the early-morning sunlight. Most of the shops won't open for at least another hour. Tourists are still sleeping off transatlantic flights or hangovers from indulging in Greece's famous ouzo.

But as Alessandra and I walk down one of Athens's most prominent streets lined with signs advertising brands like Prada and Gucci, I don't even glance at the window displays. We only have one stop this morning before continuing to Santorini.

I glance at my wife out of the corner of my eye. I didn't see her after our kiss until about an hour ago as the plane was descending into Greece. She emerged with her hair caught up in a bun at the crown of her head, a loose white shirt hiding most of her belly and black pants that clung to the curves of her legs. I let her set the tone for the morning, taking a cue from her blank face and monotone voice.

But inside, I seethe. Burn.

Her accusations last night were not misplaced. No, they were all too accurate. My mother has told me on more than one occasion she can take care of herself, that I don't need to be hovering over her shoulder like I'm the parent. Occasionally, she'll reference her week in the hospital, promise me that will never happen again.

Except it wasn't just a week. Yes, she was hospitalized for seven days. But it took months for her to recover, to lose the shadows beneath her eyes and the strain in her smile when she asked me how my day at school was. For me not to panic every time she looked even mildly worried.

Once I got control of my anger at my then-unknown father, and by extension the world that looked down on my mother and me, our lives got better. The more I controlled, from my behavior to my grades to taking on a part-time job in high school so that my mother could focus on finally finishing her college degree and getting certified as an art teacher, the better our lives became.

I know Alessandra isn't in the same position my mother was. But damn it, what good is my money if I can't use it to give the mother of my child a chance to be there for our son? To be present in a way my mother was never able to be there for me? Knowing Alessandra had to give up a job she loved is a knife to the chest.

But she's not giving up. Instead, she took on another role while five months pregnant so she could prepare for her ultimate goal of owning her own business. I admire her initiative, her tenacity. She's balancing her professional dreams with providing the best life possible for our son.

Her accusations last night cut deep. But in the light of day, I can't help but wonder if I'm insisting on helping her because it's the right thing. Or is it to make myself feel better?

"Kyrios Sullivan!"

A short, portly man with an impressive salt-and-pepper mustache leans out the doorway of one of the shops and hails us with his boisterous greeting. Alessandra's steps slow.

"You know him?"

"I do. Chances are you've heard of him, too."

She arches a brow. "Oh?"

"Kallos Boutique."

Her eyes widen. "Seriously?"

"Seriously."

Kallos Boutique has nine shops around the globe, including one on New York's famous Fifth Avenue and one prominently featured on the Champs-élysées in Paris.

"Greetings, my friend." Lucas steps forward to clasp my hand in his. "It's an honor to have you visit my original establishment."

"Thank you." I turn to Alessandra and gently grab her by the elbow, tugging her forward. "This is my wife, Alessandra."

Lucas's eyes widen. "But I had no idea. Congratulations."

"We're keeping things quiet for now."

Lucas places a finger to his lips. "I am the soul of discretion."

"Thank you. My wife needs a gown for the International Children's Charity gala in Santorini tonight."

Lucas turns to Alessandra and beams. "Madam, I have numerous gowns that you would do justice to."

Her smile is surprisingly shy. The longer I know her, the more I'm realizing that while my wife may exhibit a strong front, she has an introverted side. A vulnerability she rarely lets anyone see.

"Thank you."

"No, no, thank you for giving me the opportunity to dress you for tonight's gala." He gestures to the open door of his boutique. "Shall we?"

The interior of Kallos Boutique is a fashion designer's dream. Mannequins are artfully arranged about the floor, raised up on daises and draped in the latest couture gowns. Dresses are crafted of chiffon, silk, lace, many of them adorned with actual diamonds and rubies.

"Michail?"

Alessandra is standing in the middle of the boutique, her eyes round and her lips slightly parted as she takes in the splendor around her. I move closer, all too conscious of the rounded curves of her breasts, the flare of her hips barely visible beneath the fluid material of her shirt.

"This isn't what I had in mind when I said shopping," she murmurs under her breath.

"The International Children's Charity is one of the world's most renowned funds. The guest list looks more like a who's who of Milan's Fashion Week."

"I understand that, but surely a simple black dress will do."

"My dear," Lucas interrupts with a grand flick of his wrist, "a simple black dress will not do justice for a lady such as yourself."

Her blush deepens. "I only meant to say that—"

"Will you give us a moment, Lucas?"

Lucas winks at me. "But of course."

He disappears into a sea of jewel-toned fabrics. Instrumental music plays overhead as chandeliers glimmer above. In an hour, his shop will be filled with curious tourists and some of the world's top politicians, movie stars and otherwise wealthy elite.

Alessandra glances around, her gaze both trepidatious

and longing. "This isn't the kind of place that I usually shop."

"Lucas is a friend of my mother's."

Now I've caught her attention. Alessandra's eyes narrow as she cocks her head to one side.

"Your mom?"

"Believe it or not, Lucas used to be a teacher back in New York."

Her startled laugh warms me. "A teacher?"

"Yes. Family and consumer science with a focus on fashion."

Realization flares in her eyes. "You helped him start his boutiques."

"He was a good friend to my mother when she got her first teaching job. Loyal, supportive. He had a dream. He deserved to see it come to fruition."

Alessandra stares at me for a long moment before tearing her gaze from mine. "I see."

She moves toward a mannequin draped in topaz silk. She glances at the price tag. I don't know if it's because I've spent more time in her company or if I just know her that well, but I can tell by the subtlest move in her throat and the slight tightening of her lips that these are not the prices she was anticipating when she said she needed a dress for the gala.

I had intended to purchase a gown for her. But this is the first time in recent memory where I have to be cautious on how I phrase what I'm about to say next. Never have I met a woman who would not readily agree to my purchasing her a designer gown.

But Alessandra will. How did I ever think her capable of manipulating our meeting in Santorini for financial gain? While her fierce independence will be an obstacle to my convincing her to forgo a divorce, it's also something I'm coming to admire about her.

"I'd like to offer you a gift."

She looks at me, her face carefully blank. "Oh?"

"A dress of your choosing. But," I add before she can say anything, "I want to offer it as a gift, not a requirement. Not an order. If you decline, and nothing here meets with your approval, there are several boutiques in Santorini we can visit this afternoon before the gala."

It's a concession, one I don't like making. I take care of the people in my life. Her refusal to accept the money wasn't just obstinance. It felt like a rejection of me and what I have to offer, another setback in our relationship.

But as the plane flew through the night sky, my anger abated enough for me to revisit her words. To accept that she had, in fact, conceded a great deal. It had only been two weeks since I found out I was going to be a father. The same two weeks in which Alessandra left behind a job she was passionate about, moved out of her apartment and accepted a proposal from a man she had initially thought would shirk his responsibility as a parent.

I don't like that she's still fighting me at every turn. But I have to remind myself I will not win by pushing her too hard and too fast. If I want her to treat me as an equal when it comes to parenting, I need to offer her the same when it comes to everyday life.

"Why?"

No one I've dated before has ever asked that. They've just taken what I've offered. And what I've offered has always been material goods, things that couldn't tie me down to one person. But as I think over her question, I'm surprised by my own answer.

"Because I want to. I know that while you were very successful in your career, you live frugally."

I think back to our wedding day, the way she would run her hand over the lace of her wedding dress when she thought no one was looking. Watching her fingers stroke over the material, imagining peeling the gown away before I laid her down on my bed, made my cock so hard I had to focus on putting one foot in front of the other.

"You enjoy the finer things in life. You either haven't had the opportunity, or haven't given yourself the opportunity, to experience them. I'd like to give you this."

She stares at me for what feels like an eternity. Her eyes are probing, assessing.

Then, slowly, she dips her head. "I'll consider it." Her gaze narrows when the corner of my mouth tilts up into a smirk. "I didn't say yes."

"But you didn't say no."

Before she can argue, Lucas comes back. "My apologies, but if we only have an hour, I would like to get Mrs. Sullivan into the dressing room as quickly as possible."

When Alessandra nods, a knot loosens in my chest.

Lucas claps his hands and two women appear out of the maze of dresses. One is tall and willowy thin with dark skin that gleams against the contrasting pale lavender of her dress. The other has silver hair that falls in billowing waves to frame a round, wrinkled face.

"Yvette and Agatha, two of my most trusted associates. Ladies, Mrs. Sullivan is shopping for a gown for the International Children's Charity gala tonight. Please, take good care of her."

The older lady comes forward with a beaming smile and open arms.

"What sort of dress are you thinking?"

Alessandra returns the smile with an amused one of her own. "I'm honestly not sure. I've passed by the window of the Kallos Boutique in New York many times and always been impressed by what I've seen. It'll be hard to choose."

"Then with your permission, we will bring a few selections to you and start from there."

The taller associate places a gentle hand at Alessandra's elbow and guides her forward. The women disappear into a sea of silk and chiffon.

"Your wife is very gracious."

Lucas's observation makes me pause. "She is."

Kindness has never been a trait I've focused on in previous paramours. Why would it matter when the end goal was mutual pleasure with an expiration date? But as I think back to how she thanked the medic in the ambulance, how she interacted with the nurses in the hospital and whatever transpired between her and my mother before the wedding brought such a huge smile of joy to my mother's face, I'm struck by this unexpected side of her. Unexpected because I focused almost exclusively on those few fraught minutes in her office during the will reading where she treated me with cool professionalism.

"Please feel free to browse and select anything else you might wish to gift your wife with on your honeymoon."

I shake my head. "You've got that sales pitch down pat."

Lucas's grin is broad beneath his mammoth mustache. "How do you think I became the most respected couture designer in all of Greece?"

"Europe, Lucas. And one day, worldwide."

It's true. His dresses are worn by the world's elite. I also know he donates dozens of gowns to the school where he used to teach to be given out to those in need ahead of school dances. I don't just give my money and support to those who will use it exclusively for their own financial gain. The people I support are making a difference.

Lucas's smile disappears as he reaches out and grasps my hand. "Because of you."

Uncomfortable with his sudden emotion, I squeeze his hand and step back.

"I just saw a talent and made an investment. Nothing more."

"Agree to disagree," Lucas says with a wave of his hand. "I will check on your lovely wife. May I offer you a mimosa or champagne before I depart?"

"It's nine in the morning, Lucas."

"Never too early to celebrate. My success, your marriage and, if my eyes do not deceive me, the addition of a new family member?"

When I merely arch a brow, he gives a little laugh and disappears.

I sit down in one of the oversize chairs toward the front and pull out my phone, dash off a few emails about a software update for one of our systems, approve a press release for one of Sullivan Security's new community initiatives and review our quarterly budget. All tasks that normally have my full and undivided attention.

This morning, however, as I read over spending and profits, the numbers are a blur. My mind returns over and over again to the woman at the back of the shop. To how cold and fierce she looked in her office when she essentially told me to go to hell. How fragile she felt in my arms as I waited for the ambulance. How stunningly beautiful she looked coming down the aisle even as uncertainty flared in her eyes.

How she'd looked at me for one fleeting moment before she'd found out about the money. As if I were something more than just a partner in a contractual agreement.

I'd convinced myself the woman I met before was an illusion, just one side to a calculating, manipulative schemer. I was partially right. It was just one side of her. The more I see of my wife, the more I want to know.

But still I hold back. Even though the temptation is growing to tell her more, to share something of myself, all I have to do is think of that afternoon in the park. My seventh birthday. Sitting next to my mother on the bench even though she encouraged me to play on the playground because I wanted to meet my father as soon as he arrived. I watched every man who passed by like an overeager puppy begging for a treat.

As the hours passed, my excitement had dimmed, replaced by a slowly sinking heart. When the sun sank down below the horizon, a single hot tear had slipped down my cheek. Every now and then I can still feel the burn of its trail down my face before others followed. I broke down and cried like I hadn't in a very long time. Nothing my mother said made a difference.

I got into my first fight at school the next day.

Emotions can be good. But they can also be volatile creatures that strip away one's ability to act, to think. Add in factors like lust and a belief that you're in love, and you have the ingredients for a disaster.

I blink, realizing I've tried and failed to read the same paragraph at least three times. I glance at my watch. My eyebrows shoot up. It's been nearly an hour. Our flight to Santorini will be less than that. But I'd rather get there and have extra time than be late or, worse, miss the small window of opportunity we have to secure my mother's paintings.

I slide my phone in my pocket and make my way through the dresses toward the back. The dressing room is tucked in a corner. Skylights welcome morning sunlight and turn the cream-colored room into a glowing paradise. Plush armchairs in jewel-toned colors like navy and deep purple are angled toward the doors of the dressing rooms. Arched mirrors dominate the walls, with a raised platform every third mirror or so.

I glance around. And stop in my tracks.

Alessandra stands on a podium toward the left. Her hair is still pulled up into a bun, leaving her neck bare to my gaze. The sleeveless gown she has on is unzipped. The rich purple is the color of violets and makes her skin glow. Even though she has one hand holding two pieces together at the base of her spine, the back lies open, revealing the curve of her spine and her naked skin. I can see in the mirror that her other hand holds the bodice of the dress to her chest. The material crosses over her chest in folds that draw attention to her breasts before falling in a waterfall of material down to her feet. It doesn't frame her stomach the way her wedding dress did. But there's something carelessly elegant, even sensual about the way the fabric hugs her curves.

I stay where I am, waiting to see if Yvette or Agatha makes an appearance. But as the seconds scroll by with no one appearing, I step forward.

"Need some help?"

Her spine straightens so quickly I can almost hear it snap. Her eyes meet mine in the mirror. A blush steals into her cheeks, then traces an alluring path down her neck toward the swells of her breasts. I stifle a grown at the memory of those breasts pressed against my chest last night as we kissed.

"I'm sure Yvette or Agatha will be back in a moment." She gives me a small smile. "They've had me try on no less than a dozen dresses so far."

"See any you like?"

Her throat bobs as she swallows. "Perhaps."

I let my gaze wander over the swell of her breasts, the gentle roundness of her stomach, the swirl of fabric hiding her legs from my gaze and then back up to her flushed face.

"I like this."

Her gaze breaks from mine and she stares at her own reflection. "So do I."

Her words seem almost wrenched from within, a confession she wishes she hadn't given. I approach the platform slowly, ready to halt if she shows any signs of bolting.

"Would you like me to zip you up?"

Her shudder is so slight I almost miss it. It takes every ounce of willpower not to let my satisfaction show on my face when she gives me a slight nod.

"Please."

I step onto the dais. Inches separate us. She releases her hold on the fabric. For a moment, the cloth gapes, giving me an even better view of her bare back. I grasp the top of the dress with one hand and use the other to slowly slide the zipper up, conscious of the heat emanating from her naked skin.

I remember kissing my way down every inch of her spine, the way her body arched and twisted toward my touch. Remember her suddenly moving on top of me, grabbing me with one hand and guiding me into the wet heat of her body as she sank down, asking me to make her forget for just a little while.

I hold her gaze with mine in the mirror, never blinking as I let my knuckles graze the skin between her shoulder blades, savor the parting of her lips and the quick, harsh exhale that lets me know she is just as affected as I am. By the time I'm done, I'm not sure if I've ever been this aroused in my entire life, simply with the act of helping a woman get dressed.

"You look beautiful."

She blinks, then looks down. I see her eyes focused on her stomach. I take a risk and place my hands on her shoulders.

"Alessandra." Her eyes shoot up to mine in the mirror. "Beautiful."

She stares at me like she's seen a ghost. As if she can't quite believe I'm telling the truth. A realization that makes something twist in my chest.

Before I can reassure her, feminine voices come from outside the dressing area. I release her shoulders and take a step down as Yvette and Agatha come around the corner.

"Oh!" Yvette smiles at me as she walks over with several other dresses draped in her arms. "Mr. Sullivan, what do you think?"

"It will be a hard choice." I glance back at Alessandra, who's now watching me with caution. "But my wife has excellent taste and sound judgment. I know she'll make the right decision."

Alessandra frowns. I smile at her, nod to Yvette and Agatha and then make my way back to the front of the store. I've unsettled her. Hopefully shown her that I can offer her something more than a planned marriage of convenience. It's just the first step, but with this inter-action, I've confirmed that our desire for each other hasn't dimmed. No, if anything, it's grown, driven to new heights by our separation these past five months and the intimacy we find ourselves in with impending parenthood.

I'll use whatever I can to my advantage. But as I settle down in the chair and pull out my phone again, I can't help but wonder what price I will have to pay to secure Alessandra's surrender.

CHAPTER TEN

Alessandra

I FEEL LIKE a princess. I'm standing on a marble balcony overlooking the cerulean waters of the Aegean Sea. The room behind me is the size of my apartment, complete with a massive bed on a raised dais, a clawfoot soaking tub in the ensuite bathroom and deep blue tufted furniture that invites one to laze away an entire day napping or reading.

Too bad my nerves are wound so tight I feel like I might snap. It's not just being back in Santorini, although that certainly doesn't help. Every time I catch the sweet, floral scent of the bright pink bougainvillea flowers, I'm thrust back to the moment Michail pressed me into a tumble of blooms and branded me with a kiss I felt all the way to my soul. Whenever I stare out over the ocean, I see Michail walking through the door of the bar, his eyes locking onto mine as if he'd been looking for me.

I sigh and lean on the railing. The memories I spent months trying to suppress are everywhere. The pain is still there, but it's no longer acute. Now there's confusion. I was so convinced I wanted nothing to do with Michail Sullivan.

But each passing day ushers in realizations about the

man I married. Details like how he funded a world-renowned boutique for a friend of his mother's, or how his
desire to give me a small fortune is rooted in watching
his mom struggle through his childhood.

A knock sounds on my door.

"Come in."

Michail walks in and quietly closes the door behind
me. My heart starts beating in triple time. The more time
I spend with him, the more I question my resistance.
Yes, there's the potential for heartbreak. But more and
more I'm seeing the other side, the possibility that Michail and I could find our own version of happiness. Is
it possible that, in time, he might be able to let himself
feel more for me? The thought is simultaneously thrilling and terrifying.

"The limo will be here in an hour."

"Okay." He glances at the dress draped across the bed.
"Are you going to keep me in suspense until we leave?"

It takes a moment for me to realize he's teasing.

"Well, since you paid, I'll give you a preview."

I move to the bed.

"Why did you let me pay?"

My hand stills on the zipper as I glance at him. His
jaw is tense, his hands clasped behind him.

"Because you gave me a choice."

When I'd first walked into the boutique, it had taken
willpower to keep my anger in check. I thought he had
brought me to one of the most exclusive dress shops in
the world because he had known my budget would be
stretched to the limit by a mere belt, let alone an actual
dress. That he would present it as an opportunity to tap
into the money he'd deposited.

But when he'd offered me not just the gift of a dress but

to choose for myself, my anger had crumbled, replaced by an emotion I'm still too afraid to examine closely.

"It's been a long time since anyone other than my mom gave me a gift."

His eyes flare. "I'm glad it could be me."

I nod and quickly look away before I make a fool of myself. I unzip the bag halfway. Violet-colored chiffon peaks through the gap. When Michail joined me on the platform, I knew. Knew I had to have the dress that would always make me think of how he stood just behind me, the barest touch of his fingers on my back setting fire to every suppressed desire that's been smoldering since we first locked eyes all those months ago.

When I look back at Michail, my breath catches. He's staring at me, his gaze burning, possessiveness and lust etched into his face.

"Good choice."

My thighs grow damp as my ache returns, deepens with every passing moment. "Thank you."

Is that my voice? Husky and breathless? I hesitate for a split second, caught between self-preservation and a consuming desire that intensifies with each passing moment. Now, as we prepare to walk into our first public event as husband and wife, the need to be with him, to have him in the one way he'll let me, is a demand I can no longer deny.

"I could use some help getting into it."

His body visibly tightens. "Now?"

The word is a guttural growl that spears straight to my core.

"Yes." I reach down and grab the hem of my shirt. "It might take a while to put on."

I whisk my shirt over my head. Nerves hit, fast and

vicious. My body has changed so much since we were together, from my ever-expanding stomach to my breasts swelling above the cups of my bra.

He stalks toward me with slow, measured steps that make me want to scream at him to hurry. His gaze is scalding as his eyes linger on my breasts, my stomach, my legs. He stops in front of me, hands fisted at his sides.

"Last chance, Alessandra."

I raise my chin up even as I quake inside. "Are you going to kiss me or not—"

He wraps an arm around my naked waist, the heat of his skin a brand against my back. His other hand comes up to cradle my face with a tenderness that stings my eyes.

And then he feasts on me. Mouth on mine, firm with need, his tongue sweeping across my lips with a masculine confidence that has me opening for him. His fingers tug at my hair. When it cascades down my back, his groan vibrates against my lips and fills me with feminine confidence.

I push my hands between our bodies and tug his shirt up, thrilling at the feel of bare skin and muscle. The hand at my back moves up. One slight tug and my bra falls away. Michail pulls back and stares down at me.

"God, you're beautiful."

My teeth sink into my lower lip. I hadn't even realized how deeply my insecurities had taken root until that moment. A thought that's obliterated as he leans down and presses an open-mouthed kiss to my skin.

My eyes drift shut and I moan his name, my head dropping back as he sucks one nipple into the wet heat of his mouth. He pulls me deeper, sensation spearing out from my breast and through my body. He repeats his movements on my other breast, driving me to the edge of madness as he nudges me back toward the bed.

Slowly, he lowers me until I'm sitting on the edge. He pulls back. Cool air kisses my nipples. He hooks his fingers in the waistband of my pants and pulls down. I arch off the bed for a moment.

And then I'm naked before him.

Even though my blood feels like it's on fire, even though I want nothing more than to feel him inside me, my hands drift to my thighs, my fingers splaying to cover myself.

Michail lays one hand on top of mine.

"I woke up some nights, especially that first month, with the taste of you on my lips."

Fire? No, it's molten lava now coursing through my veins. That and the knowledge that whatever walls I thought I'd erected to keep myself safe from Michail are nothing more than an illusion.

"Michail…"

His other hand comes up, smooths strands of hair back from my face. This is the man I fell for that night. The man who could demand and soothe in equal measure.

"I want to taste you again." He shakes his head slightly. "I need to taste you."

Shuddering, I part my thighs. His breath rushes out as he places his hands on my legs and gently pushes. I lean back on the bed, watch as he lowers his head. My eyes drift shut when he places a soft kiss on my inner thigh. I cry out when he grazes his teeth just above that. My inhibitions disappear as he moves higher, higher still, teasing, driving me mad with every caress.

He places his mouth on me and I explode. I fist my hands in his hair, my hips pressing into his mouth as pleasure catapults me up so high I wonder if I'll ever come back down to earth.

I'm aware of Michail standing, feel his absence like a part of me has been wrenched away. I open my eyes in time to see him pull his shirt over his head.

"You really do have perfect abs."

His laugh is short but pleased as he pulls off his pants. "Glad those hours in the gym are worth something."

He stands next to the bed, naked and confident. Skin bronzed by hours spent under the sun. Dark hair thick and slightly mussed, adding to that hint of wildness that's always just below the surface. His body is sharp and defined, from the thick bulk of his arms to his muscled thighs. The sight of his hard arousal makes me feel satisfyingly feminine.

I hold out my hand to him. "Definitely worth it."

He joins me on the bed, gently pushing me onto my back as he kisses me. This time he's gentle, each kiss a soft promise of what's to come. His hands drift up and down my body, cupping my breasts, teasing my skin. I dimly note that he avoids my stomach. But I'm too distracted by the growing sensation, by the intensifying ache between my legs, to question it.

My own hands explore his body, my fingers sliding across hard muscle and heated skin. I reach for him, wrap my hand around his length. His groan has me smiling and pumping my hand.

He stops me. "I need to be inside you this time."

I frown. "I want to play."

His grin is quick, uninhibited. "We have all the time we need."

But we don't. The thought is fleeting, painful. We have

a year. After that… I don't want to hope for more. Hope that things can change between us.

He kisses me again. I push the thoughts away and focus instead on him—my husband—and the pleasure between us.

"Tell me what works best."

I smile against his mouth. "I've never done this before pregnant."

His laugh is warm against my lips. "A first for me, too."

He places his hands on my hips and rolls. I push up on his chest and straddle his waist, moaning as he hardens, his cock pressing against my core. I wrap my fingers around him again, lifting up slightly before easing down just enough to feel the tip of him against my wet skin. I smile as his eyes darken.

And then I sink down, slowly taking him inside. My body stretches then tightens, clamping down around him. I sigh as he fills me up.

"I missed this."

I freeze. I didn't mean to say that out loud. Ridiculous to feel self-conscious when I'm naked with my husband deep inside me.

Michail leans up, threading his fingers through my hair as he pulls my head down.

"So did I."

The kiss is a soft caress, his lips whispering across mine. Tears press against the backs of my eyes but I blink them away as I kiss him back. It changes, deepens, turns into something hard and hungry as he thrusts up into my body.

I push him back down on the bed, brace my palms against his chest, and ride. The pleasure builds once more, but this time deeper, even more satisfying. He keeps his eyes locked on mine, his hands on my hips, helping me keep the pace as we spiral up.

My release hits, sudden and devastatingly intense. I cry out his name, my fingers digging into his chest. He follows a moment later, his body shuddering beneath me, my name on his lips.

I sit there for a moment, the aftershocks of my pleasure making me shiver. I slide off and lie down on the bed next to him. Our ragged breathing fills the air. That and the roar of my blood still pounding through me.

I think I've known all along that this is where we would end up. As soon as I said yes to going back to his apartment, a part of me knew I couldn't be this close to Michail without succumbing to the passion that bound us one night.

Michail shifts and leans over, pressing a soft kiss to my bare shoulder. After what we just shared, the small gesture shouldn't touch me the way it does.

"Next time will be more drawn out."

I arch a brow at him. "Next time?"

He moves, shifts until his body covers mine again, bracing himself above me as he leans down and kisses the skin between my breasts.

"Next time." His mouth moves over, brushes one still-taut nipple. "And the time after." I cry out as he grazes his teeth over the tender flesh. "And the time after that."

"You've made your point," I gasp as he kisses the underside of my breast.

"Good."

He frowns at something between our bodies. I raise my head to see him hardening again. The ache returns, swift and deep, as if I hadn't just been made love to.

"As much as I would like to stay in bed the rest of the day…"

One last kiss to my lips and he stands, making quick work of getting dressed. I watch him, some of my pleasure ebbing away as his words come back to me.

We have all the time we need.

Something seems to have shifted between us. Some of the tenderness we experienced that first night together has returned, deepened by the intimacy of the connection we now share. As he pulls his shirt over his head, I can't help but wonder if something has changed for Michail, too.

Because I know, no matter how much I want to deny it, that those feelings I ran from five months ago are spreading, lodging themselves into the very fiber of my being.

Whether he will return those feelings, or at the very least trust me, remains to be seen.

CHAPTER ELEVEN

Michail

CANDLES FLOAT OVERHEAD, flickering against the darkness of the summer night. A full orchestra plays at the far end of the terrace. Waiters move to and fro with trays of champagne.

The International Children's Charity gala is underway.

I'm usually seeking out opportunities to connect at events like this, to network and further advance Sullivan Security. It's clients like these that keep the true purpose of Sullivan in business; providing security systems for those who need them most. It's not cheap to keep my own satellites orbiting above the Earth and providing the kind of service that reaches those communities. But when a millionaire or a world-renowned museum is willing to pay seven figures for a private consultation with Sullivan Security, and even more for a custom-designed system from a former officer in NYPD's Special Crimes Division, it goes a long way. Add in our traditional security systems for the average customer, and Sullivan Security continues to advance.

There's a vague sense of anticipation, of meeting the lawyer who will authorize the return of my mother's paintings and finally putting Lucifer behind me once and for all.

Tonight, however, I'm not thinking about new contracts or hobnobbing with current clients. At this moment, my attention is focused on the woman at my side.

Alessandra is beautiful in deep, vibrant violet. The gown is a perfect fit. Sometime between when I left her bed to get dressed myself and came back, she'd styled her hair in loose waves that fall over her bare shoulders and down her back. Diamond bobs glint at her ears, the only jewelry besides the engagement and wedding rings on her finger.

More than one man is looking at her with appreciation. I step closer to her, catching their gazes and watching with possessive satisfaction as they blanch and look away.

"You're not going to make friends if you keep glaring at people like that."

I capture her hand in mind and bring it to my lips. "I'm not here to make friends. And it's their fault if they continue to look at you like you're available."

Her smirk of a smile makes my chest clench. After having her this afternoon, experiencing her passion again and embracing everything she gave me, the thought of another man looking at her with covetous eyes sends a bolt of fury pounding through me.

"You don't have to be jealous, Michail."

"But I do. I always protect what's mine."

I mean every word. It's not just the baby. Not anymore, although I'm coming to suspect it never was just about our son to begin with. Alessandra has been a part of me since that night. I still have a long way to go in convincing her to stay after our year is up. But we're headed in the right direction. She's mine, whether she's ready to accept it or not.

Something flickers in her eyes. Before I can pursue it, a man appears in front of us. Tall, lean, his skin tanned a deep bronze and his silver hair combed back from a broad forehead, he looks every inch the wealthy lawyer.

"Mr. Sullivan."

"Mr. Lykios."

He inclines his head. "Thank you for altering your plans at the last minute. I apologize for the sudden change in my schedule." He turns to Alessandra and bows his head. "Mrs. Sullivan, I presume."

"Yes." Her smile is gracious. "Thank you for finding a way to meet with us. As you can imagine, the paintings are very important to my husband."

I jolt. It's the first time I've heard Alessandra refer to me as her husband.

"Yes." Lykios cocks his head to one side. "Formerly Alessandra Wright?"

Her arm tenses against mine. "Yes."

Before Lykios can say anything else, a woman in a black dress swoops up. Her tiny body fairly vibrates with energy.

"Alexander, you must come. Frederick Woodowitz is about to leave and you haven't finalized the terms of the new contract."

Lykios gives us a long-suffering look as he allows himself to be led away by the woman I can only assume is his wife.

"If you'll excuse me, I'll return momentarily."

I turn to Alessandra as he departs. Her cheeks are pale, her lips tense. I place the hand on her lower back and pull her closer.

"Are you all right?"

"Yes." She shakes her head. "No. This is what I was afraid of. Of people judging me, making insinuations."

Her gaze darts around the terrace.

"Why does it matter what they think?"

Her breath comes out in a rush. "It shouldn't. It shouldn't matter at all."

The orchestra strikes up another tune.

"Dance with me."

She stares at me like I grew a second head. "What?"

"Dance with me." I grab her hand in mine and tug her toward the dance floor. "Unless you can't?"

My words tease a small smile from her.

"All right."

I lead her onto the floor and spin her out in a dramatic fashion that has the chiffon flaring out around her legs. Her smile grows as I pull her close and wrap one arm around her waist.

"I never pictured you as the dancing type."

"Given that Gavriil thinks I was raised in the woods by wolves, I can understand why."

She tilts her head back and laughs, a deep, husky sound that reaches inside my chest and creates a warmth I'm not prepared to deal with. The first time I've heard her truly laugh.

"I'm glad the three of you are getting closer."

I lead her into a turn, pulling her body closer to mine as we navigate the dance floor in time to the music.

"We are. Slowly."

"I don't think speed matters in a case like this."

I tilt my head to one side as I gaze down at her. "Spoken like someone who has dealt with cases like this before."

"Far too often. I've dealt with lovers, scorned spouses, secret children, broken-hearted friends."

I frown. "That sounds terrible."

"It could be. There was also a lot of reward. Helping people figure out what kind of legacy they wanted to leave, how to help the ones they loved even when they were no longer here."

Guilt twists in my gut. Yes, our night together was one of mutual pleasure. But it cost her the career she loved.

"How did you get into it?"

"I knew I always wanted to go into something with numbers. I loved math. It was like a puzzle with numbers that was always wanting to be solved. I liked the challenge." The smile fades from her face as her eyes grow distant with memories. "When I was sixteen, my mother was in an accident. She was riding her bike and a car blew through a stop sign and hit her. She ended up with a couple broken ribs and a concussion. But it could have been worse. More like…"

Her voice trails off. My grip tightens on hers. When we met, it had only been a few months since her mother had passed from a heart attack no one saw coming. The thought of losing my own mother is something I can't even begin to contemplate, let alone so suddenly. Knowing that Alessandra had a special relationship with her own mother, that she had nearly lost her once before, is a pain I feel as if it were my own.

"When she got back from the hospital, she set up a life insurance policy. She sat me down, outlined everything she had: student loans, bank account information, the insurance policy. It was overwhelming. But I latched on to the numbers, the patterns. I looked stuff up and found a better insurance policy."

"And your passion was born."

She smiles slightly. "I guess you could say it like that. Especially once I found out the kind of salary I could earn if I work my way to the top, it seemed like a natural way to go. To not have the uncertainty I grew up with."

She hesitates, then looks up at me. My chest tightens at the naked vulnerability in her eyes. This is what I want: her trust, her surrender. My guilt deepens. Because I know that whatever she's about confide in me, I'm not ready to confide in her.

I don't know if I ever will be.

"I don't remember much of my father. The few memories I do have are usually him and my mom yelling at each other. They were college sweethearts. She got pregnant. He told her she could go back to school but should stay home with me so they didn't have to pay for daycare. He told her he would work and take care of everything."

Just like that, I have a better understanding of Alessandra's need for independence. Her mother trusted a man, just as mine did, and was punished for it.

"He stuck around for the first three years before he decided he'd had enough of working all the time." One corner of her mouth turns up into a sad smile. "I think the worst part is he had the potential to be a really good dad. I have a few memories where he was everything I wanted in a father. But he didn't have the drive to make it happen."

I glance down at her stomach. Emotion, fierce and deeper than anything I've ever experienced, fills me. Alessandra and I have both experienced what life is like without a father. Our son will never experience such a reality. He will always know that I am there for him.

"I'm sorry."

"Thank you, but I'm not," she says with a lift of her chin. Strength and defiance. "If he didn't want to be there, then it was a good thing he left. The worst part were my grandparents, or specifically, my grandmother. They weren't wealthy like this—" she nods to the glittering crowd around us "—but well off enough that they had plans for their little girl that didn't include a wastrel of a son-in-law or an unplanned pregnancy."

Blood starts to pound at my temples, a serious drum as I foresee the direction this conversation is about to take.

"What happened?"

"Once my parents split, we moved back to my mother's hometown. I don't know the details, but I know my grandparents provided some financial support." She sighs. "It came with conditions like her agreeing to have dinner with one of my grandmother's best friend's sons that she thought more appropriate as a potential husband than my father. They paid for her degree as long as she was pursuing a degree they approved. Nursing was not on that list. Not prestigious enough." Her half laugh is sharp, biting. "She made my mom feel more like a commodity than a daughter. A bargaining chip to get her into a better lifestyle. My grandmother also never let her forget the mistakes she had made, first in getting together with my father and then becoming pregnant and then getting married."

"But she broke free."

Alessandra nods, but the pain on her face cuts through me. How did I ever think her impervious? Cold?

"The night Mom cut her parents out of her life, we were over for dinner. I was six. Sitting on the couch. My mom and grandmother were arguing, but it wasn't anything that struck me as abnormal. They often argued." She shakes her head. "But that night was different. My mom was refusing to go out with the son of one of my grandmother's friends. She was furious. She told my mom that having a permanent reminder of the worst mistake my mom had ever made humiliated her. That..." Her throat works as she swallows, her eyes drifting from mine and focusing on some distant point over my shoulder. "That I looked just like my father."

Red fills my vision. I have to consciously keep my grasp gentle at her waist, my grip on her hand loose as we continue about the dance floor.

"Your grandmother is a bitch."

Alessandra's laugh is relieved, as if she can breathe now that she's shared the ugliest parts of her childhood. "That's one way to put it. I heard a crack. My mom slapped her across the face. She told my grandmother that the evidence of her worst mistake was the best thing that had ever happened to her."

I've known for my investigation that Alessandra's mother was a woman to be admired. But now, after hearing that, I want to nominate the woman for a damn sainthood. There's regret, too, that our son won't know her.

"She sounds like an incredible person."

"She was. We left my grandparents' four-bedroom, three-bathroom town house and went home. A six-floor walkup with a shower that worked half the time and an oven we used to heat the apartment in the winter because the furnace barely worked." She shakes her head. "Not that I wanted to live with my grandparents. But they knew how hard my mom was working, and they still set standards designed to hurt rather than help."

I know all too well what it's like to go to a place that should be home but is just a reminder of everything you don't have. It's not the lack of material possessions that make it hell. It's the lack of support coupled with the judgment of people who tell you all the things you could do to be better even as they hold the very resources you need with clenched fists.

"When we got back to our apartment, my mom locked the door behind us. She sat me down and told me that it was just her and me against the world. That we couldn't trust anyone besides ourselves." Her voice grows thick as I whirl her around the floor, beneath the dazzling lights among a sea of tuxedos and gowns. "She told me that night the only person we could trust was each other."

More pieces of the puzzle click into place. Alessandra's fierce independence, her unwillingness to entertain the possibility of a relationship. Her only experience with fathers has been an absent one, similar to my own, and what I'm guessing was a judgmental grandfather. She hasn't mentioned him. But the fact that he didn't intervene, didn't stop his wife's cruelty, says enough about his character. The very people she should have been able to trust, to rely on, had deemed her as nothing more than an unfortunate circumstance.

"I fought tooth and nail to get where I am today." She raises her eyes to meet mine. "Alone. I could always depend on myself."

The music draws to a close. We come to a stop. But before I can say anything, a voice cuts through.

"Mr. Sullivan."

Lykios, I think irritably, has impeccable timing.

"Apologies for my sudden departure."

"No apology necessary." Alessandra smiles at Lykios even as she shoots me a warning glance.

"Thank you for your understanding. Now, as per the

will, I needed to not only review the official documentation certifying your marriage but actually lay eyes on you as a couple." He smiles, amusement in his eyes. "After that dance, I can safely say that I acknowledge your marriage and fully authorize you to collect the paintings of your mother."

I mask my relief as I give him a simple nod. "Thank you."

"The paintings were moved into storage at Lucifer's penthouse on the main island." Lykios hands me a card with an address written on the back. "You'll have to make your own arrangements for sending the paintings wherever you want them to go."

"Thank you."

Lykios glances at Alessandra. She tenses, as do I. If the man even attempts to suggest anything seedy, I'll escort him over to the railing and toss him into the sea.

"I admired your handling of the O'Roarke case in New York."

Her lips part. "Oh. Well, thank you."

"Masterfully handled." He shakes his head. "I lost quite a handsome bet on it not going to trial."

Alessandra's smile is amused. "I would apologize, but given that I kept the family out of court and resolved it to everyone's satisfaction, I'll simply say better luck next time."

Lykios chuckles and offers his hand. "I'm sorry for the extra step in this whole process. Best wishes to you both."

Alessandra sighs with relief as he walks away. "Well, at least that's over."

"Yes." I glance down at the card, my heart thudding against my ribs. It's only a few minutes past eight o'clock. If I remember correctly, the penthouse is less than five minutes from here. There are five paintings total. The limo can easily accommodate them.

"I'll have the driver take you back to the villa."

Alessandra tenses. "What do you mean?"

"I'll have him take you back to the villa and then have him meet me at the penthouse. I want the paintings taken to the airport tonight and flown out as soon as possible. I'll feel better when they're back on American soil."

Silence stretches between us. Then, finally, Alessandra speaks. "I thought I was coming with you."

My walls shoot up. Yes, Alessandra and I have gotten to know each other much better in the last few days. But the thought of her being there when I finally take possession of my mother's paintings, of having her be so intimately involved, is a line I'm not ready to cross.

"I think it would be better if you go back to the villa and rest."

The severing of the connection between us is a cold, vicious cut. I know as soon as I've spoken that any progress she and I have made has been eradicated in one fell swoop.

"Alessandra—"

"No." She steps back, a mere foot, but it might as well be a canyon for all the distance it puts between us. "You're right. This is a matter for family. I'll see you back at the villa."

She turns in a swirl of violet fabric and moves through the crowd with her head held high. I follow at a steady pace, my eyes trained on her back as I follow her through the terrace doors, down a hallway and into a room. A library, I note, as I close the doors behind me and lock them. We don't need an audience for this discussion.

Alessandra is standing by a window, one hand clenched

onto a red brocade curtain as if it's the only thing keeping her from floating away. She's staring out the window at the sea, shoulders tense, neck rigid.

"Go away."

"No."

She shakes her head. "Of course you didn't want me to come with you to get the paintings, so you tell me to go back to the villa. Then, when I do leave, you suddenly change your mind and just like that—" she snaps her fingers "—everyone must follow Michail Sullivan's orders."

I slip my hands into my pockets, count to ten. "The paintings are a private matter."

Her laugh is sharp and tinged with bitterness. "Yes. So private the mother of your child with whom you just had sex with two hours ago can't be there."

"So I'm to allow you all the independence you crave, yet you're allowed to invade my privacy whenever you choose?"

She whirls around. "I will respect your privacy. But I thought I was a part of this." She holds up her left hand. The emerald in her engagement ring winks in the dim light. "Wasn't that one of the primary reasons for us getting married?"

"Yes, and I appreciate that you helped make this acquisition possible."

Her cheeks pale. "Appreciate it," she repeats dully. "God, I'm such an idiot. I unburden myself to you, tell you some of the hardest parts of my life, and then five minutes later, you shut me out."

I waver. Think about what it would be like to have her by my side when I see the paintings for the first time. A steady, calming presence.

I know exactly how she'd act. But the unknown factor, the reason why I can't say yes, is me. I can't have her there when I'm not sure of how I'm going to respond.

"You won't ever let me in, will you?"

The soft words cut through me like a dagger, the pain in her voice a far more powerful punishment than I ever imagined.

"Alessandra, it's not that I won't, I—"

"Can't." A mask drops over her face. The same mask she wore when I walked into her office for the first time. "There's a difference."

My spine stiffens as I advance forward. "I've told you why."

"Bits and pieces. I've been repeatedly placing my trust in you, sharing my most vulnerable moments with you, my body…" Her voice breaks and she spins away, facing the window once more. "This must be how our mothers felt."

I freeze. Blinding fury surges up, but I squelch it, summon the cold control that will see me through this.

"Our mothers?"

Slowly, she turns to face me. "I didn't mean—"

"Oh, I think you did." I step closer. "Like father, like son?"

She shakes her head. "No, that's not—"

"It is." I lean down. "I may not be as willing to disclose as you, but I've done my own share of opening up and placing my trust in you. If you can't see that, if you're demanding more than I'm prepared to give even as you compare me to the man who destroyed my ability to trust, then perhaps it's your turn to look in the mirror and see who you resemble."

I turn my back on the mother of my child and stalk out of the room.

CHAPTER TWELVE

Alessandra

MORNING SUN MAKES the white walls of Santorini glow. The bright blue rooftops that grace countless pictures on Instagram and Pinterest gleam in the early-morning light. At this hour, the streets are mostly empty, giving me time alone with my chaotic thoughts.

As I wander up and down the alleys and streets, I'm bombarded by images. Michail zipping me into my dress at Lucas's boutique. Staring at me as I undressed like he'd never seen anything he wanted so much in his life. Smiling down at me last night as if he never wanted to let me go.

Thickness swells in my throat. That brief high had made the fall even harder when, just minutes later, he drew a line between us. Part of me understands. We have a bond between us. But it was a bond forged out of circumstance, not choice.

Yet I thought the last few days we were growing closer. It felt like he respected the boundaries we had agreed on, but he had also been the one to introduce intimacy, to subtly push and draw me in. But the intimacy he's offering doesn't include himself. Only what he'll share in the bedroom.

My throat tightens. I certainly didn't help matters. Instead of taking time to calm down and talk to him, I lashed out. I truly hadn't been comparing him to Lucifer when I'd said what I did. Only that I was coming to understand how our mothers had fallen for the men who had taken everything they had to give yet refused to do the same.

I stop in front of a small nook carved into one of the stone walls. A statue of a woman draped in Grecian robes stands inside, gleaming white and cradling a baby in her arm. My hand drifts down to my belly. I can only imagine how frightened our mothers were, stranded with no resources, no support.

Remorse propels me away from the statue. There are some similarities in my situation. But one key difference is Michail's desire to be a part of our son's life. Yes, he hurt me last night. His lack of trust even as he demands more of me is something we'll have to address.

But my response—more lashing out, out of fear and embarrassment—was also unacceptable. I hurt Michail. Deeply. If he can't trust me enough to have me present for getting his mother's paintings back, will he be able to forgive me?

I continue my walk as the village by the sea starts to come alive. A couple of children scramble out onto the street, tossing a ball between them. One spies me, shoots a gap-tooth smile, tosses the ball in my direction. I catch it with a laugh and throw it back.

I start to walk again. Then stop, my steps faltering as I recognize the sign hanging a few storefronts down.

It was the mermaid that drew me in first all those months ago. One arm is stretched over the top of the name of the bar, blond hair cascading over her bare breasts. The other lies along her side. Her fingers are splayed against the green of her tail. She smiles down at passersby, a teasing smile that tells people if they continue on without stopping to see what's inside, it's their loss.

Even though the sign makes me sad, I try to focus on the happier memories made here. I reach into my purse and pull out my phone to take a picture. A quick glance at the screen shows a dozen missed calls, all from Michail in the last thirty minutes.

Worry jolts through me. The door to his room was closed this morning, so I assumed he was still sleeping. Is he okay? Did something happen to Sarah?

Before I can dial him back, my phone rings again.

"Michail?"

"Thank God." His voice is heavy, gruff. "Where the hell are you?"

"Santorini. Where else would I be?"

His breathing comes across the line, harsh and labored. "Your bed was made and your suitcase was gone. I thought you'd left."

I don't want to be touched that he was concerned I'd left him. But I am. The worry in his voice is gratifying to hear. It's not love or trust. But it's something I desperately need in the wake of his rejection last night.

"No. I make my bed every morning, and my suitcase is in the closet."

"Where are you? Specifically?"

"Um…" I glance up at the mermaid. I swear she's laughing at me. I roll my eyes at her. "The bar."

"The bar?"

"*The* bar."

Silence reigns. Then, at last, he orders, "Don't move." He hangs up. I slide my phone into my purse. I thought

I'd have more time this morning, to wander and organize my chaotic thoughts.

Awareness pricks the back of my neck. Slowly, I turn.

Michail is striding up the street, his eyes fixed on me. One of the boys playing shouts, then lobs the ball toward Michail. He looks away and catches the ball with an athletic ease that has my breath catching. A younger boy, no more than four, runs up and randomly hugs him about the waist. Michail freezes. Uncertainty crosses his face, followed by an emotion so raw it makes my heart ache. He returns the hug with one arm, pressing the boy against his side for a moment before an older child comes over to take the ball and pull the boy away, scolding him in Greek. The boy looks back at Michail and waves.

Michail waves. And then his eyes find mine again. As I stand there on the pavestones, with the morning sun threading strands of gold through his dark brown hair, my heart thuds. I can feel myself slipping ever closer to that emotional edge, toward the same cliff my mother warned me time and time again to stay away from. I should be longing for a man who's safe, stable, dependable. One who will care for me but who I can live without should the worst come to pass.

Not a man who will command not just my body but my heart and soul, even as he keeps his own just out of reach.

I know all this. But it doesn't stop my pulse from racing nor my heart from crying out as Michail draws close.

I resist the urge to step back. "How did you get here so quickly?"

"I've been looking for you for half an hour."

Warmth clashes with trepidation. "Why?"

His jaw tenses. "Alessandra—"

"You found her!"

A young woman steps out of the doorway, her smile broad and her eyes sparkling as she looks between Michail and me. It takes a moment for me to remember her as the waitress who served me that night.

"Excuse me?"

"He was looking for you." The woman points at Michail. "A few months ago. He came in the morning after you were here and asked if we knew who you were." She clasps her hands in front of her chest. "I'm so glad you found one another!"

I don't dare look around. How can I when my heart is thundering so hard in my chest it feels like it's going to break free?

"Thank you." Michail's voice sounds closer. "We're fortunate to have found each other again."

Hysterical laughter bubbles in my throat, but I bite it back. Michail's shoes whisper over the pavestones as he walks up behind me and places a hand at my lower back.

"Perhaps we'll be able to stop by for another drink before we leave."

The young woman beams, oblivious to the tension between us. "We open at five. I hope you'll join us."

She disappears back inside. The children must have gone somewhere else, because there's no more high-pitched chatter, no thuds of a ball being thrown. There's just us, Michail and me, outside the bar where it all began.

My thoughts are a kaleidoscope, tumbling and twirling as I try to make sense of what the woman just revealed against Michail's rejection of me last night. His hand moves up my back, his fingertips sliding along my spine. I lean into his touch even though I know I should be walking away.

Slowly, Michail turns me to face him. He drops his hand and takes a step back, his shoulders tense.

"I came here to Santorini because Lucifer invited me."

His voice is flat, his eyes cold. But I know that at least in this moment, it's not directed at me. It's the only way for him to talk about something so incredibly painful. I wait with bated breath, torn between hoping he'll confide in me and being terrified of what that will mean for us. What it will mean if he gives me a part of himself.

"Growing up, I was so angry that I didn't have a father. The reality of it hit me for the first time in kindergarten when our teacher had us make Father's Day cards. I told her I didn't have a father. The teasing started." His gaze shifts, travels up to the sign over my shoulder. "There was a boy who kept telling me that if I wasn't such a coward, a pip-squeak, and all the other names that young boys can come up with, my dad would still be around."

I think about all of the taunts and teasing I suffered in elementary and middle school, usually centered around my love of math, being a geek, not having the right clothes. Nothing so cruel as what Michail suffered, but enough to dig under my skin, to fester over the years and further convince me that alone was best.

"Children can be cruel."

"It didn't help that we lived in a crumbling apartment building known for its mold issues, lack of air conditioning and pipes bursting on a semiregular basis. The apartment next to us was known as the place to go to get decent heroin."

My eyes widen. A blush stings my cheeks as I remember my words last night, venting about an apartment that didn't always have working appliances. But I never had to worry about things like whether somebody was bringing illegal drugs into the other side of our wall.

"Were there no charities to help?"

"Her parents cut off her health insurance." The venom in his voice lets me know his relationship with his grandparents is fractured just as badly as mine. "They withdrew their financial support so she was left with a mountain of debt for her partially finished art degree at a very expensive university. Add in the cost of giving birth to me at an inner-city hospital, and she was drowning in debt. I remember going to food banks, but so did thousands of other people." He shrugs. "We were one of many. Every now and then, when she would come home after midnight, I would see how tired she was. I would remember that kid's words. I would wonder if I was the reason why my dad didn't stick around."

I surrender to my instincts and go to him, lay a hand on his arm. He jolts, looks down at my hand and then slowly looks at me. The pain reflected in his eyes is a stab straight to my heart.

"It wasn't you."

Slowly, ever so slowly, his hand comes up and covers mine. His acceptance of my comfort makes my heart swell even as it aches for the young boy who struggled so much. For the woman who had so much ripped away simply because she fell for the wrong person.

"Logically I know it. But I'd be lying if I said the thought didn't come back to haunt me every now and then." His smile is quick, bitter. "Not after I actually met Lucifer."

He starts to move forward, his step slow. I walk with him, matching my pace to his as we wander through the city streets. Even as my heart aches for him, hope whispers through my soul. I know this confession is not coming easy to him. That he's making the effort at all means more than I can express.

"I don't know how many times I asked my mom if she could ask my father to come meet me, or at the very least tell me his name. I later found out he was sending her a few hundred dollars every month if she kept his identity a secret and sent him occasional photos."

My eyes widen. "What?"

It's hard to picture Lucifer having that kind of interest in his children, framing photos like a proud father.

"He didn't actually care. It was like having a trophy. She still carries that guilt. Feels like she sold a part of me to keep the money he sent."

"What else was she supposed to do? Let you starve?"

He glances down at me, a faint smile on his lips. "It seems obvious to us, doesn't it?" His eyes drop down to my stomach. "But I imagine you and I will both face similar feelings of guilt and regret as we navigate parenthood."

More people start to appear in the streets. Shop owners open doors and bring out shelves, stocking them with leather shoes that gleam in the sunlight, pottery decorated with artful swirls and vivid colors, and hand-carved wooden plates, bowls and cups. We meander for a while, always touching, not speaking yet somehow more in sync than we have been since we reconnected.

We turn down a side street. The noises of the crowd dim. Olive tree branches arch overheard, creating a shadowed tunnel as we walk.

"A day before my seventh birthday, he told my mom he would be in town and would come see me."

I don't say anything, keep my eyes focused on the

curving path. But my other hand settles on my stomach. Maybe I'm offering assurance to my son, or maybe I'm seeking comfort for myself.

Because there's only one way this story can end.

"I was so excited. We both got dressed up and went to a park in Soundview. Mom bought me ice cream for my birthday. We waited almost five hours. He never showed. I cried harder than I've ever cried before. The last time I cried."

"When you were seven?" I whisper.

He nods. "After that, all I could feel was anger. One of the boys from my school had been at the park and saw me cry. He told everyone the next day and teased me on the playground. I punched him in the face."

"Sounds like it wasn't undeserved."

"He was a nasty little bastard. But I turned into one, too. I picked fights whenever I could. People didn't have time to tease me about not having a dad when they were trying to avoid me. And it gave me something to focus on besides his abandonment. It got so bad in middle school that the principal was calling my mother down several times a month. I didn't get it under control till almost the end of middle school. I put my mother through hell." His lips quirk. "Like my father."

"Michail…" I shake my head. "I didn't mean—"

"I know. I overreacted." He looks down at me, covers my hand with his. "I'm sorry, Alessandra. For that and everything I said before."

I stare up at my giant of a husband, floored by his apology.

"I am, too." It's the only thing I can say without my voice breaking.

"We got into a good place. I got a job as a 911 dispatcher my senior year of high school. That led to becoming a patrol officer, and my mother enjoyed nearly twenty years as an art teacher before she retired. I got my degree, started Sullivan Security and then it took off. We were happy. I barely even thought of my father.

"Then six months ago, my birth father reaches out to tell me he's dying and would like to meet me before he passes. My mother had never told me his name. I was shocked. I knew about Drakos Development. And then I was angry. Angry that someone so wealthy would have let us flounder like that. I debated on going. But I knew I'd always wonder if I didn't. So I went."

A shiver creeps down my spine at the banked fury in his tone.

"He told me he'd actually been at the park that day. He'd been testing me to see how I would respond to disappointment. When I cried, he washed his hands of me until I made something of myself."

Horrified by the depths of Lucifer's depravity, I stay silent as I tighten my grip on his fingers. A small gesture, but one meant to signal that I'm still here. Still listening.

"He was proud of it. Proud," he says with such disgust I can only imagine how hard it must have been for him to restrain himself in Lucifer's presence. "And he still expected me to be happy that he was finally paying attention to me. He thought I would just agree to the terms of his will for money. I ran into some of the worst people this world has to offer my first few years working patrol, and to this day, I have never met someone as cruel and selfish as him. I left with him screaming that he would make me sorry I was ever born."

We stop again. He places a hand on my hip, gently turns me to face him. My breath catches as his hand comes up. He traces a finger along my jaw before cradling me in his palm.

"When I walked into that bar and saw you, it felt like something was finally going right. My night with you wasn't expected. I needed it more than I realized. Yes," he says with a ghost of a smile, "I went back to the bar to look for you. Our time together meant something."

"It meant something to me, too." My words are barely a whisper.

"I know that now. When I walked into your office three months later and saw you, my first thought was that I had found you. You were cold, calm. At first, I thought you didn't recognize me. Then, when I realized who you were, and that you had appeared in my life right after Lucifer issued his ultimatum, the answer seemed obvious. Even if you hadn't been involved with him directly, I wondered if you had figured out who I was and decided to put your knowledge to use." A scowl darkens his face. "More than one woman has tried to trap me into becoming a father or getting married since I made my first million. It's the reason you saw pictures of so many women. I already didn't trust people in general. Why let someone get close when I had so many examples of people acting in their own interests?"

Hearing him present it now, without anger or insult, I can't say I wouldn't have drawn a similar conclusion.

"When you walked into my office… I thought the same thing." I look up at him, his handsome face that is now so familiar. "I thought you had found me."

A muscle twitches in his cheek. He looks away. "After you read the will, I wanted nothing to do with Lucifer, my brothers, you."

"What made you change your mind about Gavriil's wedding?"

"My mother. She hadn't wanted me to go see Lucifer. But as she told me, her wants and my needs were two very different things. After I told her about the will and my brothers, she told me I owed it to them, and myself, to give them a chance."

"So you went to the wedding."

"I did. I wasn't happy about it, but I knew she was right. Because I showed up, Gavriil reached out a couple weeks later when he had a problem." His voice drifts off as his gaze turns pensive. "The fact that he reached out and asked for my help meant something. It opened the door for us to get to know each other better, and eventually Rafe."

I want to point out in that moment how much that meant to him, his brother placing his trust in someone he barely knew. But I stay silent. This isn't about me. Not right now.

"When I saw you there at the wedding, all of my suspicions came to the forefront. I was convinced you were playing a long game, just waiting to somehow use our night together. I decided to warn you off."

He stops next to a low-lying wall with incredible views of the sea. He gently turns me to face him, running one hand up and down my bare arm as he cups my face with the other.

"I'm sorry. I still wanted you, and that made everything ten times worse. I lashed out at you, not just because I was angry and suspicious, but because I was angry at myself for still thinking about a woman I thought had betrayed me."

I reach up and smooth a lock of hair away from his

forehead. "I understand a little better now. I didn't deserve the vitriol."

"No, you didn't. But I also understand a little more now." He leans down and touches his forehead to mine. The simple contact makes my breath rush out in a wash. "My whole life has been tainted by betrayal. My father betraying my mother and leaving her to fight on her own. Schools that were overburdened and didn't help. The women who wanted money or clothes or a ring after I made my first million. What I saw over and over again of human nature and what we can do to each other as an officer."

I lean back slightly. "You don't talk much about your time as an officer."

"I was very proud of what I accomplished during my time with the NYPD. I gave everything I had to that job. But I wanted more, too. I wanted to make a bigger difference."

"Do you miss being an officer?"

"Sometimes I miss the work. But what I do now fills a lot of that void. When I was working for the Special Crimes Division, I saw so many alarm systems that failed. I learned a lot. Sullivan Security was born because of those failures and the lack of affordable systems for the people who need it most." His fingers drift up and down my jaw, his movements light even as they leave tiny sparks burning in the wake of his touch. "Good can come from ashes."

I suck in a quick breath as the baby moves.

"What's wrong?"

I laugh slightly at the alarm in his voice. "Nothing. He's just very active this morning."

Michail's gaze drops down to my stomach. Slowly I

reach up, tug his hand away from my face and guide it down. He inhales sharply. The intimacies we have shared so far are nothing compared to this moment. I place his hand on the side of my stomach.

"I don't feel anything."

"Give it a moment."

And then he moves. A good roll, tiny hands or perhaps a foot pushing against my stomach. Right against the palm of Michail's hand. His eyes widen as his lips part.

"Was that...?"

"Yes."

His head snaps up. His eyes burn into mine. Then he leans down and kisses me. Hard, hungry, passion flowing between us in a way I never imagined. I moan his name as I cling to his arms.

There are still obstacles between us, challenges to overcome. But here, in this moment, I make a conscious choice to let down my walls, to be more vulnerable with my husband as he's chosen to be vulnerable with me.

I don't know what the future holds. I do know that my path forward is no longer certain. That if Michail were to ask me to stay, I don't know if I would say no.

But that's a question for another day. Today, I'm going to enjoy myself and this moment of happiness that we've claimed.

CHAPTER THIRTEEN

Michail

WE MEANDER THROUGH the streets, hands clasped together, rarely speaking. More people fill the streets, tourists with cameras and phones pointed at the iconic blue domes, the churches, the caldera that cradles the sea. We duck down twisting paths with no destination in mind.

I've never felt more content in my life.

Eventually we end up at the edge of the city, whitewashed walls behind us and the sea laid out in its deep blue splendor before us.

"My mother would have loved this."

I remember the picture I saw in her office, the happy grins and pure joy on both Alessandra and her mother's faces.

"What was she like?"

Alessandra's lips curve into a slight smile, her face softening as she gazes out over the sea.

"Incredible. Strong and supportive. She worked two jobs while studying for her nursing assistant qualification. When she got her nursing degree, we went apartment hunting. She taught me to enjoy the little pleasures but live within my means."

"A wise woman."

"Those first years were hard on her. Learning how to balance a budget, how to forego things she took for granted."

"Another reason for your interest in finance?"

"My mom made mistakes early on. She never hid it from me. Since I loved numbers, she'd even have me help her with the budget, figure out how much we could afford for our new apartment. Graduating with her was the proudest moment of my life." She squeezes my hand. "Your mom reminds me of her. Both going to school and pursuing a dream to create a better life for us."

"And it was just the two of you?"

Alessandra nods. "She didn't trust others after my father left. I don't think she trusted herself, either. She fell hard when she met him. Looking back, she said it was all heat and no substance. But she ignored the warning signs, especially when my grandparents threatened to stop paying for her college."

"You never saw him again?"

She slowly shakes her head. "No. The only real memory I have of him is the day he left. He came out of the bedroom. I heard my mom crying. I was playing with some wood blocks. He walked by, looked at me and said, 'Sorry, kiddo.' And then he was gone."

I slide an arm around her shoulders and pull her a little closer. First her father walking away from her, then her grandparents labeling her as nothing more than a mistake. It's no small wonder that she has a hard time letting people in when the people who should have loved her the most abandoned not just her but her mother.

"My mom didn't go on a date until three years ago."

Alessandra leans into me. My body tightens with need. Part of me wants to whisk her back to the villa now. But

I also want to be with her now, like this, sharing pieces of herself like she did during our night together. Her confessions then were propelled by grief and passion. Right now, though, Alessandra is sharing herself because she wants to. And I want every piece she'll give me.

I've never felt this way before. Never wanted to know someone on a deeper level. But each new thing I learn about the mother of my child adds to the complex layers of a dynamic woman who's quickly becoming an integral part of my life.

"I wish they could have let themselves be happier sooner."

Her words linger as we walk down the path to the water's edge. When I had knocked on her door that morning and then opened it to find the bed made and no sign of her suitcase, I'd experienced a bone-deep fear similar to when she'd fainted outside her office in New York. Had I ruined things so quickly after we'd just finally made progress? I'd pushed her away from joining me at an event only made possible by her. And then, instead of owning up to my behavior, I'd jumped on one thing she'd said and used it as an excuse to put even more distance between us.

The relief I'd felt when she had finally answered her phone this morning had momentarily robbed me of speech. When she'd told me where she was, I'd allowed myself a sliver of cautious hope. I hadn't planned on opening up to her. There had been several moments where I'd almost stopped. But she had taken everything I'd shared and given back compassion in an instant. Compassion and understanding, although I'm not sure I deserve either. The least I could do was show her I had heard her last night. Was making the effort even if I couldn't go all the way.

As she picks up a stone and tosses it toward the waves, I can't recall the last time I was happy. There have been moments, like when I bought Mom her house an hour north of the city, or when Sullivan Security cleared the billion-dollar mark after launching our latest system.

I pick up a stone and hurl it, easily outdistancing Alessandra's throw. She laughs and accuses me of cheating. As I stare at her, the wind whipping her hair across her face, the swell of her stomach pressing against her dress, I want happiness. Not just for me, but for her.

I opened up to her this morning. Is it possible for me to open up even more, to let her in? To tell her just how closely I came to breaking my mother the same way Lucifer did?

No. She's accepted my apology. Accepted what she knows about me. But I haven't told her everything. Doubt flickers inside. Would she even want me to be involved with our son if she found out? Learned how my actions hurt my mother just as badly as Lucifer did? Even though she hadn't been comparing me to him last night, my assumption had rekindled an old, deep-rooted fear that I was far more like my birth father than I ever thought possible.

I know I can rise above his legacy and be a good father. But can I truly let go of my need to control? Place not only my trust but my heart in Alessandra's hands? Once I fully let her in, I won't just be opening the door to her and a future with her. I'll be giving her the power to betray, to hurt.

I slide my hand in hers, focusing on the sensation of her palm resting intimately against mine as we walk back up the path. For now, I'll focus on today and the woman at my side.

We find a café tucked away among a sea of houses. We

dine on a tomato-cucumber salad drizzled with olive oil and meat and grilled vegetables threaded onto wooden skewers. After lunch we continue on, passing the infamous blue-domed church before Alessandra ducks into a bookshop, the walls packed from ceiling to floor with titles in English, French, German, Chinese and Greek. There's no rhyme or reason to our wanderings, just the fun of exploring a new place with someone whose company I like. Her enjoyment of the world around us makes me feel like I'm coming out of a deep sleep, one where I've been so focused on my goals of building up Sullivan Security and providing for my mother that I've missed out on far more than I realized.

When the air cools as the sun starts to slide down in the sky, we head back toward the villa. As we pass the bar where I found her this morning, the bar where it all began, Alessandra stops.

"Care to join me for a drink?"

Something shifts in my chest. I comprehend the significance of this gesture, what she's offering me. I bring her hand up to my lips and kiss her fingers.

"I'd like that."

The waitress greets us with bright eyes and an even brighter smile. She seats us at the same long table that hugs the far wall. Beyond the low stone wall lies the half-moon bay and the rocky wall of the caldera. The view is incredible. But again, just like that night nearly six months ago now, my eyes are drawn to the woman across from me.

I grasp her hand, brush my thumb over her ring.

"The moment I saw this ring, I knew it was yours."

Her fingers tense in my grasp.

"But…you said Anthony picked it out."

I raise her hand to my lips, brush her lips across her knuckles the same way I did the night I proposed. But this time I gently scrape my teeth against her skin, savor her sharp inhale.

"No. I said he told me it was the most expensive ring he had. I picked it out."

I look down at the ring. I knew the moment I saw it I wanted it for her. Even when I told myself it was all for show, I wanted it for my wife.

"Diamonds for your elegance. Emerald for your eyes. And silver for moonlight on your skin."

Her eyes glisten in the dim lighting. She swallows hard. "Thank you."

The raw emotion in her voice seeps into my skin, wraps around my heart with a warmth I never thought possible. Music filters through the air as our waitress sets down my ouzo cocktail and a lavender lemonade for Alessandra. I smile at my wife.

"Dance with me."

I pull her on to the dance floor, gather her into the circle of my arms. I clasp one of her hands in mine, the contrast of her delicate fingers in my large grasp kindling a sense of protectiveness as I wrap my other arm around her waist. I lean my head against her hair and breathe in. Her scent, roses and that faint hint of dark, sends need straight through my body to my groin.

I hear her sigh, feel her press her hips against me as we sway to the music. My hand tightens on hers.

"Alessandra…"

She leans back and smiles at me. "What?"

I tug her closer again and put my lips to her ear. "Tease."

I nip her lobe with my teeth, drink in the sound of her gasp, revel in the way her body arches into mine.

"Maybe we should cut dinner short."

The breathlessness in her voice yanks me to the edge of my control.

"Why are you in such a rush?"

"Because I want you."

"I want you, too." I tilt my head back so I can smile down at her. "I intend to enjoy every inch of your body tonight." Her lips part as her eyes flash with lust. "And the pleasure will be even more incredible with the heightened anticipation."

"You're not playing fair."

"I don't play fair. I play to win."

If seducing my wife helps convince her to stay, I'll use every tool at my disposal.

The waitress brings us a plate of spanakopita, flaky phyllo pastry filled with cheese and spinach and served with a homemade tzatziki sauce. As Alessandra takes a bite, I brush my leg against hers under the table. Her eyes flare even as she glares at me. My amusement is short-lived when she returns the gesture, leaning over to point something out on the sea as she places her hand on my thigh, just short of my groin.

The rest of dinner continues in the same manner. Teasing touches over grape leaves stuffed with rice, herbs and beef. The brush of a kiss on the cheek as the waitress brings out a steaming pan of sautéed Greek prawns. Seductive whispers as we finish our meal with honey-drizzled baklava.

By the time we leave, I'm so hard it hurts. I started this, but she's met me at every step, driving me into a sexual frenzy until all I can see, think, feel, is her.

As soon as we step inside the villa, I close the door and press her against the wall. I grab her wrists and pin them above her head just before I slant my lips across hers. I taste honey and desire, heat and passion, as my tongue slips inside her mouth. She moves her hips against me as she groans.

"Michail, please..."

I scoop her up into my arms, startling a laugh from her. "I'm too heavy."

I kiss her again. "I'm not letting you go."

When we reach my room, I wait for her protest. When she doesn't say anything, I carry her inside.

I set her on her feet. Step away and strip my clothes off. The cool air is a balm for my heated skin. Her eyes rake over me from head to toe, her breathing harsh as she stares at me.

Then, slowly, she pulls her dress over her head. God, she's beautiful. Still the same long, lithe limbs, the curve of her waist. But the sight of her, stomach rounded with our child, is so sexy I have to clench my fists so I don't reach out and give in to the desire to rip the midnight blue lace she's wearing from her body. Slowly, so slowly it just might kill me, she slips the bra off. Her breasts are full, her nipples a dusky rose and pebbled, just begging for my mouth. A couple tugs and the panties pool at her feet.

I drink in the sight of her. Imprint this moment in my memory.

And then I take her.

Alessandra

Michail crosses the room in a matter of seconds and pulls me into his arms. I sigh as our naked bodies press together, the hair on his chest a gentle scrape against my breasts. His fingers tangle in my hair as he tilts my head back and kisses me with a firm tenderness that makes my blood sing.

He tugs me over to the bed. Cool air drifts in, carrying the scents of the sea and the bougainvillea climbing up a trellis on the balcony. I shiver.

"I'll warm you up."

Michail's promise sinks into me, warms me as my muscles tighten in anticipation. But this time, when he tries to gently push me back onto the bed, I turn and plant my hands against his firm chest.

"My turn."

With a quick push he falls back onto the bed. His husky laugh turns to a groan as I kneel between his legs.

"Alessandra…"

I wrap my hand around him, kiss the heated skin. "Please. I want to touch you."

I tease and taunt, kissing and licking my way up and down his hard length. When I at last take him in my mouth, his hips bow up off the bed as he utters my name in a guttural growl that makes me feel powerful and seductive. As I make love to him with my mouth, my other hand caresses his thighs, his abs.

His hands grab my shoulders.

"I need to be inside you."

I flow up his body, straddling him as I kiss him. I start to grab him to guide him inside, but his hands clamp down on my hips.

"May I?"

Confused and burning with need, I stare down at him. "But…"

He slowly eases me off of him, guides me onto my side on the bed. He lies down behind me. The heat from his body sears my skin as I press back against his hardness. I feel him against my core. And then, slowly, he eases inside me.

"Michail…"

One hand grasps my breast, his fingers a tease against my nipple as he moves inside me.

"You feel so good."

His breath feathers across my neck. I lean my head back, moan again as his lips blaze a trail down my neck. His thrusts grow harder, pleasure and pressure building in equal measure. As we move, his hand slides from my breast to cup my stomach.

I freeze. The intimacy of his touch, the feeling of his hand where mine so often rests, is a shock.

Michail stops. He utters a curse and starts to pull his hand away.

"I—"

"No." I grab his hand, guide it back and lay mine on top. "Please don't stop."

I turn my head to look at him. Michail is watching me with emotion burning in his eyes. He kisses me, hard and deep.

And then he starts to move again, each thrust of his hips filling my body with unspeakable pleasure.

I reach my peak, cry out as he fills me. He follows a moment later, his moan vibrating through my body.

I don't how long we lie there with his arm across my waist and his head pressed to my hair. I only know that I don't want to move. I don't want this moment to ever end.

The moment I finally accept that I'm falling in love with my husband.

CHAPTER FOURTEEN

Alessandra

I LOOK DOWN at the picturesque town spread out before us like a patchwork quilt. Crystal Falls, the small town Sarah moved to after she retired from teaching, is just an hour north of New York City tucked along the banks of the Hudson River. There's a town square surrounded by local shops and restaurants. Several parks scattered throughout the neighborhoods of cozy homes. On the perimeter, farmhouses with rolling hills and sweeping pastures, several wineries, a horse stable and bed and breakfasts. A mix of small-town America and country escapism.

"Are you ready?"

I smile up at Michail as the plane descends toward the lone airstrip just outside of town.

"I am."

The last week has been one of the happiest of my life. We would wake up whenever we wanted to in the morning, making love by the glow of the sunrise. Sometimes we fell back asleep in each other's arms. Other times we would get up and wander the streets before the tourists descended. Lunch would often be taken in whatever random cafe we happened upon. Some afternoons we sneaked into shops and picked up trinkets for his brothers, Tessa and Juliette, his mother. Several days we drifted back to the villa, lounged on the terrace or took a dip in the pool. Nights were spent in bed, exploring each other's bodies as the sun gave way to the moon.

I never imagined when our plane took off from New York City a week ago that I could find such happiness. But it's here. It's here and it's real. Each day that passes comes with Michail and I growing more and more comfortable in each other's company.

There's still so much for us to decide, to talk about. I may have accepted that I'm falling in love with Michail, but I'm not ready to share it. Not yet. There are still parts of himself that he's holding back, too.

But I can wait. He's already given me so much in a short amount of time.

I check to make sure the gift bag containing his mother's present is nearby. It was odd, picking gifts for other people, but it made me excited. There's still some nervousness about opening myself up to others. But I'm excited, too, at the thought of having a family again.

The plane touches down. A private car whisks us away to his mother's home, a stunning Victorian just down the road from one of the wineries. As we drive up, I smile. It's like a gingerbread house come to life, complete with lavender shingles, crown molding on the wraparound that reminds me of icing on a cake and colorful stained glass in the front door.

"You bought this for her."

Michail nods. "The one luxury she would allow herself in those early years was a magazine that featured Victorian homes. She'd page through and point out the details she liked." He nods toward the turret on the far end of the house. "When this came on the market, it was like it had been made for her."

I reach over and squeeze his arm. Sarah comes out as the car pulls up, smiling from ear to ear.

"You're back!"

It feels natural to walk up, to accept her hug. I hug her back before she turns to Michail.

"Hi, Mom."

Sarah wraps her arms around her son. He returns her hug with an exuberant one of his own. I step back and look away. There are still moments, moments like these when I'm reminded of my own mother, when the loss hits anew.

But it's getting better. Day by day. Michail's and my deepening relationship is helping with that.

A chill touches the back of my neck, fleeting but potent. I glance around, but there's no wind, no sign of an impending storm. No, this chill comes from within.

I frown. It's only been a week. I know this level of bliss won't be permanent. Even my mother and I, for how strong our relationship was, still disagreed, even fought. At some point, something will come up. Yet as Michail takes my hand in his and guides me into the house, I can't help but shake the feeling that something else is coming. Something that will not only test our newfound happiness, but possibly rip us apart.

I push that thought aside. This is just me trying to mentally prepare for the worst-case scenario. Something I have done ever since I can remember. If I expect the worst, I can't be surprised. But I missed out on so much living my life that way. I want to stop that, not just for myself but for my child, too.

I sit down in Sarah's living room, taking in the mix of

old-fashioned furniture like a low-lying pale blue sofa and a clawfoot coffee table. Paintings adorn the walls, stunning watercolors of the Hudson River, the nearby mountains, a farmhouse amid the bold colors of fall. On an end table next to an antique lamp is a copy of the photo I saw in Michail's apartment, him standing next to his mother with his arm about her shoulders and the sea behind them.

"You have a beautiful home."

"Thank you." She taps out a nervous pattern on her thigh. "I did want to offer after you've had the baby and settled back in to come out and stay for a couple of weeks. Help out around the house, cook, clean."

Touched, I smile at her. "That sounds amazing. Although I hope you'll be holding the baby, too."

"Of course." Sadness crosses her face. "When I had Michail, I didn't have much. There was a family who lived next door, and sometimes the daughter would come over to clean or bring me something her mother baked. It meant the world to me."

Michail tenses next to me. But when I glance at him, his face is smooth.

"We'd love to have you, Mom."

"Good." She leans forward. "So how was your trip?"

We make small talk for a few minutes, telling her about the various shops and restaurants we visited, the villa we stayed in. Her eyes grow misty when I tell her about returning to the bar where we met.

"It sounds wonderful. I'm so glad that you can make new memories there."

Michail reaches over and grabs her hand. "We have something for you."

Sarah cocks her head to one side. "You didn't have to get me a gift."

Michail almost looks like an excited young boy as he stands. "I'll be right back."

He disappears out the door.

"I'm so glad your trip to Greece was a happy one," Sarah says.

"Me, too. I wasn't sure it would be given what happened the last time we were there."

Sarah nods knowingly. "I felt the same way. But maybe this is a fresh start for us all."

I evaluate my next words carefully before I speak them. "I didn't know Lucifer long, but long enough that I saw his crueler side. It must have been hard when Michail told you he was going to go see him."

"It was. Agony. I barely slept until he got back to New York. We didn't talk about it." Her words are barely a whisper. "I would never wish anyone dead. But when I saw on the news that Lucifer had passed, I was so relieved."

She glances at me. "Michail's told you, hasn't he? What happened?"

"Some, yes."

"Eighteen, raised by very wealthy and very controlling parents. The fact that I managed to talk them into a semester in Paris was a miracle. They had already planned for me to marry the son of one of my father's business partners. When I met Lucifer…" Her voice trails off as she looks back to the clouds. "He was older, arrogant, dangerous. I thought it was love, but it was the novelty, feeling rebellious. When I told him I was pregnant, he told me it wasn't his problem. My parents disowned me."

"Michail shared some details."

Her eyes brighten. "He did?" At my nod, she swallows

hard. "I'm glad. It's a hard chapter of our lives, one he doesn't share with hardly anyone."

Michail walks in with a large black bag in hand. He moves over to a small alcove and brings out an easel.

"What is this?"

Michail unzips the bag. "This, Mom, is for you."

He pulls out the first painting and sets it on the easel. Sarah gasps.

"Michail…"

The painting is stunning, a bright blue sea with white-capped waves and a gull flying with its wings stretched out. In the distance, a mountain looms, the edges hazy and dreamy.

"How did you— I haven't seen these in years."

He looks at me. "With Alessandra's help."

Touched by his inclusion, I glance away before I give in to my own urge to shed a tear or two. Out of the corner of my eye, I see Sarah stand and slowly approach the easel. She runs a finger along the edge of the canvas.

"I never thought I would see this again."

Michail carefully sets it down and puts the next one on the easel. One after another: New York City at night, an old man fishing off the end of a dock, a field of flowers and springtime, and the Eiffel Tower, standing proud against the backdrop of Paris.

"I don't even know what to say."

Michail wraps an arm around her shoulders and pulls her close, pressing a kiss to her forehead.

"You don't have to say anything."

Worry passes over Sarah's face. She glances in my direction before smiling up at her son.

"This is cause for a toast. Would you mind grabbing

us some champagne? And I have some sparkling cider on the top shelf of the fridge."

Michail has barely left the room when Sarah turns to me. Her eyes are wide, her cheeks pale as her fingers curl around the arm of her chair in a death grip.

"Sarah?"

"What did he have to do?"

I freeze. "What?"

"What price did he have to pay? There's no way that Lucifer would have ever let those paintings out of his grasp without some sort of condition or..."

Her eyes widen, then drop down to my stomach. My body goes cold.

"Did it have something to do with you?"

Six months ago, I would have been able to handle her questions, to misdirect, buy time. But now, as I stare into her apprehensive eyes, I have nothing. I don't want to lie to her any more than I want to break my promise to Michail.

Unfortunately, my silence is telling.

"Oh, God." She scrunches her eyes tight and grips the back of her neck. "What happened?"

"It's not my story to tell, Sarah."

She looks back at the paintings. Heartbreak is written across her face in the deep lines on either side of her mouth, the tears spilling down her cheeks.

"How can I look at them? How can I possibly even have them in my house knowing that my son had to give something to that hideous man?"

"He wanted to do it."

Sarah's head whips back around.

"Michail loves you so much. It was worth it to him—"

But she's shaking her head. "Do you know why he's named Michail?"

I shake my head.

"Because I went back to that bastard one more time after my parents cut me off. I called him, begging, pleading for money, a place to stay, anything." Shame drips from her voice, but she doesn't back down. "He offered me five thousand dollars. Five thousand if I would name my son Michail. The Greek version of the archangel Michael."

Michael. Raphael. Gabriel. My heart sinks in my chest.

"And I took it."

Her breaths are coming in rapid gasps. I go to her and try to hold her hand, but she stands and starts to pace.

"It was the only thing that got us into that hellhole we lived in for thirteen years. From what little I know of Gavriil's circumstances, I imagine Lucifer offered his mother a similar deal." She throws her hands up in the air. "And I don't know what's worse. The fact that I took the money, or that that man had such a sadistic sense of humor that he wanted his sons named after archangels. I asked him why, and do you know what he said?" Her voice pitches up. "Because it amused him. It amused him and I still took that money. I accepted every payment he offered me for years in exchange for a photo, an update, even as he teased and taunted that one day he would finally meet Michail."

She collapses back into her chair, her body shaking. I go to her, kneel before her and wrap my hands firmly around her trembling fingers.

"Sarah, you were young. You had nothing."

"I still have my pride." A shudder passes through her body. "Or I did before I let that man brand my son with a name of his choosing. Let him string Michail along with promises of visiting and threatening to cut off my payments if I denied him. It took my son getting threatened with expulsion in school to realize how badly my own weakness had played a role in the pain he was suffering."

One of her tears drops onto my skin, slowly slides down the back of our joined hands.

"What did he have to do?" she whispers again.

A board creaks behind us. I look over my shoulder to see Michail standing in the doorway. I flinch at the furious anger burning in his eyes.

"Alessandra."

I stand. "Michail, she—"

He brushes past me and kneels before his mother.

"I never wanted this," Sarah whispers. "We made it. We were free of him." She reaches out and cups her son's face. "What did he make you do?"

"Mom, I made a choice. And I don't regret it."

Sarah starts to protest, but he shushes her. "I promise you the price I paid was minimal, and I would do it over and over again to get back what he stole from you." He squeezes her hands. "Are you…?"

She slowly shakes her head even as her eyes slide away from his. "No. I'm not in danger of going back there."

Confused, I glance at Michail, but he's refusing to look at me.

"All right." He stands and kisses Sarah's forehead. "Give me a moment to speak with Alessandra, and then I'll be back. We'll talk."

He turns and stalks past me, doesn't even look at me. The chill I felt on the back of my neck when we first arrived pierces my skin, spreads through my veins like ice water.

I follow Michail out the front door and onto the porch,

closing the door softly behind me. He's standing at the railing, hands braced, shoulders bunched.

"You told her."

"No, I—"

"You said something."

"She made the connection. I wasn't prepared for it."

"So you told her."

Irritation firms my voice. "No, I didn't. I told her it wasn't my story to tell."

He whirls around so fast I take a few steps back. "But you didn't deny. You didn't tell her that everything was fine. Instead, you let her fall back into a past she has worked for decades to escape."

My mouth drops open. "Are you blaming me for this?"

"Yes. She was happy, Alessandra. Happy. Content. Who knows what this will do to her?" He runs a hand through his hair. "This could set her back years, all because I trusted you, and obviously I shouldn't have."

My body goes numb. There's one split second of the most intense, heartbreaking pain I've ever experienced. And then it's gone, leaving behind a void where there's no emotion, no anger, no heartbreak. Just nothingness I wrap about myself like a shield.

Michail stills. His breath comes out in a heavy rush. "Alessandra—"

I hold up a hand. "Don't. You said all you needed to say."

He swears. "Look, I—"

"I know." I drift over to the railing, stare out over a field of flowers clinging to the fading warmth of summer. "I've made a mistake."

"What?"

"I mistook what we shared in the last week for something more."

He grabs me by the shoulders and spins me around. "Don't. Don't erase what happened between us this week."

"Why not? You did."

Something that might be pain flashes in his eyes, tightens his jaw. But I don't care. Eventually, when I crawl out of this numbness, I know the ache I will experience will be ten times what he's feeling now.

"I thought maybe something could develop between us, something that would go beyond a year." His eyes widen a fraction. "But I was wrong. You told me from the beginning that you struggle to trust, to let people in. You told me, and I should have listened."

He reaches for me, but I step back.

"I'll honor our agreement for a year. I still want you to be involved in the baby's life. But I'm moving back into my apartment."

His eyes blaze. "No."

"Yes. Unless you want to explain why you locked a pregnant woman up in your penthouse, you'll let me go. No more pretending. No more playing house. I have a job. My own apartment. You have your penthouse. I'll accept help for the baby, but that's it. Nothing unless it's for the child."

"Damn it, Alessandra, this isn't a game. I care about you."

The word slices through me. I care about him, too. In fact, a part of me was starting to embrace the depths of my feelings for him. To accept that I was falling in love with my husband. I'd even started to hope he might be falling for me, too.

But love without trust is nothing. No, it's worse than nothing. It's having the promise of something wonderful and beautiful, only to have it crumble into ashes as if it never existed.

"You care, but not enough to trust me. You said so yourself just now. I should have listened weeks ago, but you can bet I'm listening now."

I start down the stairs. Each step feels like I'm walking through wet cement.

"You're running away again."

I stop, one hand clenched on the railing. A frisson of anger darts down my spine. Slowly, I look back at him.

"It's not running away if you're leaving something that's not good for you."

I turn and walk toward the car. The driver is still waiting. As I climb into the back seat, a stupid, foolish part of me waits for him to call out. But as the driver closes the door and there's no sound but the thudding of my pulse echoing in my ears, I know I've made the right choice.

Even if it breaks my heart.

CHAPTER FIFTEEN

Michail

A HELICOPTER SOARS above Central Park, the blades whipping about in their endless circular pattern and sending a cascade of noise up toward my balcony. I lift the glass of whiskey to my lips. The noise is a welcome change from the graveyard silence of my penthouse.

I glance at my watch. Six o'clock. The florist should be delivering a bouquet of red roses to her apartment now.

My fingers tighten around my glass. It's been a week. One week since Alessandra walked away without a backward glance. One week since I went back into my mother's house to find her still sad but strong. The trails of her tears had still been evident on her face.

But instead of finding her catatonic, she'd been standing in front of the easel, her shoulders back, her chin determined. She'd looked at me, then frowned and glanced over my shoulder.

"Where's Alessandra?"

I told her part of the truth, that she'd decided to go back to the city and give us time to work through this. What I didn't mention was how much I had screwed up, how I had pushed my wife away in the blink of an eye. All because I couldn't take the risk she had and let myself fully trust the woman carrying my child. The woman who had repeatedly given herself to me, letting down her own walls even as I fought to keep mine in place.

When Alessandra said she had been contemplating more for us, a future beyond that first anniversary, it felt like someone had reached into my chest and cracked it open, releasing the feelings that had been building since that first night in Santorini.

Love. I had been falling in love with Alessandra for months. But I had been so fixated on keeping her at arm's length I couldn't see it. Then, just when she was preparing to offer even more of herself, I had once again blazed right past the facts of the situation and demonized my wife without a moment's hesitation. Had I told her before about my mother, if I had trusted her with the truth, we could have faced everything together.

Now, less than two weeks into my marriage, I'm drinking alone.

I showed up at Alessandra's apartment just a few hours after she left my mother's home. I knocked for fifteen minutes, talked through the door. I've called every morning and every night. My voicemails are short. But they're honest. Telling her good morning and I miss her. Sharing something that happened in my day, something that made me think of her, the baby. Wishing her good night.

I've lost count of how many times I've almost said, "I love you." I want to tell her in person the first time, have her see the truth of my feelings so she doesn't think I'm trying to manipulate her into coming back for the sake of the will or the baby.

But there's just silence. No texts, no phone calls, not even an email.

The worst part is, anything I would have done in the

past to get a woman's attention, to apologize, would mean nothing to Alessandra. Jewelry, clothes, a luxury trip. They don't matter.

Having my trust meant the most. Now, when I want to offer her not only my trust but my heart, she's out of my reach.

As I wrack my brain trying to come up with something, anything that will show her how sorry I am, how much I need her in my life, a ding sounds behind me. Hope shoots through me. I sit up and look over my shoulder. Then groan as my brothers step out of the elevator. Gavriil spots me in an instant and makes a beeline for the terrace door. I slump back down in my chair as I hear the door open behind me.

"We have got to stop getting together like this."

I rub the bridge of my nose. "I don't disagree."

Fingers pluck the glass from my hand.

"Hey."

"Still got it." Gavriil takes a sip of my whiskey. "I haven't pickpocketed in years, but you never lose the touch. What is this? A seventy-six?"

My growl doesn't faze him in the slightest.

"Rafe," he calls over his shoulder, "top shelf in the booze cabinet."

"When did you have time to go through my alcohol?"

"Right before your wedding." Gavriil hands me back my glass. "I must say, for a lumberjack you carry quite the selection of fine alcohols and liqueurs."

"You do realize," Rafe drawls as he walks out onto the terrace and hands Gavriil a glass, "the drop down to the street would certainly kill you."

Gavriil frowns. "Why would that interest me?"

"Because I think Michail is contemplating throwing you over the side."

I raise my glass to Rafe. "It's amazing for only spending a couple nights in each other's company that you already know me so well."

Gavriil's amusement vanishes as he sits in a chair across from mine. "Your mother called."

I roll my eyes. "Lovely."

"She's worried about you."

"Mothers never stop worrying."

Gavriil shrugs. "I wouldn't know."

"Neither would I," Rafe chimes in.

I wince. When I first met my brothers, I assumed they had lived a charmed life, surrounded by the ease of wealth. But Gavriil's earliest years had been spent as a petty thief on the streets of Athens. Rafe had grown up in a luxurious villa most people could only dream about, but his childhood had been more like psychological torture inflicted by the hands of our sire.

"I didn't mean—"

"We know." Gavriil leans back in his chair. "Your mother said she suspected something was wrong between you and Alessandra."

Just hearing her name is painful, a sharp knife that lands somewhere in the vicinity of my heart.

"There's nothing to talk about."

"What happened?"

"What part of *I don't want to talk about it* do you not comprehend?"

Gavriil cocks his head to one side. "As I recall, when I was going through my own issues with Juliette, you gave your advice freely."

He'd been utterly miserable when I let myself into his

Malibu beach house after hacking his security system. Swimming laps in a heated saltwater pool as if he could outpace his problems.

"You were there for me."

My head snaps around to Rafe. I haven't spent as much time with him. My first impression had been of a stuck-up bastard incapable of experiencing human emotion. But when I joined Gavriil in Greece to stage an intervention, it had been plain to see that Rafe's attitude was rooted more in the hellish childhood he'd experienced, and that his feelings for Tessa were very real.

"That was different."

"Where is she, Michail?"

I look over at Rafe.

"Home."

Gavriil looks over his shoulder. "She's here?"

"In her home," I retort through gritted teeth. "In Queens."

Rafe sits down in the chair next to mine, his face sober. "What happened?"

I hesitate. Then, slowly, I ease back into my chair. The root of my problem with Alessandra lies in my inability to trust. Maybe confiding in my brothers will get me nowhere.

Or maybe it will be the first step that will show Alessandra I truly want to change. To get back to those days we spent together in Santorini where I felt relaxed, free, instead of coiled tight inside a prison masking as a safety net.

"I made a mistake." I stare down into my whiskey. "One I will regret for the rest of my life."

"Mistakes can be rectified."

I glare at Rafe. "And I've been trying to fix it."

"How?" Gavriil asks.

"I tried stopping by her apartment to talk to her. I call every morning and every night. I send flowers."

Rafe tilts his head to one side. "What do you say in those phone calls?"

"Maybe I should just forward you the damn voice-mails," I snap.

"That would be helpful." Gavriil just grins when I flip him off. "Seriously, though, did you apologize?"

"Yes."

So many times. But maybe it's too late.

No. I will not accept defeat. If it takes the rest of my life, I will show Alessandra every way I can that I'm here. That I want to change, do better. I want to give her the support she received from her mother, the knowledge that I'm proud of her and everything she has accomplished on her own.

More than that, I want a life with her.

"Do you love her?"

I don't even hesitate to answer Rafe's question.

"Yes. I've loved her since that night in Santorini."

Loved her and yet ran from it at every opportunity, too scared to confront that I had finally found a woman who had snuck past my defenses, who had bared herself to me, who had driven me wild not only with her passion, but with her strength and vulnerability.

"Have you told her that?" Gavriil asks.

"No." I hold up my hand as Gavriil starts to say something smart. "I don't want her to hear it the first time in a voicemail or through her door."

"You need a grand gesture."

Both Gavriil and I turn to look at Rafe, surprise etched across both our faces.

Rafe shrugs. "I've learned a lot."

"We all have." Gavriil turns back to me. "Although you have yet to share the details of your, ahem, first night with Alessandra, what made it special?"

Her. "What do you mean?"

"Something that stood out. A detail that would be important to her while showing her how you feel."

I think back to that night, images whirling through my mind like a kaleidoscope. Alessandra sitting at the bar, the Aegean Sea and rocky ridges of the caldera a backdrop to her incredible beauty. That first smile that made the rest of the world fade away. Pulling her body close even as I told her I could only offer her one night...

Inspiration strikes. There's every chance she'll say no. But maybe, just maybe, she'll say yes.

I set my whiskey glass down. "If this works, I'll buy you both bottles of Macallan."

"The 1926?" Gavriil asks.

"The last one sold for nearly two million at auction," Rafe comments dryly.

"She's worth it." I stand. "She's worth everything."

And I'm not going to rest until she's back in my arms where she belongs.

CHAPTER SIXTEEN

Alessandra

I'M SITTING BESIDE a window overlooking the towers of New York City. The view rivals that of my former Kingston office. I'm seated in a private room of Cloud, one of the hottest and highest-rated restaurants in Manhattan. Three walls are glass, offering unparalleled views of Central Park and the surrounding skyline. The back wall is ivory, catching the colors of the setting sun and making the room glow. The square table is draped in red linen with a candle glowing in the middle.

But the view is wasted on me as my finger hovers over my phone, specifically the send button. I've written and rewritten this text a dozen times. The one where I let Michail know that I have an ultrasound appointment in a few weeks. The first version just included the date and time. But then I was worried it wasn't clear enough, so I rewrote it, asking him to let me know if he planned on attending. Then, worried it sounded too friendly, I revised it again.

Will he want to come? Or will I be left waiting? I don't know which is worse. I don't want him there, don't want to see him, be near him, be reminded of everything we had and lost in such a short amount of time. But I also want him there, want him to see the baby, to experience the same joy I saw on his face when he heard the baby's heartbeat for the first time.

I suck in a deep breath and hit Send. There. Done. My mother would tell me it's the right thing to do. I hate it, hate the anticipation, hate my dueling emotions.

I set my phone down, pick up my glass of alcohol-free red wine and take a sip. I debated on whether to accept Gavriil's invitation to join him for dinner. I have no doubt it's related to Michail's and my current predicament.

But I like Gavriil. Part of my reason for saying yes was rooted in morbid curiosity of finding out how Michail's doing without actually communicating with him. And part of it is because I need a distraction.

I set the glass down a little too hard. Wine sloshes over the rim and lands on the tablecloth. I sigh and lean back as a headache starts to drum at my temples. It's been nearly ten days since I left Sarah's house. Since I saw my husband. Those ten days have been utterly miserable. I started my job at Regent. It's a good job, and my boss has been nothing but accommodating. I've already had three successful client meetings. There's so much potential there, a chance to hone my skills in financial planning as I work toward my dream of owning my own company.

Too often, thoughts of Michail intrude. It doesn't help that the voicemails he's been leaving make me crave his presence even more. The little details he's been sharing, from a new book he's started reading to a little boy he saw learning how to ride a bike in the park. These are the sorts of things I'd wanted from him. Pieces of the man I'd married.

But how can I open myself up again? Ironically, now

that he's trying to show me he's willing to work on his trust, I'm not sure if I can give him mine again.

If I ever decide to get into another relationship, it will be with someone safe, someone who makes me happy and content but doesn't drive me to these incredible highs or drag me down to these vicious lows. The happiness isn't worth it. Not worth this pain at all.

Although the thought of going out with another man, let alone holding hands or even kissing someone who's not Michail, makes me sick to my stomach.

The thick velvet curtain that separates the private room from the hallway outside rustles behind me. I smile as I glance down at my phone.

"You're late."

"I know."

I freeze. Then, slowly, I turn.

Michail stands framed in the doorway. My heart breaks all over again having him be so close yet so far away. He's handsome, of course, in a black suit and a white shirt molded perfectly to every muscle. His hands are clasped behind his back. The top button is still in place.

"What are you doing here?"

He's staring at me as if he hasn't seen me in years instead of just a week.

"I got your text. About the ultrasound."

I frown. "The appointment's not for four weeks."

"I know. I wanted to see you."

I sag. "Gavriil set me up."

"He did. I didn't know how else to see you. I understand," he adds as I part my lips, "that I lied to get you here. If you tell me to go hell, I will turn around and leave. All I'm asking for is five minutes of your time. Five minutes to explain."

As I hesitate, he pulls one hand out from behind his back to reveal a bouquet. But unlike the vases of roses that have been arriving on my doorstep like clockwork, this one features a cascade of fuchsia-colored bougainvillea blooms.

My heart twists. "You didn't have to bring me flowers."

"Yes, I did. Not just because I hurt you. But because I realized, as much as I've offered you everything my wealth can buy, I never offered you the little things. The things that mattered."

I struggle to speak past the growing thickness in my voice. "You bought me the dress."

"I did but even then, I chose the most expensive thing and the most expensive place. I thought that I was doing so much for others. But I've come to realize that doing what I thought was best was my own way of dealing with my past. Helping others without letting them get too close by making choices for them."

I stand on a precipice. One with the fall so deep I don't know that I'll ever be able to claw my way out if my heart breaks again.

But just as Michail has made mistakes, so have I. I told him back in Santorini that I wish our mothers had let themselves be happier sooner. But I'm guilty of the same tactic they used to keep their hearts safe, of keeping myself locked up so tightly nothing got in. Not the bad, but not the good, either.

I love him. Love without his trust means nothing. But if I don't extend him that same trust, then I have accepted that there is no other outcome, no possibility, but our divorce.

I'm not ready to let go of that hope just yet.

I gesture for him to join me at the table. His body slowly relaxes, as if each muscle is unknotting. He circles around the table and sits across from me. His sheer presence envelops me, tempts me.

"I told you what it was like growing up. How I started to do better managing my anger in middle school."

"I remember." I glance down. "I thought you were holding something back, but I didn't want to push."

"I was holding back." My gaze darts back to his. "Not just because it's painful, but because it took hurting someone and pushing her to the edge for me to correct it."

"Your mother."

He nods. "One day she came down to the school. I'd punched a kid in the face in the cafeteria. Something was off. I learned later Lucifer had told her he wanted to set up another meeting. But she knew he wasn't going to come. It was just his way of making sure she was staying compliant."

My stomach pitches up into my throat.

"She barely talked, barely even looked at me. When the principal told her I was on the verge of getting expelled, she started crying. And then she couldn't stop."

I try to picture Sarah—happy, sweet Sarah—so hopeless and broken.

"The principal called an ambulance after she'd been crying for nearly thirty minutes. She wasn't talking, just crying and grunting. By the time we got to the hospital, they'd given her a sedative. It was like looking at a shadow of who she used to be."

"I'm sorry, Michail."

"She recovered, obviously." His eyes are dark with regret. "But it took a week for them to release her. She lost one of her jobs. It took her months to...to be herself again. I started applying myself in school and stopped getting into fights."

He steps back but laces his fingers through mine as he gently pulls me forward again.

"When I started controlling my actions, good things happened to our family. She stopped accepting the money from Lucifer and cut him out of her life. I started working a part-time job and brought in enough money that she was able to get her degree and become a certified teacher.

"I didn't tell you before because it wasn't my story to tell. Or at least that's what I told myself. But I never talked to my mom. I told myself that if I asked her permission to share, it would just hurt her. Just like I wanted to take care of everything with giving you spending money and buying furniture for the nursery. I've never let go of that guilt. It helped me shore up the walls I used to keep people out. I'm sorry." The words come out as if they'd been wrenched from his soul. "I hurt you, so many times, and I am sorry."

I smooth out an imaginary wrinkle in my skirt, focusing on that so he can't see the tears in my eyes. "Thank you."

He stands and comes back to my side of the table. I swallow hard as he extends a hand to me.

"Dance with me."

The same words he said to me in Santorini. I feel like I'm pitching headfirst over a cliff. Am I an idiot for daring to think that Michail could really change? That this could be something like what I dreamed about all those months ago?

I think back to that moment in my room in the penthouse when I reached for the wedding dress. The instant I realized just how much I had missed out on by living in my mother's footsteps. How much more I could let slip through my fingers in pursuit of keeping my heart intact.

I place my hand in his, my breath catching as he gently but firmly pulls me to my feet. He guides me out onto the balcony. I frown as I glimpse a covered easel tucked off to the side. It had been out of sight from where I was sitting.

"What is that?"

Michail doesn't answer. He pulls out his phone and taps the screen. A moment later, music fills the air. Deep, seductive. He moves next to the easel.

"I remember so many things about our night together. One of them was dancing under the stars with you."

I glance up at the sky, giving myself a much-needed break from gazing at my husband and fighting the urge to go to him. "Hard to see stars in the city."

"It is. So I brought the stars to you."

He pulls the sheet off. I stare at the canvas, navy blue dotted with silver. As I step closer, I see the date at the bottom.

"Is that…?"

"A map of the stars from the night we met."

My hear twists in my chest as my pulse starts to pound. "Michail…"

He crosses to me, slowly easing one arm around my waist as he captures my hand in the other. We begin to dance, swaying, our bodies drifting closer as the music weaves a spell that brings my past and present together in a moment so emotionally powerful I want to cry.

Michail rests his cheek against my hair.

"What I should have told you that night was how much you fascinated me. How much I wanted to get to know you. Not just your body, but you, Alessandra." He leans back so I can see his eyes, see his feelings blazing with pale blue fire. "I told myself I felt that way because I was raw from talking to Lucifer. More susceptible to emotions I didn't normally allow myself to feel. But it wasn't that. It was you. We should have woken up the next morning tangled up in each other so tight we'd have known right then we couldn't let each go."

"I wanted to stay." I blink back hot tears. "But I didn't want to be that woman."

"I know. I didn't give you a choice." He lays his forehead against mine. "I have been hoping and praying for days that you will give me one more chance. That you'll choose me just one more time. I will do everything in my power to be more open, to show you I trust you, I believe in you, and most importantly," he says as he stops our dancing and lifts a hand to my face, brushing a strand of hair behind my ear, "that I love you."

I suck in a shuddering sob.

"What?"

"I love you, Alessandra. Lexi." His hand cradles my face. I lean into his touch. "I didn't understand why the memory of you drove me crazy, why it hurt so much when I thought you had been working with Lucifer. But I know now that it's because I fell in love with you that first night. I fell and I've kept falling the more and more I've gotten to know you." He touches his forehead to mine. "Please tell me it's not too late."

Slowly, I reach out and grab his other hand. I place it on my stomach and lay my hand on top of his.

"I'm scared."

"I am, too. But I'm here. I'm here and I'm not going anywhere. I will be here for you, for the baby."

"Our baby."

He leans back, his eyes wide. "That's the first time you referred to him as ours."

I nod. "I thought I'd repeated my mother's mistakes by falling in love with you." I reach up and trace a finger over his lips. "I knew on our honeymoon. But I didn't want to push you. When you were so angry..." I shake my head. "I was holding your reaction up to how I felt."

"You had every right to."

"To a point," I agree. "But I did walk away. I nearly repeated my mother's pattern in the worst way possible. I almost lost out on a lifetime with you because I was scared."

He crushes me to him. "Alessandra..."

"I don't want to get a divorce, Michail." I reach up and place my hands on his face. "I want to be your wife. I want to raise our son together, and maybe another baby or two. I want to be by your side as you grow your business, and I want you by mine as I work toward my own goals. I want..." My voice cracks. "I just want you. Always you."

He leans down and kisses me, a searing kiss I feel all the way to my soul. As we stand there, bodies warmed by the setting sun and each other, I know I've found my happily-ever-after.

EPILOGUE

Michail
Six years later

"XAVIER!" I SHOUT. "Get out of that olive tree!"

"I'm just showing Simon how to climb!" my son shouts back.

I roll my eyes as Gavriil lets out a bark of laughter. "Are you seriously okay with your three-year-old climbing trees?"

Gavriil shrugs as he sips his whiskey. "Got to learn sometime. I knew kids who could filch a wallet at his age."

Adessa, Rafe and Tessa's older daughter, bounces up to us. She gives us a gap-toothed smile.

"Uncle Gavriil, will you teach me how to filch?"

Gavriil chokes on his drink as I throw my head back and laugh. I can only imagine what Rafe would have to say about his daughter learning how to pickpocket.

"Maybe when you're older," he says as he wipes two-million-dollar whiskey off his chin.

"Teach her what?"

Tessa navigates her wheelchair between our chairs.

"Nothing, Tess."

"Liar." Tessa leans over and kisses him on the cheek, then grimaces, her hand moving to her swollen belly.

"Don't do anything to stress me out. I need these babies to stay put for another four months."

Out of the corner of my eye, I see Rafe advancing across the lawn, trying to look like he's not checking up on his wife and failing miserably.

"How are you feeling?" he asks as he leans down and kisses her cheek.

"Pregnant." She smiles up at him. "And happy."

I glance around the north shore of our island. Once Gavriil, Rafe and I all officially received our inheritances, we sat down to decide what to do with all the money, properties and investments. Much of it was given away or invested.

None of us had wanted anything to do with the villa that had served as the backdrop for so much pain and suffering. But surprisingly, we all agreed we wanted to explore our Greek roots. To start a new legacy with the Drakos family. So we pooled our resources and purchased this island a few miles south of Santorini. Drakos Development oversaw the construction of a luxurious cream-colored villa with soaring pillars, balconies that curved out over the water and a saltwater pool overlooking the sea. A grove of olive trees takes up most of the east side of the island. A sandy beach lies to the west, crescent shaped with pale sand that hosts beach towels and tubs of toys during the summer. Tessa and her interior design team personally decorated every room, including twelve bedrooms. Enough for us, our wives and our growing families, as well as visitors like Juliette's honorary mother, Dessie, and my mom.

Well, at least there's room for now. Half the bedrooms are taken up by us and our children. Next year, there will be Rafe and Tessa's twins and my daughter.

Warm hands slide down over my shoulders. My body hardens as Alessandra leans down and kisses my ear.

"Hey, handsome."

I grasp one of her hands in mine and guide her around the lounge. My gaze slides up and down her body, the red sundress showing off her long legs and the swell of her belly.

"Hi, beautiful."

I ease her down onto my lap and kiss her deeply. Beneath my hand, our daughter gives an indignant kick.

"Why do I get the feeling we're going to have our hands full?" I murmur against her lips.

She chuckles and glances over her shoulder at Xavier, who is now dangling by his legs from a low-hanging branch as Simon claps his hands enthusiastically.

"Going to?"

It never fails to amaze me how much my wife accomplishes. She took the year off we'd planned to spend time with Xavier. Time I knew had not only been beneficial for our son, but healing for her. When she'd returned to Regent after Xavier's first birthday, she'd taken the firm by storm, attracting new clients and earning a reputation for her financial savviness and ability to connect with clients.

A reputation that followed her three years later when she opened her own firm. I never felt prouder than the day Xavier and I helped her cut the red ribbon on the door to her new office.

I lean back against my chair. Alessandra leans into me, her head resting over my heart.

"Dinner!" Juliette calls from behind us.

Xavier manages to untangle himself from the branch and scampers up the lawn to the porch where Juliette is setting down a plate of freshly baked pita and a bowl of tzatziki. Simon is just behind him, trying to mimic his older cousin's movements.

I tighten my grip on Alessandra and stand. She shrieks and clings to my neck.

"I'm too heavy!"

"I recall you saying that once before." I kiss her again, savor the taste of her. "You were wrong both times."

She shakes her head even as she curls into my embrace. My grip tightens on her.

"I've got you," I whisper against her hair.

My wife smiles up at me, love shining in her eyes.

"Now and forever."

* * * * *

Did you fall head over heels for
Pregnant Behind the Veil?

Then you'll be sure to enjoy
the other instalments in the
Brides for Greek Brothers trilogy,
Deception at the Altar
Still the Greek's Wife

And check out these other stories
from Emmy Grayson!

His Assistant's New York Awakening
An Heir Made in Hawaii
Prince's Forgotten Diamond
Stranded and Seduced

Available now!

MILLS & BOON®

KING'S EMERGENCY WIFE
Lucy King

'I'd like you to draft an announcement regarding the imminent change to my marital status.'

If Sofia was startled by his request, she didn't show it. She barely even blinked. 'Have you finally made your choice?'

Ivo nodded shortly. 'I have.'

'I understood none of the current candidates were deemed to be suitable.'

'That's correct,' he said. 'I had to think laterally. Outside the box. It turned out to be an excellent move.'

'Then may I be the first to offer you my congratulations.'

'Thank you.'

'The palace will breathe a sigh of relief.'

'I can almost hear it now.'

'I'll draft the announcement immediately and email it to you for approval,' she said, glancing down briefly to jot something in her notebook. 'It will be sent to all major news outlets within the hour.'

'Good.'

'The people will be ecstatic.'

'I certainly hope so.'

'Just one thing…'

'Yes?'

She lifted her gaze back to his, her smile faint, her expression quizzical. 'Who's the lucky lady?'

'You are.'

Continue reading

KING'S EMERGENCY WIFE
Lucy King

Available next month
millsandboon.co.uk

COMING SOON!

We really hope you enjoyed reading this book.
If you're looking for more romance
be sure to head to the shops when
new books are available on

Thursday 25th September

To see which titles are coming soon, please visit

millsandboon.co.uk/nextmonth

MILLS & BOON

MILLS & BOON TRUE LOVE IS
HAVING A MAKEOVER!

Introducing

Love Always

Swoon-worthy romances, where love takes center stage. Same heartwarming stories, stylish new look!

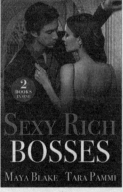
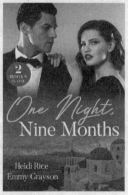

Afterglow Books is a trend-led, trope-filled list of books with diverse, authentic and relatable characters, a wide array of voices and representations, plus real world trials and tribulations. Featuring all the tropes you could possibly want (think small-town settings, fake relationships, grumpy vs sunshine, enemies to lovers) and all with a generous dose of spice in every story.

♪ @millsandboonuk
⊙ @millsandboonuk
afterglowbooks.co.uk

#AfterglowBooks

For all the latest book news, exclusive content and giveaways scan the QR code below to sign up to the Afterglow newsletter:

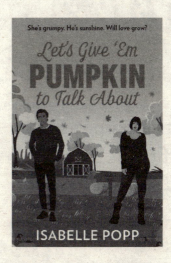

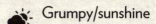

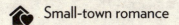

LET'S TALK
Romance

For exclusive extracts, competitions and special offers, find us online:

- **f** MillsandBoon
- **X** @MillsandBoon
- **⊙** @MillsandBoonUK
- **♪** @MillsandBoonUK

Get in touch on 01413 063 232